THE SISTERS' SONG

The God Singer: Book III

Jacob Oakley

Admittedly Bad Publishing, LLC

Editor at Large Keith Winkelman

First Printing, December, 2022

Art by Jacob Oakley

To my wife and family, thank you for supporting and
tolerating my excessive nerdiness

For my kids, don't ever stop dreaming, and write down the
really good ones.

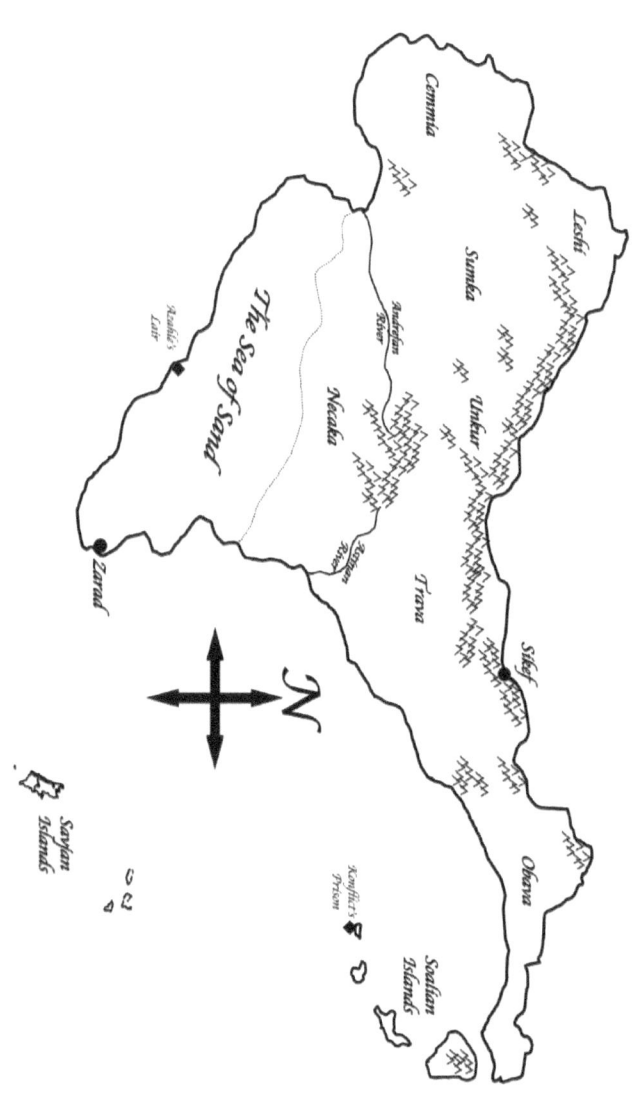

THE SISTERS' SONG

Prologue

Harpis finished dragging his tiny boat out of the frigid southern waters for the hundredth time in as many days. Goddess-ravaged ears provided a prison of silence where he could not hide from his thoughts. Perhaps worse, his voice had been burned away by the very deity he wished to curse.

Neither the chill of southern winter nor the whip of its wind could keep his thoughts from wandering to the losses he had suffered. Stepping away from the water's edge and heading north, he almost lamented that once again, the sea had not claimed him as it had his father. Stamping the cold ache from his toes and burrowing his hands under the layers of heavy, he began the ten-mile trudge back to the nearest village and its only inn.

As he walked from the shore, he focused on the scratching slide of his boots through the snow crusted saw grass and the percussion of their thud as they struck the ground beneath. Two hours later, when the inn came into view, he couldn't remember anything of the time between turning from the sea and finally seeing the yellow-orange glow of candlelight shining out of windows.

After his first few weeks at the edge of nowhere, he had learned its name when one of the patrons who could write, and there were not many, scribbled its in response to his own written inquiry. Akriven was so remote and small that it had taken over a month for the town to receive news that Kalt was again free from the grips of the invaders. That information was brought by happenstance when someone who was lost and looking for the coastal road passed through.

Pushing his way into the warm inn, he nodded and smiled at

the mustached owner behind the bar and made his way to his room. He had been given a room and food and rum each day in exchange for playing music for the other patrons. Business at the inn had nearly doubled since he had first taken up his violin in front of an audience two months ago. Not that he could hear what he played. He could only feel the hum of the notes in the instrument's wooden body and the vibration of the bow pulling across its strings.

Still, the folk of Akriven seemed to enjoy the performances well enough. He pulled the case from beneath his straw mattress and unclasped it, watching the ebon instrument's pearl-inlaid stars wink in the candlelight. Then, grabbing the violin, he walked back down the stairs, noting the feeling returning to his toes and gloved fingers. He made for the small iron stove and used his boot to unlatch the door before removing his gloves and holding his trembling fingers nearly in the flames.

He felt the plodding feet of the innkeeper walking towards him on the uneven wood flooring and turned as the man took his last step toward him. Harpis gave a forced smile as he took the half-stale biscuit leftover from breakfast service and the copper cup of rum. Using his boot again, he closed the stove door and lay his cup of rum on top to warm while he chewed the tough bread.

Brushing the last crumbs from his chest and scraggly beard, he wrapped his glove around the cup of rum to avoid being burned and sipped its contents. Closing his eyes as it scalded its way down his throat and into his belly, he took a deep breath and went to his stool.

He began this performance just like the others, with an ungifted rendition of what he hoped sounded like *Panoryla's March*. It may have sounded like animals being skinned alive for all he knew, but it made the folk of Akriven happy enough, and as far as he remembered, it felt like it had when he could hear it. His fingers danced along the strings, and he could feel the rise and fall of the notes tremble the wood of his violin.

After several Kalt drinking and fishing ditties, he concluded this evening like he had all the others by playing *Temurellin's Lullaby*. The first time he had played the lullaby was days ago. He hadn't realized he had nearly put the entire bar to sleep, stopping when he looked up and saw the crowd in its entirety had closed their eyes and relaxed. Since then, he had used the song as a finale and for a practice of sorts. He would pick a member in the crowd

2

and specifically weave his gift to make just the one-person slumber where they sat.

He had discovered the ability to weave his gift into his music while deaf and mute by accident, half-drunk and caught up in the vibrations of a song. It was one of the few times Harpis missed his former life, wishing to tell Mahala what he had discovered. He used each performance from that point on to perfect the surgical nature of specificity with his gift and practice the exciting ability to let his gift drift with the ebb and flow of vibrations felt instead of notes heard.

He stifled the cough of what might have been a laugh when the old fisherman he had been targeting fell sideways out of his chair onto the ground without stirring. As the man lay there, his chest rising and falling in measured silent snores, Harpis took a short bow as the soft drumming of the clapping crowd tickled his senses. Then, stepping over the sleeping drunk, he took the man's full cup of rum, raised it in a toast to the others, and made his way back to his room.

*****

The central city on the largest of the Soalian Islands was a burnt ruin. Enky had watched many wars and battles through the portals of his plane. Still, the carnage in the frame that hung inches in front of his face made him grimace. The less evolved and civilized a people, the more terrifying and slow their deaths were at each other's hands. Barely two months since his brother's awakening, there were none now in all of Solia to resist the army of Konflict. Now, the eyes of all Solian people glowed red, possessed by the god who never aspired to ascend.

Enky leaned back, sitting straight atop his desk in his cross-legged stance. He tapped a small finger against his teeth pensively as he watched the horde building canoes and making weapons on the coast nearest the Nysian mainland. Across the Soalian straights from his brother's army was the westernmost country on the only continent of the mortal plane.

He doubted the nearby nation of Obava or its people were ready for any kind of battle, let alone the war Konflict was about to bring to their shores. Unlike the other human countries on the continent, Obava had gone nearly a millennium without being

3

conquered or trying to expand its kingdom. Bordered on three sides by picturesque coastlines and on the fourth by sky-high mountain ranges with only a single narrow pass, the country was easy to defend. Moreover, with its plentiful wine and olive trades, Obava was easily able to acquire through economic means what others went to war to attain.

Turning away from the wall of frames, Enky slipped from his desk and onto his floor. Walking towards the blank stone wall to his left, he took a steadying breath as it shimmered and swirled, revealing the visage of The Nexus, which he strode into confidently.

He curiously glanced around at the moss-covered stone room that was manifested ages ago to connect the planes of Qisme's ascended children. While he viewed the space and audiences between his sisters often, rare was it for him to attend in person. He smiled at the three of his sisters standing in the center of the six-sided room.

"If it isn't the destroyer of the mortal plane himself," the pale-skinned, red-haired goddess of storms said sarcastically.

"It's not Enky's fault!" her olive-skinned and motherly twin-sister said, hugging him.

"Indeed, it is merely his nature," The oldest said with a warm smile glowing below golden eyes and blond tresses.

He hugged her too and cast a mournful glance at the wall that held the portal to The Great Dream.

"It was not my intention to wake our brother. Mother knows that and does not hold me accountable for breaking open the prison that took four goddesses to build so long ago. Also, if we want to be specific, it was your screeching howls that woke him, Zavesti," he explained, grinning as he watched the storm goddess seethe in rage.

"How is our mother?" the olive-skinned goddess of the wild asked in and obvious attempt to distract her twin.

"She is as she always was, Awata," he answered with a smile.

"And what did she have to say about this little mishap?" the eldest asked after Zavesti calmed.

"That I can watch him destroy the mortal plane and slowly rip devotion from the mortals until none are left on Nysia to believe in us. Our planes would collapse, and we would once again find ourselves amongst them," he answered.

"Or?" Zavesti asked, nearly spitting the question at him.

"Or I can do something about it," he said defiantly.

"Is that why you have brought us here, brother, to ask for our help in bringing Konflict to heel again?" Awata asked, crossing her arms.

Before he could answer, Zavesti walked up and put a long finger into his chest, her hair falling around her face like a lava flow.

"I will not be party to your chaos Enky. You know the rules. We cannot uninvitedly influence the mortal plan lest we be banished again. We are not fools, brother. We know you would let us end Konflict's reign again, watch as we are sent back to Nysia by mother, and then meddle from your little observatory. Just as you did when you ascended before us," she said, stomping back into the visage of storms on the wall behind her.

Enky watched her go, trying to hide his disappointment and frustration. A soft hand from Awata stole his attention from The Siren's departure, and he looked up into the almond eyes of her twin.

"I love you, Enky, but I know your nature and that you cannot elude it. If you fail, then all five of us rejoin our brother, but I'll not be the subject of your whimsy either," she said.

Kissing him on the cheek, she turned towards the woodland sanctuary of her plane, mossy footprints growing on the stone as she walked.

He looked up at the airy goddess of dawn and life, not expecting any different.

"Good luck, brother. If you fail and the six of us find ourselves on trial amongst the mortals again, you may have cause for concern. Your sisters might deem it necessary to imprison you alongside our brother to avoid this sort of calamity happening again," she said and turned to go.

Seeming to float to her glowing portal, she looked over her shoulder with a smirk.

"It appears it is time for the puppet master's greatest performance," she said in parting, her voice tinkling like bells off the now dormant stone walls.

"I never did like tragedies," he said, walking defeatedly back into his tiny abode.

Chapter 1

Savja

Aanaman finished his daily breakfast of eggs and cured ham with the same speed and zeal at forty-nine as when he was still a farmhand racing the rising sun to finish eating. Unlike four decades ago, when he would have been ushered out of the bunkhouse by the berating of older laborers, he was presently able to take a moment of solitary respite before beginning the day's work.

Attending meetings at the council chamber in Mer was no hard day of sowing fields in Ravnice, but he wasn't sure it was any less tiresome. Naming Mer the capital of the young nation of Savja had been one of his easier decisions as Chancellor. The bustling port was already the island's economic hub and previously home to the quarterly meetings of governors.

The choice also spared any perceptions of favoritism that could arise if he had picked his home city. Twisting to either side, he listened to his body creak along with the wood of the tavern chair. Regrettably, his wife might be right about taking a ship to these meetings instead of riding a horse for two days from his home in Ravnice. With a sigh of resignation, he stood from his chair and paid the server before heading out into the morning sun.

The squat council chamber was just across the street from what had become a governing bunkhouse of sorts. The tavern Aanaman stayed in was solely used by the visiting folk of the island who needed to travel to Mer for council meetings and other governmental procedures. He was reasonably sure more was accomplished at the tavern's dinner table over ales and whiskeys than they ever achieved at sessions in the council chamber.

Nodding at the guards wearing tabards of the Savjan army, he smiled at the symbol of the southern nation he had ushered into existence, navy-blue and emblazoned with orange anchor sigils. Pushing his way through the heavy iron doors Aanaman walked to the newly emplaced circular table. It could easily sit twenty, but as the doors closed behind him, he smiled at the other four attendees seated together next to each other. Of all the political meetings he had attended or overseen, this was the most friendly and competent group he had been a part of.

"Nice of you to finally show up, Chancellor Reaper," Ingar said with a wink.

"Oh, I just wanted to give the underlings time to talk about me behind my back before showing my face," he replied, rolling his eyes.

Taking his seat next to the dwarf, he leaned forward toward Lorent to view the Tormenta woman's shocked face.

"Don't worry, Governor Lorent. It is ok to jest at this meeting and any others you attend. We are not as severe as your People were in our rule or governance," he said with a smile.

Pushing his chair several paces back from the table, he motioned for the other four to turn theirs and face him. Then, as they finished adjusting their seats into an informal circle, he threw his right foot and leg over his left thigh and leaned back in his chair.

"There, less formal, and no longer a need to mention my official title. Speaking of which, Minister Rashida, how did the mayoral conference go yesterday? Any headway on determining a path forward for procedural replacement of myself and carrying forward of the chancellorship?" he asked.

The stately Tuathian woman slowly shook her head from side to side slowly before shrugging at Aanaman.

"Concerning transitioning rule, limits, elections, and the like regarding chancellorship, I feel we are still in the bickering and jockeying stage for the newly elected city officials," she answered.

He hung his head for a moment before motioning his hand for her to continue.

"What else came out of it then?" he asked her.

"The people of the cities seem just as content to have a leader called a mayor as they did one called a governor. If anything, I think it makes the cities feel like they can ignore the people of the wider island outside their cobbled streets as if they are now the responsibility of our centralized national Savjan government here in Mer. The Tormenta and folk below the Fjall mountain excluded, as governors Lorent and Ingar are undoubtedly responsible for those interests," Minister Rashida said.

Aanaman nodded thoughtfully before returning the woman's flat look.

"That is fine, and well. I expect Tawito will similarly represent the Quaji once they complete the transition of the tribes to the city of Quajillian on Lake Gitche. Please take any relevant discussion from today to day two of the mayoral conference and let me know if there is anything I can do to help," Aanaman finished.

Turning towards Ingar, he chewed his lip pensively before addressing his old friend.

"Ingar, I know we already spoke on the way here about Glasduille and the elves, but I think the rest of those gathered would benefit from hearing our joint suggestion before it is finalized and formally put forth," he prodded.

The old dwarf rubbed his calloused hand over his bald head before pulling it down past his face and speaking.

"It is not surprising that the elves desired no part in the fighting between the others of this island and the Tormenta last year. Nor is it surprising that they have opted to abstain from joining our new nation of Savja. While I don't harbor any resentment for these facts, I also don't think they should maintain the same influence on the decisions of this body as, say, myself or Governess Lorent. I propose a new treaty be drafted and ratified by our next quarterly sessions, not just by the national level but the mayors and governorships as well. Once approved, we will take it to them," the dwarf stated

Aanaman waited for the dwarf to finish before weighing in.

"The short of it would be an open acknowledgment of free passage for trade and the like but a formal delineation on policing and military affairs. This statement is so that both our nation and the elves understand what can be expected of each other in various situations. Such understanding might save lives and time in the face of threats from abroad," Aanaman explained, doing his best to keep his voice calm and expression soft so as not to add to Lorent's already understandable awkwardness and guilt.

Ingar lay his hands in his lap and switched to other topics after nodding in agreement with what Aanaman said.

8

"As for the national military fortress at Lake Gitche, it is nearly complete and is ready to serve as the center for operations whenever necessary for the government and military. I also have a hundred or so smithies and tinkerers down south with the Tormenta working to outfit and improve some of their ships with the same sort of weaponry and tools of naval combat we developed in haste during the last conflict. Aside from that, I have nothing for the group. I'll leave the talk of ships to Lorent and the military to Elliswerth," he said, sitting back in his chair.

Aanaman motioned for the older man to go ahead with his briefing, giving the young Lorent a few more moments to gather herself.

Elliswerth walked to the wall behind him that was now a massive map of Savja, from Huval Island in the south to the Quaji atolls in the northeast.

"I will say the dwarves and the island's carpenters have been impressive. The headquarters of our army is more than adequate. It can hold the entirety of the ten standing battalions with room for more within its numerous barracks. The easily defendable perimeter would serve as a safe place to operate our forces from if it is ever necessary again. We have also established horse and ship messaging systems from there to Mer, which pass by Ravnice and down to the naval headquarters in Kalt," Elliswerth said.

He walked and pointed to Lake Gitche and then traced the Fjall river to Ravnice and then up to Mer, doing the same to the southern point of Kalt and then indicating where the horse paths were.

"We currently have a battalion at each of the five cities along the coasts. We did not feel it necessary after talking with Tawito for one to be specifically assigned to his growing settlement, given that the other five battalions reside at the headquarters only a few miles from his people. Each of the nine regular battalions has ten companies comprising them. There are five companies of regulars, two shield wall companies, two having archers and crossbowmen, and a single cavalry company for each battalion. We have made every effort to mingle citizens of various areas within them as much as possible to encourage mutual trust and responsibilities as well," he finished after pointing out Tuath, Mer, Ravnice, and Kalt.

Ingar walked up next to him and pointed at the head of the Fjall river, where the entrance to his city lies and then the island's

9

southernmost point.

"My people will still maintain our own forces to protect our city and provide trainers and soldiers to the other units. Commander Shatter-Hand has been permanently assigned with a small contingent of officers to aid Field Marshal Elliswerth at Lake Gitche. Down here in the south, work is nearly complete on our specialized forces contingent under Commander Zolga. She will be attending the next sessions to outline those efforts and the accomplishments of that organization," the dwarf said, retaking his seat.

Aanaman was genuinely impressed by what they had been able to orchestrate in the months after defeating Queen Oluja Vetar's Tormenta forces.

"When do you think the battalions will be ready to begin rotating through the cities and the headquarters?" he asked Elliswerth.

The man shrugged and indicated for Minister Rashida to answer.

"The mayors and governors and I will work out how that will best function logistically and in augmentation and complement the re-working of militia and policing roles within each major city and region. My best guess is late this year," She answered confidently.

Aanaman turned to Lorent and waited patiently for the young woman to lift her gaze.

"If you would please, Lorent? How have your people fared since the treaty, and how goes the efforts in Kalt?" he asked.

"Um, as Governor Hammersmith and Field Marshal Ellisworth indicated, Zolga has taken to leading the development of a specialized force. Its purpose is to be quickly deployable via our ships to anywhere in Savja with the resources necessary to ward off an enemy or otherwise aid a city, island, or atoll," she stated before standing and walking over to the wall-sized map.

"Tormenta ships will sail in pairs of two, patrolling Savjan waters and harbors. One will be in port while the other is sailing patrols from the five major ports of Lodestar, Kalt, Ravnice, Mer, and Tuath," she said, pointing at the locations in order.

"Meanwhile, two other pairs will sail long loops from Huval to the atolls and back around the spine of Quaj, reporting in at Kalt and the naval headquarters. So, there will always be two at harbor and two at sea. With the ships we have built and the ones that

10

remained, we currently have twenty-five galleons to comprise the navy under command of your, sorry our, Admiral. That is enough for these patrols and our specialized raider force, plus nine on stand-by between Lodestar and Kalt. We plan to continue construction until we have over thirty operating galleons," she said.

Elliswerth waited for her to return to her seat before doing so himself.

Aanaman looked at the gathered group and let out a soft whistle.

"Let us hope these beginnings are a sign of what is to come for our country. Lorent, have you heard anything from Galonica as to your people's priests and priestesses and their involvement with Lorkin's planned organization?" he asked.

"Yes," she said, obviously still awkward in terms of respect and males despite her nervousness.

"High Priestess Galonica has allowed the gifted male curates to join the ranks of the priesthood. I think the gifted Tormenta are on the path to recovering their numbers between them and several young, gifted females who have come under her tutelage. As to working with Lorkin, you'd have to ask them. I have been too busy with non-gifted tasks to worry over much of our magically inclined," she answered.

Aanaman stood and put a comforting hand on her shoulder before sliding his chair back into the table.

"I would say that we should take advantage of our efficiencies and have lunch across the street together before adjourning for the afternoon and preparing ourselves for the pedantry of the next few days," he said, smiling.

*****

Lorkin shook his head at the unkempt grounds of The College of Elements as he strode through the open gates and into the courtyard that encircled the building that had the Arch Mage quarters above them. Waiting for him patiently at the center was Stone Mage Vennil, and he embraced the other mage before turning to take in the four towers.

"It is an odd thing to be here without Uridyll. It almost feels unnatural. Still, these hallowed halls of study should be more well-kept," he said.

Vennil ran a hand through greying raven hair and looked around with a similar dissatisfied expression at the courtyard. Lorkin instinctively reached for what had once been a black knot on top of his own head. He was old, even by dwarven standards, and his once black hair was starting to show streaks of age.

"It seems the stress of the past few years has caught up to us both, Arch Mage," Vennil said, laughing.

"I'll be happy to shed that title if you are still willing to take it up," he said, becoming more severe as he faced the man.

"I am, for now anyway. I will happily see to the re-opening of the college and the return of our students. I agree with you that having mage-hood bestowed at this school as a requirement for evaluation at your new organization should increase the number of students and attendance we see, which is good for the school, the students, and the people" Vennil replied.

"I think splitting those who wish to learn to fight with their gift from others who are more interested in academic pursuit is needed. Hopefully, forcing only those with the blessing of their specific gifted leader will allow for sufficient vetting and dedication to their craft. When we set up our institution alongside those of the specialized units, we will build a library of gifted knowledge and send a copy here and another to the rebuilt archives," Lorkin said to the man.

Vennil nodded in agreement before crossing his arms and looking across the Mer peninsula to the central spire of The Archdiocese of Daybreak.

"I don't much care for the new Exarch, but his point is valid on separating the gifted and non-gifted clerics to preserve the reputation and function of the Clergy. The gifted priests and priestesses of Daybreak could ask for none better to lead them than Luminary Ezera anyway," he said.

Lorkin had himself been shocked when during the height of the conflict, the Exarch had made that decision to revoke the status of Ezera's building in Fjall as a diocese. If anything, it had improved the situation of those that wield Daybreak given gifts.

"It is a little different for us, though there is certainly a need to separate the scientifically focused educational college from the craft of battle magic honed at Southpoint. I don't think the Tormenta have a line between the two. Jabruelle is still trying to figure out the future of The Sleeper's devoted moving forward," Lorkin finished.

"I wonder if any of The Wild's gifted will show themselves at your schoolhouse. They seem the least likely to be interested, but we know so little of their gift and their typically solitary devotion and worship," Vennil said.

The dwarven Arch Mage took one step to get closer to the man and reverently removed the short cloak that indicated his rank and stood on his toes to put it over Vennil's head.

"I name you Arch Mage Vennil, headmaster of The College of Elements," he said, bowing to the man.

"What does that now make you?" Vennil asked, smirking before looking appreciatively at the clasps of the Arch Mage cloak.

"For now, Stone Mage, though, I have one more favor to ask of you before I depart to the south and begin readying the schoolhouse for channelers of every gift to come learn how to fight with and against them," Lorkin said.

"Of course, anything at all, Lorkin, what is it?" Vennil asked.

"I will attempt an apotheosis enchantment, and if successful, I would like it to be you who vouches for the item, enchantment, and title of Stone Magus. After all, you are the second most senior stone mage and now Arch Mage of the college," the dwarf replied with a smile.

"It would truly be an honor, Lorkin. I have several of the quarterly sessions left to attend, as do you, but around or after those, we can hide ourselves up in the tower of stone. I wasn't planning to depart for a week or so anyway. I need to send word out to the students and faculty who fled to their homes before I return to The Hall and bring back those who went there with Stone Sage Mara and I," he answered.

*****

A millennium of peace Obava had enjoyed proved ultimately more harmful than good when the far more savage peoples of the Soalian Islands crossed the Obavan Straits and began the first steps of conquest across the wide but squat country on the east of the Nysian mainland. They were more advanced and more populous than the islanders, but far less ready to do battle.

Ornamental armor and swords that had hung above mantles or

in cupboards, dulled from centuries without use, were little hope against the frenzied humans that followed in Konflict's footsteps. Their eyes shone with the eerie red glow of devotion to his cause, one shared amongst all those he had defeated and turned towards the gods long-sought vengeance. He would not stop conquering until his sibling's devotion had fled from the mortal plane. He would not cease until he had achieved order amongst the chaos of the mortals. To Konflict, the only end to such a struggle was complete subjugation.

Enky knew that, and still, it surprised him how far his brother had come. Barely three months after departing the shores of Soalia, Konflict and his horde had already fought across most of Obava, with only a few large cities left between him and the mountain pass to the rest of the continent. Setting the frame he was viewing back on the wall hook, Enky leaned back in his chair and looked at several other scenes of people preparing for battle.

"Despite his growing army, the countries of Trava, Sumka, and Necaka have been at constant war with each other and gotten rather good at it. They also know you are coming, brother, or at least that an army of conquerors is. Perhaps they will hold you off longer, or all together," he said to his toes with feigned hopefulness.

"And how long will you wait to intervene, Enky?" a raspy female voice asked behind him.

Kicking his feet from his small desk, he spun around in his chair to face his mother.

"My apologies, mother, I did not hear you enter," he explained.

"I understand, my son, quite the distractions you have playing out across your tiny abode," she said, looking from one scene to another.

"Why would you create something as brutal as my brother?" he asked his mother sincerely.

"I did not design him. He is simply the product of his heritage, just like you and your sisters are. Life is given purpose by death. The seas and the land give contrast and depth to each other's existence. Similarly, there needs to be a struggle for order against the disorder of chaos. That is the heritage of your brother, and you" she replied.

I am not sure if that is an explanation," he said accusingly.

"It is not an explanation. It simply is. How did it go with your sisters?" she asked with a grin.

"You know full well how it went, mother. You know how everything goes," he answered grumpily.

"It sounds like you should start figuring that out, my son. Otherwise, you and your sisters will once again find yourselves amongst him, and the mortals. If that happens, the struggle for devotion will be again reset," she said accusingly.

"I have a plan for preventing exactly that," he said, staring at the frame on his desk.

"Quite the irony, you and plans," she laughed.

Chapter 2
Overture

Lorkin's stomach growled, and his back ached as he sat motionless on the floor of the college's cellar. He was partially aware of the presence of Vennil in the blackness, having heard the man open the cellar door and tiptoe down the stairs. Lorkin was struggling mightily to concentrate on the enchantment. He had just finished imparting his gift to the two stone orbs upon which his hands sat and had yet to completely pull his mind from them.

If Vennil had arrived a few moments earlier, Lorkin would not have heard him at all, so entirely within the act as he was. The dwarf had fabricated hundreds of enchantments over the long centuries of his life. However, this was likely to be the last and the best of them. He was exhausted and starving but he refused to let go of his mental connection to the magic, inspecting every bit of the area it covered, looking for a kink or a tear or anything that might allow the enchantment to rip itself apart when he fully pulled his considerable focus from it.

The act of enchanting was akin to stacking a lattice of fragile flat pieces of glass on an item. The stronger or longer the enchantment, the taller and more challenging the lattice of activations was to keep stable. These maces and the memory he had imparted upon them, his apotheosis, was more like wrapping a thin pane of glass around a sphere without it breaking. More than a few times, he had thought he evenly coated the entire item, only to race against its unraveling as he tried pulling his focus from it. Finally, feeling no instability as he let his mind roam over the magic, he let out a long sigh.

The dwarf let his hands fall from the orbs to his side and leaned back to the groaning pops of his back, straightening after an entire day spent sitting hunched over. Nevertheless, he could feel the eagerness in the room as Vennil quietly awaited a signal that he had withdrawn his mind from the items.

"It is done. Light a candle and let us see what the newest Arch Mage feels of the last one's work," he said wryly.

After several bumbled attempts at striking a flame to the wick, the small candle caught, illuminating the room in a golden glow that was almost painful to their unadjusted eyes. When Lorkin's more sensitive eyes became accustomed to the light, he stood slowly, looking down at the twin maces on the ground where he was sitting.

Vennil walked past him and gave him a comforting pat on the shoulder before kneeling and placing a hand on each mace's head. Confident as he was, Lorkin felt a moment of trepidation as he watched the second most senior Stone Mage on Quaj Island inspect his work. Vennil removed his hands reverently and stood slowly, turning to face him.

"Not only a perfect Apotheosis Lorkin but identical permanent enchantments on identical items done simultaneously. You have more than earned the title of Magus old friend. Come, let us tell the others!" the man said excitedly, heading up the stairs.

Lorkin grabbed the maces and paused to give them a smile of appreciation, twirling them deftly in his hands before following Vennil up. Leaving the cellar door behind, the orange and purple glow of sunset greeted them through the library windows as they made their way towards the courtyard. He caught sight of Ingar and several others who had been patiently waiting and threw the dwarven governor a wink.

Several paces into the courtyard, he and Vennil stood side by side and waited while Ingar, Aanaman, and a young female dwarf with braided black hair joined them.

Vennil took a step back and grandly pointed at Lorkin before bowing deeply.

"As newly appointed Arch Mage, I take great pleasure in my first official act, certifying the creation of an apotheosis enchantment and thus also having the privilege to confer the title of Stone Magus to Lorkin Kiln-Keeper!" Vennil stated, to several claps from the others.

"What will you name them?" The new Arch Mage asked, turning to him.

Lorkin looked down at the maces appreciatively. Then, tucking one of them under his arm, he ran his hands over the perfect sphere of polished brown and black stone the size of a child's head and nodded to himself in thought.

"These are The Stones of Fjall," he said, looking from the maces to Ingar.

The governor of Fjall nudged the young dwarf forward, and she walked to stand before Lorkin.

"Itka Frothbrew, the niece of the heroic Braffen, my cousin and only living relative, are you still intent on joining Ezera and The Cause?" he asked.

Itka took a knee before him, her long thick braids nearly touching the ground.

"I am, Stone Magus. Having turned thirty this year and now being an adult in my own right, I have chosen to take up the burden my uncle once carried," she said, rising to her feet and looking upon him with fierce green eyes as she finished.

"You still favor wielding two maces, I hope?" he asked her.

"I don't know a better way to bludgeon my enemies," she answered.

He presented the handles of the weapons to her, and she gingerly took them from him, running her hand over their smooth spherical heads before expertly executing several sweeping feints, strikes, and blocks. After a moment, she paused, dropped them to the ground, and gave him a crushing hug.

"Thank you so much, cousin!" she said.

"Easy lass, my back hurts enough as it is," he replied.

Ingar crossed his arms impatiently, waiting for their embrace to end.

"Well, mage, with such a lofty name, what have you enchanted these maces to do?" the governor asked.

Lorkin motioned for Itka to hand him one of them, and after she did, he clutched the handle, hoping his confidence in his work was well placed.

"Fjallinthrop," he whispered, uttering the ancient name for the mountain that was home to the dwarven city. He then let go of the handle, and when the mace head struck the ground, it did so with a resounding thud that echoed off the walls and slightly shook the ground. However, the mace did not fall or sway, and the handle sat upright at a slight angle where he let it go.

"Try and move it," he said, beckoning for Itka to grab the weapon.

After a long moment of straining her corded muscles, she gave up and looked at him with her hands on her hips, panting. The mace had not budged at all.

"I have given them the memory of the mountain that their heads were hewn from," he explained.

"Izdan," he said, feeling the tug as the mace's enchantment pulled from his vitality for a moment before relenting. With a bitter fondness others reserved for parting with a child, he handed the weapon back to Itka with a slight bow.

"Releasing them will drain you some, so don't overuse it, or you will find yourself too tired to fight, but they will never forget the mountain. May they keep you and those you protect safe from harm Itka Frothbrew," he finished.

*****

Yesterday had marked the first half a year of his self-imposed life sentence, exiled in the village of Akriven. The passage of time was a fact Harpis was only able to discern from notches scratched into his boat's starboard rail. With summer beginning to take hold, Harpis decided he could spend a day forgoing the daily ritual of self-flagellation at the hands of bad rum and rough waves. Though he felt the music now instead of hearing it, playing each night at the tavern had started becoming as important a routine to him as his suffrage at sea.

Sitting on the ground with his back against the front wall of the tavern, he held his violin to his neck, playing random notes he could not hear just to feel their vibration. He sat for hours, taking in the ebb and flow of the town's activity. Most recently felt was the rumble from the wooden wheels of a horse-drawn cart over-laden with goods. The tiny tremors of its passing flowed through the ground and into his body. That lower, more consistent vibration served as a background harmony to the punctuated stomps of hooves and the pop he sensed as the driver cracked a whip over the animal's head.

Before dawn, there was a flurry as anglers made their way towards the coast as he usually would have. The cart and horse traffic ended shortly after dawn as traders and workers made their way north or south on the singular road that ran down the middle of Akriven. He felt nothing but the wind humming past his ears and fluttering his loose blouse and cloth pants.

He was barely conscious of an impact from the door across the street slamming shut. The thud pulled his attention to where a fisher and his son struggled to carry the morning's catch. The big rock cod was then strung up on a cross-post for easier cleaning. Harpis shook his head as the boy, who must have been ten or eleven, stood next to the fish with awe at its length that stretched taller than his head.

Harpis found himself engrossed in their movements. The scene was similar to several he had been a part of with his father two decades ago in a town only hours from this one. Halfway between daydream and observation, he saw himself beside Jedren Akkeri with a similarly strung fish. Watching the father across the road drag a thin filet knife down the fish's flank, he could feel the knife-tip grazing vertebrae and pulling itself through the white flesh of the cod like the wind ripping a torn sail.

The boy disappeared inside for a moment to deposit the first filet before returning, and they did the same to the fish's other side. Harpis heard the sound of a knife pulling through fish scales from his memories just as he somehow felt the pull of steel through meat now from across the dirt street. The boy caught the other large filet, and the two walked back into the shop.

Staring at the carved-up cod swaying in the breeze, he pressed his fingers against the high-note string, almost on the bridge that suspended them above the instrument's body and pulled his bow across it as if it were a knife itself. His eyes opened wide in surprise when he watched a piece of belly fall as if partially cut, hanging a corner from the carcass.

In disbelief, he focused on the top of the fish and pulled a note from his violin with his bow as if he were fileting the fish himself. He nearly threw the instrument in surprise when the fish across the street fell to the ground, its tail still hanging in the noose around the post was cut straight across exactly where he had been looking.

*****

Sitting precariously on her short stool in the Broken Barrel Inn deep below Fjall, Sudbina stared at the bottom of her empty flagon as if it would grow a mouth and offer her answers. The bar atop the mining platform under Fjall was the last stop for workers heading into the underbelly of the world and their first stop upon returning. She was an odd patron at the squat bar full of burly dwarves. Admittedly, she was probably considered an odd patron wherever she went.

The other customers were a tough, heavy drinking crowd, to be sure, what miner wouldn't be. However, the dwarves were always respectful of her, and she could walk about as the exotically flirtatious woman without suffering the uninvited attention that usually accompanied it. To the dwarves, she was more a curiosity than a lustful morsel.

When the flagon bottom offered no opinion despite her staring, she handed it to the barkeep to be refilled and pondered her trek. Sudbina had always wandered. Recently though, it had become a relaxing and meandering existence. What was once nomadic restlessness in pursuit of fresh faces and pockets to pick had become a vacation of sorts to find purpose in a Nysia that was now free of Svenus Kalt.

After the parlay with The Tormenta and the disappearance of Harpis, she had struggled to contain her impatience at the changeless routine she found at Kalt City's wharf. So, Sudbina decided she would do what she always did and put one foot in front of another until she ran into something interesting.

She did want to visit those places that brought her the most happiness as she tried to find direction. If she did not find it along the way, her final planned stop at the sunny beaches of Tuath in mid-summer seemed like an excellent place to think on it further.

From Kalt, she had first gone to Lodestar and spent several evenings with Zolga and Galonica before bidding the storm women goodbye and heading to Ravnice. In the city of farmers, she had enjoyed herself as the charming young man. Taking Jabruclle out for a night of drinking and getting the poor boy so intoxicated, he tried converting an entire tavern full of drunks into necromancers.

That stop had not been wholly joyous, as breakfast with Kalna at The Siren's Scream had been sadder than she expected. The look in the pretty blond woman's eyes when she had no information to offer about Harpis was pure agony. No one had heard or seen anything from the bard.

"Hard to find a spy who doesn't want to be found," she said grumpily to the ale in her cup before tipping it back.

Finishing the contents in one long pull, she gently laid the flagon back on the bar, leaving twice as many silver coins as necessary for payment, and eased herself from her seat and walked determinedly towards the stairs down to the rented rooms. Tomorrow the next leg of her travels awaited, but tonight she would enjoy a raucous night of snoring on furs next to a well-fed heating stove in the stone-clad womb of the world.

Approaching her door but ignoring it, she looked before and behind her for any would-be assailants as she had since she was the young girl growing up in a brothel. Then, finding herself alone, she went to her door and let herself in. Latching it, she looked up at the ceiling barely an inch above her and smiled in appreciation that her diminutive form gave her comfortable passage in quarters built by and for dwarves. She pulled the red-haired wig from her head, tossing it towards her satchel bag before taking a wobbly step towards the smoldering stove and furs as her eyes adjusted to the dimmer light.

She froze mid-step, staring at the reddish-brown-haired boy of ten or eleven years sitting cross-legged in the middle of the furs and shooting her an unimpressed look from under a raised eyebrow.

"Who in the god's-be-damned world are you, and what are you doing in my quarters? Where are your parents?" she said in shocked exasperation, thankful that she had waited for a second longer before dropping her dress around her feet.

The boy stood and put his hands on his hips, looking her up and down.

"I fear that the answer to all three of those questions is a bit complicated and hard to believe. You are in no danger, Sudbina, I swear by all the gods. But, before we cover distracting things like the answers to your earlier questions, including why I know your name, I must tell you that I truly need your help. The entire mortal plane hangs in the balance. So, before we get to the rest, how about you throw a couple of logs in the oven and settle in for a nice chat," he said calmly, motioning towards the pile of logs.

Her mind was near panic. She was utterly awash in confusion, and every fiber of her being screamed at her to flee. Instead, she found herself doing just as the boy recommended, kneeling next to the hearth and throwing several fresh pieces of wood onto the embers. Glancing at the polished bronze panel next to the stove that served as a mirror and a heat radiator, she looked at her own shocked face and then noticed that the boy to her right was not in the reflection.

"I can explain that too if you give me a chance," The boy said wryly.

Still staring at herself in the bronze, she shook her head in disbelief and took several steadying breaths.

"You are not that drunk, Sudbina," the boy chuckled.

Unfortunately, she was well aware that he was correct. She looked from the boy now sitting next to her, holding his hands to the stove's warmth, and back to the mirror that did not show his reflection.

"I've finally gone mad," Sudbina concluded.

"No, you haven't, not yet anyway, and I hope you make it through our conversation with your sanity intact. Millions of lives hang in the balance," he said seriously.

"Who are you?" she asked without any idea what kind of answer she could expect.

"My name is Enky, and you are now the only person in all of Nysia who has heard that name, my true name, in over two ages," he answered casually.

She sat up straight and narrowed her eyes at him before crossing her arms and leaning forward to see if she could read deceit in his responses.

"How old are you then, Enky the boy?" she inquired.

Enky sat thoughtfully looking at the ceiling before exaggeratedly counting on three fingers of his hand.

"Well, this being the third age, I suppose I am some eighty-eight thousand years old," he stated.

She was incredulous at his answer but could not see a lie on his face and usually could, on non-imaginary people anyway.

"Three ages?" she asked after a long moment of silence.

"I tell you that I am eighty-eight thousand years old, and I appear before you as a young boy, and you are most concerned that there are three ages?" Enky laughed.

"Well?" she prodded

He lowered his raised eyebrow and crossed his arms, giving her an appreciative look.

"As far as Nysia is concerned, there have been three ages," he answered.

"As far as Nysia is concerned?" she questioned.

"Well, there was a time before when there were only the elemental planes and the elder gods during the Endless Eon, but there are three as far as the mortal plane is concerned. First, there was the age of discord when my sisters, brother, and I were brought here. Then there was the age of ascension, where five of us left. Currently, you mortals live in the age of devotion," he explained.

She scoffed and waved her hand at him dismissively, drawing a look of surprise from the boy.

"What are you then, Enky?" she asked, smiling slyly.

"There is the dawn of mortal life, and there is the long sleep when it is over. I am everything in between. I am that which my younger brother struggles against in futile attempts to establish order. I am chaos!" he finished eloquently.

She sat unimpressed and let out a laugh. You had me there for a bit. Now I know I am dreaming and imagining things. I hate to break it to you, Enky the Imaginary, but there are only five gods. Now, if you'll excuse me," she said, laying down facing away from him and looking at herself in the bronze mirror before closing her eyes.

"Sit back up and try to stay on topic, you need to leave first thing in the morning, and we still have much to discuss!" his voice boomed in her mind.

Sitting up in a panic, she squeezed her head between her hands and stared at the reflection of terror in her eyes in the bronze mirror. Then, after a moment, the boy appeared in front of her.

"Calm. Down," Enky stated emphatically, holding his hands up in peace.

Sudbina realized she had no way out of this ale-induced nightmare or unbelievable reality other than to hear him out.

He seemed to notice her relaxing slightly, and he sat down in front of her again.

"Look, six gods walked Nysia with you mortals during the first two ages. You are familiar with my sisters, and all living beings know Konflict by name and action. He is the only one who remained behind and also the reason I am here with you now," he explained.

"Where are you now then?" she asked, leaning to look behind him at the mirror and still finding no reflection of his form.

"I am in my own plane, sitting as you see me now. It is not much larger than this room. I do not need the grandiose of my sisters' environments. I have found it makes the conversation easier if I project my form before you. There is less a chance of my marionette going stark raving mad," he said.

"This is supposed to help me from going mad?" she asked in open disbelief.

"It has historically gone better than contacting a mortal like this!" he said once again from inside her head.

"I'll give you that," she said, holding up a finger to pause him while she collected herself for a moment from the ringing in her mind.

He sat waiting with a patient look in his eyes as she turned to face him fully.

"All right, so you are Enky, the god of chaos that no one has heard of, Some sixth god that no one knows about. You're over eighty-eight thousand years old, and you need help with something, or millions of lives may be lost. Does that about sum it up?" she asked, hardly believing that she did so in a severe tone.

He put his hand on his chin and tilted his head to the side for a moment.

"Technically, there are nine gods, but we can get into that later. Otherwise, yes, you are correct," he replied.

"Why me?" she said.

"Because you are deliciously chaotic, the most chaotic mortal on all of Nysia, it turns out, and my chosen bridge of influence to your plane. Also, because I prefer comedies to tragedies," he answered proudly.

She let out a long breath and tried to concentrate despite the apparent insanity of his statements.

"Ok then, why just me?" she countered.

"Because there are rules, Sudbina. Long ago, my mother told me that if I directly influenced or made myself known to more than one mortal on Nysia at a time, she would banish me to live amongst you all again. No offense, of course, but I prefer to pull my puppet strings from beyond the pale," he explained.

"Your mother?" she asked.

"Not important right now. At the moment, I just need you to

consider my request. If you agree to help me in saving Nysia, then tomorrow afternoon, when you check out of this room and make your way back to the surface of Quaj, call my name when you are out of eyesight of Fjall city, and I will come to you again to discuss things further," he said, standing.

"I have to agree without further details. What if my answer is no? I have free will, don't I?" she exclaimed.

"I can only influence one living mortal at a time. If it is not you, I will have to create a situation where I can converse with another. Rules and all you see," he answered, looking down at her.

"Is that a threat?" she asked indignantly.

"I would never be so direct!" he said, feigning insult before bowing and disappearing.

"Give me your answer tomorrow, goodnight Sudbina," his voice said, echoing quietly in her head.

Staring back at herself in the mirror, she stood and looked towards the door and her wigs.

"I think it would be prudent to have at least another drink or three while I think about it," she said.

Hearing a soft chuckle fade behind her, she spun around to find herself still alone in the room.

Chapter 3

Rumination

Jabruelle's pale, skeleton-like hands shakily closed the thick leather-bound tome. Then, pulling his untamed black curls out of his face, he squinted in the soft candlelight at the nearly dead fire. He did not need the warmth. Mid-summer in Ravnice made for, if anything, uncomfortably hot evenings. However, the faint crackles and dancing light made Wren's old apartment seem more inviting. He rose from the comfy chair and threw a single log onto the embers and watched as a few tongues of flame began to grow around its sides.

As the orange and red tendrils lengthened and swayed, he felt his thoughts roam along with the hypnotic twists and twirls of the brightening flames. His eyes closed slowly, and for a moment, he let out a relaxed sigh at the calming blackness his eyelids brought. His mind did not stay in the dark stillness, instead taking him back to the scene of despair at The Dreamer's Door. One after the other, his burial rights for pieces and parts of his brothers and sisters of The Sanctum raced through his mind. The images came in a quickening stream until he felt the rush of air as he once again leaped into that grim void.

This time the voice of his goddess did not halt his plunge, and as the air kept rushing past, he began to hear the deafening screams of the dead. Suddenly his feet hit the floor as he leaned forward, and his eyes pried themselves open in startlement, and he stared into the calm pirouettes of warm light in the hearth. The scream from his own throat cut off in a gurgle of surprise. Looking down at his hands, he noticed he had ripped several fingernails off, clawing his grip into the armrests of Wren's old chair.

"Apologies, Herald," he said with a sad look at the red stains on the chair and then on his own hands.

The searing pain in his fingertips brought him fully back to the present, and he clenched them into fists to slow the bleeding while looking around for some linens to use as temporary bandages. The pain subsiding, Jabruelle realized how tired he was. Nightmares were all that awaited him when he slept. Worse, in his waking excursions into The Great Dream, all he seemed to find was depressing disappointment. It was increasingly and terrifyingly frequent that Jabruelle was unsure which cathedral of slumber he was strolling through at a given time. Between being lost in The Sleeper's dream or not being able to wake from his own, he couldn't decide which of the two scenarios terrified him more. He let out a nervous laugh at the thought and then looked around, expecting someone to be staring at him like he was a crazy person. Instead, the only judging audience he found was his back-lit blotchy reflection in the glass of the lone window.

Jabruelle smiled slightly while looking towards the piles of texts he was tasked with ingesting and analyzing. He had read every book on necromancy Wren owned and some of the others that focused on devoted gifts from other gods as well. While he was still unable to reanimate the pickled cat that was left to him by the old gnome, he had learned much of the magic of his goddess. Of the two forms of reanimation, he had become proficient in the easier one. Reanimating something very recently deceased was a different and stronger form than something that's soul had already passed to the dream. Before a handmaiden takes a soul to The Sleeper, it was easier for him to reanimate their corpse with an easier but shorter-lived channeling of his gift.

Reanimating a more husk-like body whose soul was entirely in the dream was a much stronger focus of will and something he struggled to accomplish. However, reanimation was not the only channeling of his gift that he faltered with, as he had still not succeeded in attempting to pull a sentient familiar from the dream.

"Sleeper, I will keep trying. I don't believe any will join our faith if I cannot perform that feat and call myself death speaker," he said quietly to the flames.

He looked down to his lap, where his scythe lay across his knees. Notes of ancient death speakers and heralds in the texts he had finished refused to relent from his mind as he considered making his fourth attempt dominating a familiar. There were risks, not insignificant ones. Failure to maintain dominance of one's familiar could lead to summoned soul's sudden and unexpected departure from the mortal plane. If the necromancer's mind was not ready to unweave their gift from their familiar, their mind could be lost to the dream along with the sentient undead they had failed to command.

He had unsuccessfully attempted to sway apparitions of large and impressive beasts within The Great Dream in his first few attempts. In many cases, he had not even been able to get the attention of the departed spirit, let alone conquer their will. On his second venture into the grey in-between, he felt his sanity fray for a moment as he tried to dominate a vulture. Initially, he had thought it would be a fitting ward, floating over the shoulder of one who worships the lady of death.

In reality, his mind met with the singularly focused intentions of the animal and its nearly non-existent capacity for memory. Switching from one immensely felt motive to another almost dragged his mind along with it. The bird went from the urge to eat to the desire to fly so rapidly that he was unable to keep up and was barely able to separate himself from it. There had been no time to inject his own will.

"Perhaps something more intelligent would be appropriate," he said to the scythe.

Clutching it in his hands, he embraced it, intertwining his mind with the grey between life and death. Slowly the room around him lost color and became a muted darkness. Stars began winking overhead, and he let out a sigh as his mind was once again within the temple of his goddess. His consciousness floated under the vast purplish-black night sky of The Sleeper's Dream, opting to pass by several spirits he knew better than to pursue.

After a time, he came across a small but strong feline sentience. He sent out a tendril of thought to it and felt in his mind what seemed like a twitch of its ear in acknowledgment of his presence. Encouraged, Jabruelle sent another grazing coil from his mind, and he felt the hum of cat purrs in his very being. The spirit drifted away from him, not in a fleeing manner but almost coyly, and so he focused and willed his mind to pursue it, hoping desperately for another contact.

Perhaps it was finally time for him to assume the mantle of death speaker and bring forth a familiar. He followed the flicking tail and humming purr of the feline apparition for what seemed like an eternity. Each time he thought he was growing closer to it or its interest in him was gaining, it would turn away and saunter into the fog.

The distinct sound of a chainmail gauntlet pounding on a wooden door punched him back to consciousness, and he blinked several times as aching eyes adjusted to the bright light of dawn. Then, glancing about in confusion, he saw the candle he had lit the night before was nothing more than a thin pool of hardened wax on the table next to him. The fireplace contained not even the warm memory of an ember.

Gathering himself, Jabruelle headed for the door. Thankfully, there was no need to get dressed since he still wore the necromancer robe when he fell asleep. Taking the steps down to the main floor of the mortuary two at a time, he was comforted that in his careless pursuit of the potential familiar, he had not left his mind back in The Great Dream. He did wonder, with some nervousness, at what point during the night he had left the dream and simply been asleep in Wren's old comfy chair.

Opening the door, he squinted in the rising sun's light at the armored soldier standing before him. The man was not a regular militia and the sigil emblazoned on his breastplate indicated he was a member of Aanaman's personal guard.

"Sorry to wake you, sir, but Chancellor Reaper requests your presence at his residence as soon as is convenient," the guard said with a nod.

When the man did not turn to depart after delivering the message, Jabruelle realized he was there to accompany him in his trek across Ravnice.

"Ah, um right, I guess, lead on then!" he said in a fluster, awkwardly stepping outside and turning to lock the door behind him.

It wasn't like he had anything better to do at that moment than go and meet with the leader of Savja. As the guard led the way across Ravnice, Jabruelle took in the sights, smells, and sounds of a bustling summer morning in the workman-like city. Aanaman was as good a leader as the newly anointed nation could hope for, and everyone knew it. They also knew he was doing everything possible to hand his office over to someone else so he could once again retire to his crops and his whiskey. At least, everyone in

Ravnice knew it. To be fair, though, the man had said the same of his station as governor, and he had held that post for over a decade.

Jabruelle was still reflecting on the prior evening's trek into the grey of undeath when Aanaman's home came into view. It was still the same as when it was the governor's mansion of Ravnice city and state, but now it had a fifteen-foot stone wall with ramparts patrolled by his personal guard pushed out further around its border than the original wrought iron fence.

The guard stopped at the outer gate and beckoned for it to open. When the chains lowering the drawbridge-like entry stopped their clanking, he walked forward to another guard and was let through the wrought iron fence and led into the home. Aanaman's wife, whom he had only met in passing once before, gave him a warm smile and pointed up the stairs towards her husband's office.

"They are waiting for you upstairs, dear," she said with a concerned look at his hands before heading around the stairwell towards the sounds of children arguing.

He took the stairs cautiously, crossing his arms to hide his nail-less bloody fingertips, wondering who she meant by they. Jabruelle was at least confident in why Aanaman wanted to see him, and he was glad that he found the answer to the chancellor's question in his readings. The last guard at the door to the office held a hand up to stop him before cracking it open and sticking his head inside for a moment. Then, reappearing in the hallway, the guard motioned for him to enter.

Jabruelle hoped that he had kept from externally revealing his relief that the only other person in attendance was Captain Kilannry and not an intimidating unknown. He was fond of the captain, an aging native and steadfast defender of Ravnice who had graciously declined to take charge of the newly formed Savjan cavalry.

"Good morning, Chancellor, Captain," Jabruelle said, giving a slight bow to each man before returning to his awkward stance.

"Jabruelle, why do you always look like you are about to be interrogated, young man?" Aanaman asked from his seat behind the desk.

Jabruelle couldn't help himself from laughing out loud like a madman for a moment before slapping his hand over his own mouth.

"Sorry, Chancellor Reaper," was all he thought to say, and he awkwardly cringed when he heard the captain slap his own forehead.

"No need for apologies, son. Take a seat," Aanaman said comfortingly, motioning to the chair across the small circular table from Kilannry.

"Indeed, use the bard's seat. He hasn't been in it in quite some time," the gruff militiaman said with sour remorse in his voice.

As he lowered himself into the chair, Jabruelle looked across the table towards Kilannry, who sat back for a moment in feigned shock.

"Acolyte Jabruelle, have you been in a fight?" the older man asked.

Jabruelle hung his head for a moment, forgetting in his solitary existence what had transpired several days earlier thanks to one Sudbina.

"I believe a fight would involve two separate individuals exchanging blows. But, instead, the incident was more a mugging engineered by Sudbina," he said softly, staring at the tabletop.

Kilannry hooted in laughter before steadying himself and leaning in to inspect his face.

"She did that?" Kilannry asked incredulously.

"In a way," he said, sighing before turning to Aanaman to explain.

"During her last visit, she took me out to one of the wharf taverns on her last night in town. Only, that day, Sudbina was the young man. And the bald young man that was Sudbina picked a fight with several drunk sailors while indicating that his dress-wearing companion, that would be me, would effortlessly take on the lot of them if they had a problem. I don't think I need to describe how the rest of the evening went," Jabruelle finished.

After a momentary stern glance at the militia captain, Aanaman turned back to Jabruelle and changed the topic.

"Have you finished your research at the Death Herald's former home?" he inquired.

"Yes, sir. I believe I have covered all the written text regarding our goddess that he had in the mortuary several times. Though I cannot enact all the magic and rituals contained within them, I have the knowledge of them firmly in my mind," he said with rarely found confidence.

"Good, then I would ask you to take a journey to Southpoint to meet with Lorkin and the other channelers to have that knowledge transcribed and kept there. After that, they will handle disseminating it to the Archdiocese, and the clergy will spread copies to each of the cities. We should preserve as much knowledge of the gifts as possible to protect it and our people better in the future," the chancellor stated.

"Of course, sir," he replied.

"Then we will see that you get an escort and a horse to make the trip tomorrow if that is acceptable. As to the old gnome's house, consider it my gift to you for your work on our behalf. I also have news from Ingar. They have finished repairs on The Sanctum and are excited to welcome you back in Fjall to see it after finishing your business at Southpoint. Stay as long as you like in the mountains and your temple. The men I will send with you will stay at your side until you are back here if you wish. If not, send them back with word that you wish to remain in the sanctum, and I will have your things sent to you," Aanaman said.

"There will be no issue with that timing. I will prepare to depart tomorrow at dawn, sir," he answered.

"Did you find out about what may have happened to Wren at the trade bridge?" the chancellor asked him before he had a chance to leave.

Jabruelle clasped his hands in front of him and took a deep breath.

"The Death Herald carried out a ritual that brought the mortal plane in partial contact with The Great Dream. The spirits within were able to grasp for any life they could find and try to pull it into the darkness with them at the spot where the two planes met. In successfully performing *Yixia's Conjunction*, he is one of only four necromancers to conduct the entirety of the ritual. All of them died in the channeling of it. There is no doubt in my mind he knew the sacrifice he was making," Jabruelle finished in a voice barely above a whisper.

Both of the other men sat in silence for a time before Aanaman rose and walked around to stand before him, putting his hand on Jabruelle's shoulder.

"It is little in the way of consolation, but take heart in the fact that members of your order have individually done more for the people of this Island than those who worship the other three sisters combined, and at a greater cost. The trade bridge and surrounding area are being renamed Wren's Crossing. It is not much in the way of thanks, but perhaps it will add to the notoriety of you necromancers and may aid your case as you find more to worship death as you do, Acolyte," he said.

"You have my appreciation, sir. Also, if it is all the same to you, I would like to be referred to as simply necromancer. An acolyte is a title for those under the mentorship of a Death Speaker, and regrettably, I am not," he said.

"As you wish, Jabruelle the Necromancer," Aanaman said, emphasizing the singular nature of the title with evident respect that Jabruelle was unaccustomed to receiving.

*****

Sudbina waved cheerfully at the dwarven guards while departing from the mouth of the Fjall river and its cavernous entrance to the city in the mountain. The late afternoon sun was pleasant and not too hot thanks to the mountains keeping out most of the wind-carried humidity from the north. For several long moments, she walked in silence, glancing around at the peaceful woods and enjoying the flower-scented breeze that swayed the treetops.

Once the narrow dirt road wound its way around the first bend a half-mile from the city, she found herself alone and out of view of the dwarven fortress.

"All right, Enky, Lord of Mischief, let's hear more about this mad adventure I will embark on," she said to the sky.

"I am glad to hear your willingness to help our plight, Sudbina, my agent of turmoil," he said from beside her.

She jumped and held in a scream with her hand. Sudbina had honestly hoped she would just be talking to the woods like the crazy person she thought she had become and not receive an answer from the alleged deity.

"Expecting someone else?" he asked, appearing to be injured at her reaction.

"I was hoping for no one," she answered honestly, looking down at the boy walking next to her before glancing behind them to make sure no one was around to see her talking to nothing.

"Then why call for me at all?" he asked, gazing up at her with a knowing look.

34

"Because I have been wandering Nysia searching for a purpose since the invasion was put down and Svenus killed. Either I have gone insane, or a seemingly important purpose has appeared before me in the guise of an adolescent, orphaned god-thing," she said, shaking her head.

He shot her a glare before crossing his arms and continuing his trudge at her side.

"I am not an orphan, thank you very much. Aren't you going to ask me where we are going?" he said with an inquisitive look.

"I am sick of asking questions just to have you dodge or satisfy them at your leisure, and you seem hard-pressed to keep silent anyways, so I assumed you'd get around to it," she said accusingly.

"Always so titillating and frustrating all at once, my darling Sudbina! Your fickleness robs me of my rare opportunities at self-entertainment!" he exclaimed.

He eyed her up and down as if hoping that his short-lived attempt at an awkward silence would provoke further questioning.

"Fine, be that way!" he said with a harumph.

"We are heading to Daybreak's Temple in what used to be the Fjall Diocese," he explained.

"Seems a bit odd, starting our quest by visiting your sister's house of devotion," she replied, having a hard time reconciling that she was playing along with his notion of being the eldest brother to the four sisters.

"I'll be more watching you than joining you, so it would have been more appropriate for you to say your quest, not ours. That is except in the aggregate sense, in that it is a quest for all of us, mortals and gods alike," Enky said, rambling to himself.

"Ok, what does Daybreak or her diocese have to do with our quest? Whatever it may be for, I doubt you have or will give me wholly truthful answers," she asked with a raised eyebrow.

"It doesn't at all. You are heading there to meet with Luminary Ezera about joining The Cause. I believe you are aware of the spy organization run from the basement of my sister's temple?" he asked rhetorically.

"I am aware of Ezera and her agents and their organization. I am also aware, as I imagine you are, being a god and all, that friendly as she and I may be, Ezera has no reason to trust me further than she could throw me," she said.

"Ah, that is no worry because you will show up with information so valuable and important that they will be begging you to join their little band of spies," he stated with a beaming smile at his own cleverness.

"And what information might that be?" she asked, afraid to know the answer.

"That an envoy of sand elves from the nation of Zarad on the Nysian mainland will sail into the Harbor of Mer. They will arrive in just over a month. They will give you their reason for being there, which will be partially honest. However, the true reason is entirely more terrifying and the real reason I am here in the first place," he said, speaking gravely.

Sudbina stopped walking and stared at him as he paused and turned to face her.

"Is that true? Sand elves? And why are they really coming?" she blurted.

"It is true, and the fact that it is true will gain you the trust of Ezera and membership to The Cause, which will be important. I will tell you their true intentions if you complete this first task and the one after," he answered.

She stared at him, becoming more suspicious of his inability to provide complete or precise information.

"The one after?" she questioned.

"Yes. One that I think the carrying out and completion of will grow your trust in me and help your case with Ezera for what must happen next. I need you to retrieve the one you call Harpis Akkeri," he elaborated before turning to continue walking.

She could not resist the temptation of finding the lost bard and the promise of adventure in the childlike god's cryptic propositions, so she started walking after him again.

"You'll deliver her the information about the elves, and you will tell her you will bring Harpis to Mer in time for the meeting with their envoy. From there, you will head to Kalt. Ezera will assuredly have you followed. Then, when you have successfully escaped the watching eyes of The Cause, I will find you and tell you how to get to him," Enky finished.

"What if they flat out just don't believe me?" she asked sincerely.

"Sudbina, that voice of yours has never had trouble convincing anyone of anything," he said with a wink and disappeared.

"A dozen more paces, and you'll see the path to the diocese's clearing. Good luck, I'll be watching!" his voice said softly in her mind.

*****

It had been ten days since Harpis had used his gift to play a knife cut with his violin strings. Exploring this previously unknown facet of his abilities took over his full attention. Since that day, he had yet to return to the prison of solitude he found alone on the waves. Instead, he had spent his time observing and feeling the goings-on around Akriven.

Tonight he found himself sneaking out from his room to the pile of logs behind the inn by lantern light. He began mimicking what he felt in the strikes of the ax head with the pluck of his lowest note violin string and a wrap of his knuckle on the instrument's body, concentrating on weaving his gift along with the flowing resonant vibration as much as possible.

The effect was wood all over the pile flying apart in splinters, and only after dozens of attempts was he finally able to execute the feeling of an ax strike with any accuracy. He was nearly scared to death when a window from the inn swung open, spilling candle and firelight out over him and the randomly hewn log pile and kindling around him. The innkeeper looked from him to the ax wedged in a stump, to the splinters that had showered the grass.

He slid his violin as far out of view as he could. Harpis, for once, found his muteness a blessing, glad the man expected no explanation from his patron who could not speak. Harpis gave him an apologetic shrug and slinked back around and in the front door. His curiosity was aggravatingly unsatiated as he wished he could know if the plucks did indeed present the action and the sound of the ax blows.

Once back inside the glow of the inn, he paid for a drink before taking his customary seat. Then, he decided to offer a song or two to apologize for the apparent raucous he had been making. The barkeep walked the drink over himself and handed it to Harpis with a questioning and curious look.

He took it with a thankful nod and placed his violin in his neck with his left hand. Then, placing the glass precariously on the horizontally held body of the violin, he began to play while staring longingly at the dark liquor. He felt it best to provide them a sober concert of a few songs before taking the drink and retiring for the evening. As his bow pulled across the strings, he felt their vibrations reverberate down its neck and within its body.

Staring at the tiny waves that the quivering wood caused to ripple outward from the center of the liquid against the glass, he couldn't help but imagine them as swells lapping the shoreline.

Chapter 4

Momentum

Jabruelle was exhausted despite the short trip traveling from Ravnice to Southpoint. The weariness of his insomnia compounded the guilt he felt at being an encumbrance to his armed escort. The four experienced soldiers of Savja sent with him were readying five proud russet brown mares as the sun rose. Jabruelle walked over to grab the reins to his own mount from the corporal in charge of the group, and the gruff, mustached man gave him a respectful nod.

After climbing into his saddle, Jabruelle smoothed his plane black robe over his leather britches and pulled the heavy wide hood up over his head. While awkwardly clawing his wiry black strands out of his face and back underneath the hood, he was joined by the four riders who kicked dirt over the small fire that cooked their breakfast.

"We are only about two hours from Southpoint, sir. Are you ready to move out?" the corporal asked.

Still unaccustomed to being asked permission, Jabruelle fidgeted and gave a quick nod while stifling an unexpected laugh that became a snort.

The corporal looked over his mustache with concern and confusion in his tired eyes, easing his horse into a plod. Jabruelle's and the other three mounts followed its lead without further command.

"I apologize if I kept you all from getting much sleep again. My night terrors shouldn't be shared suffrage. I truly would have slept out of earshot to let you all rest," he said to the back of the corporal.

"It's all right, we're here to keep you safe and deliver you alive, and I mean to keep to those orders. God's above though lad, What haunts you so?" the man asked, scanning the horizon.

"I think perhaps your orders are a wasted effort. I don't know that she would allow me the peace of death," he said quietly, his thin hands tensely clutching the reins as he ignored the man's question.

The corporal turned until their eyes met before furrowing his brow and slowly facing forward again. They rode on for the following two hours in silence, and as he had for the previous days, Jabruelle felt entirely alone despite the traveling company. The prairies of Ravnice and then woodlands of Glasduille and north Kalt quickly gave way to the short tufts of hardy grass that claimed most of Kalt's barren southeastern coastline. Unlike the endless rows of pines encircling Kalt city, the eastern coast of the Quaj Island's farthest southern edges was home to little besides the howling wind and swaying arctic grass.

Around mid-day, the central spire of Southpoint poked above the unobscured horizon. Having just been to Southpoint before visiting him in Ravnice, Sudbina had informed him how there were plans for such towers to connect several important places on the island. The intent was to use the silent Tormenta signal language to pass messages from miles away as fast as flashes of light from the towers could carry them.

Soon the looming circular structure of Southpoint was visible around the six-story central spire. While the light tower was barely wide enough to accommodate a spiraling staircase and the watch room at its top, Southpoint itself was immense. Its exterior appeared as a single, unending smooth stone wall that towered three stories high, with ramparts allowing for the easy firing of bolts and arrows.

They halted their horses as a horn blew once from the spire. A few moments after the signal, the curved iron doors, half a foot thick and as tall and wide as a large man, rolled silently on greased bearings into the sidewalls. Through the opening strode the proud Zolga, former Tormenta officer and now Southpoint military commander.

Jabruelle let out another uncontrolled nervous laugh at the sight of the fearsome woman, drawing disconcerted looks from his escort. She was almost petite by human standards, but he had seen what Tormenta women were capable of doing. He knew the rapier on her hip had taken the lives of hundreds if not thousands. The circular blue patch and orange anchor sigil of Savja on the breast of her tight leathers reminded him that they were now on the same side.

"Well met, Necromancer," Zolga said with a slight bow before nodding in greeting at his escorts behind him.

Most people intimidated him, but Zolga did far more than others. Jabruelle swallowed hard several times before finding his voice and addressing the woman who was a member of the tribe that cleansed The Sanctum of his brothers and sisters in worship.

"Good afternoon, Commander. I do hope Stone Magus Lorkin is about?" he asked softly.

"The Prime Channeler is finishing his lunch in our shared office. I'll take you to see him. First, you all will need to dismount and walk your mounts through the entry," she said, motioning for them to follow her.

"Prime Channeler?" he asked.

"Those who Lorkin deems practiced enough to wield their gift in battle have been named Channeler. I admit Lorkin does not much appreciate the unofficial title of Prime Channeler I have given him," she explained with a smirk.

As they walked into the stone tunnel, the doors closed behind them with a bell-like toll, followed by heavy mechanical knocking as locking mechanisms fell into place. Finally, after twenty paces, they emerged on the far end of the ring-shaped building and into the courtyard that stretched several hundred feet before them. A second set of iron doors slid closed behind them as they passed out into the open, and Jabruelle looked behind him and then straight ahead to the identical exit on the far side.

"You four can put your horses up in our stable for the night. Then, any of my raiders will be able to steer you towards the mess hall. Go ahead and get some food and rest." Zolga said to his escort, pointing first at the small wooden stable building against the wall behind them and then to the small door on the left of the courtyard.

"Come," was all she said to Jabruelle before heading towards the door to the east.

Walking behind her, he looked around at the many windows that dotted the three-story interior face of Southpoint, noting that each had heavy iron shutters hanging on either side.

"No windows on the outside?" he asked, trying to make conversation with the woman.

"It was enough of a struggle convincing the dwarves to put in windows on the inside. Still, they took General Shieldborn's design concept of a singular walled circle too literally for my taste. Come, I'll show you the best view before we head inside," Zolga suggested, turning towards the far side of the courtyard, and walking them up to the curved doors.

"Open the southern gate!" she shouted to the window nearest them.

The doors slid open, and they walked into the tunnel's darkness, while light began spilling in as the exterior doors rolled back. Zolga led him outside onto the singular dock that stretched as wide as the gated tunnel out into the sea. It could easily accommodate two galleons lengthwise on either side, but now, there was only one of the giant ships moored there and several single sail schooners.

"Beautiful, isn't she?" Zolga asked him, raising her eyebrow.

"If I am honest, she looks much like the other galleons I have seen, though I certainly find all of the ships built by The Tormenta more than impressive," he answered, watching as several of the crew bustled about the vessel.

"The *Torrent* may look like our other ships, but she is the fastest boat to sail the seas of Nysia. Her hull is almost twice as thick as the others of the Savjan navy, and her masts can withstand much more strain. More importantly, the crew was handpicked from across Savja. So, what do you know of Southpoint's purpose, necromancer?" she asked, waving to the crew and leading him back into the fortress.

"I know that Lorkin intends to train gifted folk in the art of magic combat and to record as much as possible about the strengths and weaknesses and machinations of the given and inherited gifts," he replied as they emerged back into the courtyard and headed to the door to their left.

"It is that and more. It is also where we will develop and perfect tactics and techniques of leveraging magic and traditional forces in combat together. Southpoint is a school, fortress, and base for Savjan's elite raiders," she said proudly, opening the door and leading him into the lower level.

"Raiders, like Tormenta raiders?" he asked, genuinely

intrigued.

"In a way. We are focused on being deployed via our ship across the Savjan islands within a day from being tasked. We are working out the optimal contingent. Our goal is to put a forty-strong dwarven phalanx onto a shoreline that ten, eight-crewed, sculls have secured under cover of two sets of twenty crossbows and bows in concert with magically gifted protection and offense," she said.

"Sounds terrifying," he answered as they reached the third floor and walked down a long hallway.

"That is the idea," she said with a grin and knocked on a nondescript wooden door.

"Please, come in," he heard Lorkin say gruffly from inside.

Zolga walked into what looked like a small library and picked up an empty plate from in front of the chair across from Lorkin's before sitting down.

"I'll take my leave if you don't mind. I plan to oversee the drills this afternoon," Zolga said as she closed the door behind herself.

"Thank you, commander!" Lorkin shouted after her receding footsteps.

"She is not the most amiable military officer I have ever been around. However, one cannot argue that woman's intelligence or savagery when it comes to battle and tactics or effectively keeping troops humble and inline!" the old-looking dwarf said with a laugh from his seat, motioning for Jabruelle to sit.

Jabruelle reached into his robe with slightly trembling hands, pulled out the leatherbound notebook, and slid it onto the table after lowering himself into the chair and pulling straggling black hair from his face.

"The tome of the last necromancer," Lorkin said softly, reverently taking the book from him.

"It is the compilation of The Sleeper's given gift, her magics, and their workings, minus all the rites and rituals that were solely religious. I hope it is acceptable, Stone Magus," Jabruelle said quietly, staring at the tabletop.

Lorkin set the book down and laid his hand on it before lightly slapping the tabletop with his other.

"Up here, lad, show some confidence. You are the senior-most gifted necromancer and an invaluable resource to your goddess, our young nation, and your faith's future. There is no shame in you wearing the mantle of your station, lad," Lorkin stated comfortingly.

It was odd for Jabruelle to hear compliments and praise, and he struggled to accept both from the revered dwarf, but after a deep breath, he met the mage's gaze.

"Thank you, Prime Channeler. I have a request, if I may, now that I have delivered the texts," he asked, trying not to sound like he was begging.

"You've simply but to ask it, and for Sleeper's sake, Lorkin is fine," he said with a tinge of frustration at the title.

"I would like to stay awhile and learn the ways of battle magic, become a channeler under your tutelage. I am the last of my kind. Without the ability to wield my gift in combat, I will find it difficult to defend or grow my goddess's faith, I fear," he said.

"I'd do it even if just to give you more trust in yourself," Lorkin replied.

"How many other gifted people are here at Southpoint?" Jabruelle asked after sighing in relief.

"Fire Mage Lyrnah and Water Mage Helki have both earned the rank of Channeler, thanks in no small part to their role in the Battle of Wren's Crossing," the dwarf said, pausing.

"Ezera is training Dobry Hammersmith to use his cleric bulwark in combat at their temple, though they often visit here. We also have several apprentices who were with us at Lake Gitche during the invasion that are still in training," Lorkin finished.

"No others with the sisters' given gifts?" he asked the dwarf while staring at his slender fingers.

"Well, we've got you now. High Priestess Galonica sent word to Zolga only yesterday that two storm priests will be headed our way to train. Weeks ago, I sent word to Jawylap Atoll asking Moodi Shen to share his knowledge of The Wild and her magic with us," Lorkin answered.

"Do you think the troll will come?" Jabruelle asked excitedly, brightening at the thought of meeting with the kin of the former Death Herald.

Lorkin shrugged unknowingly in response.

*****

44

Sudbina was quickly tired of most situations. Spending half a week in Daybreak's Temple behaving herself while doing nothing more interesting than eating or sleeping was akin to outright torture. In the beginning, she had found mild entertainment as the lone audience member in the pews watching Dobry Hammersmith carry out rituals for the goddess of light and life.

Ingar's son was nice enough and had happily welcomed her to the place of worship when she had arrived. But flirt and prod as she tried, he had said nothing more of Ezera than that she was away on travel and would return soon and that he had no idea what The Cause was. Heated arguments with Enky had filled some of the evenings as she considered changing her mind on their arrangement, but each time he had won her back with hissed temptations of finding Harpis and traveling to the Nysian mainland.

About to begin her newfound ritual of fighting her mind into a state of slumber, she fell out of the bed when the door was flung open, and candlelight from the hall danced off Ezera's blond tresses.

"Good evening Sudbina. What brings you to Daybreak's Temple?" Ezera said with a smile on her face and suspicion in her pale eyes.

"Oh, it is good to see you too, Luminary. You embody the dawn herself!" she said, bounding to her feet and embracing the taller woman.

Sliding her hands from Ezera's shoulders slowly down the small of the cleric's back and onto her butt, her advance was halted as the other woman grabbed her wrists and looked down at her with a knowing smirk.

"Nice try, Sudbina the sly, but I do not keep the keyrings to this place in my beltline," Ezera said, handing over a thick black hood.

"Well, you'll have to forgive me for the attempt. Besides, I wouldn't consider the endeavor completely wasted," Sudbina said, giving Ezera a seductive wink and hungrily gazing at the woman's rump.

"Put the hood on, and let's go chat about what brings you to visit me here in Fjall.

"As you wish, spy mother," Sudbina said, smiling as the hood covered her eyes. Ezera led her several times in circles and turns

45

around the small building before heading down the stairs into the cellar and kitchens. At least that's where Sudbina assumed they were based on the acrid smell of Dobry's pickled cabbage that accosted her as they descended. Kind as she was attempting to be, she had not made the mistake twice of agreeing to dine with him for supper.

A pause later and the sound of heavy stones sliding against each other, they went down another set of stairs, and she could feel the air cool considerably. Ezera guided her around a table, and she heard the screech of a wood chair sliding on stone, and then Ezera slightly pushed her down into the seat before pulling off the hood.

As she squinted and blinked while adjusting to the lantern light of the temple's second basement, she watched Ezera walk to the other end of a long dining table and sit at its head and then nod while looking past her.

"You sure she is to be trusted?" a deep but feminine voice asked behind Sudbina.

Turning in her chair, she let out a whistle at the chiseled form of a petite female dwarf with maces in her belt loops that walked past her and sat along the side of the table.

"To be trusted? That depends entirely on the topic or task at hand. However, she is a friend and means us no harm. Of that, I am sure. Sudbina, meet Itka Frothbrew, a warrior of The Cause and protector of myself and Mahala.

On cue, the tiny chestnut-haired woman bard walked past and sat on the table's other side, kicking her boots upon its top with an unimpressed look.

Sudbina was beside herself as she looked fondly from Mahala to Ezera and back to Itka. Then, leaning forward, her elbows on the table, she gave Mahala a pleading look.

"Sing me a song, dear bard, your voice could tempt The Siren herself, and I miss its croon!" she asked.

Mahala rolled her eyes and looked impatiently back over her shoulder toward Ezera. The blond woman crossed her arms, and a serious look came over her face.

"Out with it, Sudbina. What brings you here, asking about The Cause and pestering poor Dobry and insulting his cabbage?" Ezera asked sternly.

"Our motivations were once aligned, and it worked out for all of us. I believe we are once again on parallel paths, and I would desperately like to join The Cause. I mean, I did want to join. That is why I came here. However, after seeing the raw beauty of its members, I would never forgive myself for not attempting to join such a society," she said honestly.

Sudbina knew lying would not get her very far, with Ezera scrutinizing every word.

"I can count on my fingers the living mortals that know of The Cause. Tell me then, from whose lips did you seduce it forth?" Ezera asked.

Sudbina panicked for a second and started looking around the room. Her nervously shifting eyes settled in shock at the boyish form of Enky standing behind Ezera's chair for a moment, shaking his head from side to side.

"I have my sources, and I choose to keep them private on that matter as I will on at least one other," she said.

She felt her calm returning and knew she had the means to captivate all three women.

The dwarf scoffed, and Mahala stood from her chair.

"Just let Itka torture it out of her Ezera. This whole charade is a waste of all our time," the bard stated flatly.

"I can find Harpis!" Sudbina yelled out, and Mahala froze mid-step, looking down at her wide-eyed. Then, glancing from the bard towards Ezera, Sudbina caught the fleeting image of Enky smacking his forehead with his hand and then acting like he was slamming it on the tabletop.

Seeing the rest of the women were in stunned silence, she decided to bring up the information Enky had instructed her to present first.

"More importantly, there are foreigners, elves, on their way to our lands. They will arrive at the docks of Mer in a month. I'll meet you there with the god singer if you promise to let me into your merry band of operatives, Ezera," she demanded as confidently as she could. The sultry tone of her voice making it hard for her to take herself seriously when speaking with attempted authority.

Mahala took a step back and sank back into her seat. Across the table, Itka slammed down the flagon she had just finished drinking and then pointed an accusing finger at Sudbina.

"Your breath smells heavy with horse manure!" the dwarf accused.

Sudbina wasn't sure what the dwarf was getting at, so she looked at Mahala with a questioningly raised eyebrow.

"Itka suggests you are a liar, and I don't think she is wrong," Mahala said with a glower.

Sudbina looked desperately to Ezera across from her, and the blond woman was deep in thought, drumming her fingers on the table and staring pensively at her.

"I don't think she is lying, though I can scarcely believe it to be the case," Ezera said after a few moments.

"What've you got to lose besides a trip to Mer?" she asked the table.

"Where did you get news of these visitors, and where is Harpis?" Ezera asked, staring her down.

"As I said, I choose to keep my sources to myself. For now, anyway," Sudbina said, hoping the offer of future indulgence would help her case.

Ezera crossed her arms and leaned back against her chair for a moment before looking from Itka to Mahala, who offered only shrugs.

"The complete audacity of your claims aside, why does the wandering rogue of Savja want to become a member of our little organization?" Ezera asked seriously.

"Because I am bored. Because I enjoy tempting, swindling, meddling, lying, and stealing. I can think of nothing more joyous than doing so in the company of such fascinating companions and for a good cause," she explained truthfully.

"Giving impossible to believe intelligence and then also refusing to accommodate any inquiry as to its origin is either the very worst or very best way to solicit entry into an espionage organization. Very well, Sudbina, if you are proven correct, and you deliver Harpis to Mer, consider yourself offered membership into The Cause," Ezera said.

Chapter 5
The Sea of Sand

Enky had so far been pleased with Sudbina's willingness to play the starring role in his personal dramaturgy. He was also surprised and impressed by her ability to keep her sanity as he communicated with her. A long line of failures in this endeavor over millennia had him more than worried about introducing himself to his most cherished marionette. Still, he had learned enough from the Sirul debacle to understand that he need not, no, he best not, leave everything in a single pair of hands, nor those hands without help.

The bare stone wall of his tiny plane had long ago turned into a portal to The Nexus. He stared into the howling cavity of more than ancient stone for long moments before deciding nervousness did not befit a deity of his station. He slipped barefoot out of his plane and onto the cold floor of The Nexus and let out a sigh as he stepped fully into the archaic chamber. Glancing about, he looked at the other six walls, expecting at any second for his sisters to appear from their planes to accost him.

Directly before him was the long inactive portal that led to Nysia, the plan that belonged to only his brother now. Enky's destination was the one on its left that belonged to one of the younger twins. Silent and swift as the shadow of a hunting bird across a field, he found himself before a stone wall churning into the swirling visage of a forest. He sniffed the perfume of flowers and the welcoming scent of dew from the air beyond the portal and snuck into his younger sister's plane.

It had not been since The Age of Ascension that he had visited any of his siblings in their realms. Walara, The Boundless Growth, was as beautiful as he remembered it, and as wild and welcoming as the goddess that lived in it. He followed the sound of a trickling stream and soon found himself sitting at its edge, bathing his feet in the cool tickle of its passing waters.

"Brother," he heard his sister say from behind him.

Enky turned and smiled up at the dark-haired, olive-skinned visage of a young woman clad in flowers, moss, and vines.

"Your Wilderness," he said, standing and bowing as if to royalty.

"A rare thing indeed to see you and not just your machinations or projections beyond the four walls of your domain Enky," she said, returning the bow and smiling.

"Not for no reason, dear sister, I have a favor to ask you, towards our shared interests in stopping our brother from eradicating devotion to anything save himself from the mortal plane," he said.

*****

Erimo sat tall in the saddle box of his camel, patting its albino white fur, shared by all those bred for the military. Staring out at the endless unmoving waves of sand that stretched before him, he took inhaled the dry, furnace-like air of the desert. Behind him, the soft plods of another camel came to a barely discernible halt, and a high-pitched whistle blew several times to signal the advance. Then, with a click of his tongue and a slight nudge of his knee, Erimo's mount obediently turned to face his senior brigadier.

Other races found it nearly impossible to tell one bronze-skinned and blond-haired sand elf apart from another, but that was because the other races did not have the time necessary do understand and identify their deviations. Erimo knew every crease in the other elf's face, the uniqueness of his expressions, and the fleck of gold that glinted in his brown eyes. Such bonds were formed and understood only amongst and between other sand elves. Even more so for Nathken and he, after eight centuries spent serving together.

"And so, for the first time in generations, a sand elven army marches forth from the fortress city of Zarad. Take a good long look, Nathken. It may be a year or more before we see her again," Erimo said with a tinge of sadness, watching his army begin its slow march out of their city's front gates.

50

Looking above and beyond the approaching column to the south, he took a moment to glance to the east and west at the fifty-foot ivory colored marble wall of Zarad that stretched in both directions. Unlike many of his soldiers, he left no family behind to miss him. In truth, The Sea of Sand felt like more of a home to him than the city itself. The city itself had not seemed like home as long as he could remember, spending nearly his entire adulthood patrolling its vastness in service to Vizier Mistis.

"Oh, I don't worry at all, High Marshal Erimo. With the great Desert Eagle himself at command, we can't help but overcome our enemies," Nathken said, giving him a playful shrug.

"I am not sure which of those titles I find more ridiculous," Erimo said, smiling at his friend.

"Well, being one of the three high marshals is quite impressive if you ask me. However, being revered by every soul under your command as the great golden eagle of The Sea of Sand is another thing altogether," Nathken said, nodding his head at the front rank of the column that was just now slowly marching past them. To a one, the soldiers tipped their spears or helms in respect of the two elven officers.

They all wore tan cloth cloaks and bleached leathers just as he and Nathken did. The only difference in their uniforms was the filigree on their saber handles, and the name and house etched along the blades. Tokens of identification for the fallen, to be returned to whichever of the five families they hailed from. The bloodlines were intrinsically important to most sand elves, a claim on the purity of one's ancestry. Those of the first house had the most direct blood ties to the first Aelar.

Erimo drew his saber for a moment and glanced down its blade with a smile. His first weapon as a foot soldier had been engraved with the family name Abda, the fourth house of Zarad. Every rank since, including being named a High Marshal, he had his new saber inscribed with the ancient Aelaran runes for Warrior and Desert. The only brothers and sisters he knew were those he served with, and the only place he felt at home was the sands.

After sternly surveying several passing ranks of elves, Nathken turned and guided his mount so that he was directly next to him.

"Did the Vizier or Commandant offer any more information when you met with them this morning?" Nathken asked, looking back at the army.

The only time Erimo had witnessed such a procession had been in parades and displays. Never in his life had such a large force been sent outside of Zarad's walls. He was ordered to go north with twenty thousand of the most experienced elven soldiers, two-fifths of their entire actively serving military. Ten elves across and with strings of camel-towed supply wagons in between every formation of five-hundred marching elves, it would take the better part of an hour for his army to make it out of the city and into the rolling dunes.

"They were just repeating what they had said weeks ago mostly. That there was a threat to all mortal races, including our own. They said a horde has been moving across the north of the Nysian mainland, conquering human nations. We are to stop or delay it as much as possible while the city prepares for an impending siege," he answered with a shrug.

"What of the wood elves? The trolls? The dwarven clans? I can understand not trying to fight alongside the humans, but surely the other elder races must be willing to join us in this fight?" Nathken asked, gazing northward.

"I have been told that messengers and emissaries have been sent to all the nations of Nysia. However, according to Mistis, there is not enough time to wait on a response. Hence, we are to march north to meet this threat and impede it," he replied.

"Where are we headed, Erimo?" Nathken prodded.

"Due north for a month and a half until we reach Necaka and its capital city," he said.

"Through the entire Sea of Sand and another two weeks further north into the mountains and valleys of the nation of mages?" Nathken asked incredulously.

"The other two marshals and I met with the commandant at length. We are to assume Soalia, Obava, and Trava will have fallen by the time we make it out of the desert. Bolstering the defense of Necaka will prevent the gifted humans from falling in line with the conquering forces. We can use the Necaka mountain ranges and the rivers that flow east and west from their peaks into the seas as a natural defensive border," Erimo explained.

"There is logic there, I suppose," Nathken conceded.

"I was told to expect an attacking force of a quarter of a million humans. But, if we hold them on the far banks of the rivers and the mountains long enough, perhaps the men of Sumka and the dwarves, trolls, and wood elves will answer our call and crash into the enemy from behind," he said.

They both looked as the last of their army made it out of the city gates, and the enormous iron portals slammed shut.

"Two-hundred-fifty thousand human fighters! What warlord could have gathered such a large force?" Nathken asked in apparent disbelief.

"Allegedly, the very worst one," he said with a defeated shrug.

"What if the rivers and mountains and then warriors and mages of Necaka are not enough? What if we fail to defend this proposed border?" Nathken questioned in an out-of-character outburst.

"If it comes to that, we will use the greatest weapon our people have, the endless miles of sand where our army can become nearly invisible. We can drag the enemy through the furnace until attrition becomes their foe," Erimo answered, giving his brigadier a stern look.

"I trust the vizier not, but you have my complete faith Erimo. I shall gather the other brigadiers and let them know we are headed for the northern sands. Perhaps it is best, for now, to leave it at that. Sir," Nathken said, nodding in respect and turning his mount away.

Erimo saluted his friend with his saber before sheathing it and nudging his camel towards the front of the army, now barely visible in the distance.

*****

While Sudbina had been all but certain that Ezera had sent an operative to follow her, she could not confirm her suspicions until she had reached the familiar confines of Kalt city. There, surrounded by the cool, drizzly alleyways and street corners, she had been able to catch glimpses and fleeting movements indicating she was not alone when she ought to be.

Sudbina had spent the better part of the morning slipping in and out of taverns she knew well. She randomly changed direction and pace, going from an amble to a sprint and back and forth. All the while, the edges of her perception were fleeting and fraying with the sensation of being watched. Multiple identity changes along the way had also been unsuccessful in losing her perceived shadow. She had entered a tavern as a blond woman, leaving it the young, bald man. Then she had flirted and drank for several hours at an inn on the wharf before donning a raven-haired wig and climbing out a window.

It wasn't until she had strolled onto the grounds of the Tormenta shipyards, formerly the Kalt family lumber yards, that she finally felt as though she was not being followed. Unless her babysitter had been a Tormenta, it would be hard-pressed to blend in with the sea's overly pale people with black and white hair. Though the invasion was over, the peace treaty signed, and the nation of Savja formed, The Tormenta were not overly fond of company, and the other races of Quaj island still gave them an understandably wide berth for the most part.

So, it was Sudbina saw only Tormenta around her as she strolled about for an hour, greeting several women she did recognize before making her way to the shipyard's lone tavern. Walking up to the young Tormenta man cleaning the bar top, she laid her hand on top of his to stop his scrubbing.

She made sure to give her most invitingly teasing giggle as he startled at her touch. She had little trouble manipulating most folk, men especially. Tormenta men, who until just recently were subservient to their womenfolk and were now enjoying the freedom of independent choice, were by far the most pliable victims she had encountered in some time.

"Well met...?" she greeted him, using the silence and her eyes to plead for him to introduce himself.

"Kallion," he said with a short bow and a nervous smile.

"Nice to meet you, Kallion. My name is Mahala," Sudbina said in a kittenish voice, trying not to laugh at how angry the bard would be at using her identity.

"How may I help you then, Mahala?" he asked, smiling, and returning to his scrubbing of the polished wood counter.

"Any chance I might be lucky enough to run into High Priestess Galonica or Commander Zolga at the shipyards today?" she asked hopefully.

"I am afraid I haven't the privilege to know the coming or going of two such high-ranking women, madam," he said apologetically.

She did her best to pout her lips in disappointment at the

young man and gave him a grin when he pressed on in a blatant attempt to provide her with something.

"I will say that I haven't seen them here in some time, and I've heard no gossip of arrivals anytime soon. Of late, the only ships at our docks are those newer galleons just out of drydock and finishing being outfitted before being crewed and deployed," the man offered.

"Very well, Kallion, that is unfortunate. I had hoped to lay my eyes upon their fine forms while traveling in the south. Maybe you can ease my disappointment," she said in a sultry voice, leaning in and cupping his chin in her hand.

"Uh, what, er how, can I give you?" he stammered in a flustered voice.

"Rent me a room for the evening and allow me to purchase a bottle of wine and some cheese and bread," she said, dropping all enticement from her voice.

She smiled as his shoulders sagged, and he nodded before bending down and straightening with a cloth-wrapped loaf, a small wheel of cheese, and a bottle in his hands. After placing twice the silver coins necessary on the bar and taking the items from him, she raised her eyebrow impatiently.

"Oh right, sorry!" he exclaimed, plucking a room key off a row of hooks on the wall behind him.

"First door on the left at the top of the stairs," he finished with a short bow.

After latching the door behind her, Sudbina looked around at the small room containing only a lantern, flame striker, and a hammock hanging from hooks on either of the walls. Ducking under the hammock for a moment, she walked up to the tiny window the room had and glanced around in the growing gloom of dusk to see if she spotted her pursuer or anything else odd.

Satisfied, she lit the small oil lantern and hung it on the hammock hook on the right wall before awkwardly climbing into the cloth and netting bed. She nearly fell as she got herself into a lounging position with one arm holding the wine, cheese, and bread. Then, rocking slowly from the momentum of the effort, she unceremoniously bit the cork sticking out of the bottle's top and pulled it out with a satisfying popping sound.

After several long pulls from the wine bottle, she leaned back into the hammock and tried to calm nerves frayed raw by two days spent trying to evade prying eyes.

"Enjoying your travels in the south?" a boyish voice said quietly from next to her.

Her eyes snapped open to the view of Enky on his tiptoes, peering out the window next to her.

Instead of immediately entertaining his question, she shot him a glare and decided it was her right to happily munch some bread and cheese before engaging with the supposed deity. After a few moments of watching her eat and drink, he grumpily crossed his arms and gave her a severe look.

"Yes, I am enjoying my trip south, thank you very much," she said sarcastically around a hunk of bread.

"Are you sure you weren't followed here? Are you sure you are alone, and there isn't an eavesdropping agent of The Cause outside that door listening to you talk to yourself?" Enky said with a smirk.

"If anyone is out there eavesdropping, it is that lustful young barkeep downstairs. But I imagine if whoever Ezera sent to follow me was here, you wouldn't be," she concluded.

"Indeed, your pursuer is in Kalt but abandoned following you when you made the shipyard. Clever girl," he said appreciatively.

"I was only playing the girl," she corrected.

"My apologies, dear Sudbina, I meant no offense," Enky offered, with his hands spread.

"Who was it that Ezera sent?" she asked, wondering what the child avatar's appetite for ambiguity was today.

"What is the fun in telling you that?" he said chidingly.

She looked pleadingly at the ceiling and took another gulp of wine before looking back at him.

"Well, I did as you bid, as I am sure you know, given that you were there firsthand and unnoticed it would seem," she said.

"Not exactly as I bid, but you achieved our desired outcome," he agreed.

"What next? How do I find the most famous bard, if not the most famous man across the Savjan islands when no one else has heard a rumor about him in more than half a year?" she asked.

"Bard," Enky scoffed.

"Not a fan of music?" she asked in confusion.

"Harpis Akkeri is a descendant of the harpies just as you are, my dear Sudbina. But, unlike that jester of a man, you need not an instrument or any music to wield your gift. It is elegantly indistinguishable on that silken voice of yours, bending the will of mortals to your wiles," he said in a sullen voice, sitting on the floor with his back on the far wall.

"See, I knew you had a sense of humor, Enky, suggesting I have a more powerful gift than a man known as God Singer," she said, rolling her eyes.

"I suppose you have another explanation for how the words that drip like honey off your tongue and lips have always seemed to get you just what you desire and always when you need it most?" he asked.

Unwilling to play along with what she assumed was a deflection by Enky she tried to turn the conversation back to her reason for being in Kalt in the first place.

"Seeing as you're the oldest thing to exist, being a god and all, I'll take your word for it," she replied.

"I am by no means the oldest being to exist! I may be as old as the mortal plane that you call Nysia, but there are creatures more ancient than I here, too," he insisted.

"Oh, and what would that be?" she asked, indulging him despite herself.

"The dragons, for one, mother brought them here from the elemental planes to help me and my siblings shepherd the elder races," he stated matter-of-factly.

Sudbina squinted her eyes for a moment and forced herself to press him on the issue of Harpis instead of letting him meander her mind down what seemed to be a history lesson.

"Why do I need to retrieve Harpis anyway? What good is a bard that cannot hear or sing?" she asked.

"He can hear fine. His mind has just chosen not to let him. But, of course, you'd be like that too if you'd heard my angriest sisters screaming firsthand!" he laughed.

"Ok, so his ears work just fine, but his mind won't let him hear. What am I supposed to do about that?" Sudbina said, frustrated at his endless conversational pirouettes.

"Do not worry, Sudbina. Harpis will hear your voice despite his mind, so long as you really want him to listen. His voice was damaged, I am sure, but I doubt it is permanent. We need him to help undo this calamity he has unleashed," Enky finished gravely.

"What exactly did Harpis unleash?" she asked in surprise.

Enky shook his head at the question before standing from his seat and moving next to her hammock.

"Harpis is in the town of Akriven. It is about halfway up the coast between Kalt city and the bottom of the Fjall mountains to the north. Find him, show him he can hear and probably speak too for all we know, and convince him to come with you. He needs to be there when the elves arrive in Mer," Enky said.

"I'll head there in the morning. Now, if you don't mind, I'd like to finish my dinner and this wine and get some sleep before dancing on your strings again," Sudbina said.

"If I am honest, the sound of your voice makes me long with nostalgia for the time when my muses flew these skies, and I could hear their songs on the ethereal winds that flow between your plane and my own," he said forlornly looking at his feet for a moment in silence.

"Remember, Sudbina. You must not reveal my existence or machinations to any other mortal. Mother is watching," he said, holding up a chastising finger before disappearing.

"You know, life was a lot simpler when all I had to do was wander and scheme to myself about killing Svenus Kalt," she said in exasperation to the ceiling before finishing the bottle of wine.

Chapter 6

A Healing Voice

Enky smiled triumphantly as he stared at his toes wiggling atop feet propped up on his desk. Sudbina, while as incorrigible as ever, had proven that despite her fickle nature, she was true to his intentions. Within the day, she would reach the town of Akriven, where Harpis Akkeri was suffering through self-imposed exile.

While Enky was unsure of the state of the man's vocal cords, he was hopeful they would heal enough in due time to play the necessary part in his scheme. As far as reaching the recluse in the sensory prison built within his own mind, Enky knew that Sudbina, a distant descendant of the beguiling harpies, was up to the task. Her intoxicating voice would be able to invade Harpis' purgatory of silence. Of that, he was sure.

"Disorder seems to be unfolding as intended. I suppose it is time to look at how the struggle against it is going," Enky said, sliding his feet off his desk and reaching for the gold frame on his wall.

In it grew the haunting visage of a town besieged. From ages of watching this plane and others, he knew that it was the town of Cherna, the first large settlement one would encounter traveling from the newly conquered country of Obava towards the capital of the Travan nation. Almost four months into his brother's campaign to bring order to the Nysian mainland, there had been little resistance to the incessant horde of glowing, red-eyed warriors that Konflict commanded.

Enky guided the frame's perspective to pull back from the immediate view of his brother's black-plated form at the forefront of the attacking formation. Enky gasped aloud at the magnitude of the newly formed army under his brother's influence. Fifty thousand Soalian and Obavan men and women bristling with various arms and many with ornate Obavan armor stood ready to charge the town that had maybe the same number of citizens altogether.

Across the few hundred feet between Konflict and the ramshackle town defenses, there was nothing but fear. A black armored gauntlet held the god's ever-dripping obsidian spear high in the air and then pointed it straight ahead at the town, and the ember-eyed horde streamed past him without a scream or bellow. There was only obedience in Konflict's army, no need for cheers and war cries to help motivate the forces.

When the throng had nearly reached the perimeter of berms and broken wagons that ringed the town's edge, several arrows and stones were loosed from the force of farmers and ordinary citizens cowering behind their makeshift wall. Dozens of Konflict's fighters died, but their charge did not slow. As they were about to reach the defenders, Enky watched in surprise as some five-hundred Travan calvary riders came sweeping up from the south into the flank of the horde.

The wall of riders a hundred wide and five deep became an elongated triangle as the lead riders were able to push deep into the melee. Konflict's forces, caught between the horses and the townsfolk, were quickly butchered as the inspired defenders rushed past their perimeter to join the fray and help their soldiers. Enky jumped to his feet and raised a fist cheering at the apparent success of the counterattack, and for a moment, the child-like god felt some hope at Nysia's ability to slow or ultimately stop his brother on their own.

His joy was short-lived, though, as was the success of the Cherna townsfolk. Konflict's armored arm pumped back and forward endlessly, each time, his black spear appearing in his and then flying forth, striking cavalrymen from their saddles at an impossible rate. Thousands of possessed warriors died in the counterattack by the horse riders and the citizens, but it was not enough. Moments after Konflict joined in the fighting, the tide had turned, and the cavalry went from being on the attack to being surrounded and helplessly butchered.

The horde then rushed forward, reaching the partially built fences and embankments of Cherna's defenses, raising weapons towards the defenders. Just as hope looked lost and defeat seemed inevitable, the fighting stopped. Where seconds ago, Enky had seen a defiant people ready to fight to the last, there were now simply more glowing red eyes as the people of Cherna became one with the dominated souls of Konflict's struggle.

There was no need for further bloodshed. Once there was no hope of struggling against the forces of order, the souls who lost their hunger for strife and independence came under the dominion of Konflict. Without the need for verbal commands or intonations, the god strode forward past the recently defended town and into its heart. The city's fittest and most skilled fighters fell in line, more than replacing those lost in the battle. Those not adequate to the pursuit of his conquest became mindless automatons that would provide the necessary supply and logistics his army would need as it swept onward across Nysia.

Enky sighed sadly at the eerie red glow in every eye that had replaced any visage of rebellious, independent resistance the people of Cherna had so recently had.

"When hope has died, there are only those at Konflict's side. I suppose the mortals should be thankful your hunger is for obedience and not purely for bloodshed," Enky mourned.

*****

It had only been a few days since Harpis cut apart a woodpile by sawing his violin bow across its strings, and he had become obsessed with understanding how he had done so and exploring what else he could play. Only two days ago, barely hours into his attempts, he realized that his inability to hear forced him to feel, making replication via his gift that much more of a puzzle.

His yearning to solve that riddle had him back out at the edge of the sea today. He had trudged away in the pre-dawn hours and spent the day watching the tide come in and then recede in the afternoon. The waves rolled onto the sand like the ripples of rum in his glass atop his humming violin the night before. Harpis felt pulled back to the sea as if she might have the answer to his questions.

While he could not hear, he could feel the thudding roar as the man-high waves curled downwardly into the sands, sending spray and white foam flying. He imagined the caressing touch of the waters quickly being sucked back into the sea as the next wave

61

pulled in the seas before it before diving headfirst into the beach itself. After a while, he ran his hand down his forearm as the next incoming wave sucked out the waters. Then, as the late afternoon sun kept sinking, he lamented for the first time in months that he did not have access to The Hall and its many instruments.

While his violin did not feel capable of calling forth the waves of the ocean, he felt sure that if he had the metal symbols to crash together or a gong to strike, he could weave his gifts on those notes to mimic the rush and crash of the sea. Though the day spent at the waters he had so often called home had been meditative, he was still frustrated at his lack of understanding of the newly discovered abilities of his gift.

Standing, he brushed sand from his trousers and closed his eyes as he gave himself to the sensation of the roaring summer winds blowing inland from the southern seas. His eyes snapped open at once, and he looked down at his violin case. He could not hope to play the notes of a crashing wave thundering into the beach or the receding sigh of waters being sucked back into the sea. The wind, however, was something inherently familiar to him. The Siren's screaming gales were a part of his very being, even before they took his voice and hearing.

The violin, his tool of choice, embodied the crying sorrow that those winds carried. It was more than capable of matching the moaning keen of their song. He hastily unlatched the case, grabbed the bow and instrument, and waded ankle-deep into the shallows while staring down a rogue swell almost twice as tall as he was. He nearly stumbled as the current tugged the waters from around him out to sea. He clutched the neck of the violin and patiently waited. Then, with the wave looming above him, he stared it down and drew his bow across the strings, summoning forth the same roaring vibrations that he had felt sticking his head over the balcony at The Hall as gusts flew up the face of the cliffs in northern Tuath.

His mouth hung agape as the wave was thrown upward and back to sea without a single drop landing near him. He barely had time to cringe as the next wave crashed in. Fed by the previous swell being flung up and onto its back, it roiled and sucked him under the surface. He curled around his instrument and bow protectively and waited with the patience of one who lived by the sea for the wave to relent its burdensome crush holding him to the seafloor.

Wading out of the water, he smiled wide. He had just played a wind gust! Wouldn't Mahala love to know that they could play acts of nature themselves! Shaking his head, he took his boots off, flung them over his shoulders, and began the journey back to the Akriven tavern. He was soaked, barefoot, and for once, truly happy, swinging his violin and bow as he walked to dry them along the way.

*****

Harpis had months ago timed his walk from the shoreline back to Akriven and the comfort of its inn. The sky was painted orange by the nearly disappeared sun as he reached for the door handle and walked into the soft din and comforting warmth. A small fire burned low in the fireplace. He leaned his boots against the hearth bricking to pull the last bit of dampness from the leathers.

His routine of late had been to eat his dinner, then perform for his audience before ordering his drinks and retiring to sleep. The people of Akriven, too, had come to follow a routine with the inn packed at nightfall to hear the bard play a few songs. Given how crowded the inn became before dinner, he must not have lost much of his musical talent even though he did not hear it to assess for himself. Either that or the people of Akriven were just poor judges of musical talent.

Sitting on the stool, he looked down at his bare feet, grinning from the thought of what he had done that day. He looked over the anticipating patrons to the barkeep and motioned for a drink. Today was one he would celebrate, even if he would do so alone despite the inn's plentiful company. When the barkeep handed him a glass, he downed it in a single gulp, held up a finger, and nodded to ask for one more. The owner, understanding his request, gave a slight bow and walked back to fetch more rum.

The drink's fire in his empty belly was followed almost immediately by the anticipated tingle at the edge of his mind. Placing dry violin to his neck, he began with several fishing jigs. If he could sing the words, he would spin the tale amongst the notes of a fisherman's fabled struggle and glorious catch, a victory at the sea's edge that mirrored his accomplishment that day.

After playing the first two songs, he noticed the grinning barkeep had returned with a second glass, and he looked out at the

63

applauding crowd. Harpis was appreciative of their silently clapping hands. He winked at the owner, threw back his second drink, handing the glass back and diving right back into the sawing of his bow and the vibrations of his violin. After several more renditions of local music, he had exhausted his repertoire of fishing ditties, drinking anthems, and Kaltese lullabies.

The barkeep returned with an unordered rum this time, shaking his head in apparent disbelief at the raucous people of Akriven and their bard-encouraged purchase of food and drink. Harpis gave the man a small salute and happily took the glass, adding it to the mind-numbing comfort already in his stomach. Welcoming the calming burn of the rum, he placed his bow across the violin strings and simply played.

There was no purpose or previously heard song he used for inspiration. He simply played how he felt and let the vibrations of his instrument carry his thoughts as he went on, eyes closed, feeling the thumps of dozens of feet stomping along with the rise and fall of his cadence. Harpis found himself mourning the memory of what music sounded like despite his newfound abilities. He would trade them all, his gift too, to hear the sea or wind again instead of just feeling them.

He could feel the pull and push of his bow slow across the strings, and he became sad as he wished too that he could hear Mahala's excitement at what their gift could truly do. He longed for the drinking company he knew could be found in Aanaman's office. He sorrowfully regretted the hurt he saw in Kalna's eyes when he left. Then he thought of his first drink at the tavern where she worked and the old gnome who had bought it, and he let out a sob.

He opened his eyes, staring down at his violin vow quivering in his hands, and looked up to the perfectly still townsfolk before him. Tears streamed down multiple faces, and to a one, they wore expressions on their faces that depicted his inner sadness. Then, placing his hand on his heart, he mouthed an apology and carefully stood from his tool and walked through them towards the stairs and his bed, trying not to weep like a child.

At the top of the stairs, he took several deep breaths to steady himself and opened his door, excited for sleep but afraid of what the recently conjured memories might summon to his slumbering mind. Closing the door behind himself, he turned to feel his way towards his bed in the darkness when suddenly the room was awash in yellow light as the hood was pulled from a lantern held by a small figure on his bed. Recognizing Sudbina, his eyes went wide before he instinctively cringed away from her. Then, dropping his violin case, he tried to cover his neck and other exposed skin with his hands or leathers while watching for her blowgun to appear in her hands.

Unmoving, Sudbina wiped a tear from her cheek before laying her hands back in her lap. He relaxed some, still looking down at the woman suspiciously.

"That may have been the most beautifully depressing instrumental ever played by mortal hands," she said in a more enthralling and tantalizing voice than any other he had ever heard.

Harpis scoffed and rolled his eyes before he realized that he had heard her words and his own rasping grunt in response. Then, slapping his hand over his open mouth, he ran over and snatched her off the bed in a giant embrace and kissed her bald head.

"Easy there, bard, or is it, dock worker? When was the last time you bathed? You reek of sea salt and rum and are a long scraggly beard away from taking the lead part in a play about a castaway that washes up on the Kalt shores!" she exclaimed.

Ignoring her, he turned back towards the door, unlatched his case, and pulled for the violin with trembling hands. He placed the violin in his neck and drew forth several cords of *Panoryla's March* before nearly dropping the instrument in excitement. Then, laying it back down, he clutched his ears and stared at her, fearful that at any moment, he would once again return to the prison of silence where he had spent the better part of a year.

"How?" he asked in a rattling whisper, sliding his hands from his ears to his throat in the same protective and shocked manner.

"Perhaps because you truly wanted to, or maybe at last you were finally ready to," she said with a shrug, glancing over his shoulder for a moment before looking back at him with a smile.

He looked at the empty wall where her gaze had gone and then back at the woman dressed as a young man. Sudbina stood and walked up to him, laying her hands softly on his shoulders.

"It was no small thing you did at Lodestar, defeating the Tormenta priestesses and dispelling their summoned storm. Tawito said it was like he heard The Siren herself screaming from the crater. It was a wonder in and of itself that you escaped with your life after hearing the Quaji's description of what happened to the priestesses around you," she said, glancing at the floor for a moment and shaking her head as if to dismiss whatever imagery the statement had conjured.

He had spent months burying the sadness and guilt he felt at outliving his dearest friends and the family he had found in The Syndicate. After so much time having only his thoughts and inner voice to battle, Sudbina's voice carried history and memories right back to the surface of his consciousness.

Still looking up at him, he could sense Sudbina reading every emotion as it passed over his face.

"Harpis, you have given decades of your own life to The Sleeper. You spent what must have felt like an eternity without your voice or hearing the music that embodies your gift after invoking the screams of The Siren herself to the mortal plane. Your sorrow is for what was lost. Instead, think of what you saved. Hundreds of thousands of people across this island are now freely living their lives because of you. Me included," she finished, pulling herself into his arms and resting her head on his chest for a moment.

Her hand went to the nape of his neck and tilted his head towards hers. Then, standing on her tiptoes, Sudbina put her lips next to his ear.

"Thank you," she whispered, her lips barely brushing his earlobe before she pulled away and sat back on his bed.

The flood of woeful emotions that had been about to overtake him were washed away by a surging torrent of more basal and instinctive feelings provoked by the sensuous assault she had just unleashed on his nearly virgin ears. It took several vigorous shakes of his head to regain his focus.

"Sudbina, how did you find me, and why are you here?" he asked through much effort after coaxing damaged and long unused vocal cords to the task.

"You forget, mighty God Singer, that I too am from The Siren cursed south of Kalt. After you disappeared, I eventually took it upon myself to look for you. Now, I will say I knew that the southwestern shores were a barren and dreary place full of only fishing villages. However, it is only when you lose count of just how many of them there are, dotting the map between the Fjall mountains and Kalt city, that you appreciate why our people drink so much rum," she said proudly.

He crossed his arms and waited for her to answer the rest of his question, still suspicious of why the woman had set out to find him in the first place.

"We can get to my motivations some other time. For now, let us just leave it as fortunate. Let us focus on what should be your reasons for leaving your Kalt penal colony and returning to the people that care for you," she suggested.

"I have come to prefer this simplistic life," he answered in a whisper, not even believing himself.

Turning behind her, Sudbina grabbed and then held up a leather-wrapped stack of parchments.

"A simplistic life doing nothing more than playing and drinking your days away with the folk of Akriven? I read through most of this while you were away today. This research into the previously unknown and fascinating aspects of the bardic gift is quite interesting. But, I wonder, was this despite your recent affliction or because of it?" she asked with a bemused expression on her face.

Harpis angrily snatched his notes from her hand and glowered back at her.

"Harpis, this knowledge should not die with you and your liver here in Kalt. If you are unwilling to leave, at least let me copy it down and take it to Southpoint to share with Lorkin and Mahala," she pleaded.

The thought of Mahala not knowing what he had learned sent a pang of guilt into his belly, as did the idea of not seeing her face when she learned of it. He looked from Sudbina to the papers he held before dropping his hands to his side.

"Southpoint?" he asked in a clawing, scratching voice.

*****

Aanaman sat alone in his office, watching the light from a lone candle dance in the caramel-colored whiskey swirling in his glass from the roll of his wrist. He stopped the waltz of light long enough to take a deep sip before closing his eyes and listening to the patter of heavy raindrops and the distant but growing thunder of a summer storm blowing across the planes of Ravnice.

Soft knocking at his office door pulled him from the

meditation found in good whiskey and the smell of rain.

"Yes?" he asked, trying not to sound impatient as he waited for one of the guards to pop their head in with whatever question or report they had for him at this late hour. He sat up in surprise as his wife's tresses spilled around her face as she leaned through the doorway.

"Shanowen, I thought you would be fast asleep by now. Did the thunder wake you or the girls?" he asked.

"No, dear, I was up talking with our guest. Mother is here to see you," she said with a smile, giving him a slight bow and turning to hug the other person in the hallway before departing to the creaks of wooden floorboards.

He crossed his arms and raised a curious eyebrow as Ezera walked in, closing the door behind her and sat in the chair across from his desk, brushing blond locks out of her fierce blue eyes.

"Come in and have a seat, mother of spies and apparently my wife's guest," he said sarcastically.

"I was merely catching up with the more amiable and talkative leader of the Reaper family before coming to see you. I do not involve your wife in my affairs, Aanaman," she said seriously.

"And why is it that one of my guards was not here to announce your presence?" he asked.

"I do not believe they are aware you have a visitor, as was my intention," she said with a smile.

"Bah," he said with a wave before taking another long sip of his whiskey.

"What brings you from Fjall to Ravnice and my home, unannounced and unwitnessed in the middle of the night?" he asked with some concern.

"Sudbina recently paid me a visit at my temple. She was there to talk of The Cause, not with Daybreak's Luminary," Ezera explained.

"How is the mysterious vagabond? That she called upon you hardly seems like an event worthy of your visiting me so hastily and in person," he stated.

"She said she was off to find Harpis and that she would bring the bard here," Ezera replied.

Aanaman sat his glass down harder than he meant to as he looked at Ezera in shock.

"He lives? She knows where he is?" Aanaman asked, unable

to contain his excitement. He had all but given up his friend for dead, as Harpis had so entirely and quietly disappeared.

"Allegedly," Ezera said, turning to grab an empty glass and the decanter of whiskey from the meeting table behind her.

"As meaningful as the bard's livelihood is to you and I and many others, that is not what brings me here to see you in this way. It was the other claim she made that sent me here so quickly and secretively," she said, pouring herself a glass and then handing him the decanter.

Chapter 7

Erudition

Jabruelle stood atop Southpoint's ramparts with his hands snugly shoved across his chest and into his armpits. Even in summer, southern Kalt's early morning chill and coastal wind caused his slight frame to shiver despite his thick black necromancer robe. He calmed himself, knowing that before long the sun would crest over the horizon to his left, and the warmth of its rays would ward off the cold.

"You'd think a lad who grew up in Kalt city and then lived for years in the Fjall mountaintops at The Sanctum would be more accustomed to the bluster of a coastal morning," Lorkin laughed, looking back out to sea.

Jabruelle let out an uncontrolled nasally laugh before bridling his unabated outpouring of nervousness.

"Er, ahem, sorry, Stone Magus. Admittedly, I did not spend much time outdoors at either location," he said, taking in the sea.

"You don't say?" Lorkin said, looking him up and down with a raised eyebrow.

"I do say…" he responded awkwardly, unsure of whether the dwarf was serious or not.

Lorkin let out an exasperated sigh and turned towards the waters himself with squinted eyes.

"Your young eyes see anything?" the mage asked, and Jabruelle was glad for the change of subject.

He pulled out the looking glass Zolga had lent him the night before and scanned the horizon for a moment before taking a break and looking up at the sky above them.

"Not yet Prime Arc… er…Lorkin. When did she say to expect them?" he asked, hoping to avoid beratement by the old mage at the use of formal titles.

"She said the first rays of morning," Lorkin replied.

Looking upward, the dwarf pointed an old, gnarled finger at the sky.

"There, see? Slight tinges of orange and yellow in the blue above. It should be any moment now," Lorkin exclaimed.

Jabruelle looked at the magnified horizon through the looking glass tube and did a short skip jump in excitement.

"Ah, as if on your very cue Lorkin, I see the blotch of their blue and orange sails now!" he shouted.

Soon after, the lookouts of the fortress, whom he knew were not privy to the exercise plans, started sounding the alarm of assault. Southpoint became a blizzard of activity as hundreds of Savjan soldiers busied themselves. Within minutes, a column of two hundred warriors wielding padded staffs, swords, and shields marched out the gates and onto the Southpoint dock, and another hundred filled in the ramparts around the mage and he with quivers of flat nose arrows.

The great galleon of the raiders was now closing in on the empty docks below, and Jabruelle caught himself painfully gripping the stone rampart in anticipation.

"Will any magic be channeled during today's assault?" he asked the mage.

"No, that comes later, after the visiting battalions from Lake Gitche garrison have had a few walk-throughs. Pay attention, though, and see where you think your gift could play a part or where others may be applicable," Lorkin responded.

The mage was staring intently, arms crossed in front of him, while he scrutinized the unfolding scene with the discerning gaze of a military general.

"Do you think Zolga will take Southpoint?" Jabruelle asked eagerly.

"I have yet to see the commander and her raiders fail," Lorkin replied with a widening smile, winking at the few archers nearby who heard him.

Jabruelle looked on in fascination as the ship swept near the dock that was now bristling with defenders before turning sharply to circle back out to see. In its wake, it left the now vigorously rowing swarm of ten sculls that went after one side of the dock while two larger assault boats were then dropped and rowed towards the other. The attackers quickly forced the soldiers on the pier to retreat from its furthest end as dull crossbow bolts peppered them from the several members of each scull while more were raining down on them from the dozens of crossbows on the assault boats.

No sooner had the defenders begun to backpedal than the galleon finished its sharp, wheeling turn. Zolga masterfully brought it in, broadsiding the end of the dock. Before mooring off, wide drawbridge-like sections of the vessel's upper railing and first subdeck fell with thuds. The elite phalanx of dwarves rushed out into a shield wall formation and began quickly stepping their way towards the now fully retreating defender formation.

Shaking his head in amazement, Jabruelle spotted something beyond the galleon and pulled the lens to his eyes.

"I did not know a Quaji ship was taking part today. How exciting!" Jabruelle shouted.

When he looked down at the confused dwarf holding out his hand for the looking glass, he grew concerned.

"There was no Quaji ship planned for today's operation," Lorkin said evenly, looking out to sea.

*****

Jabruelle was unsure about the exact source of Zolga's frustration as the woman finished her exasperated verbal abuse of several of her officers before glaring at the newly arrived company and storming off. The arrival of the Quaji catamaran caused the training exercise to conclude early. Still, it was apparent to even his infantile understanding of military tactics that the docks were already lost, and the fortress would have fallen. The iron doors of the front gate slid on their tracks to let the Tormenta woman stalk out into the tent city of the visiting units to join the other officers in discussing the day's exercise and lessons.

The receding sound of her stomps somewhat calmed his ever-frayed nerves, and Jabruelle looked back to Southpoint's newest guests. He had met the Quaji representative Tawito before, during the Tormenta invasion while they were both at Lake Gitche. He knew the man was originally an associate of The Syndicate and a longtime friend of the famed and fabled Turin Deadeye. The hulking form of a mountain troll that traveled with Tawito though, was unknown to him.

"Ever the perfectionist, that one. Come, let us talk in my study," Lorkin said with a nod of his head after the departing commander.

"I better go smooth over her ruffled feathers. After all, I interrupted her mock orchestra of death," Tawito said with a grin as he walked towards the gate.

Jabruelle and the troll that introduced himself as Moodi Shen followed Lorkin into the circular fortress and the dwarf's study. The whole while, the steps of the troll reminded Jabruelle of the death herald who had welcomed him to The Sanctum. She had allowed the adolescent young man from Kalt to shed the burden and shackles of his family name to join in the worship and service of The Sleeper.

Reaching the third floor, Lorkin opened the same door Jabruelle had passed through upon reaching Southpoint a week earlier and motioned them in. They stood around his desk while the dwarf quickly pulled a third chair from a writing station on the other side of the study before bidding them sit.

"I must admit, I did not expect the great shaman Moodi Shen to answer my call to build a body of knowledge on the magical gifts," Lorkin stated.

"Moodi answers her call, not yers good dorf!" the troll said with a guttural laugh before turning in his chair to face Jabruelle fully.

Moodi leaned in, his lanky, sinewy form almost falling out of the chair that was barely large enough to hold it, and Jabruelle leaned as far back from him as his own would allow. With their noses almost touching, the troll flashed him a grin and then put his greyish pointed ear to his robed chest. Jabruelle tried not to squirm like a child and looked pleadingly at Lorkin for help, but the dwarf only grinned at him over the troll's enormous head.

After a few seconds of listening to his chest, Moodi lifted his ear from Jabruelle's black robes and looked him in the eyes.

"Heavy with the sadness in there," Moodi said somberly, poking him in the chest with a long finger.

The troll then placed his palm on Jabruelle's forehead. The action was one that he usually would recoil from. However, an odd aura of comfort seemed to surround Moodi Shen. The troll slowly pulled his hand back and shook his head mournfully.

"Sleeper's chosen can't find slumber, and nightmares tear his dreams asunder!" Moodi said with a chuckle, and Jabruelle couldn't help but expel tension with a cackle of his own that caused Moodi to erupt into further laughter.

Lorkin sat, mouth open. The dwarf looked like he was about to speak when Moodi interrupted him.

"S'okay, Lurking, Moodi, show them Awata's blessings!"

*****

Harpis hadn't questioned the plentiful coin Sudbina had produced when they procured horses from a stable keeper in Akriven. For all he knew, the coin had belonged to the man himself or some other victim of the woman's sticky fingers the night before. Though he was happy not to be walking, his groin and legs ached mightily from the two-day ride towards the southern tip of Quaj, where she said this Southpoint castle was.

At sunset, the pink and orange sky provided a starkly contrasting backdrop as the towering circular fortress came into view, and Harpis shook his head in awe.

"It would seem the dwarves have been very busy these past eight months. What was the purpose of this place?" he asked, looking at the impressive three-story structure.

"As I told you, Aanaman has begun building signal towers and fortresses at strategic places around the island to allow for an improved ability to defend against would-be conquerors. Southpoint was the first and, as far as I know, the only one completed so far. Lorkin trains battle channeling here to those that pass his assessment, and this is where our young country's raider battalion resides and trains," she said.

They were almost in the long shadow of Southpoint's signal tower when a horn blew, and he watched as the heavy curved doors slid wide, revealing a tunnel-like entrance into the courtyard.

"You say Lorkin is building a library of texts regarding the gifts here?" he asked, hoping for further reassurance at his motivation for coming out of hiding.

"What, don't you trust me, Harpis Akkeri?" Sudbina asked in a mischievous purr.

"I trust you to be you," he said, shaking his head and trying not to smile as she feigned injury.

"You wound me so!" she exclaimed as they walked their horses through the tunnel.

"I don't think you do it on purpose, but chaos itself seems to swirl around you and follow in your wake," he replied with a wink.

Harpis tilted his head at the curious expression that flashed across her face as they came into the dusk-lit circular yard. He did not have time to prod her about her reaction, though, as Moodi lifted him from his feet in the crushing embrace of leather-clad, greyish-green sinewy arms.

"Hair Piss!" Moodi Shen shouted in his face before looking at him with concern.

Harpis turned to look accusingly at Sudbina for not telling him the addle-brained troll was at Southpoint. Still, when he saw the complete shock and confusion on her face at the sight of Moodi, he suspected she was unaware of his presence at the fortress or even who he was, for that matter. Harpis' suspicions were confirmed when the troll dropped him to his feet. Moodi then stepped towards her, dropping to his knee and kissing her hand before touching it to his forehead.

Reverent formality turned to an aghast look of curious intensity as Moodi hastily returned to his feet, clutching his face with both hands while staring over his fingertips at the bald woman.

"What's wrong with him?" Sudbina asked with a sharply raised eyebrow.

"I wouldn't even know where to begin," Harpis replied honestly.

He watched on, confused, as Moodi looked past Sudbina, his eyes at her waist level with his mouth open in surprise and his eyes wide. Sudbina glanced from the troll's odd expression behind her almost fearfully, and after a second, the troll wagged his finger, chastising the emptiness behind Sudbina.

"Told you his name, did he?" Moodi asked Sudbina. For the first time since he had met the woman, Harpis watched in wonder as she seemed unable to come up with any sort of response.

Moodi then turned back to him, crossed his arms, and gave a disapproving look.

"Should be no sad. The screamer's pain is fading, and the gnome is happy with the dreamer! Got tea to help you voice Hair Piss!" the troll said, rummaging around in one of his leather satchels.

It was the bard's turn to be caught off guard as he struggled to respond to the mention of his healing wounds and Wren's passing.

"Uh, I am ok without your tea Moodi. Thank you," he said and sighed in relief as he saw Lorkin, Jabruelle, Zolga, and Tawito making their way to them.

Harpis found the whole reunion almost overwhelming. He had spent two days steeling his nerve to be around folk he had abandoned and to talk with Lorkin about what he had discovered about his gifts. Seeing Moodi, Tawito and Jabruelle had him wavering between sobbing and cheering. Sudbina nearly tackled Zolga, and the Tormenta woman then led her away after waving at him in greeting.

The dwarven mage and two men joined them and Lorkin gave him a slight bow before embracing him.

"It is good to see you all," Harpis rasped, a tear rolling down his cheek as his crackling voice broke with emotion.

"By the Sleeper Harpis, you have your voice back!" Lorkin exclaimed.

"I can barely whisper, but yes, and my hearing has returned in full, it would seem," he said, straining.

"It is good to see you, bard!" Jabruelle said, bowing low in plain black robes.

"You as well," he whispered to his departed friend's last pupil.

"Come, this is cause and company for an ale or three and a tale or five! Lorkin proclaimed and motioned them all to follow him into Southpoint.

Harpis found Tawito walking at his side as they went down several hallways and up multiple stairs.

"What brought you back? Not many choose to find their way back into their old lives after completely disappearing from them." the Quaji man asked.

"I've discovered knowledge that I feel I must share. I have been led to understand this is where to do it," he replied.

"Why now?" Tawito prodded.

"I suppose I had finally found that I missed some of you," Harpis whispered with a smile, and Tawito gave him a slight shove.

"In truth, though, you'd have to ask Sudbina. She found me and it was her voice that finally reached me," he said, raising his hands in resignation.

"I doubt the goddesses themselves could discern that woman's intentions," Tawito said with a laugh.

*****

Sudbina followed excitedly as Zolga hurriedly led her down several hallways before pausing at the door and knocking.

"Galonica will be so deliciously jealous that you were blessed with my company for dinner while she sits at damp and sullen Lodestar lording over her priests and priestesses!" she said to the Tormenta warrior.

Zolga's only response was shaking her head and running a hand through her stiff, short-cut hair as the door swung open.

"Hello, Sudbina," Galonica said, her arms crossed over her blue-robed chest.

Sudbina squealed in delight and leaped into the arms of the High Priestess.

"Oh, but the two of you storm goddesses will be more enjoyable dining and drinking partners than Harpis. I'll enjoy torturing smiles forth to your faces much more than I did trying to cheer up the gloomy bard," she said, grinning.

Sudbina gave Zolga a pouting look and pursed her lips as the warrior rolled her eyes and shut the door behind them.

*****

Harpis leaned back in his chair, feeling unburdened for the first time since before Turin's funeral. He even laughed out loud at the comical exchanges between Moodi and the nervously cackling Jabruelle. Raising his tankard of ale in a toast at Lorkin, he joined in the back and forth.

"Is it Prime Channeler or Stone Magus then? I guess Arch Mage wasn't good enough for the mighty Lorkin!" he chuckled quietly.

He wasn't sure if the dwarf, staring at the study's doorway, didn't hear his struggling voice or if Lorkin was ignoring him.

A second later, there came rapid knocking, and the door was thrown open before Lorkin could even bid the caller enter. Harpis nearly fell out of his chair as the petite form of Troubadour Mahala

Shelta strode into the room with an oddly familiar looking blond female dwarf, Zolga, Galonica, and Sudbina in tow.

"So, you weren't lying after all," Mahala said, looking Harpis up and down and then turning to give Sudbina an appreciative nod.

"Ezera will be glad to know you've held up your end of the deal so far.

Harpis looked from the oft glowering Mahala to Sudbina and back again.

Zolga strode into the room and took the ale from Harpis, handing it to the female dwarf, who downed it in one gulp and placed it on the table, smiling at Lorkin.

"I'd switch to water if I were you. We depart in force at sunrise for Ravnice to meet with the Chancellor," Zolga said, leaving.

Harpis crossed his arms and shot Sudbina a glare, and the bald woman shrugged sheepishly before disappearing out into the hallway with the two Tormenta.

Mahala looked down at Harpis, and he couldn't tell if she was happy or angry to see him.

"You can once again hear and use the gift?" she asked

"Yes," he said quietly.

"And the wonders pile up!" Mahala exclaimed.

Harpis wanted to protest. He had only agreed, begrudgingly, to come with Sudbina to Southpoint. But, joyous as his evening had been, sharing drinks and dinner with old friends, his stomach churned with nervousness at the thought of returning to Ravnice and the memories the city held.

"Aanaman said to let you know that he is glad you are not dead. Shanowen Reaper said to tell you that they both miss you and that their daughters are expecting a God Singer sung lullaby in the next few days," she said sternly.

He decided that there were limits to even how sorry he could feel for himself, and those limits were disappointing Shanowen Reaper's daughters.

Chapter 8

Amends

Harpis sat alone with his thoughts on the bow rigging of Zolga's raider galleon, *Torrent*. The visiting battalions from Lake Gitche stayed and garrisoned Southpoint while the entire contingent of raiders were onboard, per Aanaman's request. Mahala and Itka, whom the Troubadour had introduced to him only this morning, traveled with them. Jabruelle seemed happy to travel by sea back to Ravnice, sending his escorts back at their leisure with the horse. Lorkin had opted to stay behind, saying someone had to babysit the new fortress and record Moodi's knowledge of The Wild's magic before the troll and Tawito departed.

Anxiety, guilt, and excited anticipation dominated Harpis over the eight-hour sail north to Ravnice. The rushed visit at Southpoint had been somewhat more of a reassurance than he had expected. No one had shouted him down as a coward for fleeing into hiding after the events at Lodestar.

Harpis accepted responsibility for silencing the Tormenta's final attempt at causing death and destruction. He had endured for months with the cost of once again uttering the true name of a goddess. Still, he could not hide from himself, his soul. He knew that Harpis Akkeri had chosen exile, surrendering to its habitual, austere comforts. Aanaman and others had been working to rebuild the peace of Quaj and unite diverse peoples into a nation. He, their supposed hero, the one they called God Singer, allowed himself to retreat to the sea like a giant Kaltese hermit crab with an empty rum bottle for a shell.

As Ravnice came into view on the sear's horizon, he took several steadying breaths against the pain of happy memories sailing into the city. Then, he made his way deftly off the rigging and joined Sudbina and Jabruelle at the ship's rail.

"Jabruelle, would you mind if I stayed with you at Wren's while in town? I haven't decided how long that may be yet, but if it is more than a few days, I will talk with Aanaman about getting a room at the tavern where I lived before," he asked the necromancer.

"Of course, Harpis, it would be my honor. I've never had a guest!" the odd man answered in a jittery voice.

"You don't want to stay at The Siren's Scream? I'll pay for a second room for you if you don't have any silver, though I doubt Kalna would charge you at all, not in money anyways," Sudbina said in a teasing voice.

"She still works there?" Harpis asked, trying to keep fear and hope from cracking his already soft and raspy voice.

"Work there? No, the pretty thing owns the place now, turns out she had a pair of exceptionally generous over-tipping customers whose coin she had stuffed away over the years. When the owner died a few months back, she had bought it from his son. You best find your way there to see her," Sudbina threatened.

"I am not even sure what I should say to her, Sudbina," he said in resignation.

"Well, you have ears to hear any berating she may deservedly have ready for you and at least some semblance of a voice you could use to apologize when she finishes. So, make amends with that beautiful woman, or I'll get Zolga to lend me a few raiders to drag you before her," Sudbina said with a smirk, patting the blowgun sheathed in her boot.

Giving her only a grunt in answer, he looked to Jabruelle and noticed the leather belt that looked big enough to wrap twice around the man's waist slung over his shoulder with leather pouches Harpis was sure he recognized from somewhere else.

"Where'd you get that Jabruelle?" he asked, tapping the slung strap.

"Oh, Moodi Shen gave me some herbs for tea. I have…trouble sleeping, but not since he gave me these and the recipe for more! I'll make you some tonight when you come by the mortuary!" he said over his shoulder as the vessel bumped against the Ravnice dock, and he stepped off.

Sudbina nudged into his shoulder and threw him a wink while adjusting a brunette wig.

"Don't worry, Harpis. You'll come to thank me for bringing you back. I'll be following up to see if you've shown your face at the tavern," she said with a finger raised in warning before jumping from the ship to the dock.

Harpis turned as the galleon deck got more crowded while Zolga's raiders moored the boat and began security patrols around the Ravnice wharf and the ship's deck. He saw Mahala and Itka quickly converse with Zolga and Galonica before the commander, and the High Priestess disappeared back into the ship's cabins. The bard and warrior stopped at his side before disembarking.

"Get yourself some dinner and some sleep, Harpis. Aanaman is expecting you after breakfast, we'd join you this evening at The Siren's Scream, but we have a few things to attend to first. We'll find you after your talk with the chancellor tomorrow," she finished, and the two of them headed to the wharf.

Harpis looked down at his boots, standing inches from the edge of the ship. Then, letting out a soft breath, he began another chapter of his life by once again stepping from deck to dock.

*****

Standing outside The Siren's Scream, watching the sign swaying in the lazy summer breeze, Harpis felt more trepidation than he had facing down enemy armies. He stood alone, and he felt alone. Still, he knew this would be the first step in many on his journey back into a life that had brought him undreamt-of joy and caused him unimaginable pain. With the sun not fully set, he opened the door to the quiet buzz of a few conversations and the clanging and bustle of a kitchen and bar preparing for the busy din that befell all wharf bars at dusk.

Inside, he let his eyes adjust to the lack of sunlight and peered around, inspecting the place for signs of Sudbina. He walked slowly, dragging his hand along the smooth bar top as he headed for the rear of the inn and his and Wren's customary booth at the back behind the stairwell. The kitchen door creaking open and bouncing off the wall as it swung wide captured his attention, and he quickly hid a look of confusion as an unrecognized young brunette woman curtsied at him and walked up to the bar.

"Afternoon, sir, have a seat where you like. I'll be right with you," she said with an easy smile that he struggled to return.

81

Turning towards the back again, he rounded the stairwell wall and froze in his steps when he looked to sit in the booth. Where his and the gnome's habitual meeting place had been, a large vase now sat on a stool with a few flowers in it under a painting of the sleeping goddess of death. He quickly wiped tears from his eyes as he heard footsteps behind him.

"Sir, there is an empty booth here," the serving girl said, holding a warm loaf.

He let her lead him to a small two-person table next to the larger back corner booth where he had once watched Sudbina hold court over a dozen drunken would-be suitors. It now held stacks of parchment and pens, an inkwell, and a basket of napkin-rolled silverware. The girl reached for one of the rolls and handed it to him before placing the loaf on the table with a small chunk of butter.

"What will you be having? It's a bit early for dinner yet, but the stew has been cooking all day if you'd like some, or a drink perhaps?" she asked with a warm smile.

"I'd like to see the owner please, if she is in," he whispered as loudly as his vocal cords would allow.

She straightened, giving him a confused look before walking away with her head tilted and arms crossed.

Hearing the kitchen door swung wide again, he clutched the tabletop in front of him to keep his hands from trembling and could feel his skin burning flush with anxiety at the sound of two sets of footsteps.

"You haven't even served him yet, what's he got to complain about?" he heard Kalna grumble as she approached.

As soon as she came around the stairwell, she slapped her hands over her mouth in shock. Sliding out of the bench, Harpis stood, and she ran to him and wrapped him in the most welcoming hug he had ever felt before pulling back and punching him in the chest.

"Meera, fetch two bowls of stew and two glasses of our finest Reaper vintage!" she yelled back at the serving girl before going to the corner booth and grabbing charcoal and parchment, which she began furiously writing on.

Harpis walked up behind her and stayed her hand with his own.

"I am sorry for everything, Kalna," he said in a choked

82

whisper.

She dropped the parchment and grabbed his face, tears falling down her cheeks.

"You have your voice back!" she exclaimed.

"Not all of it," he said hoarsely.

"And you can hear?!" she shouted happily, boxing his ears with slaps of her hands before kissing his cheek and punching him in the chest again.

"Where in The Siren's cursed seas have you been! I'd given you up for dead!" she demanded.

"Then where are my painting and flowers?" he said quietly, pointing at the mural of The Sleeper after they slid into the booth.

She stared at her hands, lacing her fingers on the tabletop before looking at him with tear-rimmed eyes.

"Maybe I hadn't quite given up hoping you'd show your ugly face again, you horse's ass," she said accusingly.

The walls of staunch emotional armor he had built in defense of his decision to stay hidden on the Kalt coast crumbled at the shakiness in her voice. He looked away from her and wiped fresh moisture from his eyes, looking at the memorial to his friend, realizing that she had given him a small semblance of closure by removing their old table.

"What made you get rid of it?" he asked, turning back to her.

"A booth in a bar is useless if none of the regulars will sit in it, nor let anyone else use it, regardless of how crowded this place gets," she explained.

"Besides, now you can't sit there alone and feel sorry for yourself across from an empty seat no one could ever hope to fill. You'll have to deal with me for company now," Kalna said, trying to cheer them both up as Meera returned and deposited two bowls of stew and their drinks before bowing and tending to other patrons.

"Pretty little thing, isn't she?" Kalna asked, and Harpis flushed, unsure of how to respond.

"That is where you say, not compared to you, Kalna," she said, shaking her head and grinning at him, her blond hair falling around her shoulders.

"Sudbina certainly won't leave the poor girl be. Sailors, soldiers, and other drunks Meera can disarm with ease, but watching that girl squirm under the Sudbina's gaze is quite the entertainment," Kalna said with a laugh.

"Is she renting a room here?" he asked, surprised he had yet to see her.

"Rent? No. Sudbina owns a room here. We keep it cleaned and such for her. She stops by now and then when she tires of wandering or wants to harass my staff or chat me up. The last time I saw her, she dragged that poor lad Jabruelle here and got him roughed up by the crew of some ship out of Mer. That one is trouble incarnate," she said, shaking her head.

"You know, that is where we came to celebrate our victories, and now it is a mausoleum to the cost of the last one," he said sadly.

"You are back here in Ravnice, and for me, that is another victory worth celebrating. Given all that has happened, I think Wren would agree," she said, looking at the depiction of the gnome's goddess.

"You were right to scold me when last I was here," he said, finding relief in the admittance.

"I know I was," she said firmly.

He picked up the glass of whiskey and raised it to her, truly glad to be in Kalna's company and happier still that she did not harbor hatred for him as he had been sure she would.

"To you, Kalna of Ravnice, purveyor of the best drink in Nysia," he toasted.

"To sharing it with you," she said, staring him in the eyes.

He tipped back the glass and felt the fire hit his belly a moment later, hoping it would burn away the butterflies fluttering about in his stomach.

"What kept you away, Harpis? No one has heard nor seen the faintest clue that you were on Quaj or still breathing. And believe me, I'd been asking, and people had been looking," she asked.

"Fear," he whispered and shrugged.

"What does the great God Singer fear so much that he keeps himself from those that care for him and would help him most?" she prodded.

He opened his mouth to speak several times but found himself unable to confess to the woman the things that haunted him.

"Another time then," she said, clasping one of his hands across the table.

"For now, I am happy to enjoy that you came back. To what

do I owe thanks for accomplishing that great feat?" Kalna inquired, sitting back in her seat.

"A fated and perfectly timed visit by trouble incarnate herself. Or, so it would seem," Harpis said, laughing a little at the look on Kalna's face.

*****

Harpis stood at the door to Wren's and now Jabruelle's mortuary and apartment, staring at the handle for long moments. He wavered at the thought of stepping inside his old friend's former home. Part of him desperately looked forward to sharing a drink with the gnome's last living apprentice and finally moving beyond the sadness of the past. However, another part of him wanted to continue clinging to the memories of spending dozens of evenings in the same chair, sharing drinks and verbal barbs with the old gnome, and refusing to admit that it could ever be otherwise.

The opportunity to flee back to the comfort of Kalna and her inn disappeared when Jabruelle opened the door.

"Good evening, I was tidying up the apartment and caught a glimpse of you! I hope I did not keep you waiting long. Unfortunately, I did not hear you knock," the necromancer stammered apologetically.

Harpis gently placed a hand on Jabruelle's shoulder to dispel the nervousness that the necromancer seemed to wear as naturally as he wore his black robe.

"Thank you for letting me stay here," he said, following the man up the creaky staircase to the apartment.

"I've already made you up a bed. Those are normal sheets, not burial linens, I swear on The Sleeper," Jabruelle said, pointing at the blankets and pillow next to a low-burning fire.

"That will do just fine, Jabruelle. Thank you again for accommodating me. Hopefully, I will be out of your hair before long. After meeting with Aanaman in the morning, I'll let you know," Harpis stated.

"Would you like some tea?" the necromancer offered.

Harpis looked from the man's kettle to the leather pouch on the small round table.

"Is that the tea you got from Moodi Shen?" he asked with

genuine worry.

"It is wonderful stuff. It knocks me right out," the man said, setting the kettle back on the table.

"If you've some whiskey, I would prefer that instead," he requested hastily.

"Of course, the last unopened bottle of Reaper Vintage Wren bought before the invasion seems appropriate, and what sort of student of the gnome's would I be if I let you drink alone. If you don't mind the company," Jabruelle offered.

Harpis smiled at him and lowered himself into the comfy chair by the fireplace, taking the brimming glass from Jabruelle with a smile and watching him awkwardly drag one of the two wooden chairs over while trying not to spill his own.

"Jabruelle, would you mind telling me of Wren's burial rites? I am woefully embarrassed that I did not come to The Sanctum," he asked.

Harpis' fear at hearing out the act of his friend's burial ritual wilted under the unbelievable sorrow and horrors that followed. Jabruelle described what he had found upon reaching The Sanctum with Wren's body. Harpis listened, mouth agape in shock as the man retold his day-long task of committing his fellow necromancers' frozen and charred remains to their goddess through The Dreamer's Door.

After Jabruelle finished the tale, Harpis realized his pain was indeed a small thing. After almost a half bottle's worth of staring at the smoldering fire in silence, Harpis finally found the courage to speak.

"I am so sorry, Jabruelle. I had no idea. I had no intention of making you relive that agony or immerse yourself in that sadness again," Harpis said, his voice close to a whimper.

"It was agony, for many reasons, but I weep not for my family at The Sanctum. They are where they always wanted to be, with The Sleeper," Jabruelle said in a stoically calm tone that Harpis had not known the man was capable of.

"You wear the mantle of the last necromancer well, Jabruelle," Harpis said, toasting him.

"Some necromancer I must seem to you. I have yet to summon a familiar from The Great Dream," Jabruelle lamented.

"You've pulled forth your scythe, though?" Harpis asked, more than familiar with the traditions of those gifted devotees of the goddess of death.

Jabruelle shifted uncomfortably at the question and finished the last of his glass, refilled it, and described his final moments at The Dreamer's Door that day.

When the Jabruelle told him of his attempted suicide and The Sleeper's refusal to welcome him home, Harpis could hardly believe what he was hearing.

"It is a wonder you have remained sane at all. You are a stronger man than I," Harpis said softly.

Jabruelle merely cackled nervously at the complement and pulled forth the scythe, laying it across his lap and watching the dancing reflection of the flames dying in the hearth.

"Would you like to hear her song?" Harpis asked, opening his violin case and pulling out the instrument.

When Jabruelle leaned back in his chair after nodding vigorously, Harpis lay the bow across the strings and pulled forth the sad melancholy of The Sleeper's Serenade. Sparing his vocal cords, Harpis only played the instrumental portion of the song. The moaning cry of the pearl-inlaid black violin, given to him by Wren in this very place, seemingly more mournful without the accompanying vocals. It may have been that he had not heard himself perform in nearing a year. Or maybe it was what he had endured in the months of silence. Either or both, he could no longer separate the feel of the notes from their sound, and it was a transcendent sensation.

*****

Enky stepped foot into The Nexus for the second time in as many weeks.

"It would seem I am in the very beginnings of developing a bad habit," he muttered, peaking around the damp stone chamber to see if his presence was noticed.

"Not long from home," he said in self-reassurance as he turned to the portal wall directly beside his own.

Curiosity was tugging at his senses, and he decided that a quick stopover with his youngest sister in Walara would provide information well worth the trouble. A short sneaky scurrying later, he found himself once again breathing the humid air of The Boundless Growth. However, this time, he did not get the opportunity to wander and wait for his sister, as she met him almost as soon as he entered her plane.

"Two visits and not millennia apart. Enky, have you finally found a fondness for family, dear brother?" she asked playfully.

"I cherish you all dearly, little sister," he answered in a voice that echoed uncommon solemnity.

"Of course," she said, reaching out and pinching his cheek before putting her hands on her hips.

"Did you not trust me to do as you asked?" she asked in feigned insult.

"Of course, I trust you, but did it work? Do you think he did as you bid?" Enky inquired.

His sister merely shrugged and smiled at his frustration, placing her hand on his small shoulder.

"You are the one who has the ability to see all that transpires," she deflected.

"Well, that does not mean I always do watch every event on every one of the planes!" he replied, growing annoyed at himself for not paying closer attention.

He shook his head and looked up at her, his features softening at the unavoidable motherly comfort in her gaze.

"It was odd. I was projected into Nysia to check up on my schemes for a bit. It seemed like he could actually see my presence there. Is that even possible?" Enky asked.

"That old troll eats so many mushrooms each day. I imagine he sees a great many things that are real and imagined. My guess would be he sensed the periphery of your manifesting and simply associated one hallucination or another with the direction he felt it from.

Enky decided he was growing uncomfortable being this long gone from his abode, and with still one errand and another sister to visit, he gave her a quick hug and excused himself from her plane. Then, tiptoeing back towards the other side of The Nexus, he tripped over his own feet as he turned in surprise upon hearing movement from the other side of his portal.

"Where exactly are you headed, Enky?" came the question from the eldest of the sisters, her blond hair spilling like sunlight around her pale face and the warm expression it wore.

Hearing a giggle behind him, he turned to see that The Wild had followed him out into the Nexus and her red-haired twin joined them.

"Maelara," he answered, crossing his arms at The Siren's raised eyebrow before turning towards the one who asked.

"What business have you in The Great Dream?" Daybreak asked him.

"The same business I seem to have everywhere right now, fixing this mess!" he half-shouted in exasperation, cringing as his voice reverberated around the stone chamber.

"You know the rules, Enky. Mother is most certainly watching. Don't get us all cast back to Nysia in your attempts to stave off that very same eventuality," The Siren sneered from behind him.

He turned towards the blustery goddess of storms and seas and pointed an accusing finger at her.

"The bard's voice reached your own ears in Valara. You heard it amongst the eternally roaring winds and crashing waves of The Endless Sea, all the way from the mortal plane. I would hopefully assume that means his gift could also reach our brother's mind," he finished proudly.

"How exactly then do you intend to get Harpis to sing *The Sisters' Song*?" The Siren countered, disbelief in her voice.

"And what does Lilynth have to do with that?" Daybreak asked concernedly.

"That is for me alone to figure out and not the three of you or mother to know," he proclaimed, steadying himself for what he expected to be further interrogation from the three before being allowed to visit the fourth sister in her dream.

None of them said a word. Instead, the sisters all bowed low and did not straighten. Enky spun around smiling and gave the wispy form of his mother a long hug.

"Please, no need for formality, my daughters," Qisme said, giving him a wink.

"Is everything unfolding as you expect?" she asked, a grin forming on her face.

"More or less..." he answered, unsure of himself at the manner of her questioning.

"Very well then, carry on, my son," she said, motioning towards the swirling vision of The Great Dream appearing on the stone wall in front of him.

Enky turned back to see her talking with his sisters and paying no attention as he walked towards it. He stopped for a moment, shaking his head in confusion before shrugging and heading into the starry night of Maelara.

Chapter 9

Captivate

Walking across Ravnice city as the sun rose and the summer warmth chased the morning chill, Harpis felt at peace with the present and the past. He had mended emotional wounds just as his body had healed his physical ones. His conversation with Jabruelle the night before had put his suffering in perspective and reminded him that the toll of the Tormenta invasion was a shared one. He felt a kinship with the odd necromancer, mostly from their shared grief for the loss of the old gnome. However, they had also bonded through the battle at Wren's Crossing and their days behind enemy lines in Kalt City pretending to be the band called The Sea Goats.

Aanaman's home came into view around the last street corner, and he let out a low whistle at the walls and guard contingents that bristled around the former Ravnice governor's mansion now that he was chancellor. The guards that recognized him nodded respectfully and saluted as he passed with a reverence he felt he did not deserve.

One of the two guards at the home's front door opened it for him with a smile.

"Good to see you back in Ravnice, bard!" he said as Harpis walked by.

"Good to see you indeed, Harpis!" Shanowen shouted when he stepped inside, giving him a big hug.

A second later, the two Reaper girls nearly bowled him over as they rushed into the foyer and grappled both his legs.

"Sing us a song before you leave again!" they shouted in unison while their mother pried them from his legs.

"I will," he whispered, riding the roil of emotion at seeing them again and guilt at having kept himself away.

"Don't be such a stranger! We missed you, perhaps Aanaman, more than anyone. You know where to find them," Shanowen said, hugging him again and chasing the girls off.

At the top of the stairs, the last guard gave Harpis a grin and a light punch on the shoulder before walking ahead of him and opening the door to Aanaman's office without bothering to introduce him or wait for the chancellor to bid them enter. Harpis could not help but smile at the near-permanent fixture of Captain Kilannry sitting at the small table against the wall in Aanaman's office, holding a glass of whiskey.

"Bit early for that, isn't it, Captain?" he said hoarsely, pointing at the man's drink as the guard shut the door behind him.

"Nonsense, we are celebrating the return of a dear friend, long thought dead. To you, God Singer!" he said, lifting his glass in a toast while Harpis tried not to cringe at the praise.

Aanaman dragged his chair from behind his desk to sit at the small circular table. Harpis noted slight streaks of white in the red-haired man's mane as Aanaman embraced him before holding him at arm's length, staring at his face.

"I am glad you are not dead," Aanaman said, taking a seat and motioning for Harpis to do the same.

"I had my silver bet on you hiding out in the warm and sunny climates of the atolls with some scantily clad Tuathian woman or something. That or fishing away the rest of your years," Kilannry said with a laugh.

"For your sake, I was happy to hear that you got your hearing back and your voice somewhat. I figured we could sit close together so you did not have to strain your vocals. We have much to discuss, my friend," Aanaman said seriously.

"Starting with the fact that you impressively unified the peoples of Quaj, the Tormenta, and the Quaji tribes into a new nation, Chancellor Reaper," Harpis said, feeling happy to annoy the former farmer with his formal title.

"You had already guided that ship into the harbor. I merely tied her off at the docks," Aanaman replied.

"The both of you, so absurdly and aggravatingly humble," Kilannry said.

The older man then rolled his eyes, reaching for the decanter and a glass for Harpis.

"No, thank you, Kilannry. I have a long day ahead of me, even after this meeting. I like the name you and Tawito conjured up for this new country, by the way," Harpis said, holding a hand up to pause Kilannry from filling the glass.

"It is the future of Savja that we need to discuss. First though, as your friend, Sleeper below us, as your family, why did you disappear?" Aanaman asked with sadness in his voice.

Harpis sat back for a moment before answering, meeting the gaze of both men in turn and seeing only concern and no condemnation in their eyes.

"I dedicated everything I had to vindicate Wren's death after the battle at Kalt River. Waking up from what happened at Lodestar, I was rudderless. Without the ability to perform or hear my gift, I felt I had no purpose," he admitted, pausing to judge the reaction from either man, yet their expressions were understanding and unchanged.

"I felt lost and incapable of being the man and bard that everyone on this island celebrated me to be. There were no expectations of me on the bleak southern shores of Kalt. I did not have to run. I could simply hide in plain sight and drink myself to death," he finished.

"Well, then, that is one thing you seem to have failed at!" Kilannry chuckled to lighten the mood, which earned a severe look from Aanaman.

"I don't know that I or any other man could have done better or otherwise in your situation, bard. But we are here for you, my friend. This whole nation owes you whatever it can do to help, even if that means simply leaving you alone. However, I am responsible to the people of Savja and therefore must ask a favor of you," Aanaman said with apparent resignation.

Harpis could sense that Aanaman felt guilty in asking anything of him and shifted uncomfortably in anticipation of what the Chancellor would request.

"I want you to be Savja's chief diplomat. You more than proved your capability in bringing Tawito and the Quaji to us in our time of need," Aanaman proposed.

Harpis leaned with his elbows on the small table, staring at the swirls of knotted wood grains before looking up in confusion.

"What need do we have of a chief diplomat when you have united the people of the southern seas into a peaceful nation?" he asked.

Aanaman paused to look at Kilannry, who offered only a shrug in support.

"We will allegedly be met by a delegation of sand elves from the Nysian mainland far to the north. Now that I know you aren't a pile of bones being picked clean at the bottom of the sea, I can think of no one better than you to help me navigate and develop this new relationship," Aanaman stated evenly.

Harpis sat in silent contemplation of the request, completely surprised at what Aanaman had just claimed.

"What are sand elves? Why are they coming here? How do we know that?" Harpis asked in rapid-fire succession.

"Ezera passed me the information, and I sent for you when one of her operatives informed her and thus me that you had arrived in Southpoint," Aanaman replied.

"Her operatives?" Harpis asked, not letting Aanaman dodge the implication.

"She runs an organization for me, with the blessing of the nation's representatives. If we are ever attacked again, we will need the communications and intelligence capability The Syndicate commanded, minus the whole assassination bit," the Chancellor explained.

"And how exactly did Ezera get this information?" he asked, looking at Kilannry as the old soldier grew even more uncomfortable with the conversation.

"Sudbina told her but would not reveal how she was aware of these sand elves or their intentions," Kilannry said, his hands upheld in exasperation.

"The two of you, and Ezera as well, believed the most mischievous, deceptive, burglary prone human any of us have ever met at her word when she wouldn't even attempt to explain away her method for obtaining this knowledge?" Harpis said as loudly as he could, incredulous at the claims.

"She also said the same source told her how to find you and that she would get you to us before the elves arrived," Aanaman said, crossing his arms.

Harpis froze at the comment, struggling to process what his friend had just revealed.

"She told me she had been looking for me for months, across every drinking establishment in every small town across the Kalt coast," he countered.

"She met with Ezera in Fjall ten days ago and said she was off to fetch you. Maybe you are the one who shouldn't believe everything she says. After all, she is the most mischievous, deceptive, burglary-prone human any of us have ever met," The chancellor finished with a grin.

Less than an hour ago, Harpis had felt confident about his meeting with Aanaman. Now he was reeling from its revelations. What caught him most off guard was his friend's request amidst the backdrop of what was soon to arrive. He slid his chair back and hung his head in his hands before slowly exhaling and looking up at the man he would give his life for without hesitation.

"Aanaman, I can't. I am so sorry," Harpis said, his shoulders sagging as he watched Kilannry look down at the tabletop in disappointment.

The father and former farmer stood from his chair and pulled Harpis to his feet.

"Harpis, you need not apologize. It was my duty as chancellor to ask. Forgive me. As your friend, I do not wish to see you in pain or wear guilt like a cloak. Perhaps Sudbina is indeed telling half-truths, and there are no sand elves. In either case, I think I speak for all of us, that we are just glad you are back from death's shores," Aanaman said firmly.

"I am glad I returned," Harpis replied honestly.

"I do have one demand of you, Harpis. Come and play the girls a song or two tonight," Aanaman asked, smiling.

"You have my word," Harpis replied without hesitation.

*****

After taking lunch with Kalna, Harpis had returned to find an excited Jabruelle and impatient Mahala waiting for him at the mortuary.

"I found the Troubadour taking lunch on the *Torrent* with Zolga and Galonica. I told her you had bardic knowledge you urgently wished to share with her. Oh, it is so nice to have The Sea Goats back together again and under less dire circumstances!" the skittish man exclaimed, leading them down into the second basement at Harpis' request.

"This time, please spare us your attempts at vocally contributing, Jabruelle," Mahala said, wearing a tight smile on her typically angry face as she addressed the necromancer before turning to Harpis.

"How did your talk with Aanaman go this morning? Did you accept his proposal?" she asked.

He looked at her for a moment, confused at her knowledge of what Aanaman had said to him.

"Please, I'd rather not get into that now. I asked Jabruelle to find you to show you what I learned in the months without hearing," he said, turning back to the necromancer as they reached the bottom floor.

"Feel free to observe Jabruelle, but if you have other things to attend to, please don't stay on our account," Harpis offered to the man, taking his violin from its case and laying it on the long-unused preparation table.

"I asked him to stay. You are not the only one with something to share," Mahala said, producing her violin.

Not wanting to overshadow whatever she had been able to find in her research at The Hall, Harpis motioned for her to go first.

"It took much translating from old Tuathian dialects, but I have uncovered the words to a unique form of gifted song. It is one that warned of similar dangers and consequences faced by other magically gifted channelings," she said, placing the instrument under her chin.

The slow but cheery song she conjured from the wooden body of her violin was captivating unto itself. The dance of Mahala's small frame strutting and kicking along to the alluring melody made it impossible for him to pull his attention away from her. So enamored with the feel of her song and the twists and swings of her steps, he barely noticed her considerable gift being woven among the notes of her silk-like voice.

It was evident to him that he was not the intended target, and his gaze followed her threads of influence as they wrapped Jabruelle like an invisible net. Jabruelle was enthralled, staring at the woman bard without blinking. Suddenly Harpis noticed that the sounds of Mahala's voice and violin had disappeared from the room, replaced by the exact hypnotizing words pouring forth from the mouth of a wild-eyed Jabruelle. Then, he stopped singing and glared at Harpis with an eyebrow sarcastically arced as he had seen Mahala often do.

"Maybe you'll be as talented a bard as me one day," Jabruelle's mouth said awkwardly before the man shook his head and shivered, turning to look at Mahala as Harpis did.

She held the violin at her side and bowed to them before pointing her bow at Jabruelle.

"What was it like to be the subject of *Bienavor's Beguiling*?" she asked.

"Please don't ever do that again. I've enough trouble keeping my sanity with just myself to deal with in there," the necromancer said, slapping the side of his head.

"You and Bravit are no fun," she said, rolling her eyes and looking at Harpis.

"I had no idea we were capable of dominating another being," he said, somewhat shocked.

"It is impressive and surprisingly easy to perform, though, as I said, the texts warn that it carries the same risk of mindlessness if interrupted as mages and necromancers have when connected to their familiars," she warned.

Harpis shook his head in appreciation of the woman's abilities and looked around with concern for a minute.

"Jabruelle, where is Wren's pickled cat corpse?" he asked, not seeing the glass jar that usually sat on the workbench.

"Ah, Timot is upstairs. I will be right back!" the necromancer said, hurrying up the stairs. He returned to concerned stares from both the bards, and Harpis slowly put his hand to his face.

"You named the preserved corpse of a cat that has been dead for longer than you've been alive?" Harpis asked, knowing some of the history surrounding this particular feline oddity the old gnome kept in his home.

"I thought it would help me connect with him and pull him forth from The Great Dream as my familiar," Jabruelle said sheepishly.

"Jabruelle, this is a female cat...." Mahala said as she took the jar from the man and turned it in her hands.

Saving the necromancer from further embarrassment, Harpis took the jar from Mahala and placed it on the display table.

"I will do all of us a favor and get rid of this thing once and for all," Harpis said, motioning for them both to stand behind him.

Staring at the jar, he steadied himself and did his best to mold his stress toward the effort of replicating what he had practiced back in Kalt.

Harpis' fingers clutched the strings tightly, ensuring the highest register possible would shriek forth from the instrument. Then, slowly, he slid the bow along its length across the strings until his finger touched them and then unleashed several short screeching notes that cut the air like the blades of a sword.

The top of the jar flew off as though a razor sliced it, and then the jar cracked in half when another invisible knife edge slashed across the middle. As the jar shattered, Harpis altered his grip on the bow. Next, he played a roaring coastal wind, blowing the remnants of the jar and the cat corpse against the back wall of the room where several more of his violin conjured blades eviscerated the long-dead feline body into pieces as it tried to fall to the ground.

When his song and the sickening plop of pieces of wet flesh hitting the ground ended, he turned triumphantly to look at a horrified Jabruelle and a shocked Mahala.

"I am sorry for doing that to your pet Jabruelle, but Wren always told me they were bad luck anyway. I am not sure why he kept the confounded thing in his basement anyways," he apologized.

"By the gods Harpis, how were you able to do that?" Mahala asked after a stunned silence.

"I don't know exactly, but I don't recommend going deaf and mute for half a year to see if it helps you figure it out," he replied, looking around for something that would help him show them what he had learned.

"When I couldn't hear, I could still feel the sound of things happening. After a while, I tried to replicate that feeling, ultimately finding out I could play that feeling even though I couldn't hear it. For instance, a sword strike or a gust of wind," he explained, motioning at the mess on the floor.

Harpis then grabbed the bucket in the corner of the room and filled it with water from the small well in the basement.

Placing the bucket of water on Wren's old workbench, he grabbed a few pieces of parchment and folded them into tiny boats.

"I lay in the ocean, feeling the waves hit me again and again, and when I placed a glass of rum on my violin. I saw the tiny waves the notes created even though I could not hear them, and they matched the hum I felt from the body of the violin wood," he said, placing one of the parchment boats into the bucket and grabbing a fire striker.

He flicked the metal several times against the flintstone it lay with until the parchment boat caught fire before sinking.

"Fire mage," he said, grabbing another boat and placing it in the bucket. Then, he took the flintstone and held it over the ship before dropping it on the tiny vessel, driving it below the water's surface.

"Stone mage," he explained, placing the third boat in the bucket. He cupped some water in his hands and then let it fall onto the parchment, soaking it before ultimately sinking it.

"Water mage," he said.

"Harpis, we know how mages can use their elements to destroy parchment ships," Mahal said impatiently.

"Not parchment boats. Pretend this is a person," he said, placing the fourth boat in the bucket.

"This, this is music, or our gift, or however you want to name it," he said, pointing at the water in the bucket. He pulled the flintstone from the bottom and held it high above the boat, letting it fall into the water away from the parchment.

The waves from the impact of the stone rolled over the edges of the parchment ship, pulling it below the surface as well.

"See?" Harpis exclaimed, pointing at the bucket with both hands before sighing in frustration at the dumbfounded looks the necromancer and Troubadour wore.

*****

Harpis concluded his second day back in Ravnice at The Siren's Scream after stopping to play the Reaper girls no less than six lullabies. He decided today was the best day he had had as long as he cared to remember. Though he had turned down Aanaman's request, he was glad to find the man still called him a friend after that and everything else. He felt a weight off his chest at having shared his newfound knowledge of his craft with Mahala, and he was happier still that Kalna had invited him to stay at the inn when they'd had lunch.

Sliding into the booth he and she had shared the day before, he decided it was time for a new tradition in The Siren's Scream, maybe one that could become a daily habit, he hoped. The serving girl Meera walked over a moment later with a basket of sliced bread and a glass of whiskey.

"Compliments of the owner," the girl said with a smile and a curtsy.

"Thank you, very much," he returned, sitting back against the booth.

"Kalna said she will join you shortly after she's done overseeing the night's preparations," the girl called back over her shoulder as she returned to the bar.

*****

Sudbina was almost asleep in the bed when she heard the door handle jiggle from the hallway.

"It's about time," she said quietly to herself, fingering the blowgun that lay on the mattress next to her bare thigh.

When the door opened, and candlelight from the hallway illuminated her nude form, she smirked at Harpis' failed attempts to dodge the dart delivered by her sharp puff into the tube. Then, as his body went limp and began falling to the floor, Itka deftly appeared from the side of the door to catch him and silently lower him to the ground. Ezera's blond tresses danced in the hallway light as she stepped into the room with a lantern and closed the door behind her.

"Why is she naked?" Ezera asked Itka and the dwarf merely shrugged.

"I tried to tell her to put her clothes back on, but she was insistent," Itka said, raising an eyebrow at Sudbina.

"Sudbina, for Daybreak's sake, why are you naked?" Ezera asked again.

"The bard is about to spend the next day and a half in a deep sleep while we wait to see if these sand elves are as real and timely as my informant says. I feel bad, having done this to him a second time. I thought he would be better off with inspired dreams of flesh than nightmares of death," she said, reaching for her pants with a wink.

100

Chapter 10

Familiar

Aanaman woke just before dawn. Whether he was a farmhand, governor, or chancellor, he did not seem capable of sleeping longer than Daybreak. He had dressed and kissed Shanowen and the girls goodbye before heading towards the wharf with a small escort to watch the sunrise over Ravnice harbor.

He was joined by Kilannry just as the sun passed entirely above the watery horizon.

"Today should prove most interesting," he said to the militia captain, closing his eyes and enjoying the warmth of the morning sun for a moment.

"That is one way of putting it. Do you intend to wait out here on the wharf all day to see if Sudbina is a liar?" Kilannry huffed.

"No, I believe that might be a bit obvious in revealing our pre-knowledge of their arrival. But, if Sudbina spoke true, these sand elves should be intercepted outside Mer harbor any time now, if they haven't been already, and our ships on patrol have orders to escort our guests here. I would say that we have until lunch then," Aanaman said to the grumpier and older man with a smile.

"Do you think they will be peaceful visitors?" Kilannry asked in a more serious tone.

"I hope so. Either way, we will find out sooner than later. If it is more than just a vessel or two, they'll be allowed into Mer harbor and then blockaded there by an ever-growing number of galleons from across Savjan. Field Marshal Elliswerth has the entire regular battalions ready to move out. We have riders ready to spread any necessary word, and you have ensured the Ravnice militia is prepared," he said, acknowledging the gruff warrior's efforts.

"Bah, like the men would get any action at all with Zolga's here," Kilannry said, pointing at *Torrent*.

"See, nothing to worry about. Now, how about we go wait for our guests somewhere more comfortable," Aanaman said, walking towards The Siren's Scream at the edge of the wharf's cobbles with his friend and personal guards in tow.

Entering the inn, he gave a respectful nod at Kalna as she shouted into the kitchens to herald his arrival.

"Thank you for opening early on our account," he said, heading towards the large corner booth at the rear of the establishment.

"What and miss the profits from having you, your personal guards, and several other of Savja's finest folk holed up in here for half a day? It is I that should be thanking you," she laughed before helping the serving girl bring steaming coffee and sweetbreads to him and Kilannry as they took their seats.

Two of his guards went to stand at the back door to the alley, and Aanaman shooed the rest to tables by the wharf-side door, telling them to eat some breakfast while they waited.

"Anyone else joining us, your highness?" Kilannry said after a long sip.

There was a knock at the door to the alley behind the inn, and the guards let Ezera and Galonica in.

Both men stood in respectful greeting and waited for the two to take their seats before returning to theirs.

"Spy Mother, High Priestess, good morning," Aanaman said and motioned for coffee for them as well.

"Zolga and her crew are ready and waiting on *Torrent* for whatever comes of this morning," Galonica said in confirmation.

Ezera sat quietly staring at the portrait of The Sleeper where Wren and Harpis' habitual drinking table had been.

"It would have been nice to have had the luxury of his attendance or Turin's," Ezera said quietly.

"I couldn't agree more, but here we are," Aanaman replied before laying out his expectations for the day's events.

*****

With noon come and gone, Aanaman was beginning to doubt that their mysterious visitors would show up at all, if they even

102

existed. He had decided to at least make the most of his morning spent at the inn and asked Kalna to bring out some lunch for Ezera, Galonica, and him. Kilannry had long ago given in to impatience and headed out to check on the militia stationed in and around the harbor. It was probably for the best. The old warrior was not the most suited individual he could think of to attend the first encounter with a foreign people.

The serving girl walked out and lay three bowls of fisherman's stew before them and a still steaming loaf of bread. Aanaman picked up the bread, cracking it into three separate chunks and handed one to each of the women before dunking his in his soup and slowly chewing the soaked and delicious morsel. He reached for his spoon, but alarm bells and several horns sounded from outside on the wharf before his hand grasped it.

"I believe that would be our cue. Apparently, Sudbina's source is proven correct again," he laughed.

The women glared at their yet-untouched lunches before standing and following him out the back door to the waiting guard contingent. Then, with a wave at the officer leading his escort, they began walking the long way around several blocks before making it to the main road to the wharf so that it would appear as if they were summoned by the alarms being sounded and not already in wait for the arrival of their guests.

Minutes later, they rounded the last corner and the wharf once again came into view. Aanaman was surprised to see only a single smaller ship tying off at the dock with two galleons from Mer floating intimidatingly behind it.

"They made it across the widest of The Siren's seas in that little boat?" Galonica asked skeptically

"Now, now, let's not be quick to judge our new visitors," Ezera said with a laugh.

As they neared the water's edge and waited for the arrivals to disembark, Aanaman had a similar assessment of the elven ship. Even to a lifelong farmer, the ability of the vessel to sail the open sea was questionable. It did have three masts, but they looked like saplings compared to the four massive tree trunks that towered over the galleon *Torrent* moored across from it. Aanaman wasn't sure their boat was even a third as long as the Tormenta built ship.

His analysis of their craft was interrupted as a gangplank slid to the dock, and two elves with small, round shields and long spears followed another in flowing robes towards them.

"Lieutenant, take your men down to their vessel and see if Zolga needs any assistance helping their crew. See what you may see of them. I expect a report after this is over," he said, raising his eyebrow as the man frowned at him.

"I am more than protected from two spear-wielding elves," he said, with a nod at the storm priestess and cleric to his left.

The departing guardsmen passed by the three approaching elves on the stairs up to the pier's edge, and the robed figure gave them a curious look as they went by before stopping a few paces in front of him. They had the angular features of their woodland cousins, but there, the similarities ended. The sand elves were taller, skinnier, and had bronze skin and sun-bleached-blond hair tied off in a high knot above their heads.

"Welcome to Ravnice city. I am Aanaman Reaper, Chancellor of Savja," he said, prompting the elf.

"I am Emissary Keptis, speaking on behalf of his eminence, Vizier Mistis of Zarad. I must say this is quite the odd reception, Chancellor Reaper," he said, narrowing his gold-speckled brown eyes.

Aanaman noted that Keptis and his two guards carried themselves with an air of superiority in their stature and their eyes but seemingly had the self-awareness to keep it from his voice.

"Well met, Emissary. This is Ezera, my chief political advisor and High Priestess Galonica, one of our people's religious leaders. If your leader intends to visit in person, we will assemble the extent of our governing council and happily host you in the capital," Aanaman offered.

Keptis gave a respectful nod to Ezera before looking with some concern at Galonica, his eyes roaming from her hair, slowly down to her feet before looking back at Aanaman.

"The impure descendants of the Valar are known to us, though I did not expect to find them here," he said flatly.

"You must forgive our adherence to caution towards visiting foreigners," Ezera stated, changing the topic.

Aanaman hoped Galonica would let the elf's comment go unheeded.

Keptis seemed lost in his thoughts for a moment before taking in a deep breath.

"If you are anything like the impatient and abrupt humans of the Nysian mainland, I will cede to your typically hasty inclinations and get to the point," Keptis said in a confident but high-pitched voice.

"I do not know enough to acknowledge the comparison, but we are happy to hear you out," Aanaman replied.

"As I said, I am here on behalf of his eminence, the Vizier. He has decided that after centuries of inadequacy, the recently united island nation of Quaj is finally ready to receive an offer of economic and military alliance from the nation of Zarad," Keptis stated proudly.

Aanaman crossed his arms across his chest and glanced at Ezera and Galonica before turning back to the elf.

"Well, I am certainly happy that the islands of the nation of Savja have found themselves finally above inadequacy in your eyes," Aanaman returned, noting the look of confusion that flashed across Keptis' face.

The elf looked thoughtfully at the sky with his finger on his lip before looking out at the harbor.

"You have named your country after an old Quaji word for the south. How quaint," he commented.

Aanaman tried not to cringe as he could feel Galonica tensing at his side and breathed a sigh of relief as Keptis seemed to understand her agitation at his dismissiveness.

"I truly apologize, you see, in Zarad, there are only sand elves, and we interact with other races rather infrequently. Therefore, if I speak rudely, please correct me. I intend no offense," he said with a slight bow to Galonica.

"Vizier Mistis has extended an offer of welcome, requesting that you send a diplomatic contingent north to discuss potential partnership and alliance with Zarad, the southernmost nation of the Nysian mainland and your nearest neighbors," Keptis said warmly.

"Do we have to send this contingent on your ship? I understand that the southern coast of the mainland is almost a week's sail due north of here," Galonica asked skeptically.

"We welcome as large a contingent as you wish to send and on however many vessels you feel necessary," Keptis answered, opening both of his hands in peace.

"Then I shall have our galleon *Torrent* return with you as it had just finished being resupplied for departure on patrol," Aanaman said, pointing at the ship.

105

"I will send riders for my senior diplomats. They should arrive by late evening and will be ready to leave as soon as you would like," Ezera said.

"Would you like a tour of Ravnice city or to visit any other portion of the islands before departing?" Aanaman asked with a smile.

"I must apologize for my assuredly uncharacteristic urgency, but the Vizier has asked us to return with your representatives as quickly as possible. I do not wish to keep his eminence waiting," Keptis said, bowing.

Very well, I shall have the *Torrent* ordered to follow you out as soon as tomorrow morning," Aanaman offered.

"I do have one more favor to ask. Would it be possible to quickly restore our foodstuffs and water and some other supplies this afternoon? I have gold or silver to offer as payment," Keptis requested.

"Please, take whatever supplies you need from the wharf or the stores of one of the galleons that escorted you here. Commander Zolga will be able to arrange anything you should need. There is no need for payment, Emissary. Consider it our own offer of goodwill as we begin to see how our relationship may better each other," Aanaman answered.

"Most gracious of you, Chancellor. I will be on our ship if you have any further questions or correspondence as we prepare ourselves for departure in the morning!" Keptis said excitedly, bowing low and heading back towards the elven ship with his guards.

"That was awfully brief for the first meeting between a new people and hopeful allies," Galonica said with her eyes narrowed.

"You don't need to be a spy to see that they need something from us, perhaps even desperately," Ezera observed.

"It would certainly seem so, but what exactly that may be, I have no idea. However, I do find it odd that Keptis seemed aware of our unification and yet not of the fact that the atolls or the Tormenta were party to it. Will our diplomatic envoy be ready in time?" he asked Ezera.

"Oh, one way or another," she said, glancing at the *Torrent*.

*****

106

Jabruelle strolled about the harbor most of the afternoon, trying to glimpse as many elven visitors as he could before walking back to the mortuary as dusk fell on Ravnice. He was down to his last pouch of Moodi's tea and had made sure to follow the list of ingredients the troll had given him while shopping at the wharf stalls. Thankfully the herbs, most of which were grown in Tuath and the atolls, were readily available. Taking the stairs back to his apartment, he clumsily opened it with his one spare hand while trying not to drop the day's purchases. After laying the various ingredients next to the staged mortar and pestle on the table, he closed the door behind him and went to the fireplace to fan embers into flames and get a pot boiling.

While scanning over the instructions, his eyes fell upon the one unopened pouch and decided he should make the last batch from the troll for comparison. Pulling the drawstring, he shook out a few curled purplish flakes into his strainer and paused to glance at them, not recalling his other tea having the same type of leaf. Pouring the hot water over the glass and small strainer, he took it in its entirety to his comfy chair and leaned back to relax before beginning the task at hand.

The tea felt and tasted slightly different but still carried the heavy notes of coconut and fruit as the previous pouches, and he drank half the glass, breathing deep the intoxicatingly sweet steam each time he did. Then, setting the glass on the table next to him, he gazed into the fire for a moment, trying to blink away the images he was seeing. Where there had been struggling flames before, there were now red and orange images of The Sleeper herself dancing on the lone log in the hearth.

Pressing his palms to his eye sockets to try and get his sight back to normal, the pressure of his hands and the blackness they brought made him feel like the entire world shifted for a moment under him. Then, snapping his eyes open, he stared back into the normal-looking hearth and tiny fire, shaking his head vigorously.

"I must be overtired. That or going crazy!" Jabruelle said to himself with a nervous chuckle.

"Don't you mean going crazier?" a familiar voice asked from across the room.

Jabruelle's eyes widened in panic and joy at the sight of the recently deceased Death Herald sitting at the small wooden table looking over the herbs before picking up the bottle of whiskey from the wall shelf next to him and taking a pull.

"Why are you not yet a death speaker, Jabruelle? The Sleeper needs a new herald," Wren said, hopping from his stool and walking over, pouring the glass next to Jabruelle full, and clinking the bottle against it in a toast.

"I uh, well, it is not for not trying," he said nervously, picking up the glass and drinking deeply of the warm whiskey to try and calm his shaking nerves.

"And what creature is it that you have been trying to pull forth from the great dream?" the gnome asked, returning to the stool.

"I, um, I have tried several times unsuccessfully to cajole a cat from The Great Dream as my familiar," he replied.

"I thought I warned you about cat's Jabruelle. I wouldn't dare to try and dominate such a creature, let alone summon it forth under my control as a familiar. They are fickle creatures," Wren said seriously.

"All the same, I have been unsuccessful in those attempts and others. Even if I had a familiar and become worthy of being one of The Sleeper's speakers, I do not ever hope to achieve the honor of being her herald," Jabruelle replied with a hung head.

"What exactly do you think the senior-most living death speaker becomes? They become her herald. Such is your duty on this plane, Jabruelle, last of the necromancers. Why else did she keep you from her bosom and dream?" the gnome asked.

Jabruelle had no other response but to hang his head lower. After a moment of thought, he decided he might as well make the most of Wren's visit from the afterlife and ask the gnome about the ritual that had brought him to their goddess. When he lifted his head, though, he was alone in the room again. Glancing at the bottle on the shelf, he noticed it was still sealed and full. Nervously he picked up the tea glass he'd only half-finished off the table and saw that it was empty. He had consumed the liquid and dried flakes too.

"I do not think this was tea for sleeping," he said to the glass as if it would respond.

Looking up at the hearth, he noticed that it had long gone dark, not a single ember glowed in it, and he felt the chill of night in the room around him for the first time. He stood to fan the flames and make some actual tea for his slumber, but before he took his first step, clouds were blown across the moon outside, and the room went almost entirely dark

As his eyes adjusted to the gloom, he found himself once again within the shadowy tendrils of The Great Dream. Nervously he looked around for the cat that had taunted him across the expanses of The Sleeper's realm on previous occasions. He saw no feline demon but did notice the flutter of a bat not far ahead.

"Worth a try, though it does seem a bit archetypal for a worshiper of the dead to have a bat as a companion," he said with a nasally laugh.

He suddenly felt the cool touch of his scythe handle in his palms, and he focused his mind on the spirit of the bat. Its wings fluttered again, and then it allowed itself to land on the ground ahead of him as if Jabruelle's attempts to dominate it were too distracting to allow it to continue floating in the air. Jabruelle felt his mind pushing against the animal's consciousness when suddenly he felt the hot burn of panicked thoughts and heard the mad screeching of the trapped bat as if it were alive in his very hands and he was squeezing it nearly to death.

Distraught, he forced his hands and eyes open, abandoning the terrifying visage of the shrieking bat and The Dream. Yet, as his eyes took in the once again moon-bathed apartment, he noticed that the shrill outcry of the animal had not ceased, and he slowly began to realize that he had pulled forth the being from the great dream.

"Oh, but Wren will be so very pleased I was finally able to do it! I have pulled forth my familiar from The Great Dream. I am at last Death Speaker, nay, Death Herald Jabruelle!" he shouted at the top of his lungs in excitement.

It was then that he realized the shrill noises from the bat were, in fact, verbal screams of beratement.

"Sleeper below us, Jabruelle Kalt! What, in the name of all that is dead and will be, am I doing on the mortal plane in Wren's apartment," the high-pitched voice finished.

Jabruelle let out a scream of shock, jumping onto the gnome's old comfy chair like it would somehow protect him from the diminutive undead fire sprite raging at him from the now immolated contents of the hearth.

Without thinking, he picked the small pillow next to the chair and chucked at her in the fireplace. She caught it with fiery red hands and lit it ablaze before casting it to the side. Seeing the pillow on the floor, he ran over and kicked it into the fireplace before yelping and hopping on one foot like a piece of burning cloth fell on his bare toe.

Clutching his foot in his hands, he fell on his butt and stared at the silent but angry-looking fire sprite.

"You aren't a hallucination like Wren was, are you?" he asked, his voice catching with fear.

"No, I am not a hallucination! What am I doing back on Nysia Jabruelle?" she demanded, stalking towards him with a threatening finger.

Cowering in fear, he wished the tea would wear off, and Xissay would disappear like Wren had and leave him to his now less sane but soberer mind. Instead, he smelled sulfuric smoke and looked up to see he was alone once again.

"Oh, thank the goddess below. Perhaps I finally am coming out of it," he said, taking several deep breaths.

"I wish I had pulled forth a familiar from the dream, though. It is lonely being The Sleeper's only minion," he said forlornly, coughing as he once again smelled sulfur and then cringing again as Xissay reappeared and started in on him again.

"What did you do!?" she asked.

"I was just trying to summon a familiar, I found a bat in the great dream, and I did as the texts described, dominating and pulling it forth as my familiar,"

"Your familiar?" she howled, slapping her forehead with her tiny hands so hard that sparks flew off them.

"You release me and send me back this instant!" she ordered.

"I don't think that is something that can be done. I don't even know how I summoned you in the first place!" Jabruelle whined.

She raised her tiny fist again as if she was about to attack him and then glared at him in silence for a moment.

"You thought I was a bat!?" she raged.

"In my defense, I think I was hallucinating from the tea I drank. I swore I was talking to Wren like he was right here with me, not minutes before going into The Great Dream," he replied, his hands held wide in a shrug.

"Hallucinating from tea? She asked incredulously.

"I got it from the troll named Moodi Shen," he explained.

"Oh," was Xissay's only reply, a terrifying look of understanding coming across her diminutive features.

110

Chapter 11
Involuntary Obligations

Sudbina lounged on the bow point of the *Torrent,* watching the crew of the sand elven ship busy themselves in preparations for casting off. Then, hearing the familiar and purposeful clicking of boots on the wooden deck, she looked over her shoulder at the approaching Tormenta commander. She rolled over to face Zolga fully and gave the woman a grin.

"Last chance to grab anything from the wharf. I've ordered the crew to push off as soon as the elves do. I plan to track them closely all the way to this Zarad they speak of," she said, with a glance at the elven boat.

"Are you worried about losing them at sea?" Sudbina asked curiously.

"Some of my crew helped the elves restock their vessel late into the night. It runs a surprisingly shallow and sharp draft. I imagine that they are quite quick across the water, albeit via a very rough ride through any kind of heavy seas. No, we won't lose them, but we will be stretching out every inch of sail these four masts can hold to keep them in view if there is a good wind," Zolga commented.

"Do you think it wise we travel alone? Won't Galonica be worried?" she asked the commander playfully.

"We'll have several galleons shadowing us. We'll keep far enough back from the elves, and they'll keep far enough back from us that they'll be beyond the horizon to our new friends the entire time. The night before we are supposed to arrive, I've instructed them to patrol out at sea and await word from us. Which reminds me, we have a full raider contingent aboard, so you'll have to double up," Zolga stated.

"Ooh, and do I get to share the captain's quarters with you?" Sudbina asked hopefully.

"Ezera may have accepted you into The Cause, but Itka is its senior operative on this trip. I am afraid she will have that privilege," Zolga said, departing with a smug look that Sudbina acknowledged by sticking out her tongue rudely.

Several whistles blew on the elven ship, and she watched them cast their lines. The rustling of cloth unfurling and the pop of ropes going taut surrounded her as the *Torrent* readied itself to follow when she noticed a frantic commotion from the pier. She spotted the plane black robe of Jabruelle as the necromancer haphazardly ran down the steps to the dock and up to the ship's rail.

"Is it too late to come aboard?" he asked between labored panting.

"It's about to be," Sudbina said, pointing at the growing gap of water between the deck and the dock.

Jabruelle leaped, his feet barely making it into the ship. Sudbina had to grab the front of his robes while he flailed madly, trying to regain his balance.

"Oh good, so good to have made it. This will be such an exciting adventure! Destiny awaits!" he said triumphantly, looking out to sea.

The docks were several lengths behind them when Sudbina once again heard Zolga's boots, stomping more angrily than usual as they approached.

"By The Siren, what is he doing onboard?" Zolga asked her, pointing at Jabruelle.

The man held a hand up to speak and waited in awkward silence for Zolga to look at him.

"Well?" she prompted.

"Ah, yes. I had the most interesting evening, and well, I went and woke the Chancellor before dawn trying to find Harpis as I had already checked The Siren's Scream. Aanaman said that Harpis was on board and that I should feel free to join you all on this quest of diplomacy!" Jabruelle stammered excitedly.

Sudbina did her best not to laugh as she and Zolga exchanged glances at the man's statement.

"Fine, he can come along, but he's staying in your cabin, Sudbina," Zolga said, heading for the stairs to the helm.

Sudbina put her hands on her hips and stuck out her tongue at

112

the Tormenta woman again.

"All right then, necromancer, what did you pack?" she asked, pointing at his satchel bag and leather pouches.

"Oh, tea, and um, a few tomes on necromancy. Perhaps on the Nysian mainland I may find new devotees for The Sleeper," he answered proudly.

"Tea and books?" she asked, and he confirmed with a nod.

"You realize we will be gone for two to three weeks, Jabruelle?" she asked.

The necromancer meekly shrugged in reply.

*****

Harpis tried not to gag on the cloth tied around his mouth as he opened blurred eyes that took longer than expected to focus due to the pounding in his head. His jaw ached, and his lips were cracked from being held open for gods knew how long. Judging by how his muscles ached as he sat up gingerly in the wide hammock, it had been many hours. He tried to get his bearings even though his mind was still swimming with the dwindling effects of whatever had knocked him out.

He felt the rolling of the sea and quickly realized he was in a cabin onboard a ship. By the looks of the bulkhead, it was a Tormenta Galleon. He arched his back in a stretch and bumped against something in the hammock above him. Seeing a lanky form and black robes above him, Harpis immediately recognized Wren's last apprentice. He angrily struck the man in the behind several times with punches from his bound hands.

"All right, all right!" Jabruelle said, hopping out of the hammock with a fearful look before apologetically holding up a finger at Harpis.

"One moment!" he shouted before disappearing into the hallway.

No sooner had he lost the sound of the man's receding footsteps did he hear several sets approaching, and the cabin door was flung open. Zolga, Itka, Sudbina, and Jabruelle all piled into the tight cabin standing around him. He raised his hands and pointed at his mouth in irritation.

Itka looked from Harpis to Jabruelle and put her forehead in her palms for a moment.

"Necromancer, why is his mouth gagged?" the dwarf asked.

"You didn't see what he did to my cat Timot," Jabruelle exclaimed, looking at Harpis with concern.

"I did not see it, but you haven't stopped talking about it. Bard, do you promise not to cut us to pieces with your eviscerating word powers?" the dwarf asked sarcastically.

Harpis rolled his eyes before shaking his head and shrugging angrily.

Zolga snapped her rapier from its sheath and deftly cut the rag gagging his mouth and the rope around his wrists before handing him a skin of water. He guzzled the contents and took a moment to find his breath before addressing his captors.

"Sudbina, by the gods, I swear that if you shoot me with another one of those darts, you had better kill me because if I wake up, I will show you exactly what happened to Jabruelle's pickled cat," he threatened in a strained whisper.

"What's that, dear? I can't hear you," she said, snickering as he glared at her.

He chucked the empty waterskin at her head, but she easily dodged it and blew him a kiss.

"I'll be in my cabin. The four of you have fun figuring this whole situation out. Harpis, welcome aboard the *Torrent*. We are tight on cabins, so you'll be bunking here with Jabruelle and Sudbina. I'll have some food sent down for you," she said, departing the cabin.

Harpis crossed his arms and looked grumpily at the three left in the cabin.

"How long was I asleep?" he asked, looking directly at Sudbina for the answer.

"It is almost midday, so, about a day and a half," she answered cheerfully.

He sighed to himself, rubbed his stiff neck, and rolled his shoulders against the ache of immobility.

"Today, I was supposed to have lunch with Kalna," he whispered accusingly at the woman who turned her guilty eyes away from him.

"I know it was your plan that got me here on this boat, Sudbina, but who's idea was it for me to go along? I assume Aanaman and Ezera?" he asked, looking at the dwarf he knew worked for his former Syndicate colleague.

Itka nodded at him before answering the knock at the door and taking a plate of grilled fish and another water skin from the crew member in the passageway.

"It was a contingency that we set in motion after Ezera and Aanaman met. She asked Sudbina and me to get you aboard the *Torrent*. We had to try to convince you one last time, especially after how odd the meeting with the sand elves went," the dwarf explained, handing him the food.

Harpis ignored the statement for a moment, slowly chewing the warm fish. Living life as a poor man scrounging on other people's leftover scraps at taverns as a deckhand had taught him that the best-tasting food was the meal had after not eating for a day or more. He took the small moment of solace, savoring the fish as his stomach came alive, and informed him just how long it had been since he'd eaten.

"And what if my answer is still no when we arrive? which it continues to be now," he said to the dwarf.

"Then you can spend the next couple of weeks relaxing on the *Torrent* as the single greatest waste of talent and abilities I have ever heard of. Meanwhile, less qualified people will struggle to perform delicate work you are aptly suited for," Itka answered grumpily.

The knowing and well-placed barb hurt more than he expected, especially coming from someone who he had only recently met. Maybe Ezera's senior operative was indeed an heir to the legacy of her kin, Braffen Frothbrew.

"I know why you are here," he said, nodding to Itka before uncrossing his arms and pointing at Sudbina.

"No need to explain why you were involved in my abduction, but I am curious to know why you are playing along with the plans of others and seeking membership in The Cause? I never took you as one to follow another's path," he asked, probing Sudbina for information.

"I've roamed every inch of sea and land across the islands of Savja. What could be more interesting than meeting these sand elves and seeing their city?" she returned.

Harpis stared at her for a long moment after her explanation, and for a second, he thought she almost looked nervous. He felt that she was lying, attempting to distract him more than usual. Deception and conniving were things Sudbina performed as readily as she did breathe, but her response to that simple question was a clumsy deflection by comparison. Harpis decided not to push the issue here in front of the others, so he turned his accusing finger to Jabruelle.

"Which brings me to you, Jabruelle. What makes the last necromancer decide to get on a boat full of warriors and spies headed for the land full of sand elves?" he asked with a raised eyebrow.

Jabruelle let out a skittish cackle before quieting. Fidgeting, he summoned his necromancer scythe into his hands.

"The Death Herald may travel where he wishes! And we are brothers in pain, you and I. Our common bond and suffering bind our fates, and I feel it is my duty to remain at your side," Jabruelle said in a more confident voice than Harpis expected.

"I am sorry, did you claim to be The Sleeper's Herald?" he asked the man, skepticism heavy in his quiet voice.

"I do believe that is the responsibility of the senior death speaker," Jabruelle explained.

"You were able to pull forth a familiar from The Great Dream?" Harpis asked excitedly, genuinely happy for him.

Jabruelle did not answer but closed his eyes for a moment. The tiny cabin filled with a sulfuric stench, and a tiny cloud appeared, dissipating and revealing the fire sprite floating above the necromancer's shoulders.

"Xissay!" Harpis exclaimed hoarsely in disbelief at seeing Wren's companion at Jabruelle's side.

"Well, did he agree to help?" Xissay asked Jabruelle in her high-pitched nasally voice, fiery hands indignantly resting on her hips.

"Not yet," Sudbina said, answering the familiar.

The sprite floated in front of Harpis' face, fires flickering in her angry eyes.

"The old gnome must be tossing and turning in his eternal slumber, grumbling under his breath right now!" she seethed.

His shoulders sagged, and he hung his head. The mention of her former master quickly replaced the joy of seeing the long-departed fire sprite. He felt the heat on her tiny hand as she pulled his chin upward to look into her eyes.

"You know, he told me you were the greatest apprentice he'd ever trained. Wren loved you like a son and knew you were the

116

best chance the people of Quaj had at finding and maintaining peace. Now, quit feeling sorry for yourself," she finished.

*****

After Jabruelle had dismissed Xissay, they'd agreed to leave Harpis alone, so Sudbina found herself in her favorite spot on the *Torrent*, if not her favorite place anywhere. She perched on the bow, lounging against rigging lines and staring out at the calm sea under a moonless, star-filled night sky. The void-like scene made her feel like she was staring into the abyss beyond Nysia, as it became almost impossible to tell where the purplish-black expanse of the night ended and its reflection in the waters began.

Her head spun around at the sound of a long sigh behind her. She nearly fell off of the bow as she caught sight of Enky.

"I watch nights like this in many of my viewing frames from my home, but it is never as pretty as when I project myself here and view it first-hand. The stars of Nysian nights are a sight unto themselves," he said from the rope rigging above her.

"Thank you for taking the opportunity to interrupt my peaceful relaxation," she said as quietly as possible, looking back ahead of the ship but unable to discern the elven vessel ahead of them in the darkness.

"Do you mean now or in general?" Enky asked with a laugh, and she shook her head resignedly in response.

"Well, I must say Sudbina, you have done quite well. We may yet save Nysia!" he said happily.

"Save Nysia from what exactly?" she asked, not expecting an answer that held truth or substance.

"Oh, my dear Sudbina, that will be revealed to you soon, and when it is, you will be less responsible for guiding Harpis where we need him to go," he said.

"It better be revealed soon, he is no fool, and he knows me well enough to suspect something," she replied.

"Just put more of your gift into it. Never have I heard a mortal so beguiling as Sudbina when she is lying," he said with a laugh.

"I get the sense that Harpis can notice that as well. His understanding of his, our gift, has changed considerably after what happened to him," she admitted honestly.

"You mean after what he did to himself by calling for my

117

sister," Enky corrected.

"The Siren is as terrifying as she is captivating," Sudbina agreed, staring at the undeniable allure before them.

"It is beautiful out tonight," the voice behind her said.

"You said that already," Sudbina replied.

"I said what already?" Harpis asked.

Sudbina felt her cheeks flush in panic, and she kept herself looking straight ahead and changed the subject.

"Did hearing what Xissay had to say bring you closer to being a voluntary participant in our little adventure?" she asked him as he joined her at the bow.

"I will not spend the next two weeks in that cabin with Commander Zolga babysitting me. I think I can stand to serve as the third most senior operative," he chuckled.

"Also, Ezera told them that you were the Savjan representative that would arrive in Zarad and be responsible for handling diplomatic relations," she said with a cringe as he sat up abruptly from his lounging to glare at her.

Not one to be put on the spot by other people, Sudbina felt herself struggling not to squirm as he continued to stare at her, even after the fierceness in his eyes softened into a look of understanding.

"Sudbina, why do I get the sense that you are as helplessly trapped in this whole predicament as I am?" he asked, and she found herself unable to keep up her façade, turning away from him so that he could not read her face.

"How did you know where to find me? Who told you of the sand elves? It is almost as if fate itself is guiding you. Do they have spies? Did they contact you? Are you working for them?" he asked in an unrelenting stream of whispered questions.

She decided that she would not be able to continue dancing lies around him.

"Harpis, I know it is against your best judgment, but I need you to trust me. We are doing the right thing, and it is something that you and I must do. I cannot say more than that, so please don't ask me to," she desperately asked.

He leaned back against the rigging, resting his head again on his hands.

"That's the first believable thing I've heard you say since you found me in Kalt," he said quietly.

Chapter 12

Zarad

The visage of Zarad from the sea had been breathtaking as the thousand-foot-high marble cliffs came into view over the horizon. Harpis and the others stood at the railings of the *Torrent* while the ship's crew awkwardly tied it to one of the stone docks. The piers were obviously built for smaller sand elven vessels like the one they had followed north. There was barely enough room for Emissary Keptis' ship to join them along the length of the smooth polished marble causeway.

Standing in the shadow of the city with the sun setting far above, the seaward cliff-wall was a truly incredible spectacle. Looking up, Harpis could see hundreds of intricate windows cut into the faces of the smooth, tan and white swirled marble cliffs. There were only a few docks beside theirs and not many vessels tied to them. Ahead was a cavernous opening as wide as the mouth of the Fjall river and city with a stone passage rose and curved quickly out of view, big enough for ten men abreast on horseback to ride up.

His and the others' gawking gazes returned to the dock as Emissary Keptis disembarked and walked before them with an officious-looking attendant holding parchment and charcoal.

"I do not believe we had the chance to meet. I am Emissary Keptis," the sand elf said, bowing to Harpis.

"Well met, Emissary. I am Harpis Akkeri. While we are here in your beautiful city, I will speak for Chancellor Aanaman and his advisor Ezera," Harpis said, returning the bow.

"How many of your contingent will need lodging within the city?" The elf asked.

Harpis turned to Zolga, who was still scanning the docks like a bird of prey.

"How many?" he asked her.

"My crew and I will stay here on the galleon as a precaution. We will be ready if you need us," Zolga assured him, letting her gaze slide to the elf for a moment.

"I think that is prudent. For now, though, do send four raiders with us. I will dismiss them when we reach our quarters. That way, they can return to you with instructions on how to find us," Harpis said quietly so Keptis could not hear.

"Done," she said, turning to one of her officers.

Harpis smiled at his odd diplomatic party and turned back to the docks.

"Eight of us, if that is not too much to ask. The rest will spend at least the evening refitting and stocking the ship," Harpis said.

Keptis snapped his fingers and dismissed the still scribbling attendant and waved for them to follow. Then, with one last look at the relative safety of the Galleon, Harpis took in a steadying breath and led Itka, Sudbina, Jabruelle, and their four raider escorts down to the dock and towards the city with Keptis.

It took them twenty minutes to ascend the spiral ramp that wound its way up the entire height of the cliff face, windows letting in the fading light each time it curved towards the sea again. When they finally emerged onto the flat ground, they were greeted by the warm, dry air constantly blowing out to sea and a view that took their collective breath away.

Zarad was the most fascinating place Harpis had ever seen. What he thought was flat ground when seen from the sea was the top of a hundred-foot-tall hollowed-out plateau stretching away from the coast cliff face. Keptis walked them towards the inward edge, where he leaned with his elbows on the carved stone rail before waving his hand at the white and tan stone city, glowing pink in the setting sun. The city stretched for miles in every direction like a mile wide bowl of stone. He could barely make out the rising edge of the opposite plateau wall.

"Emissary Keptis, are all the cities of your country so beautiful?" Harpis asked the smiling elf.

"Master Harpis, there are no other cities. What you see before you is Zarad. Beyond the marble walls, there is nothing but The Great Sea of Sand for weeks as you head away from the sea," Keptis said, beaming.

"The buildings are so beautiful. How many elves live here?" Harpis asked, unable to pull his gaze from the growing shadows and fading glow over the city.

"Half a million of us live here. We carved this city from what was once a single plateau of marble. Nothing in Zarad is built. Instead, our artisans free the inner beauty of the marble to reveal the city of the sand elves. The higher ranking and more pure-bred members of the five families live within the walls of Daybreak's Rampart which curves around Zarad," He said, motioning for them to follow him again.

They did not walk long, arriving at a staircase that descended a single floor into the immense marble rampart.

"Here is one of our finest accommodations for visitors. The view over the city at night is as beautiful as the stars above it. Unfortunately, there are only four rooms in the suite. Your escorts will have to stay in the one next to it. I apologize," The elf said.

"You have been a very gracious host. I see no need to keep armed guards in such a refined place. If anything, I fear I risk offense at having them with us tomorrow when we meet with the Vizier. Could I inconvenience you to have someone lead them back to our ship?" Harpis asked.

"But of course," the elf said, seemingly pleased that Harpis was thoughtful enough and comfortable enough to make the request.

He whistled, and a moment later, two spear-carrying elves appeared and led the raiders back to the docks. Keptis turned towards them as his attendant from the docks climbed the staircase from the suite.

"It is prepared, Emissary," the elf said with a bow.

"Harpis, friends, we have food, water, and cactus wine laid out for you and an oil lantern lit for your convenience. Phynrit here will be in the adjacent suite. If you have any concerns during the evening, please do not hesitate to call on him. He will bring you to meet with Vizier Mistis and me in the morning," Keptis said with a bow, and he headed down into another staircase, conversing with the attendant.

Descending into the lavish quarters, they found themselves in a rectangular room with food and drink sitting out on a large table in front of a long lounging bench, all carved from the stone, just as the room was. Harpis and Jabruelle followed Itka as she walked through one of the four doors into the connected bedroom, onto its balcony. The floor of the bowl-like city was at least four stories below them. As dusk fell over Zarad, winking golden lantern lights mimicked that white of the stars above against the growing darkness.

"Can you believe this whole place has been carved from a single stone? Including the buildings, furniture, and all. Gods, even my bed is a marble relief with bedding atop it! And I thought us dwarves were the true masters of stone. They won't believe me back in Fjall when I tell them of this place," she said.

Sudbina joined them with a crystal decanter in hand that was filled with a clear liquid.

"Fancy water dish," she said, tipping it back and then spitting out an alcoholic-smelling cloud of mist.

"That is no Siren's cursed water I've ever had," Sudbina said, and Harpis took it from her, smelling the slightly citrusy contents and wrinkling his nose.

"I would say it is safe to assume this is the cactus wine Keptis spoke of, though I do not exactly know how this qualifies for wine," Harpis said, handing it to Itka's outstretched hand.

He tried not to laugh as she made the same face Sudbina had, but instead of spitting it out, the dwarf grimaced and swallowed.

"Straight fire, that stuff. It's probably the same liquid burning in the lantern inside," Itka said, shaking her head and going inside with Jabruelle to pick at the food.

"Care to have a look around?" Sudbina asked him, looking out at Zarad.

"I think it would be beneficial, but I do not want to insult our hosts by sneaking about on our first evening in their city," he replied.

Sudbina leaned her head on his shoulder and put an arm around his waist.

"What do you mean, dear? We are simply two innocent human lovers strolling about a gorgeous city on a romantic summer evening," she said with a wink.

"What now?" Itka said, her eyebrow raised as she walked out onto the balcony again, and Jabruelle and her shared water skins and some fruit with them.

"Sudbina thinks we should go have a look around," Harpis offered.

"That is a terrible idea, and it will end badly," Itka said, crossing her sinewy arms across her chest.

"Itka. Aanaman and Ezera knew what they were getting when they sent Sudbina and me here with you. Good diplomacy is informed diplomacy. Currently, they are the ones that seem to have all the information. So, I'd think some mild espionage and reconnaissance are in order," he said, trying to sound disarming in his raspy whisper of a voice.

"All right, smart guy, how do you plan to find your way down there without Phynrit noticing you? What if you get caught?" she asked in frustration.

Harpis took the decanter from her and took a sip, trying not to cough.

"Jabruelle, what do you think?" he asked and shook his head as the necromancer cackled nervously.

"I can summon Xissay and ask her to have a look around instead," he offered.

Itka looked hopeful at the idea until Harpis shook his head at the necromancer.

"I don't think sending out an undead fire sprite from the deep fires of Nysia to scout in a foreign land amongst people we know nothing about is a good idea. I don't presume the elves to be like some of the Tormenta, but there seems to be a widely held malaise towards The Sleeper's devoted outside of Savja," Harpis replied.

"I shall be in my room reading my texts if you need me!" Jabruelle said, excusing himself and refusing to participate in the argument.

Harpis handed Sudbina the decanter after splashing his hands with some of the cactus wine and rubbing it on his neck.

"Here, get some of that on your breath and person," he said before going room to room, grabbing sheets from the beds and tying them into a makeshift rope that he then handed to a glowering Itka.

"Itka, sleep here on the balcony, we won't be long, and when we return, we will call for you to lower this for us. Don't worry. If we get lost or caught, we are simply two young humans who are drunk and strolling about their city. I imagine these elves are like other over-long-lived races. In that case, they'll be as dismissive of humans as we are of our children," he said, patting her shoulder reassuringly before following Sudbina over the balcony railing and down the other end of the make-shift rope.

*****

Sudbina and Harpis had spent almost an hour strolling around the streets of Zarad. As expected, they had run into several groups of sand elves and been greeted by a smattering of welcomes and curiously raised eyebrows, all from elves looking down their noses at the brash human couple. A pair of armed elves had stopped them, but Harpis had bothered them effusively for more cactus wine, and eventually, the two went on their way, shaking their heads at his apparent stupor.

They had walked over a mile and were at the center of the city where there was a giant well-like structure big enough to hold a galleon in its water. A spiraling ramp along its inner wall went down two levels before leveling out and ringing the water.

"Do you think this is how they survive out here at the bottom of the desert?" Sudbina asked, looking down at the water.

Harpis was about to respond when they both turned towards the lowest level, hearing softly walking voices. He quickly put his back to the well and pulled Sudbina in for a kiss. Harpis appreciated that she understood his intent and kept one of her eyes open, surveying the scene below during their embrace. However, he was less than amused at her overly enthusiastic alcohol-flavored tongue in his mouth.

Thoughts brought on by their feigned romantic embrace fled from his mind, and he watched her eyes grow wide. It took every ounce of control for him not to turn and gawk with her. His entire body began to tingle with the pull of a gift stronger than he had felt from any mortal being. The voices then faded back into the small archway at the waterside platform a moment later. Sudbina's eye kept roaming for another moment, and she refused to relent her lips from his at first, but eventually, she pulled back from him and leaned in with her head on his chest.

"Did you feel that?" she whispered, caressing his chest with one finger as if she were saying sweet nothings.

"You felt it?" He whispered incredulously, unaware until now that she could sense the use of gifted magic.

She did not answer, instead of nodding her head into his neck in response.

"I haven't felt anything close to that since I spoke The Siren's

124

true name. Whatever that was made Lorkin's channeling seem like a drop of rain falling amongst a southern gale," he said quietly. She leaned up, putting her lips to his ear.

"You're going to have to kiss me again. Two of the three are walking up the ramp," Sudbina whispered, her breath tickling his neck and sending a shiver down his spine.

They returned to the performance as he heard a door close and lock below and then footsteps reach the top of the ramp, pause and then recede into the distance. When they separated again, she looked into the well with a frown, and when he turned, he saw that the door at the lower level had been closed and a giant lock on it. They both nearly yelped in surprise when the metal shutter of a window above it but below ground level clanged open, and lantern light from inside made the waters in the immense well glow and dance.

Sudbina walked him around to a spot on the encircling wall right above the open window and motioned for him to sit with her, feet dangling over the side barely and arm's length above the window itself.

"Hold on to the wall tightly," she said.

Harpis barely had time to clutch the stone rim and brace himself as she slid forward, turning as she fell to grab his ankles and swing herself into the room below.

"Oh, hello there," Harpis heard from below, and in a panic, he slid himself off the edge, spinning and grabbing the windowsill as he fell past the window and clumsily pulled himself into the room with a heave, closing the shutter behind him.

"Two visitors, I have not had guests in as long as I can remember!" the room's inhabitant said cheerily, seemingly unfazed by their burglary-like entrance into his home. He was dressed unlike the other plain tan or white-clad elves they had come across. Instead, he wore an azure robe, a darker blue than the deepest sea waters in the south of the world. His skin mostly matched that of the other elves, but his eyes were not the gold speckled brown, they were the intense blue of his garb, and something about his pupils seemed odd.

"Welcome to my abode. My name is Parafano," the elf said, bowing low.

"Nice to meet you, Parafano," Sudbina said in a voice that made Harpis' spine tingle again as she curtsied and bowed to the elf who took her hand and kissed its back, lightly touching it to his forehead as he bent.

"It is so nice to meet you, Sudbina. I tell you, I do not know how long it has been since I heard the harpies' voice on human lips, but I miss it immensely," Parafano lamented.

Harpis was completely confused at the exchange, but Sudbina's face seemed more concerned than shocked at what Parafano said to her.

"Quite the coincidence that one of mischief's muses would fly into my window on a day such as this!" he exclaimed, motioning for them to join him at the small table with four stone pillar stools in the center of the room.

Harpis decided that the whole encounter could not get any weirder and that they might as well play along with the elf that had decided not to cry out at their intrusion.

"Parafano, why is it a coincidence?" he asked, unsure how humans breaking into the elf's home on the day they arrived in his city was a coincidence and not simply a cause.

"Ah, another muse, this is a fine day indeed! Unfortunately, though, unlike Sudbina here, it appears your voice is not your instrument of choice," the elf said with a warm smile.

Sudbina glanced at Harpis and shrugged as he fumbled with his words, unsure how to proceed.

"Parafano, why is it such an odd coincidence that we arrived today?" he pressed, though what Harpis truly wanted from the elf was how Parafano knew of his gift and what he meant by harpies.

"Oh, it is troubling, Harpis. Today, when I checked on the conqueror's prison, it was unsealed, broken, and cracked as if from the inside. So, how fortunate that on the very same day, two descendants of those who inscribed *The Sisters' Song* on his cage would flutter into my home with their voices so sweet," he said, motioning at the plain-looking brass mirror that hung on the wall near the window.

She noticed that he was struggling to keep up and prodded Parafano in a different direction.

"Parafano, what were you doing when you dipped your hand in the well? We both felt what you did. It was incredible," she asked.

He rose from his seat and brought them three stone cups. He poured water from a pitcher and handed one to each before

126

touching their cups in a toast and drinking deeply.

"They need me to keep the water flowing this direction, you see. Without it, there is no elven city on the sea," he said forlornly, shaking his head as if troubled by something.

"He will come here first, bringing subjugation and sadness. He likes the sand elves least of all the elder races," Parafano said, almost to himself, joining them at the table again with his head in his hand before looking back up to them.

"I am sorry little birds, but I really am very tired. It has been a joy to host you this evening. Would you be so generous as to give me your word that you might return tomorrow and play me a song? Remembering the times when harpies still sang and the sisters still walked Nysia is a happiness I have not held in my mind in ages,"

"Of course, Parafano, thank you so much for your hospitality. You won't be bothered if we depart as we came?" she asked, nodding for Harpis to follow.

"Oh, not at all. What other way should winged creatures come and go if not through an open window?" he asked, walking towards the small bed on the room's inner wall and laying down, a content smile on his face.

*****

Halfway through the city, neither Harpis nor Sudbina had said a word as they held hands, meandering their way back to their quarters. He still struggled to make sense of what the elf had said.

"That is by far the oddest situation I think I have ever been in. I am not boasting but that claim encompasses an expansive list of unbelievable events, including singing to two goddesses," he said, shaking his head before looking at Sudbina, surprised that she did not immediately second his statement.

"It was definitely unexpected," she said, and he felt that it was honest.

"Are we just going to ignore that he seemed to know I, sorry, apparently we, are gifted? Or that he called us harpies or birds or whatever he meant by that." He said in exasperation.

"Based on the power we felt surging through the city when he enchanted that well, I think it is safe to assume he is attuned to the gifts in a way we are unaware of. Maybe it allows him to sense it, even when passive, in others," she offered, letting go of his hands.

127

She turned to him with a look on her face that was more serious than he expected.

"What do you think he meant by the conqueror's prison was broken open today?" she asked, looking almost as troubled as the elf did.

"I think that maybe we should be asking our hosts why they reached out to us and what danger this apparent aggressor might pose to newly propositioned allies of Zarad," Harpis returned with a shrug.

"But he said, the conqueror, the one banished by the sisters?" she continued.

"Well, unless Parafano meant the actual ages when he said he hadn't heard voices like ours, I don't think he was talking about Konflict. You were there. The elf is clearly addled, perhaps by the very power he wields. Maybe Vizier Mistis or Keptis himself will have answers to these questions. For now, I am going to assume Parafano drinks way too much cactus wine," Harpis replied.

"If that makes it easier for you to fall asleep tonight, I guess we can wait and find out tomorrow if the world is indeed ending," she said sullenly.

He stopped and put a hand on her shoulder, inspecting her face for signs of cracking into laughter or a smile in jest. When she did not, a tinge of fear crept into his mind.

"I've never known you to be one to worry like this," he returned concernedly.

Chapter 13
Invitations and Inquiry

Harpis and Sudbina had quickly recapped what they had done and learned during their excursion to a horrified Itka and a curious Jabruelle as the sun rose the following day. Before the dwarf had too much of an opportunity to criticize them for being so overt, a knock came at their door. Phynrit led them out onto the lip of the giant marble bowl that was the city of Zarad. Phynrit referred to the outer rim as Daybreak's Rampart, and after a moment gawking at the dawn-lit city, they began the long walk around it. He led them from the view looking down across the city to the outer edge, affording them views of The Sea of Sand and its endless dunes stretching past the horizon.

An hour later, when they went back below the surface level of the former plateau and out of the dry heat, Harpis' brushed what he thought was sand carried on the breeze, only to discover that it was salt from his evaporated sweat.

Phynrit noticed him and paused them, disappearing into a corridor and returning with several water skins.

"My apologies. I forget that other races are not as accustomed to the desert as we are. Please, forgive me. I will lead you back to your quarters through the corridors instead of out in the open," the elf said.

"No need to apologize, Phynrit. The views of the city and the sands were well worth the walk in the heat," Harpis replied.

"Three pale humans from Kalt and myself, a dwarf, spending most of my life below the surface, I could do with staying out of the sun the rest of the day," Itka said after finishing the water skin, her cheeks and lips slightly red from being burnt.

Taking them down two more long stone hallways, Phynrit

walked up to an intricate, gold-inlaid marble door and struck the gong sitting outside it. A minute later, the door slid soundlessly into a pocket to the side, revealing a wide room with an expansive window that ran its entire length, affording a view over the sands. Standing at the open window ledge were Emissary Keptis and four other elves. All were wearing the whiteish-tan cloth garb he and Sudbina had seen worn by every elf in the city besides the strange Parafano. The colors were the same, but one wore a flowing robe while another had a similar outfit to the Emissary. The last two Harpis would have bet his life on being military officers.

Keptis dismissed Phynrit to the hallway and walked the four of them the last few steps himself.

"Vizier Mistis, I present you the envoy from Quaj Island, representatives of the nation of Savja. This is their lead diplomat Harpis Akkeri and his advisors, Jabruelle, Itka, and Sudbina," Keptis said with a sweeping bow.

The vizier eyed them shrewdly before motioning at those standing with him.

"Welcome to Zarad. This is Exarch Vetlostis and High Marshals Araho and Selarom," he said, and the other elves nodded as they were introduced.

"What do you humans think of Zarad, the jewel in the sand and home of our people?" Vizier Mistis asked.

Unlike Keptis, Harpis noted Mistis did not keep his air of superiority from his voice. Something that would make it all the more enjoyable when he put the elf on his heels with what he presumed would be an unexpected line of questioning.

"Truly, Vizier, it is a wonder unto itself. It stands as a literal monument to the noble sand elves that created it and those that still thrive within its walls," Harpis said, trying not to smile as Mistis was visibly enjoying the flattery.

"Which brings me to question, what possible reason could such an advanced and self-sustaining culture have in reaching out to the virgin, juvenile nation of Savja for alliance?" he asked innocently.

"As I am sure Emissary Keptis explained, we have finally come to see the residents of Quaj Island and this nation of Savja as worthy partners," Mistis answered.

The elf's overtly patronizing tone caused Itka to huff and Sudbina to stifle a giggle behind Harpis. He hoped his ill-equipped advisors would keep themselves together for just a bit longer.

Mistis, his opponent in this verbal dance of negotiation and politicking, was arrogant, blind to any surprise that might come from the young infantile human man before him. So Harpis assumed his first swing would land like a strike from Itka's maces when he replied.

"The good Emissary was succinct in his explanation of the motive, including ample conveyance of the haste with which you would like us to return. Still, with powerful mages such as Parafano at your disposal, I can't reconcile what we might bring to you aside from a pet curiosity or a target for philanthropic altruism?" Harpis asked, pausing for a moment.

"My, aren't we wordy today?" he heard Sudbina whisper behind him, and Jabruelle stifled one of his nervous cackles. Harpis clasped his hands behind his back and angrily waved his finger at them.

He watched Mistis' mouth grow pregnant with a response before holding his hand up to quiet the elf, whose eyes went wide at the brash rudeness.

"Unless, of course, it has something to do with the conqueror on his way to your lands? What are we to be then? Fodder for your cause? Corpses to stack up on the outside of Daybreak's Rampart?" Harpis finished in as loud a rasping whisper as his damaged vocal cords would allow.

He watched the stately facade fade away as Vizier Mistis glanced nervously at his advisors.

"I get the inclination that time is an issue in this engagement. So, I would ask that you cast aside frivolity and tell us why you were so desperate to get us here, or we will depart from your shores and leave you to deal with this aggressor yourself," Harpis concluded.

"Leaving my shores will not save you from the fate of this aggressor, Harpis Akkeri, nor will it protect the people of Savja. Normally, I would be insulted at participating in the brevity and conciseness required in conversing with short-lived humans, but you are correct. We are desperate. Not just Zarad, but all of Nysia is in danger, whether it knows it or not," he said sternly, walking them over to a table full of maps of the Nysian mainland and the seas surrounding it, bidding them all sit.

"It would seem you are more familiar with my people and

Zarad than I expected," Mistis said, glaring at Emissary Keptis while he spoke, turning to Harpis as he finished.

"How is it that you know so much about us? You knew that we had unified as a country. However, not the extent of that unification or its reason?" Harpis asked, probing to understand further.

"Turin Deadeye told us as much. He sent us a message in the tenth month of last year, telling us that in a year, his agents on Quaj would have followed the instructions he recorded at The Archdiocese of Daybreak in Mer and completed the steps necessary to unify the island. Unfortunately, he'd said that his death would be required for the plan to work and asked us to make contact in the tenth month this year," Mistis explained smugly, obviously enjoying Harpis' attempts to control the contortions of surprise and confusion across his face.

Harpis turned towards Itka for a moment, hoping perhaps that Ezera and The Cause were somehow aware of this, but the dwarf only shrugged at him, her eyes wide and mouth similarly agape with surprise.

Vizier Mistis calmly laced his fingers and placed his hands on the marble table between them.

"However, as you have found out, our timeline was shortened somewhat as on the eighteenth day of the eleventh month last year, The Siren's scream was heard at every corner of Nysia and by the god-conqueror Konflict himself. That same day, almost eight months ago, Parafano alerted us that he had seen the prison was no longer intact through his mirror of farsight," Mistis explained.

Harpis thought he had taken the advantage in this war of words, but it now felt as though he had simply set himself up to be run over by a horse. Instead, the implication of his responsibility in freeing Konflict shattered his concentration.

"Parafano said last night that he had seen that vision just yesterday?" Harpis asked, still reeling.

This time the robed elf that Mistis introduced as Exarch Vetlostis spoke.

"Parafano is not well. His memory deceives him. If you went to him again today, he would likely tell you the same tale again, but the truth is that he told his caretakers of Konflict's return on the eighteenth day of the tenth month last year, Vizier Mistis stated," he explained.

"You know Turin Deadeye?" Harpis asked, still trying to comprehend what the sand elves told them.

"I tell you the god of war himself has risen and has been moving and growing his horde for nearly a year, and you ask me about a dead wood elf? Perhaps despite his advice to do so, we were wrong to involve the humans of Quaj," Mistis countered.

"The actual god, Konflict? You ask us to believe that he is on his way here and that we can somehow help you against him? I don't know which is harder to take as truth," Itka asked in frustration.

Mistis snapped his fingers, and one of the High Marshals unrolled a giant map of the Nysian continent before them while the other placed weights on the edges to hold it flat. Vizier Mistis stood with an ornate cane and pointed at the map as he spoke.

"This is us here, the southernmost tip. Here to the north and east, on the southernmost Soalian isle, is where Konflict was banished. By now, we assume at least the human nations of Solia, Obava, and Trava have fallen, with Sumka likely to follow. I have sent messengers, but they take months to return from the more distant cities. I assume the wood elves and trolls will hide in the forests of Cemmia and swamps of Leshi in the east, and the dwarven clans will hole up in the mountains. Our most conservative estimate is that if left unchecked a horde of at least a quarter-million humans will be at Zarad's gates come winter," Mistis said, sitting and handing the cane to High Marshal Araho.

"I don't know what you think we can do against a force that size. Our standing army is maybe ten thousand strong," Itka explained to the military officers.

High Marshal Selarom spoke while Araho pointed along as they explained their intentions.

"As you can see, the Necakan mountain range, the Astinan River to its east, and the Andrefan River to the west split the continent nearly in two. It is not your army we need but your armada. We do not have much in the way of ships, nor do any other Nysian countries. The Soalians are too primitive for seafaring, and the mainland nations do not need a naval force. Unlike Savja,"

"Our galleons would bottom out in a river and be easily boarded," Harpis stated, looking over the map with the others.

Mistis took the pointer back and slid its tip to the eastern

Astinan River.

"Perhaps a river on Quaj. The Astinan is over three miles wide in parts, never narrower than a mile. It would be impassable if patrolled by your galleons, especially by such a large force. That would force Konflict's hordes north and west to a small bottleneck between the Necakan and Unkur mountain ranges. There, they will be slowed more easily by Sumkan forces, who have hopefully received our warning," Mistis finished.

"Will these Sumkans be able to hold them there?" Harpis asked, looking at Jabruelle and Sudbina to see if they would participate in the conversation, but the two kept staring at the maps.

"The humans of Sumka will likely fall too. However, we have sent our most talented and experienced general, High Marshal Erimo, and the bulk of our forces to Necaka. The plan was to stop the enemy from crossing the land bridge at the north end of the Andrefan River with the aid of the Necakans. Then Erimo will harass the enemy down the river's length to the coast, forcing them to cross the shallows of the river's delta in the next most strategically viable location, where it meets the sea. Crossing there will allow Erimo to use the desert against the Konflict-dominated human forces. Perhaps if all goes well, those that make it to our walls will be unable to take them despite their godly commander," Mistis concluded.

"Why not use other mirrors like Parafano's to show us these enemies or Konflict himself?" Sudbina asked, finally breaking her silence.

"Parafano is the only one with such a mirror, and he only ever uses it to look upon Konflict's prison," Exarch Vetlostis answered.

Harpis decided to speak again after looking to his companions for support.

"I believe we will find it difficult to convince our people to join you in this war just months out of their battle for our own peace and survival. That said, we will do our best. I assume you would prefer we leave as quickly as possible to inform Chancellor Aanaman and the others?" Harpis asked.

"If you cannot return within the next month, or can't agree to what we have asked for, do not bother to return. Wait out your last few months hiding in the southern seas waiting for Konflict to find you," Vizier Mistis said.

The elf then stood, giving them a curt bow and nearly stomping out of the door.

The High Marshals stood to follow, and Araho paused at the entryway.

"Forgive his abrasiveness. He worries for the fates of the five families. We have strategized for a year on this, and the only way we potentially endure is with what we described to you today. Without your help on the eastern flank, we are lost," he said, with a nod at Emissary Keptis.

"We have provisioned your vessel. You may leave as soon as you are ready and willing," Keptis said when Harpis finally looked back at him.

"If you would grant me a favor, we will leave immediately," Harpis asked.

"Simply state it," Keptis agreed.

"We gave our word to Parafano that we would play him a song or two. You must understand, my word binds me," Harpis said gravely to the sand elf.

"Meet with him as you please. I will notify his caretakers that you will be by, and then I will let your ship's commander know to expect you. Be warned, you may have given Parafano your word, but he is likely to greet you the same way he greeted you last night," Keptis replied.

*****

Having headed hastily to their suites to get his violin, Sudbina, Jabruelle, Itka, and Harpis were crusty with the evaporated salt of their sweat when they reached the center of Zarad. Again, they took the stone ramp that curved along the inside of the giant well to the archway on its lower level after filling waterskins and drinking until they caught their breath. This time instead of slipping in through Parafano's window, the two caretakers unlocked the door and welcomed them in, taking them upstairs and then unlocking Parafano's door after a knock.

"Is he here against his will?" Harpis asked, surprised to find that the powerful mage was a captive in the city of his own people and that he seemingly allowed them to keep him that way.

The younger-looking sand elf caretaker said nothing and headed back downstairs. The older of the two gave Harpis and the

135

others a stern but solemn look.

"That is a very complicated question and an even more complicated answer. One which I am not within my rights to give. The Exarch may speak to that if you've time to talk with him before you depart," he said before heading down the stairs.

Harpis exchanged surprised and concerned glances with the other three before walking in and greeting Parafano.

"Well met, Parafano," Sudbina said as they entered.

The mage scurried about, grabbing them each a cup of water as he had the night before, asking them politely to please join him for a respite before standing between Sudbina and him.

"You know, it has been so very long since I last heard the chirping songs from the descendants of the harpies. They have vocals that fly so sweetly from their lips!" he exclaimed, turning to Harpis.

"My, and you have your violin. You must please play me a song or two before you leave. This is really quite the coincidence," Parafano said.

Harpis intently watched the faces of the others after he introduced them all, and Parafano went into the same odd recollection about the tomb that he had given them the night before, just as Mistis had suggested he might.

"Parafano, why would Konflict come here first, to Zarad? Why not go after the other descendants of the elder races along the way while he subjugates the human countries?" Harpis asked.

"The sand elves of Zarad are the closest living relatives to the elder races that resisted him during the Age of Discord. At this point, it is simply in his nature to remove the most problematic opponent first," Parafano answered matter-of-factly.

Then, the blue-robed mage walked over to stand behind Jabruelle, who hunched his shoulders almost fearfully.

"Don't worry, Herald, I know what you are. She must care about you ever so dearly for you to have such a budding gift of devotion roiling within you. Do the other inhabitants of Zarad know?" Parafano asked, and all Jabruelle could do was stammer an awkward laugh.

Parafano then stopped and looked like he was sniffing the air before turning to Itka and holding out his hand.

"May I see one of your weapons, lady dwarf? They are so tantalizingly delightful to my mind!" he said with a warm smile.

136

Itka paused for a moment, and Harpis raised an eyebrow hoping she'd see it and indulge the elf.

She handed a mace to him, and he closed his eyes, gripping the handle and slapping the spherical mace head once in his other hand.

"Oh, this is very nice! Very nice indeed!" he exclaimed, holding the mace with its head towards the ground, just an inch from the marble floor.

"Fjallinthrop," he whispered in perfect dwarfish, and the mace hit the floor with a resounding thunderclap from the impact, cracking the marble surface a little and crushing some of the stone beneath it to dust.

"Izdan," he said, closing his eyes and lifting the mace, handing them back to an astonished Itka.

"Very wonderful. Is the elementalist that crafted these here with you? I should very much like to meet them," he asked, and Itka shook her head.

"Will you get involved if Konflict does come here to Zarad? Surely one of your powers would be a huge boon to the city's defense," Jabruelle asked quietly.

"I do not think I would be permitted to do so, necromancer," Parafano said with an almost confused look.

"Parafano, are the other mages of Zarad as powerful as you?" Harpis asked, hoping to get some information out of the elf before he played the powerful mage a few songs as he had promised.

"Harpis, there are no other mages in Zarad. It is a sad thing if you ask me. You see, the five sand elven families are purists of sorts. They never interbred, even in the prior ages when they were known as the Aelar. They never allowed themselves a dalliance with others, and thus their bloodlines were never seeded with the gift that is given and not earned," he explained, looking at them as if they should already know this as a common fact.

"The gift was seeded? By whom?" Sudbina asked.

Parafano turned to her and gave her his biggest smile, clasping her hands in his.

"The dragons, of course. At first, it was quite a scandalous thing, dragons taking humanoid forms and mating with the elder races out of boredom," Parafano replied before growing visibly tired like he had the night before.

"I am sorry, you are all such wonderful guests, but I must be getting some rest," he said, eyeing his bed.

"As you asked, I shall play you a song before we go Parafano.

Putting his violin in his neck, he looked to Sudbina and motioned for her to come closer.

"Do you know the song about the Kaltese fisherman in The Siren's cave?" he asked hopefully.

When she nodded yes, he put as much into the performance of the tune as he had when he played it in desperation, hoping to become a sanctioned bard of The Hall. He channeled every ounce of his gift at Parafano, braiding it along with the drifting notes and feeling the ebb and flow within the rhythm. Shortly after he began, he looked to Sudbina and noticed her slowly swaying back and forth with the plucks of his violin while holding the gaze of the grinning Parafano.

When they finished, Parafano clapped several times before laying his hands on his lap as he sat at his bedside.

"You know, I must ask you to do something for me, children of the winged women. I have a friend, alas, I struggle to recall his name, but he really must hear your music. Like me, I am certain he misses it greatly," he asked.

Harpis nodded his head in agreement without a thought. The mage then raised his hand as if something occurred to him, and he pulled out a tome from his shelf, ripped a page out of one that had a map of the Nysian mainland on it, and blotted a spot on it with an ink quill. He grabbed Harpis and Sudbina's shoulders with one of his hands before taking the page from the marble table and handing it to Sudbina, pointing at the dot and speaking to Harpis.

"You will see them from the coastal seas, giant stone pillars. There are four of them in a line out to sea, carved from millennia of wind. There is an entrance to a cave. You can find my friend there," he explained as much as pleaded.

"It is best our hosts do not know," he said, grinning and laughing before laying in the bed.

"Rest well, Parafano. It was delightful to spend this time with you," he said, but Parafano was already snoring.

"By all the gods and The Sleeper below us, that was the most surreal encounter I have ever been a part of," Itka said, staring at the slumbering mage.

"I felt him ask us to visit his friend. Isn't that more of a bard sort of thing?" Jabruelle asked Harpis, looking in surprise at the sleeping Parafano.

*****

Harpis leaned on the *Torrent's* back railing, hanging over the stern as the tops of Zarad's seaward cliff slipped beyond the horizon, and turned to the gathered contingent standing by the helm.

"Are we in agreement then?" he asked, looking to Zolga as he caught Sudbina, Itka, and Jabruelle's heads nodding out of the corner of his eye.

"I still say that you should be the one to convince Aanaman to send our ships north," Zolga said, her hands crossed in front of her.

"It will be enough to tell him what we shared with you about the identity of this enemy and its motivation," Harpis replied.

"Including what likely led to Konflict's awakening," She asked with a raised eyebrow.

"My personal involvement in what is happening to Nysia is why I must go. Parafano is the most powerful mage, perhaps the most powerfully gifted being any of us have ever encountered. If this friend he cryptically spoke of exists and is in a better mental state than Parafano himself, it could prove an invaluable ally. At worst, we may learn more about what we will face in the coming months," Harpis rasped, unable to hide his guilt from his voice.

"I will not stop you, then. Looking at the maps, I feel comfortable speaking to Aanaman and Ezera on the validity of the sand elf conceived military plan as well," Zolga admitted.

Jabruelle and Itka gave parting words to Zolga and headed over the rail to their smaller ship. Sudbina took a moment to kiss Zolga on the cheek and give her a flirting wink before disembarking.

"My work as a diplomat is successfully concluded, I would think. It is time to try and make some personal amends. Even if we come up empty-handed from our trip east, we will return to Zarad around the same time you and the others, I will meet with Aanaman then," Harpis said, assuring Zolga before climbing over the stern rail into the single sail sloop that hung from the rear of the galleon.

Chapter 14
Request and Response

After Aanaman finished begrudgingly writing letters to the representatives of Savja's cities and Field Marshal Elliswerth he sat at his desk rubbing his aching hand. The tightness from an hour spent scribbling on parchment faded, and he ran his fingers across a palm that no longer carried the callouses and fresh scars of a life spent tending fields and livestock.

"Truly, I don't know if I was introduced to my younger self whether I'd be a disappointment or an unbelievable success," he said ruefully to his hands as he cracked his knuckles.

He eyed the whiskey decanter on his meeting table and then a stack of yet reviewed correspondence on the desk before him and sighed to himself as he stood from his chair and arched his back. Thoughts of a mid-afternoon drink were shattered when a horn blew from the direction of the harbor signaling a friendly arrival.

"No respite to be found in a glass today, but perhaps a message passed to one of our galleons from Zolga will prove more interesting than the day's planned activities," he said to the stack of parchment.

He walked to his door and poked his head out, asking the guard to let his wife know he would likely be taking his dinner in his office, and returned to his chair to impatiently await news from across the sea.

The wait was just long enough for him to reluctantly resign himself to reviewing the top letter stacked before him when there was a knock at the door.

"Come in, please." He replied, thankfully letting the letter fall back to his desk.

When Commander Zolga walked in, he was almost as

surprised at her very presence as he was at the look of uneasiness on the typically calm woman's face.

"Where is my conscripted head of diplomacy? Did he remain in Zarad? I had not expected your return for days or weeks yet. Did you even slow down when you threw Harpis overboard?" he asked with a laugh, hoping her expression might soften some.

"We spent only a single night in Zarad before returning with all possible haste. The bard and his companions will meet up with us later," she replied, her eyes unwavering.

"Please, take a seat Commander Zolga," he said, and the Tormenta woman gave him a slight bow before glancing at the whiskey on the meeting table.

"May I?" she asked, motioning at the table.

"By all means," he replied before raising his eyebrows in surprise as Zolga poured herself several fingers of whiskey into her glass that she then emptied before refilling it and then grabbing another that she handed him before pouring him the same amount.

"I get the feeling I am not going to like the discussion to follow," he stated, swirling the contents of his glass.

"You are as likely to like what I am about to tell you as you are to believe it. However, I must ask that you hear what I have to say in its entirety," Zolga stated.

"You know, I sat in this very chair, awoken in the middle of the night to hear from the bard that I had recently grown fond of and trusted that he did not work for me. Instead, he worked for a secret organization that had been manipulating and killing the people of this island in the name of the greater good for centuries," he said, taking a long sip from his glass and observing that Zolga at least raised an eyebrow at his statements.

"Then Harpis told me that he needed my help in working a secret plan to stop the mass-murdering, assassin-gone-rogue killer who had taken the identity of Tuath's governor. I heard him out then, even after his admission of espionage. I think I can hear out the commander of the Savjan raiders, returning from a mission I sent her on to a foreign land," he said to reassure her.

"To the end of the world then," she said, raising her glass and clinking it gently against his.

The dumbfounded look he felt his face make at her statement went unchanged as the commander of his special military unit recounted what had transpired during their short visit to Zarad.

Halfway through, she had slid him the map Jabruelle had copied over to several other parchments. He examined it in stunned silence both at what she had said, the hopeful ambition of the sand elf presented the plan and the scope of the presumed campaign by the attacking horde and the size of the Nysian mainland.

Another knock at the door returned him from his stunned stupor to the present, and he tried to force a smile as Shanowen walked in and put a plate of food on his desk for Zolga and him to share.

"What's wrong?" she asked after looking from his face to the Tormenta's.

"Everything, it would seem," Aanaman answered with a sigh of resignation that he was unable to keep anything from his wife.

Shanowen's face went from fear to stoic resolve so quickly he would have missed it had he blinked. She leaned in, kissed him on the cheek, and squeezed his shoulder.

"I am sure you'll see us through it, Aanaman," she said in a way he felt could have meant either their family or the island as a whole, or both.

When Shanowen closed the door behind her, Zolga took cornbread from the platter and ate it with her eyes closed in obvious enjoyment.

"All folk should yearn for a partner such as yours," Zolga said when she opened her eyes and finished chewing.

"No argument there," he said, taking another long sip of whiskey.

"You say we only have a month to send them our response?" he asked, forcing himself back to the discussion.

"Not to respond, Chancellor. We have a month to act from the day I set sail. So, more like three or four weeks," she answered, grabbing a wedge of cheese from the platter.

"Three or four weeks? It will take me that long just to get those that govern this island to meet and make a decision, let alone call up forces or anything else, should we decide to get involved," he said, sinking back in his chair.

"As far as getting involved, Harpis believes that we will become involved through helping the sand elves or become involved after they are no longer available to stand beside against the forces of Konflict. Regarding the issue of time, I hope you don't mind that I took several...liberties on my way back," she

142

said around bites of Ravnice cheese.

"What sort of liberties?" he asked, feeling he was not going to have much of a choice in any of this after all.

"I sent the two galleons circling the northern seas waiting for word from myself to go to Tuath and Southpoint and facilitate the spreading of an order that every available ship is redirected immediately to Tuath. It is our closest port to the mouth of the Astinan River," Zolga said, pointing at the eastern river on the map of Nysia.

"Our entire fleet is heading to Tuath, but we are in Ravnice, and our battalions are spread out across the cities and Lake Gitche," Aanaman replied.

She finished eating and the rest of her drink before looking him in the eye.

"Two ships from your harbor are already headed north on the Ravnice river to Fjall and Quajillian. The battalions garrisoned at Lake Gitche, and the dwarves will meet us in Tuath in five or six days, just in time to jump aboard resupplied and crewed galleons and head north to the mainland. The wind is already blowing, and I have taken the initiative to let out the sails. It is on you to decide if we drop anchor and pull in sails or let destiny carry us northward," she finished and sat back in her chair, challenging him to argue.

"Commander Zolga, your initiative and military prowess are beyond reproach. The fact that you feel the need to add dramatics to convince me makes me take this more seriously. However, I have a hard time with sending the hastily called up and ill-prepared entirety of our navy and much of our total military forces north to battle what most consider a superstition at best," he said, raising his palms in apology.

"Your friend has sung the true names of two of the sisters, and the call was answered both times. What do you think will become of that tale over millennia? Maybe it will grow into legend, later repeated as myth before fading into superstition and evening stories to scare children to their beds like we view the story of Konflict and his banishing? Thousands of your people and mine have seen with their own eyes the God Singer's songs answered by the goddesses themselves. If the sisters are still sentient and attendant over Nysia, why is it so hard to believe their brother was banished here, as the stories tell? She asked.

Aanaman sat silent, unable to argue her point, desperately

143

hoping that he would wake from what he wished was the nightmare of an afternoon daydream.

"I can't just tell Savja what to do. That was the point of all we have done since the unification," he said, frustrated at being once again in the position of directing the entire nation.

"Aanaman, I believe your wife. You should believe her too. You will see us all through this," she said, standing from her chair.

"Where are you going?" he asked.

"To meet up with Ezera. She is waiting for us on the *Torrent*. We head for Tuath as soon as you are on board," she said and departed.

*****

Sudbina had been sitting at the rudder handle on the stern of their small schooner for several hours of her evening watch. The coming morning would mark the sixth day of their journey to the west, and the task of taking shifts steering the small vessel had become almost routine. If Parafano had been correct, sometime in the next four or five days, they should spot the four giant pillars he described as marking the entrance to a cavern where his friend lived. Sudbina was not as hopeful as Harpis had seemed to be when they decided to venture west while Zolga returned to Quaj to rally Aanaman and Savja.

Perhaps her lack of hope in comparison to Harpis was because she didn't feel responsible for waking the god of war and thus desperate to defeat him, she reasoned. Sudbina would never have believed the tale herself, even being there around the intriguing Parafano and having felt his power. However, she had her own interactions with an alleged god to lend credence to the insanity that had transpired since.

Seemingly summoned by her thoughts, the childish figure of Enky appeared lying on the top of the small cabin under the boom of the boat's single sail.

"Good evening Sudbina. Have you found the Nysian mainland as exotic and beautiful as you'd hoped?" he said in a yell, his arms sweeping across the cliff faces to her right.

She raised a finger to her lips to quiet him as she heard the rise and fall of three individual snores from the cabin below him.

"Bah, do not shush me. They can't hear my voice!" Enky said

boisterously, hopping down and walking to sit across from her.

"If by exotic you mean six days straight sailing along marble and sandstone cliffs, then yes, quite exotic," she said, rolling her eyes.

"Now, you seemed to find the city of Zarad quite enjoyable. I can tell you. It has come quite far in the thousands of years they've spent carving themselves vaunted spires and cathedrals from that giant rock!" he exclaimed.

She narrowed her eyes at him, deciding it was time to put the godling on the hook for confirmation of what she already assumed, if not some outright answers, for once.

"You told me you were only allowed to meddle directly through one mortal at a time, and as far as I know, that means me, correct?" she asked, checking the moon and the cliff face and touching the rudder slightly while she waited for his response.

"I am many things, Sudbina, but not a liar," was the only confirmation he offered.

"You've said as much, though I must inform you that some folks consider the omission of information akin to lying itself," she said, observing his expression as he dismissed her accusation.

"Some folks being other mortals, I presume," he said, rolling his eyes.

"If you are honest, explain to me how the mage Parafano knows about the harpies and identified Harpis and me as their descendants. Such information would seem limited to the gods and those they chose to tell about it. Especially given that they left the mortal plane some eighty thousand years or two whole ages ago, according to you," she finished in a voice that was no longer a whisper.

There was stirring from the cabin, and she slapped a hand over her mouth while he taunted her with a chastising wag of his finger and click of his tongue.

"There were other beings around in those times besides my siblings and I. Beings that also happen to have quite lengthy lives. Perhaps Parafano's friend is one such creature, and they told him about it," was all he offered her, aside from a smile and a wink.

Growing tired of his games, she stared out to see in silence for several movements listening to him hum to himself.

"Why are you still about? Aren't I doing as you wanted?" she asked in frustration.

"Go on, Sudbina. I know you mortals yearn for confirmation so ask me what you really want to know," he grinned.

She resigned herself to his verbal game and decided to play along. It was more entertaining than sitting by herself, watching the cliffs drift by to her right as the coastal breeze carried them westward.

"Was Vizier Mistis truthful when he said your brother Konflict has arisen on Nysia?" she asked.

"Yes," Enky said, offering no riddle for once in a voice with a graveness that caught her off guard.

"Is it Harpis' fault that he broke free?" she continued, wondering how long the unpredictable deity would cooperate.

"I think, if we are all honest, that you, he, and I had somewhat shared responsibility in that," Enky admitted with a shrug.

She looked at him with a raised eyebrow, unsure of how to interpret the implications of his answer.

"Do you think the sand elves have a chance at stopping his horde with the help of Savja's forces?" she asked, afraid of the answer and almost hoping he wouldn't share it.

"Perhaps, though I don't find it likely. Mortals did not put up much of a fight the last time, though the sand elves did well in preserving the lessons of the Age of Discord," he replied.

While not as devastating an answer as he could have given, she still could not stop her shoulders from slumping at his observation.

"Do not despair, though, Sudbina, for your current course should deliver us an alternative means if the four of you can survive the journeys ahead," he finished, and his projected image faded.

Sudbina blew out a sigh, looking from the empty seat across from her to the growing glow behind them as Daybreak greeted Nysia.

*****

Though Shanowen and the girls had traveled with him to Tuath, Aanaman walked the wharf, alone save for his guard. The morning sun had just cleared the wave tops, and the shadows cast by the galleons in the harbor shortened by the minute. Following a conversation after dinner the night before, he had agreed that they could not wait any longer to decide if their ships were to reach the Nysian mainland in time to be of use.

If the ships left tomorrow morning, Zolga told them they would reach the opening of the Astinan River in ten days and have a presence along its entire length after another four. If they moved ahead, the sand elves would receive word of their planned movements in less than a week. The Tuath wharf came alive with the sun, not just with the usual vendors and marketplace of the sprawling seaside bazaar, but the crews of ships making last-ditch supply efforts.

Nodding at his escorts, he turned from the bay and headed for the nearby building that was once Tuath's naval command building to meet with those who had been able to arrive in the two days week. After leaving his guards at the door and taking the stairs, he found himself on a crowded balcony overlooking the waters. He regretted that Ingar had yet been able to arrive but could delay no longer. He turned back to the group and bid them join him at the round table.

Zolga was present, lounging on the balcony railing behind where Field Marshal Elliswerth sat. Lorkin had arrived from Kalt by ship the day before along with the Tormenta leader, Governor Lorent, and High Priestess Galonica. Minister Rashida and Ezera rounded out the group of eight. He looked hopefully to the lone true politician at the table and Tuath native first.

"Minister Rashida, where are we at in trying to reach the mayors of our major cities?" he asked the olive-skinned woman.

"Aanaman, you know as well as I do that even if we had them all trapped here, it would take weeks to get them to agree to anything, and it will be several days before they all arrive," she stated shaking her head at him.

He raised a hand in peace and gave her an understanding look before turning to his bleary-eyed Field Marshal.

"Elliswerth, I am glad you were able to make this meeting. Where do we stand on the movements of our battalions?" Aanaman asked.

"I nearly killed four horses as I swapped and ran them into the ground on my way here, and I only arrived just before dawn, Aanaman. A thousand soldiers of the battalion stationed in Tuath and Zolga's raiders will be all we can send forth in the interim if we must decide today," Elliswerth answered.

"Well, Governor Lorent, please, deliver us some positive news in all this," he asked the young Tormenta woman.

"When we last met at the council, we had the twenty-five galleons in our fleet, we completed two more, and three more are in drydock. They could be completed next month if we worked day and night. The entire Savjan fleet is anchored in Tuath Bay save the two ships patrolling the atolls and the one we sent to fetch them," she responded quickly and quietly.

Zolga slid from the balcony railing, slamming her boot heels into the decking before walking over to the table and then pointing at the map Aanaman laid out.

"So, we sail twenty-two Savjan galleons up this river with the forces we have. Suppose it's indeed miles wide, as the elves stated. In that case, we should have no issue keeping a large army from crossing between our ballista, crossbows, and the priests and mages willing to join the armada," she said with a knowing nod to Galonica and Lorkin.

Squinting his eyes, Elliswerth looked at the map one last time and then met Aanaman's gaze.

"If you approve, we will then use the three late arriving and the other three-to-be-completed galleons to ferry out battalions from here to Zarad, or to the river if that is where we are still holding our position. I will send word to Tawito to ask that the Quaji vessels, which wouldn't survive the open seas to the north anyways, begin taking up supplementary patrols with the galleons gone. Similarly, I'll leave Commander Shatter-Hand and Militia Captain Kilannry to keep order while we are away," he finished.

Aanaman closed his eyes and leaned forward, placing his head in his hands as he contemplated what they said. Then, after long minutes of silence, he looked up at Ezera.

"Well, mother of spies, any advice?" he asked the blond cleric.

"Send us forth, or do not. However, the decision must be made today, and it must be you that decides," Ezera replied.

"This is exactly the type of unilateral governing our unification was supposed to absolve the people of the southern seas from," he said sadly, pausing.

"As my last act as Chancellor of Savja, I order our forces north," he stated evenly, taking in the reactions from around the gathering.

"Minister Rashida, I name you Chancellor, with the sole task

148

of ensuring the delivery of a government that represents the interest of the people of Savja. Are there any objections?" he asked.

Pausing only briefly before continuing, knowing full well they would all readily agree, save perhaps Rashida herself, whom he shot a wry smile.

"I will sail north with Field Marshal Elliswerth, Stone Magus Lorkin, and Ezera to the city of Zarad to deliver the message of our intentions," Aanaman stated.

"If we are headed for Zarad, I will place Mahala in charge of The Cause to keep an eye on our budding nation," Ezera said quietly enough for only him to hear.

He nodded to the blond woman and turned back to the others.

"Zolga, inform Admiral Galanis of our intentions. Then, when you have sailed the length of this river, the two of you decide how it can best be defended, return to Zarad, or send word," he ordered.

He bowed to the room and headed to the more difficult task of telling Shanowen that he would be leaving them in Tuath to enjoy the tropical beaches for a while.

Chapter 15
Hope & Discovery

Harpis climbed from the hold after shouts from Jabruelle had woken him and the others. His eyes were still blinking away the brightness of the morning sun, but he quickly saw what had the necromancer so excited. Before them stood four gargantuan stone pillars marching out to sea in a straight line. Following them back to the coastal cliff, he could see the opening of a crack in the plateau that wound its way into the distance.

"Guide us in, Jabruelle. This must be the place Parafano spoke of," he said, and the other man nodded.

The first week of their journey had been easy-going, drifting with the breeze along cliffs of the coast towering above them to the right. However, they had spent the past three days in rolling treacherous seas as a procession of summer storms blew in. It took everything they had to keep from being smashed against the vertical rock wall. Had the three of them not grown up sailing on the coast of Kalt, Harpis was not sure they would have kept from wrecking. Itka had been useless during the rough seas, spending as much time hurling the contents of her stomach overboard as she had shivering in the small one-room cabin.

As the hull of the sloop scraped the smooth rock bed carved by a long-ago dried river, Itka jumped from the rails and hugged the nearest stone, kissing it several times.

"I swear by all the gods that you'll have to kill me to get me back on that confounded vessel," she shouted back at them as they lowered the anchor and tied their ship off.

"It's a long walk back. You'll miss the war Itka," Sudbina said, playfully, taunting the dwarf who spat in response.

Shaking his head at their exchange, Harpis looked to the

narrow canyon that curved quickly out of view, barely wide enough for two to walk abreast. He wondered how long it had taken whatever river once flowed here to carve the snaking hallway from the stone that stood dozens of feet above them.

"We've got maybe four or five hours of daylight left, and it will quickly become difficult to see down here once the sun starts sinking," he said, looking up to the ribbon of blue sky above them.

"Let's get going then," Itka said, patting the heads of her maces and heading down into the canyon.

The dwarf led the way as they walked along the eerily quiet canyon for half an hour. The only sounds to be heard were the echoes of their voices and footsteps. The canyon ended suddenly, widening into a circular area with a cave mouth on the far side big enough to build a house within. Nearing the entrance, they noticed a constant warm breeze flowing from the cave like some eternally exhaling beast with desert winds for breath.

Itka looked up at the sky above them and back to the cave entrance.

"There must be a windward opening to the deserts ahead and above. There are dwarven tunnels built with such vents to keep the air moving," the dwarf offered.

Harpis was about to step forward into the cave and bid them follow when his skin tingled, and he felt a slight pull at his senses. Turning to Jabruelle and Sudbina, he noticed they shared odd looks on their faces.

"Jabruelle, can you perceive and identify magics as Wren could?" he asked.

The necromancer nodded and pulled his scythe forth. He stood in the middle of the opening, and closed his eyes, opening them again almost immediately.

"Oh, there is magic in there, but it is too immense and numerous for me to pick out anything specific," he explained.

"I wonder if this host will be as welcoming as Parafano was?" Sudbina asked.

"I could at least sense that some of the stronger magics within the cave were moving," Jabruelle replied with a shrug.

"That is not very encouraging," Itka returned, pulling her maces from the belt loops around her waist.

Jabruelle nervously cackled in response and clutched his scythe with whitened knuckles. Harpis decided being prepared was not bad and unslung the case off his back, retrieving his ebony violin from it before slinging it back over his shoulder.

They all looked at Sudbina expectedly, and she gawked back at them before shrugging in exasperation.

"Obviously, my charisma and charm are my greatest weapons," she said, crossing her arms and motioning for them to lead on.

"I'll retake the lead. I don't want you soft-skinned humans getting hurt," Itka said with a grin, stalking into the quickly darkening cave with a few deft spins of her maces.

They were almost to the point where Harpis could not see his own feet or the blond braids of Itka in front of him when the gloom seemed to lessen as they kept moving down the narrowing stone corridor. Then, rounding another bend, they were bathed in sunlight again as a skylight in the stone high above them let warm rays paint a spotlight on the ground before them. As they continued for another few minutes, there were openings above at a regular enough interval that they could easily see once their eyes adjusted.

The warm breeze they felt at the entrance never faded or altered. After a few more steps, they heard stronger winds from up ahead. Sudbina quickly stepped forward and put a hand on Itka's shoulder to halt her and then hushed them all with a finger to her lips. When they all stopped, she stuffed her wig in her satchel bag, leaving it with them, and silently padded forward, disappearing around a bend in the corridor like a fleeting shadow in the sunlight. When her small form reappeared, she shook her head in concern and motioned for them to join her in a huddle.

"There is an air elemental ahead. It is in the form of a giant hunting cat and is plodding along in circles in the wider chamber a few paces past the next turn in the cave.

"Do you think it is friendly?" Jabruelle asked hopefully.

"I don't know. Why don't you go have a word with it and ask for yourself," Sudbina whispered in response.

"Unfriendly I can handle," Itka said, walking slowly forward in a crouch, and Harpis sighed and followed her, the others behind him.

When the elemental came into view, they silently gasped at the horse-sized feline form. The tan sand that rippled with the churning wind of its body made it seem almost lifelike. Itka stood and stepped into the elemental's chamber, giving a slight bow as it noticed her.

"We simply wish to pass, not fight," she stated, lowering her mace heads to the ground.

In return, the cat made of swirling sand let out a silent roar and stalked angrily towards her.

"Then again, I am happy to fight if needed," Itka shouted, her voice booming around the chamber

The dwarf's mace heads went into a circular dance before her as she charged the elemental. Itka ran right through the cat, her maces sending puffs of sand flying but not altering the form of the animal as it clawed her back with a swipe of its paw. Shrieking, she spun about angrily, but the cat turned back towards Harpis and the others as Jabruelle screamed. Xissay appeared in the air between him and the elemental, her hands glowing red and her face gleeful.

The charging elemental engulfed and then passed the fire sprite unscathed, leaving several glass droplets from melted sand on the ground as the only indication the two had touched. Finally, Jabruelle flattened himself against the wall, surrendering to the approaching elemental. Harpis slid his bow across the strings of his violin with abandon, calling forth a howling seaside wind that blew the wind-rippled, sand free of its magical bindings and dissipating the cat in a blinding shower of turbulent sand grains and dust.

"Why didn't you just do that in the beginning?" Itka asked angrily, looking at the thin lines of blood where the cat had caught her shoulder.

"You didn't give me a chance," Harpis replied with a shrug.

"Fine, next magical monster we encounter, you play it a song first," she said, pointing her mace at him and walking towards the corridor opening at the other side of the elemental's den.

Xissay floated over Jabruelle's shoulder as he and Sudbina followed Harpis and the dwarf.

"Where are we?" the undead familiar inquired.

"I am not sure, but the residents do not seem too friendly," Jabruelle responded.

Before long they heard an almost deafening roar of wind ahead, and Itka straightened, waving happily for Harpis to take the lead. He was not as stealthy as Sudbina, but he had been trained by The Syndicate, not that he thought there was much need to sneak about as the howl from the chamber ahead would cover any sound

153

they could hope to make. The corridor they were in ended at a ledge and a five-foot drop to a long narrow cavern with an almost entirely open ceiling.

When he finished blinking away the brightness of near-full sunlight, Harpis and the others caught sight of the source of the howl. Two human-height tornados of wind were spinning across the smooth stone floor. Instead of a shining surface made of sand, the dervishes had twenty or thirty large rocks, from the size of a fist to the size of his head, swirling about inside them at blinding speed. They were lazily drifting towards the other end of the cavern, but when they reached it and turned back towards the party, he noticed their pace pick up as they took a direct line towards them.

"Well, here goes nothing," Harpis said, hopping down to the ground below.

Placing his violin in his neck, he ducked as he heard a shrieking Xissay speed overhead directly at the two whirlwinds. She met them halfway across the wide passageway. Though she had a negligible effect on the sand-formed wind elemental, the dervishes did not notice her. Unfortunately, Xissay was not so unscathed as a fist-sized rock struck her, slinging her into the other swirling stones, where a larger rock knocked her clear into the wall.

Jabruelle grunted behind him in concentration, and Harpis saw the puff of smoke as Xissay was dismissed back to The Great Dream. Gritting his teeth, Harpis played a memory of the gusts from Kalt's windward coast. His violin sent forth a roaring wind of its own, but it passed by the dervishes without altering the flight of their funnel-slung stones. He turned back to the others in time to see Itka leap above his head, landing before him and running straight at the two sentient tornados.

When she reached them, she became a third dervish in the stone hall as she turned circles amongst their spinning stones. Her maces were boulders to the monster's pebbles as she dodged, ducked, dipped, and dove her way into their midst. She went on dodging and smashing the swirling stones to dust with blinding speed as her maces wove protectively around her. In the span of a few breaths, the swirling of the winds remained, but there were no longer stones amongst them to cause injury, and the four of them made their way across the hall and climbed over the ledge at the other end, and Harpis noted happily that the disarmed dervishes did not follow.

They came immediately to a cathedral-like chamber obscured by a churning wall of steam that swept around the edges like a whirlpool. It was not as loud as the roar of the dervishes, but based on the steam's speed, it was traveling exceptionally fast.

Itka walked up to it and put the point of her finger into the flow of steam, pulling it out slowly.

"It is warm. There must be a geothermal vent in here. It is moving fast, but I think we should be able to step through it," Itka said, holding her maces ahead of her and walking into the steam wall.

Her back foot leave the ground as she trudged forward and she was immediately swept from the floor and flew with the steam in a circle around the chamber. Harpis looked at Sudbina and Jabruelle, who shrugged hopelessly as Itka's shouting grew and faded several times while the cyclonic wind whipped her around. Harpis looked back to see her plummet to the ground as she activated the enchantment in one of her maces.

She flapped about like a banner in a storm as she activated her other mace a few feet further towards the other side of the steam. After releasing the first mace, she was able to pull herself out of the rotating barrier and took a moment to survey the empty circular room on the other side before turning back to them and shrugging.

"How are we supposed to follow?" Sudbina asked incredulously after slipping her finger into the steam and then pulling it out in awe.

"I have an idea, actually, but I do not know if you will like it," Jabruelle said, stepping between Harpis and her with his scythe held before him.

"Oh?" was Sudbina's only response, and Harpis waited for the necromancer to explain himself.

"I read of a channeling called shadow stepping, wherein a necromancer can walk short distances through the grey and appear back in the mortal realm a short ways away," he said, looking back towards Itka.

"The grey?" Sudbina asked in confusion.

"The place between life and death," Harpis explained, not excited about what Jabruelle proposed but seeing no good alternative either.

Jabruelle held his scythe horizontally and nodded in rare confidence at them.

"Grab hold and walk with me," he said.

No sooner did Harpis' hands grasp the scythe did the color fade as it had years ago when he went before The Sleeper. The chill of the grey was almost painful as they together took the few short steps past the roiling steam and then released the scythe, warmth, and color, returning to their view.

"That was terrifying," Sudbina said, clutching her shoulders and rubbing them to return warmth.

Harpis shivered slightly and flexed his hands before looking at Jabruelle.

"How many times have you done that? It is worse than unpleasant.

"That was the first," he responded, nervously cackling as Sudbina punched him in the arm.

Their bickering quickly ended as the steam wall around them funneled towards the ceiling, where a huge downward gust of wind sent them all off their feet and to the stone floor. All four stood on trembling legs, and even Itka did not charge forward. Instead, the galleon-sized form of a cream-white scaled dragon towered above them, its golden eyes narrowed as it securitized them before rearing up on its hind legs, stretching its wings across the chamber and raising its front claws before it as if to pounce.

They cringed as one, awaiting their deaths, but when Harpis peaked back after the moment of their impending doom passed, he saw a somewhat human, somewhat elven being standing before them, lowering his arms.

"Impressive and entertaining as your traversal of my home has been, I tire of your trespass," he said.

The four of them straightened as the creature approached, his shimmering white silk robe floating just above the surface of the cavern floor. Standing before them, he furrowed white eyebrows, looking them over, his bald head wrinkling in concentration.

"We meant no offense," Harpis said, trying to lace the statement with his gift.

"Surely, you are not yet tired of our entertainment," Sudbina purred from behind him.

The being bent over in laughter that boomed around the chamber before straightening and wagging a finger at them.

156

"That was clumsily done," he said, pointing at Harpis before turning to face Sudbina with a curious look in his eye.

"You, though, your voice drips with promise like the Siren's own," he said to her with a smile before turning to the rest of them.

"Very well, you may find yourselves welcome, for now, in my home. I am Azahle, or rather, that is what you may call me. Your lips would trip over themselves trying to pronounce my full name," he said and motioned for them to follow him into a side chamber revealed by the dissipated steam.

"How did you find the entrance to my castle? There have been no visitors here in many thousands of years," he asked, showing them to the luxuriously appointed sitting room.

"Are you truly a dragon?" Itka blurted as they joined their host.

Azahle paused and smirked at her before sitting at a small table with them.

"We once were not so foreign to the races of Nysia. But, I must admit, after millennia spent amongst the elder races and those that sprang from them, we became bored. A few of us have died over the history of this plane. However, most of us have let the past age slip by in slumber. This day is the first I have spent awake in some time. Now, answer my question," he asked again, and Harpis could feel the pull of his request.

A friend of yours told us to visit you. He also told us how to find your home," Harpis answered.

Azahle's eyes narrowed in suspicion as he surveyed them one at a time before standing from the table and walking to a cabinet.

"I call no mortal of Nysia friend, and none still living have seen a dragon, as the lady dwarf has confirmed," he said, blowing dust from a bottle and returning to the table with five small glasses.

"I do not have food, but I can offer you a drink at least. This is wine brewed by the Walar of old. The children of The Wild are unsurpassed in the skills of fermentation," he said, filling and handing them cups.

"What was the name of this alleged friend?" he asked after distributing the glasses.

"He called himself Parafano, a water mage we met in Zarad," Sudbina answered, sipping the wine with eyes closed in enjoyment.

Azahle dropped his glass to the floor, where it shattered into

157

pieces that then blew out of the chamber altogether with a gust summoned by his waving hand.

"As in the blue dragon Parafanonilphynorsinosus?" Azahle asked, concern on his face.

"He only called himself Parafano, and the sand elves called him that. He appeared similar to how you are before us now but closer to looking like an actual sand elf. He seemed to have issues with his mind, we met him on two separate days, and he greeted us as strangers on both, repeating most of what he said," Harpis explained.

Azahle's shoulders sank for a moment, and he looked at them with rage glowing in his golden eyes.

"The children of the Aelar will be lucky if I do not punish them for this," he seethed.

"Parafano did not seem there against his wishes. We only found him because of his use of his gift to enchant the well in the city center. He said he did it daily to keep freshwater flowing into Zarad," Harpis explained, hoping to calm the dragon.

Azahle retook his seat, not bothering to get himself another glass.

"As you can see, we may take the shape of the Nysian races, this allowed us to be more effective watchers, and shepherds as the gods gained devotion and eventually ascended. However, spending too much time in forms not our own frays our sanity. It would seem that my old friend has lost himself in his own mind while trying to keep the elven city from drying up and dying," Azahle explained.

"He seems protective over all of Nysia. Every day he checks on the prison that held Konflict with what they called a mirror of farsight," Sudbina interjected.

"Held Konflict?" Azahle asked in obvious concern at her statement.

"It is why we came, Azahle. We hoped the friend of the mighty Parafano would be able to help in the coming struggle against the god of war," Harpis said.

"God of order," Azahle corrected, and all four of them tilted their heads in confusion.

"His struggle is for order amongst chaos. That is what he seeks. The easiest way to create order amongst the mortal races of Nysia happens to be through conquest," Azahle said, answering

158

their puzzled expressions.

"Were I to get involved, I would be pulled from this plane and sent back to my own before being able to influence the tide of conquest," he explained.

"Is there anything you can tell us that may aid our efforts then?" Harpis pleaded.

Azahle looked at him pensively and then stood and went to another cabinet where he retrieved several blank leather canvases and an engraving quill.

"I will shadow you on your return to Zarad, and you will show me where they are keeping Parafano. In return, I will tell you a way to find the words to *The Sisters' Song*. Perhaps two descendants of the Harpies together may use it to help in the coming struggle," he offered.

Harpis looked around at his companions for affirmation and then nodded his head in agreement.

Azahle smiled and unfurled one of the rolled leathers and began etching with the quill an outline of the Nysian mainland Harpis had seen the sand elves draw. He then drew several islands off the eastern coast of the mainland and then an X along the northern coast.

"Here, on this island, is the spot Parafano watches. On the stones that sat above Konflict's prison, the words the sisters sang when they banished him are written in the tongue of the winged women," he explained and then pointed at the X he drew with the quill.

"Here is the entrance to Sikef. The Maelar, and the deep elves after them, kept translations of every language from their own and vice versa. Copy down the sigils you find at his shattered prison and translate them with the texts in Sikef, and you may have a powerful weapon to wield with your voices," he said, looking at Harpis and Sudbina.

"Sikef, as in the city of the dead?" Jabruelle asked excitedly.

"Sikef, as in the abandoned city of the Maelar, yes," Azahle corrected, turning to face Jabruelle.

"I trust The Sleeper's Herald can read the language of the deep elves?" he asked, and Jabruelle nodded meekly in agreement.

"How will we know where the entrance to the city is?" Itka asked, staring at the map.

"You will not be capable of missing it from the sea. It is much

159

more obvious than what marked my own. Now, it is late, and you all appear weary. Sleep and the wine I gave you will find you more than recovered in the morning. You are welcome to bed down here until tomorrow. You have nothing to fear in my home. I will be in the chamber outside. As I said, it is not advisable to stay too long in this form," he finished and departed.

*****

With the others snoring behind the doors of Azahle's palatial guest rooms, Sudbina snuck out into the open area where they first encountered the enormous wind dragon, and the warm steam had returned. Wisps of it wafted and spiraled about the vaulted stone ceiling and walls. Then, still standing in the archway from the foyer where he initially entertained them, she pulled her shirt and tunic over her head and let her trousers fall to her ankles before stepping out of them and walking softly towards Azahle's immense form.

As she neared him, he turned towards her, amusement in his golden eyes as he reared up and took on the human-like form again. Striding forward, she slowly touched his face, flushing at the surging heat she felt along her spine as her gift sensed his.

"Is it true, what Parafano said, that the elemental magics were seeded in our bloodlines by the dragons?" she asked, staring into his golden eyes.

"It is indeed, just as you and Harpis carry the heredity of mischief's muses," he said with a laugh before becoming more serious.

"Sudbina, no mothers survive the birth of a first-seeded. A fact which was lost long before the knowledge of the identity of the source of elemental gifts," he explained with a look of sadness.

"I am not interested in surviving the birth. I have lived longer than I ever expected and exacted the revenge I was born to deliver. What I want is to leave a legacy. I want the world to know that Sudbina, whore's daughter, was the one that birthed into Nysia one who will wield the gift of the wind and the muse. Give my life a greater purpose Azahle," She pleaded.

Unsure if Enky's rules applied to dragons and idiot Kaltese bards alike, she kept her ulterior motivation hidden from the dragon. She may be Enky's Marionette, dancing on the strands of fate and chaos pulled by the child god. Tonight though, Sudbina decided it was time for her to tug back on those strings. She would put an unavoidable expiration on his ability to influence Nysia through her and she would give rise to an unrivaled mortal lineage.

Chapter 16
Friends in Far Places

Erimo was not overly fond of interacting with the five human nations of north Nysia. Of the humans, the Necakans and their almost appalling obsession with the hereditary gift of elemental magic were the most difficult. His army had made better than expected progress through The Sea of Sand and to the capital city of Necaka, where he now sat in the tallest of many spires that towered over the rocky hills of the mountain range. They rose like enormous, branchless man-made trees from the carpet of pines that coated the small mountainous country.

Across the unnecessarily grand desk before him was the shrewd and strange Grand Arcanist of Necaka, Ekith Wikenmal. Erimo had met only one other Grand Arcanist, the woman who held the seat of power in Necaka several centuries before, and he found them to be frighteningly similar. He wanted to judge the Necakans for the almost frenzied inbreeding they had taken to in hopes of growing the ranks of the gifted within their bloodlines. However, he decided that the purity-focused practices of his own people's couplings and the bickering of the five families of Zarad were not so different in comparison.

"Grand Arcanist, I speak the truth, Konflict's hordes are on their way to High Pass, and from there, they will descend upon your people. But, powerful as your arcanists are, can they withstand a hundred thousand strong army? Twice that?" he asked.

The man sat back in his chair, rubbing the cuffs of his forest green robe in concentration. Erimo was also thankful that compared to the other human nations, the Necakans were tedious studies of history, myths, and legends. He was hopeful those studies would sway the humans towards working with him against their foe.

"Why would he lead them there, High Marshal?" Ekith asked, rubbing his hands together in frustrated thought at Erimo's suggestion that the enemy might use the land bridge within his very borders to cross the Andrefan River.

"It is the most tactically sound place to move such a large force at once across either of the rivers without going all the way to the Andrefan delta at the coast," he replied honestly.

"What is stopping them from simply swarming across the Astinan somewhere? It is wide, but slow-moving enough to move across with barges," the man countered.

"We have sent a separate force to prevent just such a crossing," Erimo said in what he hoped was a true statement.

"You are aware that we keep little conventional military units aside from those which police our streets, yes?" he asked, and Erimo nodded.

"I will have to think about whether to send the arcanists north with you. They are not an easily swayed bunch and are just as likely to fight amongst themselves as they are to aid in your predicted battle at the pass," he said, crossing his arms and scratching his wiry white beard.

"If anyone can unite them, it would be yourself and the prospect of the foe we seek to ward off," Erimo offered in hopes of appeasing the man.

"Indeed," was the mage's only response.

"Do I at least have your permission to move my troops within your lands and take up a defensive posture at High Pass?" he asked, and the man nodded in agreement and waved him away dismissively.

When Erimo finished descending the five-story tower, he took the reins to his camel from Brigadier Nathken and looked around at the gathered officers of his army.

"Well, how'd it go?" his old friend and trusted general asked.

"I would say that we can only count on them to stay out of the way for now," he said with a sigh, pulling himself into the saddle box of his white camel.

"Gentlemen, return to our tents. We move out at dawn and will head for High Pass. With or without the Necakans, we will defend the land bridge over the mouth of the Andrefan river. We have a weeklong journey ahead of us, and the quicker we get there, the more time we will have to prepare the battlefield to the enemy's disadvantage," he said sternly, and at his nod, his generals broke ranks and headed to their soldiers.

*****

Harpis breathed a sigh of relief when the protruding marble docks of Zarad came into view, and he saw several Savjan galleons moored to them. The ten-day journey from Azahle's home back to the sand elven city had proven much smoother sailing, and he wondered if it was due to the unseen but palpable specter of the air dragon's presence. He also found the company of their small party that much more enjoyable after they had bonded during their adventure into the white dragon's lair.

More than that, he had found hope in the information Azahle had shared with them. Finally, a glimmer of a chance that he may be able to help set right the pain he had helped unleash on Nysia. Maybe it would let him shed some of the guilt that still weighed across his shoulders from surviving where so many of his friends had not.

When they had set out, the three humans saw Itka as more a babysitter than anything else. However, after her numerous endeavors fighting their enemies and keeping them from harm, they realized that they could trust her as a friend. Harpis had enjoyed the few nights on the way back that he had been able to exchange tails of her uncle, Braffen Frothbrew, grappling and contorting him during his time training at Lodestar.

When they finished tying off, they left the sloop in the competent hands of several Tormenta crewmembers from one of the galleons. They were informed that Aanaman, amongst others, was waiting for them on the top level of Daybreak's Rampart.

With the ache of climbing the upwardly spiraling entryway to the city still throbbing in his legs, he walked up to Aanaman. Harpis gave the man a huge hug, lifting the greying but still very much auburn-haired chancellor from the ground.

"Nice to see you too," Aanaman responded as Harpis set him down.

"I am surprised you came yourself. Don't you have a country to run, Chancellor?" he asked his friend.

"I happily admit I shirked that responsibility and left it on

Quaj Island with Minister, now Chancellor Rashida. So, I have simply come to claim the right of chief diplomat from yourself," Aanaman said with a wink.

Ezera walked up to him next after she finished talking with Sudbina and Itka, embracing him and looking into his eyes for a long moment.

"It is good that you found yourself again, Harpis." She said, squeezing his arm.

"Well, tell us, was your trip what was expected?" she asked, and Harpis watched as Vizier Mistis and his advisors and Jabruelle and Lorkin stopped conversing and looked at him.

Harpis could only assume that Azahle had somehow been listening and waiting unseen, hiding in the light of the sun above as the dragon then came crashing down to the ramparts at that very moment, sending all of them flying from their feet. His talons, longer than Harpis' arm, dug trenches into the marble rampart as his head flicked back and forth from one sand elf to the other as they all fought their fear to stand again.

Azahle reared up as he had in the cavern, but there, perched atop the sea wall of the marble city, his cream-whiter scales glinting in the afternoon sun, the dragon was a marvel to witness. The elves and the others cowered as he lifted his claws to the sky, only to look in surprise as the elf-like form of Azahle stood before them, his robs rippling in the breeze.

"By all the gods and especially Daybreak above, what is that" Ezera uttered under her breath as Azahle stood to face the sand elves.

"The answer to your question about our trip," Harpis said, calming her and Aanaman somewhat.

Azahle strode to the stone railing of the rampart and looked out to sea before turning back to face them all.

"You know what I am, don't you, elves? Who amongst you rules Zarad?" he demanded.

Vizier Mistis stepped forward, and Harpis was impressed at the elf's courage.

"I am Mistis Zara, seventy-ninth Vizier of Zarad. I know what you are. May I know your name, dragon?" Mistis asked in a voice that was both respectful and defiant.

"Seventy-ninth? I have been asleep for quite a long time indeed," Azahle said with a smile at Sudbina before looking back to the Vizier before him.

"You may call me Azahle. I have come for Parafano, and you will release him to me so that I might try and free his mind from the prison of his own delirium," he ordered.

Vizier Mistis bowed low and then stood before Azahle, his arms behind his back in respect.

"It is not that I would not. It is that I cannot," Mistis stated apologetically.

"Do not cross me, elf," Azahle growled, and Harpis half expected him to return to his scaled form and rend Mistis in half.

Exarch Vetlostis strode forward with his hands upheld in peace.

"Vizier Mistis meant no offense, but without Parafano, Zarad would perish. We must do everything possible to keep the blue dragon here. He visited our people in The Age of Ascension. When he found no sand elves willing to accept his hereditary gift, he asked if there was anything else he could offer our city," Vetlostis explained.

Vizier Mistis placed a hand on the other elf's shoulder and continued.

"At the time, our well still filled itself and supplied the entire city with fresh water, but it was dwindling. He spent many days among us, keeping the form of a sand elf. Eventually, he began to forget things here and there. We asked if he needed to go. Knowing of the mental sickness, he told us he would keep the well flowing, for now, enchanting its waters each day to flow into Zarad instead of from it,"

"And you just let him forget who he was?" Azahle snapped angrily.

"For the sake of half a million sand elves and the five families of Zarad, we did," Mistis responded calmly.

Azahle seemed to find patience as he looked from Harpis and the others and then back to the elves.

"Is it true what the humans and dwarf told me, that Konflict has arisen?" Azahle asked.

"It is. Parafano first saw the broken prison months ago. We have been preparing to meet Konflict ever since. We know you are not permitted to participate in the coming struggle. Still, to rob us of the lifeblood Parafano provides our people at this time would doom us to certain defeat," Exarch Vetlostis replied.

Azahle nodded his head in understanding and ran a hand over his scalp.

"If you are defeated, I will free him from this place as his presence will no longer be needed. But should you succeed, I will give the sand elves a century to find a way or a place to survive without his benevolence. After tens of thousands of years, another hundred is not long for him to wait. First, though, I will meet with him to verify what you have said about Konflict and see that you keep him cared for," Azahle finished before taking his immense draconic form again and flying towards the center of the city.

*****

Harpis had spent supper talking over the intended plans for the Armada and the transition of Savjan forces to Zarad. He informed his former governor about what they had discovered through Parafano and then Azahle as well as their intention to visit Soalia and Sikef. After meeting with Aanaman, Harpis returned to the same guest quarters the four of them had shared on their first night in Zarad to find Sudbina had been gone, and no one knew where. Jabruelle had spent the afternoon pouring over tomes from Wren's apartment and others in preparation for their departure tomorrow, and Itka had told Ezera and the sand elves about the events of the past ten days and their planned excursion north.

Hearing light footsteps coming down their marble staircase into their suites, he walked to the foyer and greeted the blond-haired cleric who had taken Turin's mantle of spymaster.

"Come, there are things Exarch Vetlostis has promised to tell me of Turin's grand vision. I insisted we wait for you to arrive as you are the only other one who served under the one-eyed navigator," she said, and he nodded and followed her out with a parting glance at Itka, who shooed him out the door.

Expecting a long walk to wherever the senior sand elf cleric called home, Harpis was surprised when Vetlostis greeted them at the top of the stairs. The three walked a short distance to the railing of the stone Rampart, and the elf stared southward out to sea for a moment before turning to sit on the stone wall and face them, his bronze face and gold-flecked eyes lit by the pink of the setting sun.

"Please find me if I can be of assistance as we grow to learn each other's ways and strengthen our resolve as we prepare to face Konflict himself. Harpis, I wish you the best of luck on your journey to Sikef and genuinely hope you find something to help us all in those ruins," Vetlostis finished.

*****

Sudbina sat on the edge of Zarad's giant well, her feet dangling over the mirror-like water two stories below. She heard Parafano's caretakers respectfully bid farewell to Azahle and smiled as the dragon's humanoid form approached.

"Is your friend as you expected?" she asked with concern. For she did find Parafano to be one of the warmest and gentlest beings she had ever come across.

"All things considered, they have kept him happy and healthy, aside from his mind. I hope it is not too late to reach him, but I will keep my word to the sand elves. They have a century to free him, or less, should you all lose the coming battle," he said in an almost fierce voice before softening as he looked at her with his jewel-like, gold-rimmed eyes.

"I hope you are as firm in your resolve when the time comes for you to go to The Sleeper and birth our child, Sudbina, my muse. You should know that carrying a first-seeded means that the child will mature twice as quickly as you humans expect. I will visit you when the time nears. I genuinely hope that you mortals prevail. Nysia is boring enough as it is without Konflict bringing order to the chaos," Azahle said with a smirk before backing away from her and appearing again as a towering white dragon.

His scales shimmered nearly translucent in the moonlight as he took to the air and, with several heaves of his great wings, drifted silently westward back towards his home like a dragon-shaped white cloud.

Chapter 17
Positioning

Aanaman sat on his balcony overlooking Zarad with Lorkin and Ezera. He'd had difficulty digesting what the blond Savjan spymaster had recounted of Turin's experiment with Quaj and the Quaji themselves. He despised the elf for his methods and arrogance, playing with hundreds of thousands of lives and nearly a hundred human generations just to prove a point. But, as much as he tried, he could not argue the results. Especially as the three had moved their discussion from Turin's machinations to their present-day dilemma and the role they would be playing in the battle for Nysia against the god Konflict and his forces.

For the tenth time in as many minutes, he raised the glass before him and tried to take a comforting sip of what the sand elves called cactus wine. Scrunching his face at its burn, he set the glass down and looked at Ezera's still full glass and Lorkin's empty one.

"What is your assessment of our ability to fight alongside the elves of Zarad?" he asked the woman.

"The Stone Magus and I have had several conversations with Exarch Vetlostis regarding their people's nonconventional and gifted methods for defending themselves. The only gifted amongst the purebred sand elves of Zarad are those devoted to Daybreak. I am supposed to meet with him to demonstrate their abilities," Ezera said.

"Will the enemy have mages?" Aanaman asked Lorkin, and the dwarf shook his head.

"Vizier Mistis said that the humans of Necaka were gift-crazed pursuers of elemental power but that they were the only nation of humans to have trained gifted at all as the others long ago stamped out gifted bloodlines out of superstition and fear. Based on his description of what they know about Necakan mages, they seem to differ from ours," Lorkin said, pouring another glass of clear cactus wine.

"How so?" Aanaman asked.

Ezera shifted as Lorkin down the entire glass before setting it on the table and answering his question.

"It would seem thanks are in order to our elven deity Turin Deadeye, shaper of nations," Lorkin said, spitting in disgust before continuing.

"The mages of Necaka and the elementally gifted of the Nysian mainland have no formal rules or system for learning their craft. They work much in an apprentice and master relationship. They can wield potent spells with their element, beyond the elemental familiars and enchanting we are familiar with,"

"Such as?" Aanaman asked, motioning for Lorkin to spit it out.

"Such as, they can sling fireballs and gales of wind and shake the earth with their influence of stone. They don't simply maintain a channeling as we have learned on Quaj Island. Instead, they hurl their gift and their minds with it. Although we fear the mind loss that comes with being unable to release our channeling, they look at the potential loss of their sanity as the cost of doing business," Lorkin stated, shaking his head, and turning to Ezera.

"I hope you and these elven clerics figure something out. I don't know what myself and the few battle channelers I brought with me will do in the face of such magics if they fall into Konflict's horde.

"Maybe their plan will work, and between our galleons on the eastern front and their army in the west, we can dwindle the enemy until they can be defeated," Lorkin finished, shrugging helplessly.

"Maybe Harpis will succeed in his quest to find another way to end Konflict's appropriation of the mortal plane," Ezera said quietly, picking up the cactus wine and downing the glass in one frowning gulp.

*****

Zolga Stood with Admiral Galanis aboard the *Torrent* as they planned the next day of patrolling along the length of the Astinan

River. They had arrived at the coast almost a week ago, and their ships had strung out in a long line as they made their way north to the river mouth. It had been a surprisingly uneventful patrol until they had gotten to the very northern reaches of the waterway, within view of the thousand-foot-high waterfall that fed it. It was there that they first saw Konflict's Horde, an army whose terrifying enormity had Zolga questioning whether victory was at all possible, no matter how long they were able to draw out the war.

Half their galleons sailed up and down the river to ensure they did not miss any movement or other gathering forces. They reported to Admiral Galanis, who had anchored in its midsection. That was until two days ago when he set out to get an updated understanding from Zolga. She had not had much of an update, simply showing him the view of the slowly growing crowd that was amassing several hundred feet from the river edge.

"What do you think they are waiting for?" Galanis asked, and she offered a shrug in response.

"I am not sure. They haven't done anything but sit there since we arrived. Their silence is almost maddening. You'd think they'd shout or jeer or something," Zolga said, squinting her eyes as if they deceived her.

"Are they moving?" he asked.

"It looks like some of them are breaking camp. Are they abandoning the rest, you think?" she asked in return, and they both grabbed looking glasses from the helmsman and surveyed the enemy forces. The unexpected movement's cause became apparent, and she and he both gasped simultaneously, removing the lenses from their eyes and exchanging worried looks.

Zolga had never seen anything as imposing as the slow and deliberate march of the giant, black-armored god carrying a spear as long as a horse. Konflict was more than intimidating, wading through the horde head and shoulders above the humans. He pointed his spear at the *Torrent* from several ranks deep within the edge of the army. Immediately, there was a deliberate approach to the river's edge by what must have been several thousand men and women. As they got closer, the patchwork makeup of Konflict's forces made the scene all that stranger. Some wore ornate plate armor, others only leather or cloth, some were olive-skinned, club-wielding islanders, and others were pale and bearded pike-wielding warriors.

"I'll disembark for my ship at once and bring the rest of the fleet north as quickly as I can. Good luck, Commander Zolga," Galanis said with a stern nod and was quickly over the railing with several of his officers, untying their sloop.

Her crew started signaling the other ships under her command. Zolga watched as the ten other galleons started cycling between the *Torrent* and the portion of the horde that was now slowly walking through silty shallows towards them. What progress the horde had made was quickly erased as the fifth galleon circled past, the horde was decimated by arrows, bolts, and ballista shots from the vessel's crew.

Corpses piled high, forcing the army to split around a growing mound of corpses that became a floating barge of death. As the eerie, red-eyed soldiers continued to press further towards the middle of the river, the only sounds were the striking of weapons, dying gasps and splashes of water as the dead collapsed. As the last of the ten ships sailed past and loosed their missiles into the enemy, Zolga signaled for them to form a tighter grouping so that their next pass would be an almost continuous barrage as they floated by and rained down death. Then, while the other ships circled, she ordered her priests and priestesses to unleash The Siren's rage.

Flash after flash of lightning flew forth from the deck of the *Torrent*, and the enemy began dying by the hundreds. Zolga looked to her right to see her other ships approaching for their second pass before looking back to the coastline. It was now free of enemy fighters. They had all stepped back, far out of range of even the ship's ballista. The imposing figure of Konflict himself stood knee-deep in the river, and Zolga flinched as several more forks of lightning streaked forth from her decks and slammed into the armored behemoth.

As steam of evaporated river water and cloud of sand settled, she caught sight of Konflict as he let his spear fly and barely had time to flinch before it impaled one of her priests, sending the young Tormenta man screaming to The Sleeper. She immediately signaled for the ships to break off their pass, but as the galleons turned in an about flank back towards the middle of the river, she realized perhaps they had done their part.

The entire horde was on the move now, slowly and

purposefully shuffling northward towards the foothills of the Necakan range. Not their leader. He stood like an onyx statue, holding his spear vertically before him as he guarded the movement of his forces away from her ships.

*****

Enky had been unable to turn away from the scenes playing out before him over the past days. He had assumed that the older races of the Nysian mainland would have remained uninvolved in the contest against his brother for dominance of the mortal plane until they were forced. The god had then found himself inspired by the courage and resolve of the soldiers of Sumka and the dwarves of Unkur as they stood together atop the rising slopes of the Unkur mountains, where they came within miles of the Necakan range that was to their south.

The natural bottleneck and favorable rise in elevation had given the dwarves and humans more than a fighting chance. In fact, for several days now, Enky had watched on in horror and hope as men and dwarves died by the tens of thousands. Only a quarter of his brother's horde had been sent north and east to probe the will of the hardy men of Sumka while the rest trudged towards the banks of the Astinan River. The smaller force was still more than enough for the task. Even with the dwarven formations from Unkur, the defenders were outnumbered three to one.

Enky could not keep sadness and disappointment on his face as he viewed the weariness and desperation in the eyes of the ranks of Sumkan men that stood behind dwarven shield walls, ready to meet another charge of Konflict's red-eyed minions. Yet, the dwarves still stood unwavering, tower shields planted firmly in the ground, ready to meet the incoming tide.

Having spent the better part of three ages watching the mortal races of Nysia wage war with each other and seeing worse on different planes, it was a rare thing for Enky to find himself unwilling to watch as they played out. It may have been the weight of guilt in the responsibility he felt for this particular war that made him look away, or simply the hopelessness and senselessness of the slaying that caused him to waver.

As the red-eyed subjects met the shield wall, it was pushed back in places, and in others, the charging humans were able to force their way through holes in the front line and engage with the human forces of Sumka that stood behind the dwarves. At that moment, the Sumkan soldiers lost their appetite for battle. Just as in other conquered areas of Nysia, they immediately subjugated themselves to his brother, their eyes turned red and they became one with the horde.

Enky could not hold his gaze to the frame as the butchery began in earnest. The stalwart dwarves, who never lost their hunger for battle or their will to fight, were engaged by the original attackers before them and the newly dominated red eyed Sumkans from behind.

When he looked back to the battlefield later, not a single dwarf had lost their spirit to his brother, and so there stood no dwarves with glowing red eyes of Konflict.

*****

Erimo stood shivering at the cliff edge of High Pass, looking down the hundred-foot drop into the rushing source of the Andrefan River. Maybe twice that distance in front of him was the winding road from the Necakan range's western end in southern Sumka. To his right, it hugged the cliffs in a loping curve that eventually brought it to where he stood before broadening and flattening out as it went deep into Necaka and the country's capital behind him to the east.

Still looking ahead, he smiled at the grumpily stomping feet he knew belonged to Nathken as the brigadier approached.

"What does Zarad's great golden eagle think of High Pass?" his old friend asked.

"I think it is probably the most defensible parcel of land in Nysia," he answered honestly.

Glancing at the older sand elf, he tried not to laugh at the shivering bronze-skinned native of the desert clad in every scrap of cloth and leather he owned.

"You are aware that it is summer and abnormally warm for this area?" Erimo asked.

"It's colder than a mid-winter night in Zarad even when the sun does manage to shine through this thick fog that seems to cling to the mountain peaks like a hungry babe to its mother," Nathken replied sharply before shooting Erimo an apologetic glance.

"Are the soldiers as miserable as you are, old elf?" he asked his general.

"They are. So far, the grumbling is still your typical griping amongst troops. I sense no misgivings or disheartening. Do you believe we could hold this pass against a quarter-million strong army?" Nathken returned

Erimo peered ahead of them at the pass that could accommodate a column that was at most ten soldiers wide.

"We could hold it until our longbows ran out of arrows or our archer's arms fell off," he confirmed.

"Then why don't we make this our final stand?" his friend asked in a tone that belied he knew the answer.

"Because the enemy will probe this passage into Necaka only as long as it thinks it is the quickest way to force the last humans or our folk to heel. Then they will march south to the shallows of the Andrefan delta, where it will take longer but where their massive numbers will mean they have the advantage," Erimo said.

"Let us hope we don't lose many elves to the enemy or the cold," Nathken said.

"Forcing them from the pass will be the easy part. Scouting their movements south and then catching up with them to harass them along the river's length as they move will be the trick," Erimo stated.

"Still no sign of the mages. But, hopefully, a few of them show," the old brigadier said, rubbing his hands together furiously.

"I doubt the Grand Arcanist will get the mages of Necaka to unify fully, but we can hope at least some will show their faces and prove useful," he answered with a shrug.

"I wonder if we might be better off without power-crazed, over-gifted human mages, to be honest. What are your orders for the day High Marshal?" Nathken asked.

"Set up a relay of messengers back towards the Necakan capital and send scouts along the riverbank and across the pass. I want to know when the enemy nears or if they decide to bypass this crossing all together and simply turn south when they take Sumka," Erimo commanded.

*****

Harpis was thankful that one of the Savjan galleons that had arrived in Zarad with Aanaman was carrying a larger two sailed sloop. He had happily commandeered it with Aanaman's permission, and they embarked on the newer, bigger boat instead of the dingy they had precariously sailed west to find Azahle on. Jabruelle, Sudbina, and he could still crew the vessel despite its size, and Itka was a quick study. Harpis had enjoyed the time with his companions. He also found that the more time he spent conversing with them, the more his voice was slowly recovering. He wondered if perhaps his self-imposed loneliness and inability to hear in Kalt hadn't prolonged the poor condition of his vocal cords.

It would be a month-long endeavor to make it to Soalia and then around the northeast corner of the Nysian mainland to Sikef. They had no idea if they would be able to resupply before returning to the sand elf city. If the elven strategy worked, they still had at least three or four months until Konflict's army reached the walls of Zarad so he hoped time was still on their side.

"Is it the right island?" he asked, looking up to Sudbina's unmoving form, perched with arms and legs wrapped around the top of the mast.

"I see no other land out to the horizon in any direction. So, this would seem to be the most southern island, where Azahle told us to look," she confirmed, sliding down to the top of the ship's cabin where he stood.

"I can send Xissay to look," Jabruelle offered, and Harpis nodded in agreement.

It did not take Xissay long to return, bringing news that the tiny island was empty. Jabruelle dismissed her as they anchored offshore and swam to the beach. In the middle of the small island, the sand was cleared away from huge chunks of glinting cooled lava strewn around a cavity in the ground.

"Not a very impressive place to trap a god," Sudbina stated, peering into what was once a sealed lava rock prison.

"I believe the intention was that the location stay nondescript," Itka replied, looking around at the chunks of stone cracked and flung outward when the god had burst forth.

Though it looked plain enough, the enormity of where they now stood was not lost on Harpis.

"Ages ago, the four sisters stood on this sand and banished their brother for what was supposed to be an eternity," he said, looking down in awe.

176

"Enough gawking. We need to clean up this mess," Itka said, arranging the pieces of the slab that had stood above Konflict's tomb-like prison together.

Harpis pulled a face at the statement before realizing the dwarf meant the mess of stones and not the apocryphal mess of a god he himself helped awaken.

It had taken them nearly an hour to gather and arrange the pieces of the slab, and he was thankful Itka was the physical specimen her uncle had been, as several of the pieces weighed more than he did.

Chapter 18
High Pass

Erimo walked along the berms his army had created as defensive positions while camped at High Pass. Row after row of mounds taller than he was bristled with sharpened pike poles made from mountain pines. An attacking force would have to swarm over them or advance in a path that would expose them to a continuous barrage from archers.

The road across from him stretched in a giant curve that ended at his feet and began two hundred feet on the other side of the river gorge. The entirety of its visible portions was within range of his longbows, and he could not fathom the losses it would take for the enemy to reach the berm beneath him.

"Maybe it would be better if they did make it to these berms," he said, surveying the maze of mounds and trenches behind him.

"Is that so?" Nathken asked him, the old elf's hands were on his hips as he stood next to Erimo.

"The more we take here, the less we have to defeat closer to home," Erimo answered, crossing his arms and turning back towards the gorge.

"I think I speak for most of our kin here under your command in stating that we would all prefer to fight the human horde in the desert heat of the south instead of the bone-chilling dew and fog that seems never to leave this gods-forsaken mountain range," Nathken grumbled.

"There will be a lot of dying today, my friend," Erimo said, shaking his head.

"So long as it's lots of human souls going to The Sleeper, I am not so upset about it," Nathken said with a shrug of his own.

"They did not ask to be conquered and invaded by Konflict

and his aggressions any more than we did ourselves. I regret every life we take. Each is a soul that likely attempted to slow the very horde they are now part of," Erimo said, sadness in his voice.

"You are commanding the forward-deployed army of Zarad in defense of our people Erimo, do not wear the guilt of the warlord god yourself," Nathken said.

Erimo knew well, as did his long-time fellow soldier, the reason why they were there and that it was for the sake of Zarad.

"If Vizier Mistis was right and we face down a quarter-million humans or more, I cannot help but feel some guilt at that cost. Over two hundred thousand human lives sacrificed on the altar of war for our own sake," he said, clenching and unclenching his jaw.

"You speak with the luxury of having no family back in Zarad. To you, this army is your kin, but to most of your soldiers, they would happily kill humans to preserve the lives of their children and friends back home," Nathken stated, and Erimo held up his hand to acknowledge the point and end the discussion.

"Is the rear ready to move as I instructed?" he asked, knowing the answer but wanting the experienced brigadier to walk him through it again as a distraction.

"Yes. A quarter of the troops and all our mounted units are with the supply wagons, enough to move and protect our entire supplies at a moment's notice. If needed, the mounted soldiers could return here, but for now, they are ready to move southward on our signal to shadow the horde along the river," he answered.

They both grew quiet as a pair of elves slid down ropes from the cliff that stood above the road across the chasm. The scouts landed in a sprint, running around the curving road, and up to their position several minutes later.

"Report," Erimo demanded when they climbed before him.

"Sir, they are only a few moments away. Our best guess is their force is near one hundred thousand strong. They are marching up the mountain road ten abreast, we counted several thousand ranks deep, but their column stretches in and out of view down the slopes," The elf reported, and his fellow scout nodded in agreement.

"Any sign of their commander?" Erimo asked, and the two shook their heads.

"All right, off with you," Nathken said, sending them towards the rear before returning.

"Give the preparatory orders and send scouts further south and east. This is not even half the force we expected, I don't want to get flanked, and I need to know if those cursed mages show their faces," Erimo said as Nathken slid down the berm and started bellowing at officers.

In a few breaths, long bow wielding sand elves crowded the top of every berm for as far as he could see. Half as many, carrying shields and spears, stood in the valleys between the berms, their front rank standing next to Erimo at the foremost defensive embankment. The entire force, Erimo and his generals included, could wield the sabers on their hips as deftly any other weapon.

When they were all in place, Erimo closed his eyes and listened to the sounds of his livelihood. Like a wood elf listening to a soft breeze in a forest, he took in the sounds of his army. Though they were standing in formations, they rustled just like the leaves in the wind. Arrows shuffled in quivers, hands patted sword pommels or squeezed and released sword handles as thousands of warriors stood, fidgeting against adrenaline.

Erimo opened his eyes at the collective intake of breath from around him to see the full charge of the column across the way. He drew his saber, raised it over his head, and then pointed it across the gorge. Ten thousand arrows lofted into an arc at nearly the same time, and for a moment, the distant road and the humans running on it were shaded from the sun by the cloud of death. Then, before the first volley struck, he heard the hornets' nest of thousands of taught strings releasing at will as the longbows continued to unleash their fury.

The horde died by the thousands but still inched forward. Not all were killed under the hail of missiles the elven army sent forth. The more armored of the red-eyed humans still stood after the initial volley emptied the road in a flood of blood, and pin-cushioned corpses sent tumbling a hundred feet to the rapids of the Andrefan below.

Though they died by the thousands as arrows flew across the gorge, the enemy column seemed endless. Worse, as some of them did make progress, they widened the area the marksman needed to target, further reducing the toll each volley took on the charging horde's momentum. Within a few minutes, they were at the furthest point of the curve to his right, and Erimo knew they would soon be advancing head-on towards his position, and their shields

180

and armor would make his archers less effective.

Brigadier Nathken rejoined him atop the initial berm and cursed several times under his breath.

"They've no regard for their own lives. Daybreak preserve us, it's been minutes, and they must have lost five thousand already. Yet, they didn't utter a single scream or battle cry the entire time," he said in bafflement.

"Their minds are not their own, Nathken. They are Konflict's. We risk being forced into a wider battlefield if we don't halt some of this momentum. It is no good to kill many of them if we are still overrun in our position. There are still half of Konflict's forces and the god himself unaccounted for," Erimo said.

The brigadier shook his head in bewildered agreement as the human column snaked closer along the road to High Pass.

"It would seem more than just the humans will be paying the cost of Zarad's safety today," Nathken said softly.

Erimo surveyed the road, now a clogged ledge full of the dead and dying being trampled by fearless subjects of Konflict.

"Sound the signal horns. I want four staggered volleys concentrated on the furthest part of the road within effective range of our bows!" Erimo shouted, pointing his saber.

The scattered sprinkle of arrows along the entire mile-long length of the road turned into a pulsing thrum of death on the portion of the path where he was pointing. When the archers adjusted their fire, those of the human column already passed that position charged headlong towards the defensive positions.

Nathken bellowed the order, and as soon as the initial wave of red-eyed fighters crashed into the pike-pole ramparts, elven foot soldiers began their advance. The elves were like surgeons with their slim spears, opening throats and piercing hearts with deft thrusts and twists of their weapons. Only when an enemy clutched the shaft in death or their wooden handles of their spears broke did the elves draw their sabers and hypnotically weave their steel amongst the clumsy bludgeoning swipes of the enthralled human horde.

The difference in skill aside, the elves suffered significant losses in the initial clash due to the sheer enormity of the numbers they faced. It did not take long for the distance between those trying to pass the concentrated volley of arrows and the rear of those left on the other side to grow.

Erimo signaled an all-out charge with momentum lulling, and thousands of elven soldiers rushed past him. They were in equal numbers to the humans left to face them, and the horde was quickly put down or pushed over the ledge as the elves advanced, clearing the curving mountain path as they went. He did not halt their advance until they had made their way to just beyond where the archers were firing, cutting down the survivors that made it through the hail.

Nathken climbed back alongside him, looking over the carnage their army had left in its advance.

"I don't like it. We are overextended well beyond our defensive posture against a numerically superior force," he commented to his friend.

"I don't either but what was happening before was a far more dangerous situation," the brigadier commented.

"How much longer will our arrows last, do you think?" Erimo asked without turning to his friend.

"Not more than another ten or twenty minutes at most, and then we will have to engage the grind of melee unless I send for the supply wagons to bring the rest of our stock," Nathken offered.

"No, we will need that later," Erimo stated firmly.

"Let us just hope there is a later," Nathken said, drawing a severe look from Erimo.

Both elves flatted to the dirt in a hasty duck as the shadow of a giant boulder passing overhead momentarily blocked the sun before the rock crashed into a formation of archers on a nearby mound.

"By the gods, what was that?" Nathken shouted, and they both saw four catapults were wheeled and tied just out of arrow range. Swaths of human fighters clambered over them to proceed up the road while others set to work loading and winding them.

"Should we fall back out of their range and let them come to our embankments?" Nathken asked as another stone flew by them and took several more of their archers to The Sleeper.

"If we do, they'll keep moving them closer amongst their charge. They could just keep at it until they soften us enough to push beyond our fortifications and into the open where they will overwhelm us," Erimo shouted back, squeezing his forehead in frustration at his next order.

"Have the archers stand by, all foot units, all-out charge. We

182

have to get those siege engines taken care of before we can fall back here safely," Erimo commanded.

"We'll lose thousands!" Nathken shouted.

"War has never been convenient, my friend," Erimo returned, surveying the wretched display of devastation that High Pass had become.

The fire of the catapults did not cease, but most of their volleys resulted in rocks hitting now-empty mounds where archers had stood rather than claiming elven lives. The same could not be said where the columns of elves and humans met each other off to his right. The front seemed to constantly shift between a handful to a dozen as the two lines inflicted loss after loss on each other. Nearly as many fighters plummeted into the gorge to their deaths as were killed by enemy weapons.

It did not take long for the glowing red eyes of the catapult operators to turn towards the ledge instead of the far side where Erimo stood, and they began hammering the curving road without regard for their forces. The effect on the elven lines was devastating. They almost halted as rows at a time were taken out of the battle by crushing rocks. However, Erimo quickly countered by deploying volleys of arrows from his archers, forcing the catapults to address his ranged threats once again.

"We've only a few arrows left per quiver," another general shouted up at Erimo from behind the mound where he stood.

"Save them for when they turn their fire to our brothers and sisters once more," he commanded.

A thunder and shouting from behind him drew his attention. He and Nathken cursed together at the prospects of being flanked somehow. Erimo quickly realized the cheers were those of hope, not battle, as several dozen green-robed arcanists from Necaka halted their thick-furred mountain horses and dismounted.

A middle-aged mage with brown hair and a red beard strode forward and up onto the hill with Erimo, extending his hand in greeting.

"High Arcanist Revlis, at your service, High Marshal," the man said, staring, mouth agape across the gorge.

"Erimo is fine," the elf replied, placing a hand on the man's shoulder to get his attention.

"How far out are the rest of your forces?" he asked.

"This is all you're getting, I am afraid. However, thirty-odd

183

mages are certainly something," Revlis said, barely maintaining his composure at the bloodshed and screams of dying men falling from the mountain ledge.

"Revlis, are there stone mages amongst you?" Erimo demanded, and the man nodded.

"Yes, five of us are stone mages," he answered

"I need to use your elementals to destroy the road as soon as my soldiers are clear. Then, I'll sound a retreat and launch the last of my arrows. If your other mages could help with the catapults and keep the enemy at bay, I would much appreciate it!" he shouted.

The man nodded vigorously, hopping down from the mound, and began yelling to his mages.

The last few volleys hammered the enemy as one, and the elves on the causeway beat a hasty retreat. They ran past four massive rock elementals that began hammering away at the road to High Pass not far from Erimo's position. At the same time, the other mages went to the very precipice of the gorge and began their assault.

Balls of fire and fire elementals flew across the gap, killing hundreds of the humans moving and operating the siege engines. More died leaping from the edge in pursuit of water to quench their burning clothing and skin. Air elementals and summoned gusts of elemental wind too began clearing even more of the enemy from the road as the stone elementals finished their work, destroying a hundred-foot-long section of the road.

A few crossbow bolts were loosed from the other side and went unnoticed until they struck several of the mages who were in the middle of casting another rending ball of fire or buffeting surge of wind. The mages that were hit, even non-mortally wounded, went screaming mindlessly over the edge, their sanity splintered by the loss of concentration mid-spell. Finally, six of the mages on edge motioned as one, and the river surged up a hundred feet from below and crashed onto the far side, sweeping many more red-eyed men and women off. Again, a peppering of crossbow fire came from the far side, and Revlis pulled his mages back behind the mound with Erimo.

"The elements protect us. Is there no end to them?" Revlis asked.

Erimo was going to respond but instead held his hand up as

the forces on the other side had ceased any advance. Instead, the horde stared at the gap that had been a land bridge. Then without warning, they simply about-faced and slowly marched away down the mountain road.

"Where are they going?" Revlis asked fearfully.

"Along the river, looking for a place to cross, which will be down at the coast if I have anything to do with it," Erimo said, turning to face the mage.

"Will you stay here with your mages to check if they probe the pass again? I will leave several mounted scouts and a hundred elves to protect you," Erimo questioned.

"You have my word. Thank you for what you and your elves did here today," Revlis replied grimly.

"The day may have been lost without your timely arrival. I would recommend sending a warning to your Grand Arcanist. Unfortunately, that was not even half the force we suspect Konflict will eventually bring to bear on Nysia," Erimo said, waving for Nathken to move their forces out and south to catch up with their supply lines.

"Good luck to the south, elf, quite the battle you waged here," Revlis said, in awe of the blood-soaked stone and dirt all around them.

"The dead deserve your thanks, not me," Erimo replied and walked down from the mound after his generals.

A few paces later, he was met by one of his stewards and handed the reins to his white camel.

"Thank you," he said with a curt nod to the young elf before climbing atop the beast and urging it into a trot until he was next to Nathken and several of the other senior generals.

"I wish you had entertained Exarch Vetlostis when he suggested we take some of the clerics with us from Zarad. It would have been helpful to have had their help back there, if not their healing," Nathken said with a glance back at the receding battlefield.

"How many did we lose?" Erimo asked without looking back.

"Best estimates, we lost a few hundred archers to the catapults and almost two-thousand-foot soldiers," Nathken reported with sadness.

"How many did we send to The Sleeper?" he asked, and Nathken raised his hands in frustration.

"Your guess is as good as mine, between our wholesale slaughter and the last hammering by the mages, maybe twenty or thirty thousand? Too many to count. More death than I could have imagined seeing in an hour of fighting, but they were as mindless as they were persistent," his friend replied.

Erimo slowed his mount and let the other senior officers ride ahead before turning to Nathken.

"Even if it was thirty thousand, it was not enough," Erimo said quietly, rubbing his temples.

"It is still a tenth of their force or more, and we denied them a bunch of ruby-eyed mages to add to their ranks," Nathken said, giving Erimo a stern look before giving a tug on his reins to urge his camel forward.

"I guess you'll have to spend our trip along the river to the sea thinking about how to deprive the rest of them of their lives," the old brigadier offered.

Chapter 19

Sikef

Harpis sat at the rudder of their sand elf loaned ship, keeping their track parallel to the coast just as he had every day since they rounded the northeastern corner of the Nysian mainland. If the map drawn by Azahle was as accurate as he thought, and if they were navigating as well as he hoped, they should come into view of Sikef's entrance before the afternoon. The three-week voyage from Konflict's former prison in the islands of Soalia had given the four of them an appreciation for just how vast the mainland was.

Listening to Vizier Mistis and the others talk of months-long troop movements had sounded almost unbelievable when hearing it and pointing them out on the map. Watching the slowly changing scenery of the coast drift by for weeks, Harpis was surprised people could move from one end of the continent to the other on foot at all. Itka was beginning to complain about being imprisoned on a floating woodpile. Even Sudbina and Jabruelle had grown tired of the confines of their small vessel. They hadn't dared to venture onto land as they went but several stronger storms had forced them to find sheltered anchorages.

Jabruelle had taken to reanimating the remains of freshly caught meals when fish did find their hooks. Harpis still found it funny enough, but the dwarf and Sudbina had threatened, to no avail, to start using pieces of Jabruelle for bait if he kept it up. Since dawn, when he had taken over at the helm, black stone mountains had begun marching out of the surrounding northern pines and were growing in height to the point where Harpis felt comfortable declaring it a mountain range and not foothills.

"Goddess below us!" Sudbina called out, pointing into the distance ahead from her perch above, and Harpis tied off the rudder before walking to the bow to join Itka and Jabruelle.

"Goddess below indeed," he said, and the others nodded in agreement.

A set of three mountaintops formed the head, shoulder, and hips of The Sleeper, appearing as though she were slumbering afloat on the sea. The relief of her body cut into the black rocks of the mountains ahead looked surreal. Harpis guessed that at dusk, one might imagine they were drifting in The Great Dream with the deity herself. The immense size of the sculpture was breathtaking, reminding Harpis of when he had stood before the mountain-sized goddess in her dream after singing her true name on his lips at the battle of Tuath.

Nearing the godly sculpture that adorned Sikef's entrance, they could not spot the city's doors until they were well within the shadow of the mountains above. The eye closest to the hand upon which her head rested had steps carved up to it. The stairs ran along her hand and arm to the sea at a small landing. When they were only a hundred feet away, they could spot the stones and iron posts that must have once supported a vast dock structure. However, looking around now, they found no good place to tie their vessel.

"Looks like we are rowing ashore," Harpis said with a smile, noting the disgruntled looks of his companions, particularly the dwarf.

"How long do you think we will be inside?" Itka asked, grumpily rummaging about and packing several leather satchels with food and water skins.

"How long do you think it would take to wander around Fjall without a guide?" he asked.

"A day or two," she said, finishing stowing supplies.

"I wouldn't say completely aimlessly!" Jabruelle countered as he flipped through several tomes and stuffed them in his bag.

With the boat secured, Harpis looked up at Sudbina, who stood biting her lip after they had untied the dinghy from above the ship's cabin and lowered it to the water.

"What's wrong? Scared of the abandoned city of deep elves?" he asked her.

"I think you mean scared of the city of death. The answer is admittedly a yes. But, unfortunately, I've no gifted songs or spells of necromancy or fancy enchanted maces," she countered.

188

Harpis hadn't appreciated that the experience in Azahle's lair, where she had likely felt entirely defenseless, may have been different for her than the rest of them.

"If monsters are waiting in the darkness for you, I'd just be getting in the way. Besides, the dead don't have ears and are not so gullible, so I don't know how I'd be able to contribute," she replied before clutching her stomach and vomiting over the rails.

"Are you ill?" he asked with a raised eyebrow.

"I am fine. Breakfast just isn't sitting well with me," Sudbina responded.

"Well, keep the boat safe. We will be back in two or three days at most. If someone from the shore notices you, pull the anchor and start sailing circles further out to sea, we will ask Xissay to light a signal at dusk when we return if you are gone," Harpis instructed as he climbed into the small rowboat with Itka and Jabruelle.

"Should you three be gone much longer than a few days, I'll go ahead and assume you're dead and join the others in Zarad for the end of the world," she said with a wink.

Harpis shook his head at her, only mostly sure that she was joking, and crowded behind Itka in the aft of the dinghy as the dwarf rowed them to shore. After Jabruelle and Itka clumsily climbed out of the boat and onto the stone landing a few feet above the water, he handed the dwarf the rope and leaped out. They pulled it out of the water and flipped it upside down on the landing before heading up the black stone stairs towards the five-foot-tall eye of the goddess.

The stairs were cut for gnomes, and their shorter and narrower than expected rise, coupled with the moisture of the sea, made them a perilous climb.

"Glad I am short for a dwarf," Itka said as they looked upon the beautiful obsidian door.

It was ringed in hand holes that had been invisible to them until they stood before it. Itka tried several times to push the door inward or pull it outward to no avail before Jabruelle stepped past her, putting his hands in two of the holes and rolling the big stone eye almost effortlessly. It moved left and behind the eyelid of the sculpture revealing a tunnel that stretched downward into blackness.

They were only a dozen steps in when it was already difficult to see. Itka enjoyed several laughs at them scraping their heads on the low ceiling.

"Jabruelle is the entire city like this?" he asked, rubbing the crown of his head.

"No, according to Tegyt's journal here, once we are in the main chamber of the city, it is quite expansive. Well, expansive according to gnomes, but still, the city is a series of large, vaulted caverns with buildings in them connected by tunnels such as this. This passage should take us into the main city, then we will take a tunnel to the cemetery chamber which lies between the city center and book home," he said, hunched and glancing in the dim light at the book held in front of him.

"Book home?" Itka asked.

"Sorry, er, um, I guess we would just say library. Sorry, the language of the Maelar is an odd one, and I am at best a novice in translating it. That is where they would keep texts on other races and languages," he said, putting the tome away.

"How about summoning Xissay until we see just how abandoned the city of Sikef really is," Harpis asked.

A puff of smoke and sulfuric odor later, the undead fire sprite sat floating before Jabruelle, looking from the necromancer to Harpis with a grin.

"Do you find the city of Wren's ancestors comfortable?" she asked sarcastically.

"I do, thank you. Unfortunately, it is difficult to see, so I asked Jabruelle to summon his floating talking lantern to guide the way," Harpis returned.

Xissay glowered before floating ahead of them to hang near Itka's shoulder as the dwarf drew her maces and led them down into the city. The stone corridor grew colder as they descended. Ahead of them, there was only blackness beyond the light of Xissay's fiery hands as the path transitioned from tunnel to cavern.

They weren't more than a few steps into the cavern when they heard grating and scuffling behind them. Harpis immediately reached into his satchel and threw several mage stones Lorkin had enchanted for him onto the ground and at the noise, illuminating an area the size of a large home. Xissay darted to Jabruelle's shoulders, and Itka spun around towards the tunnel they had just exited before charging the two moving armored forms standing guard at the city's entrance.

When still living, they must have been mountain trolls from the northwest of Nysia. In death, they were imposing armored guards held together through some long-dead necromancer's enchantment. Harpis slung his violin case around and pulled forth his instrument, nearly gagging himself with the force that he slammed it against his neck. When he was ready to pull his bow across its strings, he realized his assistance was unnecessary.

Itka flung the mace from her right hand into the shambling armored creature approaching her from that side. It struck with enough force that it caved the helmet in, the mace stayed wedged into the metal when the lumbering creature thudded to the ground. She then went into a forward roll under the sweeping arc of the other's ax, coming up in a crouch behind its extended weapon hand. She grasped the outstretched wrist in her empty hand, swinging her other mace down, crushing its elbow with a sickening crunch and pop.

Without tendons or bones to hold it upright, the ax clanged to the floor, followed by the other creature's knees, and she swept the mace head down into its nearest ankle. Harpis tried not to vomit at the sound of the strike as the ankle shattered between the mace and cavern floor. Kicking the wounded sentry towards the ground, she similarly flatted the helm of the second troll before walking over to the first foe and wrenching her mace free from the remnants of its skull.

Jabruelle and he let out low whistles of appreciation in unison, and Itka gave a slight bow.

"Just happy to have something I can fight normally for the first time on this adventure!" she shouted in a voice that echoed far into the distance.

Harpis bent and picked up the hand ax. It was heavy, definitely made for the troll that had once owned it, but it would do better at fending off enemies than his violin might at times, so he loped his satchel strap around it to keep it in place alongside his bag.

Jabruelle pulled out his tome and squinted in the mage light to read the text, so Xissay obliged him by summoning a dancing flame in her hand.

"Ah, yes. So, apparently, the inhabitants of Sikef were particular about their undead wards, choosing trolls as almost a rule.

Harpis was about to ask why that was when the one with the shattered elbow started twitching its forearm muscles.

"They still regenerate after they are reanimated?" he asked incredulously, his eyes turning away from the growing flame from Xissay setting both corpses ablaze in a hissing flaming stench.

"It is a bit more complicated than reanimation. These guardians of Sikef are spectral enchantments. Essentially at the moment of death, a highly gifted necromancer can shepherd the being's soul to one of The Sleeper's handmaidens and then force the body to remember what it was like to live, lying dormant, waiting to be triggered into action. Safe to say we might run into more of those," Jabruelle finished with a shrug, bending to inspect the smoldering remains.

"Anything else about potential wards, traps, or other undead friends we might run into down here you care to share ahead of time, necromancer?" Itka asked, gathering the mage stones up and handing them to Harpis.

"Uh, erm, well, there are many things we might run into down here. The deep elves and their descendants were quite paranoid. Even here in their sanctuary, they feared prosecution by superstitious surface races," Jabruelle replied.

"You two can follow me using a small glow from Xissay. I see fine down here," Itka said to Harpis before turning Jabruelle.

"Why were the deep elves and gnomes so prosecuted and not the dwarves?" she asked.

"The dwarves came from mixing with the Boritis, those were the earliest humans in Nysia, and the deep elves in the same way ancestors of the wood elves bred with Boritis in the mountains leading to the trolls. So, I would say that the dwarves were largely left alone because of their appearance being closer to humans," he said with a shrug.

"Where did you learn that?" Harpis asked with a raised eyebrow.

"Oh, there is all kinds of information Wren did not share with us. So much is contained in his tomes and scrolls. For example, did you know he and his cousins fled Sikef as adolescents when the city was abandoned?" Jabruelle asked.

Harpis remembered seeing the gnome's deeply scarred body and troubled mind on the island belonging to Moodi Shen and shook his head sadly.

"There were many things Wren kept buried from himself and his friends," Harpis said to them while looking at Xissay, who hung her head for a moment.

Itka led the way through the upper city, and Sikef looked to Harpis like the most enormous and terrifying children's playground he could imagine. There were windows and doors and balconies in the stone face as well. The buildings they walked past were all crafted from the same black stone of the mountain, sitting at most slightly taller than Harpis' head. They made their way to the other end of the chamber without encountering any more of the sentinels left behind by the gnomes and necromancers. Finally, they arrived at a tunnel that angled downward after Jabruelle had checked his map and misled them several times.

"This is it," Jabruelle said confidently, pointing at an inscription in the language of deep elves above the tunnel arch.

"Pathway of the dead and the devoted. This will take us to the deep city, where the library sits in a wing of The Mausoleum," he said happily, excitedly stepping ahead of them down the passageway.

Itka just shrugged at Harpis and followed the black-robed man and his familiar.

"Xissay, do you know if he is correct?" he asked, barely able to see the sprite's head shake as her tiny flame bobbed over Jabruelle's shoulder.

"Wren did not find me in The Great Dream and become a Death Speaker until he was on Quaj Island and living in The Sanctum," she answered.

Itka halted Harpis at the lower opening of the tunnel as Xissay flew ahead with Jabruelle.

"Necromancer, you said this is a cemetery for the city?" she asked, looking slowly around the long chamber that stretched into the darkness ahead.

Jabruelle bobbed his head in acknowledgment, bending and examining several raised stone caskets nearest the small road that went straight ahead.

"Like, a cemetery for real dead, not partially or halfway dead, right?" she asked.

"We can look inside one and check if you'd like!" Jabruelle asked, and Harpis felt the man was just looking for an excuse.

"No, that's fine. There are just an awful lot of coffins in here," Itka said, stepping down into the cavern, and Harpis followed quickly behind, almost feeling the darkness behind them.

No sooner did the two of them take their first step onto the pathway Jabruelle had walked on did they start hearing popping and cracking sounds ripple down to the far end of the chamber. Harpis quickly deployed his mage enchanted light stones again, illuminating the nearby portion of the grave cavern. A moment later, a tide of child-sized gnome skeletons and a few other races, all in various stages of decay, flooded past a surprised Jabruelle, charging Harpis and Itka.

The dwarf's maces went into a flurry, smashing the tiny, reanimated skeletons to pieces three or four at a time in sweeps of her weapons. Then, looking over the sea of skeletons before them, Harpis dropped the ax, grabbed his violin, and immediately began playing the sounds of sword strikes and ax chops he had perfected in Akriven. He felt the vibrations of his strings under the pull of his bow mimic the sweeping whistle of the wood ax and hiss of knife blades through the air and into flesh. He closed his eyes as he played, feeling the memory of the woodpile outside the tavern that was turned to kindling by his gift.

When he opened his eyes, the air was thick with the bone dust of demolished skeletons. Itka and he had mounds of unmoving remains before them, but there was an endless supply of more to come as far as he could see. It was as if Jabruelle did not exist to them, flowing right past Xissay and he, barely disturbing the wild-eyed man's robes.

"Jabruelle, do something!" Harpis shouted at the man.

"They are already reanimated. So, what else do you want me to do?" Jabruelle replied in a shrieking cackle, and Xissay slapped her forehead before diving forward, hands ablaze and lighting the nearest skeleton on fire. The three of them were then blown to their feet as the particles of bone dust in the air caught flame and then became a roiling fireball that engulfed the entire cavern for a second before disappearing.

Smacking embers and a flame from his hair, Harpis nodded at the cursing and growling Itka before glancing to where Jabruelle lay on the ground. The skeletons were blown to the sides of the chamber. Their bones and what was left of the clothes they had been buried in were all burning low.

194

"I am having a hard time breathing," Harpis shouted.

Lying flat on his stomach, he sucked in precious cool air, glancing at the thick cloud of smoke above them, flowing towards the tunnel they had just exited.

"Crawl to the other side. Stay as low as you can!" Itka shouted, and the two of them headed towards the shimmying Jabruelle.

"Living this deep, the gnomes surely have ventilation shafts carved as we dwarves do in Fjall. When the kilns have an overburn at the mining areas below our city, the dwarves have to retreat lower and let the hot air and smoke drift up and out of the city before it becomes breathable again," she explained between heavy breaths.

Harpis nodded in agreement the next time his crawl turned his face towards hers.

"Jabruelle, why didn't they attack you?" Harpis asked.

"Perhaps The Sleeper's devotees do not disturb some of the traps left behind," he shouted back at them while he crawled.

"I am about to take the books from him and read them myself to save us from another near-disaster," Harpis whispered to Itka after brushing soot from his mouth.

*****

Sudbina lay atop the sailboat's cabin under the stars of a cloudless night. After a month stuck aboard the vessel with the others, having the peace of the evening to herself was blissful. She was happy for having the opportunity to think long about the past, present, and future as she laid her hands gently over her navel.

"What are you doing, Sudbina? Why are you not with them in Sikef? We need to make sure they find the texts to translate the song so Harpis may sing it," Enky demanded, and she opened her eyes to see him propped up, sitting at her side.

"I will not endanger my child, for you or anyone else," she said, still lying on her back.

"Does Harpis know?" Enky asked, seemingly enticed by the mischief.

"Why should Harpis know?" she asked innocently.

"I assume you would tell the father," Enky reasoned.

"It appears the god of chaos does not see as much as he should

195

in his personal plots and schemes. Harpis is not the father. It is Azahle. I assumed you had been watching," she said with a playful laugh.

"You bed the dragon! Sudbina, you won't survive the birth, which could be before we rid Nysia of my brother," he shouted in frustration.

"That sounds like it would then be a problem for you and your next Marionette. I serve no one, not even you. I am Sudbina, and I obey only myself. My life will end on my terms, not yours, your brother's, or anyone else's. But, most importantly, my life will have had a purpose greater than exacting vengeance upon Svenus Kalt or toiling as a god boy's plaything," she finished, smiling, and closing her eyes again.

Chapter 20
The Lowest Point

Harpis looked across at the soot covered Jabruelle and Itka, who were catching their breath and then to the stone passageway that led down into the deep city.

"At least your robe made it through that unscathed," Harpis said with a chuckle, pointing at the other man's raggedy black cloth robe.

"It does hide the burn marks well," Jabruelle said with a nervous laugh.

"Former familiar of Wren, The Sleeper's most cherished Death Herald in generations, now stuck blundering about in the dark with you two idiots," she said, shaking her head and sighing before looking towards Itka.

The dwarf was bent low, looking at the floor in front of her, and Harpis and Jabruelle hurried to join her, light from Xissay's flame illuminating writing etched into the floor.

"Ah, I recognize this script! It is an enchantment known as *Wehn's Decomposition*!" Jabruelle eagerly said while Xissay rolled her eyes.

"Do share. What does *Wehn's Decomposition* do?" Itka asked the necromancer, who was busy running his hands over the writing.

Xissay floated behind his shoulder and grabbed a potato from inside it, hovering just above the stone's surface, and rolled the vegetable across it. They watched as each portion that touched it started rotting before their eyes, turning into a soil-like substance and then dust before disappearing.

"Fairly self-explanatory," Xissay said in her high-pitched voice, floating back to hang above Jabruelle's shoulder.

"Is the whole tunnel enchanted?" Harpis asked, his voice revealing his concern at not being able to go further into the city.

"I would think there will be another script at the far end of the enchanted surface as a similar warning," Jabruelle replied.

The necromancer then nodded at Xissay, who flew off into the corridor, peering at the ground, stopping only a few paces ahead.

Harpis pulled one of the mage stones from his bag again, illuminating the corridor, and even he could see the second set of writing on the floor six or seven feet from them.

"How do we get past without walking through the bridge between this plane and The Sleeper's?" Itka asked hopefully.

"Perhaps I can withdraw the intimation of necrosis from the stone. I am The Sleeper's Death Herald, of course!" Jabruelle said, rubbing his hands together and opening one of the leatherbound books from his bag, reading over a page several times and then kneeling before the engraved stone, his hands held several inches above it. He closed his eyes and began softly murmuring while Xissay crossed her arms with an unimpressed look on her face.

"There, the surface should no longer hold the memory of death!" he proclaimed, standing, and lifting his foot over the cavern ahead.

Itka yanked him backward onto his rump, pulled a second potato from the man's pack, and threw it to Harpis.

"Cut a piece of that and test it again," she said, releasing Jabruelle's collar from her grip.

Harpis obliged. Using the ax donated by the undead troll, he cut the small potato in half and threw it onto the floor, where it quickly blackened and shriveled before turning to ash-like dust and disappearing as the first had.

Jabruelle looked at the floor and then his hands, mortified.

"Thank you!" he said to Itka.

"You don't get to go visit your goddess until you get us back out of this city-sized morgue," she replied.

Harpis stared ahead and then looked at the other half of the potato.

"It did not start being affected until it touched the floor," he commented, throwing the vegetable across the hall and beyond the other set of script, holding his mage stone higher to view it as clearly as possible. It sat unaffected on the cavern floor beyond the enchanted section.

"So, all we have to do is jump across the short distance?" he stated as much as asked the others.

"Well, yes, *Wehn's decomposition* only affects the surface, not the air above it. That would be silly," Jabruelle said, his nose nearly touching the pages in front of him.

Itka squeezed her face with her hands in frustration before glaring at Jabruelle.

"Throw him right in the middle and release me from this profound torture," Xissay said, floating to the other side.

"Can you make the jump, or am I throwing his eminence the Death Herald across?" Itka threatened.

"I can make the leap," Jabruelle replied defeatedly.

Harpis tossed the mage stone across and pulled another from the bag that he set on the near side of the other script to gauge the jump and then took a running start and leaped across, sticking his tongue out at Xissay when he successfully landed on the other side. She held a palm under her chin, and together they observed the awkward display of Jabruelle's running, stumbling jump aided by a shove on the rump from Itka that sent him flying well beyond them. Itka took only a single step and then easily leaped the distance, glancing back at the script.

"Shall we?" she asked.

"I believe we should allow his holiness the Death Herald to go first, as long as he promises to be observant and look for anything that might attack, maim or kill the undevoted," Harpis said.

Jabruelle and Xissay took the lead down the descending and turning tunnel. They walked for several uneventful minutes heading deeper below the mountains before finding the end of the tunnel ahead, opening into the darkness of another chamber.

"This should be it, the deep city. It will contain only The Sleeper's Temple, referred to in these texts as The Mausoleum," he said, poking his head out of the tunnel and looking from side to side.

"Sentinels?" Itka asked, and he shook his head, indicating that there were not any, before walking out into the gloom.

Harpis pulled his last glowing stone from his pack as they walked out into the cavern and the great cathedral-like structure of The Mausoleum rose before them, its polished black stone glinting like onyx in the pale light.

As they approached the entry to the building, Jabruelle held out a hand to stop them.

"The vault that houses texts and knowledge the deep elves gathered, and the gnomes later curated and expanded upon, is kept in the rear wing. This is the one place where I know about a potential foe we may face. Wren had several scribbled notes about a tale his parents told him when he was young and newly arrived in Fjall, about how a lich was left here to protect The Mausoleum," the necromancer stated.

"Lich?" Harpis asked.

"Yes, Mael Tarrebult is said to have chosen to undergo the ritual," Jabruelle said.

"No, Jabruelle, what is a lich," Itka questioned impatiently.

"Oh, of course, sorry. A senior necromancer uses the liching ritual, trading the greatest gift of all in return for immense power and sentience in death and preservation of their body," Jabruelle explained.

"So, this thing is an undead necromancer who gave his life for power?" Harpis asked.

"No, no, he gave his death for power. The necromancer must commit the suicidal rites but then refuse The Sleeper's handmaidens. This Keeps their soul trapped in their recently deceased corpse while preserving it as it was at their death. I believe the correct term is undying, not undead," Jabruelle clarified.

"So, just send Xissay in there but burn this dancing corpse to ashes and we can be on our way," Harpis said hopefully.

"I will be unable to do anything about this particular adversary, we are both her servants, and she would not permit me to harm a lich. I will, however, enjoy watching you two try and defeat it," Xissay said, grinning

"The two of us?" Itka said, confused.

"As with the previous entities we encountered, I can't do much with my gift to the already reanimated. It isn't like I could send him to the great dream, as he is not exactly living," Jabruelle stated before continuing.

"Which reminds me, a lich cannot access The Great Dream, and therefore can't do some of the more powerful things we have seen Wren do, such as force the life from a living being or converging death with the mortal plane. A lich is more like an extremely intelligent, undying puppet master," Jabruelle explained.

"Then what can we expect it to do?" Itka demanded, pulling her maces from her belt and spinning them in her hand.

"I suppose that will depend on the puppets," Jabruelle said, shrugging.

"How about you just try walking past this servant of your goddess and go look through the tomes and scrolls in the back wing until you've translated the song from Konflict's prison?" Harpis asked hopefully.

"I am happy to try, though the lich will be sentient, as thoughtful in undeath as it was in life. A human walking into The Mausoleum of Sikef's deep city, claiming to be a necromancer, let alone The Sleeper's Herald might be greeted by violent suspicion," Jabruelle said with a shrug and headed up the steps towards the entrance.

"If he happens to leave you alone and we happen to fail here, make sure you exaggerate when you tell the tale of our final battle," Harpis said, turning to follow him after throwing a hopeful wink at Itka.

"It must be past midnight. I am just happy we are near the end of this little foray," the dwarf said.

With his mage stone wrapped in a dark cloth in one hand and his violin and bow in the other, Harpis tiptoed behind the catlike steps of Itka. They crept among the shuffling of Jabruelle's sandals several steps ahead of them, Xissay's tiny flame providing the only light as they stepped down into the bowl-like center of the antechamber. They collectively came to a halt when Xissay's lantern-like glow illuminated a gnome in a black and purple robe with lifeless grey skin sitting cross-legged in the room's center between two stone-lined pools of an oil-like liquid.

The gnome's eyes snapped open, revealing a simmering purple, ember-like glow.

"You dare bring enemies into our holiest of places? You forsake our brothers and sisters by leading outsiders here!" the lich shouted.

Realizing they were not going to talk their way out of the situation, Harpis uncovered the mage stone and tossed it at the feet of the now laughing lich. The light barely reached the edges of the antechamber revealing several hulking shadow-like figures moving on either side of a balcony that rimmed the room under its glinting black dome ceiling.

There was a resounding clang of two hammers striking at nearly the same time and then the rattle of large chains echoing around them, followed by the boom of heavy iron portcullises crashing to the floor over the entrances to the left in the right. No sooner had they fallen than another set of hammer strikes by a shadowy figure across from them, trapping them in the antechamber, its four exits covered by heavy iron doors.

Harpis noticed the pool to their left ripple, and then Itka and he jumped back together as a fully plate-armored dwarven warrior with a tower shield, and immense war hammer sat up, stood, and stepped from the pool, dripping the slick oil-like substance as it went.

Harpis immediately played several chops of an ax from his violin, frowning as tiny sparks flew from the thick armor as they bounced harmlessly off. The possessed dwarven corpse took a step towards him and Harpis took another step away, noticing the other pool was also beginning to churn.

"That one looks to be all yours," he shouted to Itka, looking curiously as an undead, green-robed human woman rose before him from far pool.

"Oh, quite splendid, an amazing feat, he is using both as a familiar, tying his sentience into both simultaneously, magnificent!" Jabruelle cried from behind them.

Harpis barely had time to glare at Jabruelle. He caught a few flurries of movement among the constant tolling of a gong that was Itka's maces ringing off plate armor and tower shield as she tucked into a roll to avoid her opponent's plunging hammer swing. The woman murmuring before him drew his attention, and he saw the outstretched palm of her hand erupt in a pillar of flame in time to throw himself backward and out of the way.

His violin lay on the ground toward the reanimated fire mage, so he decided to pull his borrowed ax from his satchel straps instead. He threw it as hard as possible at the cross-legged lich, watching as it buried itself several inches deep in the gnome's shoulder. The lich's only response was a burst of laughter that then became echoed by both of its deceased servants. The woman held a roiling ball of flame above her head that she hurled in his direction.

Diving onto his face, he snatched up his violin and bow and rolled into a run across the other side of the room, where he began playing *Clario's Cacophony* as quickly and loudly as he could. Within moments of calling forth the discordant and jarring notes, he noticed that the green-robed mage and lich were both sharing the cringe he did. The woman's hands fidgeted, and her mouth tried to work, and Harpis saw the gnome's face twitch with the effort of maintaining its connection amongst the disharmony of his song.

Harpis kicked the mage in the chest and stood with his boot on its throat, turning to see Itka take advantage of the lich's faltered control. The small and sinewy dwarf spun into a backward leg sweep that cleanly sent the hulking armored fighter to the ground with a heavy thud. She then put one of her maces on its breastplate and uttered the activation of Lorkin's enchantment. The mace came to a rest after caving in the front of the armor into the backplate, pinning them to the ground, trapping the armored dwarven warrior's corpse to the ground.

Harpis could barely maintain the notes of the raucous song. He was thankful as Itka strode past the lich, yanking the ax from where it was buried in the gnome's shoulder, striding purposefully over to him, shoving him away from the green-robed corpse before promptly decapitating it and cutting off its hands.

Harpis stopped playing and bent at the waist in labored breaths while trying not to vomit at the results of her ax swings.

"Why?" he asked incredulously

"Possessed corpse or not, I've never known a mage to sling spells without a mouth or hands," she said, turning back and walking to the lich with the ax. Both the corpses went still, and Harpis walked up to Mael Tarrebult with her. The lich opened his eyes again and laughed.

"I have more pets than those!" he exclaimed.

A moment later, two immensely muscled trolls jumped down from the ledge ringing the chamber and walked towards them. Itka stepped before them with Harpis' ax and her other mace in hand. Harpis looked from the lich before him over to the headless mage and smiled. Then, bending over the corpse, he undid the leather belt around its waist. Next, he grabbed the flint and striker the mage had used to conjure forth fire.

He noticed a small dagger sheathed on the other side of the belt and quickly removed it, slipping it into his boot and standing before the lich, whose attention was on trying to pummel a spinning, slashing, and crushing Itka to death with the fists of his two trolls. Harpis cupped oil from the pool next to the lich, splashing the sitting gnome and then striking flame to the blackish purple robes.

Immediately the lich's eyes snapped open, and the two troll corpses went lifeless.

"What have you done!" he screamed as flames engulfed him, turning him into a pile of ash within seconds.

"Well done, bard," Itka said, retrieving her mace after releasing its enchantment.

"I believe we are still trapped here," Jabruelle said, striding forth and joining them.

"You two were so brilliant!" he said.

"And here, I thought I'd be returning to The Great Dream for good," Xissay said with a snicker as Jabruelle dismissed her.

"Come, I think the chains to raise the gates are on the ledge above.

The three of them climbed the stairwell off to the side against the chamber wall that led up to the second-story ledge. Finally, they found the chains to raise the portcullis. However, try as they might, Harpis couldn't even sense a budge as Itka, Jabruelle, and he pulled together as hard as possible.

Jabruelle then held up a finger and summoned his necromancer scythe.

"Hopefully, you did not damage them too badly!" he said, closing his eyes.

The two troll corpses Itka had been battling stood together and climbed up to them, joined by two others operating the other gates. The four reanimated mountain trolls began dragging the chains, slowly raising the gate and securing the chain to the release lever. A few long moments later, the other three barriers were raised again. Jabruelle then used the trolls to return the dwarf and human corpses to their pools before walking the trolls back around the second-story ledge and putting them each in similar stone tubs near the gate levers.

"There, good as new!" Jabruelle said, climbing down and heading for the rear wing, retrieving Harpis' mage stone as he passed the middle of the chamber.

"Excited, isn't he?" Itka asked as they went after Jabruelle.

"I would be if I were in the hall of long-lost bards about to have access to ages worth of knowledge," Harpis agreed.

They halted alongside Jabruelle, who had stopped walking forward, holding the mage stone above his head in silence.

Harpis felt his stomach twist and had to grab the wall next to him to keep from passing out as his head spun, sending him down on a knee. Itka let out a low whistle, and Jabruelle slowly lowered the enchanted light, hanging his head. The rear wing of The Mausoleum had row upon row of stone shelves that contained nothing more than ashes and scorch marks while the floor was littered with charred scraps of leather covers and bindings.

Harpis took the stone from Jabruelle and circled the room, desperately hoping there was a scrap of text that remained. He was unable to accept that they had come so far for nothing. Unwilling to admit that there would be no goddess written song for him to sing. His only hope at putting the evil he had unleashed unto Nysia back in its cage was lost to the flames of some long-ago fire. Harpis lowered himself to the ground, his back against one of the stone cases, and wept.

Chapter 21
Resolve

Harpis sat on the stern of their vessel, his feet dangling off the back as he watched the mountain-sized sculpture of The Sleeper fade in the growing darkness of dusk. They had arrived back at their boat just before dawn, awakening Sudbina and sharing with her the news of what they had found and had not found at the bottom of Sikef. Jabruelle had energetically described the journey, the traps, and the battles to an engrossed Sudbina and then agreeing to a short rest before setting sail.

Jabruelle and Itka were still asleep as night approached. However, recurring nightmares of their impending doom and his inability to prevent it had long since taken Harpis' appetite for slumber. So, he found himself sitting across from a too-cheery Sudbina, watching the water slip by under his feet.

"So, you didn't find the texts needed to translate the words from Konflict's tomb. What if we had been able to, and they just read something like, here lies Konflict, god of being a horse's ass," she said.

He appreciated that she was trying to cheer him up. In a way, he supposed she owed him that. It was her fault he had found hope again only to have it crushed in the charred and empty vaults of Sikef. He pulled the dagger he had lifted from the mage's corpse in the antechamber and turned it over in his hand. The sheath was hardened leather-wrapped in gold and inlaid with rubies. Drawing the blade, he appreciated the craftsmanship of the red leather grip and knuckle-sized uncut ruby lashed to the bottom of the handle with gold wire as a makeshift pommel.

"What's that?" Sudbina asked, leaning over the rudder and nosily inspecting the weapon.

"The lich's mage puppet had it on her," he replied, pulling out a mage stone and turning the blade in its glow.

"It says Fire Magus Renia along the blade, and it looks like an activation word on the other side," he said.

Before he could argue, she snatched it from his hand and uttered the word etched along the flat of the blade, gawking as the metal immediately began to glow red hot and the air around it smelled like burnt dust. She dropped it in surprise, where it singed the decking as the heat and glow faded.

"I wouldn't just pick up random enchanted items in a foreign country and utter their potential trigger words. What if that was meant to do something worse?" Harpis warned, not expecting the brazen woman to heed his words.

"It is very pretty," she said as if the dagger would flirt back with her. After retrieving it, she looked it over before handing it back to him, handle first.

"Keep it, Sudbina. It will be better suited to keeping you safe than that cursed blowgun you keep along your calf," he said, handing her the sheath and returning his mage stone to its cloth.

"Seems to be quite effective against epically powerful bards, though," she said in a purr, and he laughed despite himself.

"We have failed Sudbina," he said, finding comfort in sharing his hopeless thoughts aloud.

"We have not failed until Zarad, and then Savja have fallen. We are returning to our friends. Do you not think they will appreciate the help of the great warrior Itka Frothbrew, Death Herald Jabruelle, and Harpis Akkeri, the god singing bard?" she questioned.

"Your list of heroes is missing Sudbina, child of the harpy and greatest muse Nysia has ever known. Perhaps you should just walk up to Konflict and ask him to leave us alone," Harpis returned.

"Promise me you will be there in the end, to face down the conquering god?" she pleaded in a voice that felt as if it could pull his heart from his chest.

Harpis sighed in resentment at the request and looked the bald woman that he had grown to see as a sister in the eyes.

"I don't know that I have the strength to keep that promise anymore," he said, hanging his head.

She slapped him across the face, and he sat up straight, staring at the worry and rage in her eyes.

"Promise!" she demanded, "You owe it to my child to make sure that she is born into a life no longer besieged by Konflict!" she finished, laying a hand across her belly and staring at him.

"I promise," he said as soon as he found the focus to speak again.

"Good," she said with finality, staring out to the sea behind them, the waters shimmering under a sky full of stars.

"When, who?" he asked, unable to restrain himself from wanting to know more.

"Azahle. He says dragon seeded children develop almost twice as quickly," she said, looking at him with a smile.

"Why did you lay with the dragon?" Harpis asked, gawking at her.

"So that I will die as more than a whore's daughter and the killer of Svenus Kalt," she replied defiantly.

"Sudbina, you are already far more than that. You always have been. You might as well be family to me, and I am sure by now, Itka and Jabruelle feel the same. You are too young to be so fatalistic about your life," he exclaimed.

"I could allege the same of you, God Singer," she said, arching an eyebrow accusingly at him.

Harpis waved a hand at her dismissively.

"I don't know if I will survive the coming month," she said quietly, and he sat up straight, looking into her eyes.

"I was just moping about Sudbina. Itka, Jabruelle, I, and all the others, we won't let Nysia be conquered," he said, feeling guilt at the fear in her claim.

"It is not the enemy that will claim my life, Harpis. It is the dragon seeded gift of the baby growing inside me," she explained.

"Bah, that's just a myth told by superstitious mothers," he said.

"I don't consider it a myth when a dragon himself warns of it," she whispered, and he leaned close, pulling her into a hug.

"Sudbina, it can't be true. I am not ready to lose any more friends," he said quietly, his voice cracking.

She pulled back from him, holding him at arm's length before speaking again.

"You can and you will. This war will not come to an end without further sacrifice. Besides, you will lose a friend but gain a daughter," she said, a tear rolling down her cheek.

"A what?" he stammered, finding it hard to breathe.

"After seeing what the sand elves did to Parafano for the greater good, I don't want my child to become enslaved or turned into an experiment. You must raise her as your own. As if she were ours. People will brush off her gifts as coming from the fabled God Singer and not see her as a fresh bloodline to be tapped for its magical gifts," she pleaded.

"Sudbina, I don't know what to say," he said, taken aback by their discussion and revelations.

"You can say thank you, Sudbina, for giving me a purpose in life that will keep me from returning to the drunken exile in gods forsaken Akriven where I found you three months ago," she said, kissing his cheek and leaning into his chest as he hugged her again.

*****

Sudbina found herself alone not long after revealing her pregnancy to Harpis as he returned below into the cabin to join the other two in exhausted slumber.

"I know you're watching," she said aloud.

A moment later, the childish figure of Enky sat where Harpis had, his feet dangling above the sea over the ship's stern.

"Turn the boat around, Sudbina. You must tell them to look in other places. The Maelar may have left behind texts in their homes or other places besides just the vault," he said in quiet exasperation.

"No," she said, smiling as he hopped up and down in frustration.

"Please, you must," he begged, and she lounged back against the aft rails.

"Why don't you just tell us the words to the song, patron of harpies? I am sure you could translate, that is, if you don't simply remember the words yourself," she said, toying with him.

"If I did that, I would bring about the very thing I am trying to prevent," he whined, clenching his fists.

"The death of innocent mortals?" she asked, presuming the truth was something far more selfish.

His lack of response confirmed that assumption as she looked at the petulant god through narrowed eyes.

"How did you come to err so badly?" she asked

"What?" he returned with his eyes open in shock at her implication.

"Why did you send us on this fool's errand? How was the powerful god Enky unaware that the Maelar texts had been destroyed?" she prodded.

"I am only capable of watching living beings. There are limits to what I can perceive through my sight. The last living being I watched in Sikef was a gnome departing the library, full of texts. Perhaps the lich your friends fought, or its pet, had something to do with the destruction," he said, shrugging before standing and crossing his arms across his chest.

"I am not permitted dominion over the goings-on of domains belonging to my sisters. I could no more watch the lich than I could a bear in the woods or a fish in the sea. Good luck in Zarad," he replied curtly and disappeared.

"That's it? No more plans to defeat your brother. We are on our own?" she asked the empty night.

"It appears that chaos is best wrought without a strategy in mind after all. Only when free of fates fetter can the marionette dance better," he whispered in her mind.

*****

Zolga pulled up to the crowded docks of Zarad and disembarked before her crew even finished tying up the *Torrent*. It had been a month since she had witnessed the tremendous power of Konflict and grasped the inevitability that seemed to surround the size of his horde. The ships had patrolled the river's length without further sightings for almost two weeks before Admiral Galanis had sent her back to Zarad with half the fleet at her back to see if they would be better used elsewhere.

She glanced at the line of galleons anchored further out to sea before heading up to meet with Aanaman and the others. When she reached the top of the city's outer wall, she found a sand elf waiting for her on Daybreak's Rampart.

"When we saw the ships on the horizon, we sent word to gather the leaders to hear word of your experience on the Astinan," the elf said.

He then motioned for Zolga to follow, leading her to a meeting room directly below the rampart, announcing her arrival, and then bowing as Zolga entered.

She ignored the large gathering waiting expectantly for her at the table. Instead, she went to the far end and wrapped her arms around Galonica before kissing the woman deeply.

"I missed you too," The high priestess said, holding her hand up and indicating for Zolga to take the seat next to her.

As she eased herself into the chair, she glared around the room, daring any of the male sand elves to show impatience.

"How has the fighting been along the eastern front?" Aanaman asked, flanked by Lorkin and General Okliff Shieldborn.

"All quiet, since we first encountered Konflict and his horde anyways," she replied honestly.

"How did your galleons fare in the fighting?" Vizier Mistis asked.

She recounted the battle on the river, particularly the terrifying power of Konflict himself and the unsettling red eyes of his devoted warriors.

"Admiral Galanis and I spoke at length in the days after that. We believe he turned north with the tens of thousands, if not more, fighters he had along the river and sought passage on the other side of the Necakan range as you expected," she said to the sand elves.

She felt Galonica clasp her hand under the table. She looked at her partner briefly before addressing the table again.

"The admiral felt comfortable patrolling the river length with his and ten other ships. So, I sailed with the other half of the fleet here. How can my raiders and our ships best serve the war effort? Galanis will send a ship if there are any sightings along the riverbank," she finished.

"Very well done and very much appreciated, Commander Zolga," Aanaman said from across the table, and she nodded in thanks at his statement.

"How did they fight?" Okliff asked, leaning forward in his seat.

"Mindlessly, General. It seems there is only one commander, and that is Konflict himself. There was no adaptation or response by the forces that engaged with us, even when it would have been simple and saved many of their lives. They appear to exercise his will and nothing more," she explained.

"We must hope that the ideal outcome is still possible until we learn otherwise," Vizier Mistis stated, turning to High Marshal

211

Araho, who stood and walked over to her with a map of the mainland.

"High Marshal Erimo should be shadowing the horde's movement as they make their way to the easy passage at the Andrefan delta by the sea. We want you to take as many dwarves and humans from Savja as possible and see what you can do to slow the enemy's progress. They'll be forced to keep their supply lines along the rockier coast as the dunes would be largely impassable for their horses," he said, indicating the coast between the mouth of the Andrefan River and Zarad.

"If they keep their supply wagons along the coast, we can easily perform hit and run raids on them to keep them tied up as long as possible. What of enemy ships?" she asked

"They may try using boats from coastal villages of Sumka to aid in their logistics, but they will be smaller than even our own and forced to keep close to land. If possible, only reveal the presence of one galleon at a time as you go. Revealing your vessels and disembarking your army all at once only once the horde has arrived here at Zarad and begun their assault," High Marshal Selarom said from his seat.

"I'll leave as soon as the galleons are restocked," Zolga said, squeezing Galonica's hand.

"You'll be taking the four recently finished galleons tied off at the docks with you. General Shieldborn will command the assault on the rear flank of the horde when the city becomes attacked. His thousand dwarves and another three thousand of our more experienced fighters will depart with your fifteen ships. Send word as quickly as you can if you spot the horde or can make contact with Erimo," Aanaman said.

"Of course," she replied.

"We will send a handful of sand elves on board the *Torrent* with you. They know the coast and the desert and will help you perform your raids. As we said, preferably keep the other vessels out of view of the coast. However, if we receive word from you that the bulk of the horde is moving down the western coast, we will send word to Admiral Galanis to return here. He would then pick up as many troops as possible and join the flotilla in preparation for the battle here," Vizier Mistis finished.

Lorkin pulled the map in front of him and glanced it over with furrowed eyebrows.

"Zolga, with your permission, Fire mage Lyrnah will join you and your raiders on the *Torrent*. She is the most battle-ready channeler besides me. Ezera and the storm priests and I will remain here to help defend the city walls. Plenty of good rock at my fingertips here," he said with a smile at Aanaman.

"It would be my pleasure to have her aboard," Zolga replied, honestly appreciative to have the talented fire mage aboard.

"Water Mage Helki will stay with general Shieldborn on your armada's second ship. His elemental is better served to support the landing in any case, and I don't want to put all our gifted in one effort," Aanaman said.

*****

Erimo sat atop his camel alongside his senior staff and their mounts as they surveyed the marshy expanse of the Andrefan River delta. He had been more than impressed by his army's ability to outmaneuver the horde in the month spent traveling along the banks of the Andrefan. He had expected them to halt at some point and try to make a turn east across the river and head for Necaka across open land. However, scouting reports streaming in from his soldiers indicated the horde had a singular direction in mind, west, towards the coast where the elves now waited for them.

"It will be some doing, them crossing. Even here, we could inflict heavy losses from a distance," Nathken offered from his right.

"I agree, but I fear we would run out of arrows and time well before we could do enough to matter. We'd then be stuck trying to outrun them with some of their forces already across the delta," Erimo said, nudging his mount into a turn with a soft tug of the reins so that he faced the handful of brigadiers and twenty-some officers.

"What word from our scouts?" he asked the commander in charge of their reconnaissance efforts.

"Sir, the group that engaged us, has swelled to at least double its number at High Pass. Our best guesses are that the horde is somewhere over two hundred thousand strong. Still, no sign of Konflict among them, nor any green-robed Necakans," the elf reported.

"I do not know whether to take it as a good or a bad sign that

213

their godly general is not amongst them and that no mages have fallen in with the horde," Erimo said, looking back to the delta.

"How far out are they?" he asked.

"They'll reach the delta the next day," the same elf responded.

"Nathken, see that you and the other brigadiers have your units ready to move by nightfall. I want to keep two days between the enemy and us until they string out along the coast. Once there, we will find ample opportunities to hamper their movement. It should take a day for them to get that many across the marshlands of the delta. Especially as the silt and mud are likely to become more treacherous with that much traffic,"

"Our forces will be ready to move out. We've only been set up for two days now. Not enough time for them to get comfortable and lazy," Nathken confirmed after a shared look with his fellow generals.

"It is time to see how the unfathomable army of Konflict deals with the immeasurable barren wasteland that is The Sea of Sand," Erimo finished.

"I'd take you with the desert as your weapon over the god of war any day," Nathken replied with a smile.

"It looks like you'll get to see if that ends up being a good wager or not, my friend," Erimo replied.

Chapter 22
Harassment

Months after first arriving awestruck at the seaside marble cliffs of Zarad, Harpis guided in their vessel without more than a passing glance at the city above. One way or another, he realized it would likely be the last time he would sail up to the stone docks. Either they would be victorious, and he would sail back to Quaj and hope never to leave again, or they would all be skeletons in the sand or worse yet, mindless subjects of Konflict.

While Itka busied herself tying them to the moorings, he glanced up at Sudbina, noting that her belly was to the point that there was no other explanation for it than the truth. He wondered if it was as apparent to others as it was to him or if he only saw it for what it was because he knew that truth. Neither Itka nor Jabruelle had said anything about it, and Harpis wondered how they and the others from Quaj would react to the news.

No sooner had they finished securing the vessel to nearly empty docks did several elven guards meet them and hurry them up the spiraling ramp to the top of the rampart and into the city to report to Aanaman and the sand elven leaders. Harpis did his best to remain stoic as he watched the disappointment on the faces of those gathered at the news that there would be no defeat for Konflict through *The Sisters' Song*.

Harpis and the others were more than thankful when Mistis quickly waved them off to take their supper with the others from Quaj. As He descended the steps from the rampart into their suite with Aanaman and his companions, Harpis looked forward to a full belly and sleep. However, upon entering the central room, his eyes lightened at the sight of Ezera and Lorkin waiting at a set table for them. He embraced Ezera and received a shoulder slap from

Lorkin as he and the others hungrily took their seats at the table like greedy children.

"I am going to eat until I pass out. After months of nothing but dried preserved fruits and freshly caught fish, this looks delicious," he said, pulling a handful of still steaming bread from the loaf on a platter before him.

After he finished chewing the first bite with his eyes closed, he looked at Aanaman.

"I expected to see more galleons at the docks. How have our naval forces fared against the horde?" Harpis asked.

"Very well. They were able to quickly repel the horde's initial attempts to cross the Astinan River to the east, forcing Konflict's army the long way around the mountain range of the country called Necaka. Unfortunately, you just missed Zolga and Galonica by a day. She resupplied here with half the armada before heading out west with half our forces, General Shieldborn at their lead," Aanaman finished, grabbing some bread.

Sudbina pouted at missing her two friends before turning the sad look to the table full of food she had yet to touch.

"What is Okliff's intent for the battle here?" Itka asked, and while Ezera explained the strategy for the city's defense and their own planned counterattacks, Harpis turned to Aanaman quietly.

"Did Zolga deliver the message from me to Kalna in Ravnice?" he asked in a whisper.

"Truth be told, I don't know, lad. If you asked her to, I presume she did, but we headed north to Tuath as soon as she arrived to debate the decision on heading with our forces. I doubt she'll have word of a response for you," Aanaman apologized, pouring them both a glass of whiskey from a bottle he brought with him and raising his cup to Harpis.

"I am glad you made it back safe from your journey and that you are at our side to face the darkness of the days ahead," he toasted, and Harpis gladly sipped the smooth golden-brown liquid that he had not tasted in too long.

"I hear there are quite the tales to be told regarding fighting your way through an abandoned city of death and fighting a lich no less!" Lorkin said, looking at each of the four companions before crossing his arm and waiting for one of them to speak.

Instead, Sudbina stood from the table after her first bite of dinner and ran to the balcony, where she promptly threw it up over the rail.

"Are you all right?" Ezer asked, standing to go to her.

"She's just had a stomach bug or something off and on for most of the trip home. Perhaps her gut was quicker to tire of our unchanging diet than the rest of us," Itka offered, resulting in a cackling laugh from Jabruelle.

Sudbina stood and faced them after cleaning her face with the napkin Ezera gave her.

"I am not ill. I am pregnant," she said, smiling as Ezera wrapped her in a hug of congratulations before placing her hands on Sudbina's belly.

"I am so happy for you! How far along?" Ezera asked her.

"Seven months now," Sudbina lied, and Harpis did his best to keep his face straight.

"You are hardly showing, you lucky wench! Why didn't you tell us? Is that why you stayed outside when we ventured into Sikef?" Itka asked, also rising to embrace her.

"Who is the lucky father? Do we know him?" Aanaman asked, turning in his chair to face the women.

"He's sitting right next to you, Aanaman," Sudbina said in a cat-like purr with a look in her eyes to match.

Harpis froze in his seat as Aanaman and Lorkin slapped his back roughly in congratulations before pouring him another glass of whiskey. Finishing the first glass, he looked up at Sudbina, and the pleading look in her eyes made all thoughts of correcting the lie of fatherhood flee from his mind. Instead, he pulled the bottle from Aanaman's hand and took another long pull. Then, as the fire rolled into his belly, he closed his eyes and wondered if it would just be easier for Konflict to kill him. Then he would not have to explain the baby to Kalna when he returned to Ravnice.

She would understand. He would tell her the secret, or at least enough of it, or figure out another way to explain that he had not been with Sudbina.

"What a lucky child to have the God Singer himself as a father!" Lorkin said with a grin at Harpis.

"And The Sleeper's Herald as an uncle," Sudbina said, walking over to Jabruelle and giving the man an awkward hug, summoning further nervous cackling from the wiry-haired necromancer.

*****

Zolga stood on the gently rolling deck of the *Torrent* as it cut its way through the calm seas off the mainland's southwestern coast. Night had fallen almost an hour ago, and tonight just like last, the flicker of lanterns and torches jumped to life along the rocky slopes. After being attacked several times for stretching out in broad daylight, the horde supply lines hunkered in a large protective circle for the past few days.

They still had to stretch out in long lines. Only two wagons abreast could make their way along the sea, but Zolga admitted it was more challenging to determine where they started and ended. Tonight though, they had to light more torches due to the cloud cover keeping the moon and starlight from illuminating the desert's edge. As soon as Zolga saw the lights, she nodded to the helmsman to guide the galleon closer to land.

"I still wish you had remained in Zarad," she said quietly and for the twelfth time in as many days, keeping her eyes focused on the shore.

"And let you have all the fun, I think not," Galonica said, and Zolga could feel her smile in the darkness.

"It is ok for you to admit you missed me, High Priestess," Zolga returned, nudging the other woman with her hip.

"Oh, it was more the prospect of spending the weeks leading up to the greatest battle the mortal plane has ever seen by being bored to death listening to arrogant sand elves plan and replan every detail of battle," Galonica replied.

"I suppose they'll find out as all do that what unfolds is likely barely reminiscent of what they planned and plotted," Zolga said.

"Maybe it is Commander Zolga who should have stayed behind to help and not the High Priestess," Galonica countered playfully.

"I am just surprised Aanaman and Lorkin were willing to part with Nysia's most devoted and gifted storm priestess," Zolga stated, blinking her eyes several times at the darkness as lantern lights came in and out of sight along the rock ridge at the top of the sloping coast.

"I did not ask. Besides, they still have seven other, more than capable, storm priests and priestesses at their disposal. Someone needs to make sure you and your raiders don't bite off more of this

218

horde than you can chew.

"Fair point made. I feel this will be the last night we hit them. If I even order an attack. We are less than a week's forced march from Zarad now, and at this point, I imagine they are close to just giving up on maintaining their supply lines and making their go for the city. I also fear the possibility of a counterattack is growing as they have begun altering their approach due to our harassment," Zolga said.

"Do you hear that?" Galonica asked, cupping her ear and leaning over the vessel's rails.

Zolga walked and joined her, straining to hear over the background of waves rolling over the rocks.

"Are those battle cries?" Galonica inquired.

In answer to their question, torch after torch sprang to life along the several-mile-long supply wagon convoy and the silhouettes of the horde's forces. They were clumsily scrambling in a chaotic response to being attacked from inland.

"Infighting?" the priestess asked with raised eyebrows.

"I doubt it. Based on what I saw on the Andrefan River, the forces of Konflict's army are dominated and mentally subjugated to the point of complete obedience, and silence. They are likely being hit by the sand elven army tracking the horde through the desert," she said, releasing her hand from the rails and turning to one of her officers.

"Have someone tell our contingent of sand elves it's time to meet up with their brethren and pass a message from home. Ready the assault boats," she said, frowning as she glanced at rocky slopes steeper than the others their phalanx had surmounted on previous attempts and with a beach that looked unwelcoming to the deep drafted galleon.

"Lieutenant High-Forge!" she shouted, and a moment later, a gruff mustached dwarf stood before her and Galonica on the steering deck.

"Commander?" he asked.

"What do you think of assaulting those cliffs? If I can even get us in close enough to land your dwarves," she asked.

"Respectfully, charging uphill on terrain like that would be risky at best without the element of surprise or concealment. Hard to maintain a shield wall going up uneven slopes in the dark," the lieutenant said, and she nodded in agreement.

"We will pester them with crossbows and arrows from the two assault boats and hope that is enough distraction for the skulls to make the beach and deposit the sand elves unnoticed," Zolga said.

She dismissed the dwarf as the sounds of two large assault boats crashing to the water and the plops of disembarking sculls surrounded them.

"I think I can provide the necessary distraction, if Commander Zolga approves," Galonica said playfully.

Zolga rolled her eyes and waved an outstretched hand at the shoreline where the sounds of battle had started to fade, and more of those guarding the supply lines seemed to be returning to the wagons.

"By all means, don't let me stop you from introducing more Nysian land-born to The Siren's rage," Zolga said.

She felt her skin prickle and her hair stand up on her nape as Galonica held her outstretched hands above her. Blue robe cuffs slid down to her elbows, and a swirl of lightning began slowly between them. No sooner than it had appeared, the lightning grew and forked and became a pillar of white-hot destruction, slamming into the front-most torchbearers along the supply line.

The beachhead turned into madness after the first strike. Wagons and those guarding them fled away from the coast and the source of the lightning. Galonica sent several more thundering strikes further inland as they fled, but they were far less effective, serving mostly as a distraction. The sculls had deposited their sand elf passengers and were rowing back from further back in the lines.

Zolga heard the mechanical clicking that signaled the assault boats had already reached the hooks along the ship's sides, their bows, and bolts ineffective as soon as the enemy turned away from the beachhead. She gave Galonica a look of thanks and turned to the helmsman.

"Turn us towards the flotilla as soon as the sculls are on board, and the assault boats are pulled out of the sea," she ordered.

*****

Erimo waited in tense silence with some of his other officers for the small raiding party to return. He had been growing more concerned with the potential for the enemy to lay a trap after their supply lines had been raided for several days. This time, instead of

220

a full-on assault and immediate about-face as he had done the past two times, he had deployed only a small force.

No scouts had brought news of the horde itself turning from its southerly course to address the attacks on its support system. Perhaps he was being worrisome, and the single-mindedness of his enemy meant they would not turn from their goal of taking Zarad regardless of how impacted their supplies got. He would soon determine whether the enemy would turn to an obvious threat. In the morning, his army would move across the sands as quickly as possible to catch the horde several days from Zarad still. He would engage them with all of his forces and tempt them into the sands in a last-ditch effort to give the city more time.

He blew out a sigh of relief as he heard a commotion from the edge of their near-silent camp, hoping it was the three thousand archers he had sent on the raid. Not long after, the three commanders of the units sent out were before him and the brigadiers.

"It went well?" he asked, and all three heads bobbed in unison before the senior of the three stepped forward.

"Your plan worked flawlessly. We crept close from three separate directions and engaged them in alternating volleys from only one of the three formations at a time, retreating randomly after firing each volley until we were out of range. It was all over in a minute or two. No elves lost. We broke cover and made our way back here as soon as they went back to tending their wounded," he reported.

"How effective were your volleys?" Erimo asked.

"It was hard to tell. The convoy was traveling with very few lanterns and torches. There was certainly a lot of chaos, but I don't know how many died from our volleys," the commander explained.

"Was there some other source of damage to their convoy?" Erimo asked in confusion at the elf's statement.

The older elf fidgeted as if trying to find words before the commander to his left stepped forward, placing a hand on the other elf's shoulder.

"Sir, the convoy was struck by lightning," the commander stated.

"Lightning? We saw no storms in the sky this evening," Nathken asked in disbelief from Erimo's side.

"Actually, the lightning came from the sea several times," the older commander replied, finding his tongue again.

A few shouts and a moment later, a handful of sand elves with the emblem of the vizier's personal guard were standing before him.

"I wasn't aware Mistis had such a lack of faith in my ability to send his personal escorts amongst my troops," Erimo said sternly, crossing his arms.

"High Marshal, we arrived from the sea. We were on a galleon from our new allies, waiting to catch sight of you and make contact. We tracked your forces through the sands from the beach," the elf explained.

Erimo tried to keep his military bearing and not smile like a child receiving a new toy at the welcome news of the vizier's plan.

"Did you happen to see the lightning that struck the supply convoy?" he asked, raising an eyebrow at his commanders.

"We did, sir. The storm priestess on board drew attention away from our arrival on the beach," the elf explained.

"A storm what?" Erimo asked in surprise.

His eyes grew, and despite himself, a smile spread across his face as the newly arrived messenger described their new allies, the navy at their disposal, and the gifted talents they brought with them. He was especially hopeful when he heard the planned welcome for the horde at Zarad and his force's role in it.

"Well done in following my troops here," Erimo said, shooting a look of agitation at the three commanders.

"Find some water and a place to sleep. We move out in the morning to catch the horde," Erimo said, dismissing them.

"Quite the plan they just outlined for us and others at Zarad," Nathken said in a pessimistic voice once the messengers had left.

"High Marshals Araho and Selarom have had months to prepare the ground around the city for the eventual siege. Also, it appears we have gained formidable allies," Erimo said.

"It would seem our new friends, or at least this General Shieldborn, have quite the mind for strategy and tactics," Nathken observed, clearly trying to goad him into admitting the same, and Erimo obliged happily.

"If we can successfully divide their forces and trap a large portion of them between us and these forces from the sea, there may be hope for Zarad after all," Erimo agreed.

Chapter 23
The Desert

Erimo was tired, his muscles ached badly, and he saw the same fatigue in his soldiers around him as they neared the end of their sleepless night spent catching up to the horde. The task was made more difficult by the horde had abandoning its attempts to stay within reach of its supply lines, embarking on a forced march for Zarad instead of a cautious one.

Regrettably, he would now have to engage the bulk of Konflict's army with nearly exhausted troops. His responsibility was to victory and Zarad, as much as it was to the elves under his command. If their feint bought even one more day for the city, if it meant one more day passed with the enslaved humans of the horde away from the food and water they had left behind, then it would be worth it. That would be one more day for the desert to take its toll. Lack of water and sun poisoning was as effective a killer as the blades, spears, and arrows his soldiers wielded.

Erimo lamented that their attack would have to be convincing enough to bait the horde from its advance. To be compelling it would mean the loss of many elves as they pretended a pitched battle against the enemy forces. The commanders and the soldiers would be responsible for keeping the elf to the left and right of them alive and seeing them through the fight to come. The burden of the losses they would suffer, the burden of victory, was a far lonelier one. One that Erimo carried himself.

Hearing the plods of Nathken's camel as it trotted up to him along their advancing column, he turned in his saddle box.

"Are we ready?" he asked, knowing he need not inquire but wanting to hear confirmation from his friend all the same.

"Our own supply lines are far enough back that if the humans take our bait, they won't stumble across our wagons. They are hunkered down under the camouflage of their cloaks, and the wagons are blanketed under tarps and sand," Nathken reported.

"Any change in the disposition or composition of our enemy?" Erimo asked one of the scout commanders.

"There is still no sight of Konflict among those ahead of us, sir," The elf answered.

Erimo took in a steadying breath and forced his fear of being ambushed by the god general from his mind.

"How far ahead?" Erimo questioned.

"Four dunes, moving purposefully south within view of the sea in an unorganized mass," the scout said, riding off as Erimo dismissed him.

"The wind has shifted," Erimo said, closing his eyes and facing inland.

"I felt it too. Some of us discussed the fateful change over breakfast," Nathken agreed.

"No sight of it yet. We will shadow the horde until it arrives. The Sea of Sands blesses our cause to pay us such a favor," Erimo said, flashing a grin.

"I'll pass the word along the lines," Nathken said, bowing at his waist from his perch atop his camel before tugging the reins and riding off to meet the other brigadiers.

They did not have to wait long for the desert to deliver its blessing. After only an hour of staying just out of sight of the horde's stragglers, Erimo began to feel a grittiness to the wind, and when he opened his mouth to speak, he could taste the dryness of unseen dirt and sand in the air. The horizon seemed to grow and move amongst the shimmering haze of the heat in the distance, and within minutes the wind began whipping cloaks and cowls.

As one, the elves cinched and tightened their shawls around their faces, covering their mouths and leaving only slits for their eyes to squint through. Then, with the front of the sandstorm now clearly visible, Erimo signaled their charge. Staying a dune behind their advance, he watched his two-thousand soldier wide formation flow over the sands like a spring flood.

Five rows of elven foot soldiers followed the first two volleys from the longbows behind them, crashing into the rear flank of the horde to devastating effect. In the span of a breath, they had pushed dozens of feet into the writhing mass of red-eyed fighters.

224

They were overextended to the point that they risked being enveloped on three sides as the horde turned as one to address the threat.

"They're pushing too far. Signal them to hold!" Erimo yelled in a muffled shout, and horns blew in response.

The inertia of the elven charge halted by his command soon began to be forced backward as the sheer force of almost a quarter-million humans pushed back and dying began in earnest on both sides.

"Daybreak forgive me," he whispered in the confines of his headscarf.

"Erimo, call them back!" Nathken shouted from beside him, the older elf shaking his head at the butchery unfolding on both sides.

"This cannot appear as just another raid!" he shouted.

He could no longer see a separation in the ranks of his soldiers. It looked like he had already lost almost a fifth of his fighters in the melee.

"Signal the archers to retreat to their second position!" he shouted, and Nathken obliged with a look of sorrow and impatience.

Erimo glanced behind to the sky-high towering wall of sand that was nearly upon them, noting the darkening of the air as it became more and more clogged with debris from the sandstorm. The three lines of archers sprinted to the tops of the dune he stood upon, drawing their boys taught as they fell in line.

"Pull them back," he said, and Nathken eagerly blew the next signal himself.

The retreat of their forces was less abrupt than he had wished as the elves did their best to pull themselves from the throng of charging and fighting humans. The elven fighters were almost halfway to the valley between the dune Erimo sat atop and the one currently being climbed by the horde. He drew his sword and chopped it in the air at the enemy as the wall of sand engulfed them, and he barely caught sight of the volley of six thousand arrows flying amongst the sand.

"Full retreat!" he shouted, and horns answered as he spun his mount and kicked it in the ribs.

His entire army would be joining him in the sprint, at least those not dead or dying. After a minute, he slowed his mount, and as soon as he felt the elevation stop rising as his camel topped another dune, he halted, slipping from the saddle and hugging its neck while tugging its reins. The well-trained animal bent and then kneeled before placing its belly onto the sand. The camel then curled its head against its body as Erimo pulled the enormous cloak-like tarp from his saddle box, draping it over the animal and him, leaving only a tiny gap to look through.

Erimo could feel the sandstorm depositing dust and sand all over the creamy tan cloth above them and once again thanked the desert for what it provided his people. He struggled to hear over the rush of the wind and the rustle of sand and dirt as it blew by, but his ears found no screams of death or clanging of blades and shields. Then, a little over an hour later, the wind let up and passed. Through his eyehole, he watched as the wall of dirt passed them by and blew out to sea.

When it was gone, he could see the endless mass of the horde milling about several dunes away, ambling about in confusion as to where the thousands of elves fighting them went. Finally, after another hour, the red-eyed humans obediently turned back towards Zarad, taking the rest of the afternoon to filter out of view.

Pulling himself from his tarp, he spent several minutes unburying his animal as he watched thousands of elves pull themselves from under the sand and dirt-covered cloaks all around him. If not for the bloody wounds on many of his soldiers, he would have chuckled at the sight of the desert birthing thousands of spear-carrying elves like a winter cactus bloom.

He sent those that were able back to the sight of the battle to bury their dead. The spot was easily found as hundreds of vultures had already begun circling overhead. In his exhaustion, he felt himself being lulled by the hypnotic circles of the scavenger birds when Nathken hastily approached him with one of their scouts.

"Tell him!" Nathken instructed, and the other elf looked up with fear in his eyes.

Erimo gave Nathken a look for his gruffness and nodded at the scout.

"High Marshal Erimo, we were perhaps a few days from here, we spotted a second red-eyed force, an unnaturally tall, black-armored warrior in their midst,"

"Konflict," Erimo whispered, and the elf nodded.

"We believe it was. We counted maybe forty or fifty thousand total among its ranks. The group he is traveling with also has several hundred green Necakan robes among it," the elf finished, and Nathken sent him away.

"He's vulnerable, Erimo, the men are tired and exhausted, but they will go where you lead them. We could end this here and now by taking him down before he joins the bulk of his forces!" Nathken stated excitedly.

Erimo wanted to agree with his friend. He knew that tired as they were, his forces could likely dispatch the force that was only double their number. On the other hand, he did not know if they would fight as mindlessly as the horde they had just faced or, with their general among them, would they prove as tactically proficient as his forces.

"And what if the god general is cleverer than the elven high marshal?" he asked his friend.

"Bah," Nathken responded, spitting at the question.

"We do not know how to fight Konflict himself, Nathken. As much as I want to lead the charge now, we would be fools not to keep with the plan brought to us from Zarad. Let us trap them against the city, break their ranks and fight the god with the magic gifts of our clerics and our allies to aid us," he said, watching Nathken's shoulders sink in disappointment.

"We will avoid Konflict's second force. At nightfall, we turn and head deeper into the sands to prepare for the end of this war," he said to his most trusted general, patting the elf's shoulder and climbing back into his saddle box.

*****

Since returning, Sudbina had become more and more bedridden, attended by elven nurses and Ezera when possible. Harpis had primarily stayed with her in the suite. He often found himself playing and singing her songs to try and distract her from the pain and aid her in falling asleep. The baby inside her was clearly taking a toll. Though her belly continued to grow, Sudbina became thinner, almost frail. It did not help that she struggled to eat or keep any food down.

When Aanaman visited that morning with High Marshal Selarom, he asked if Harpis would like to tour the defenses. He had initially refused, saying he needed to stay with Sudbina, but she

227

had threatened to shoot him with her blowgun or stab him with the knife he gifted her. Only after she promised several times not to die while he was gone had he given in and left with the sand elf and his old friend. As they walked out of the immense, foot-thick doors of Zarad's front gate, Harpis was happy for the distraction.

High Marshal Selarom walked them out almost a mile from the city, and the midday sun and furnace-like air of the Sea of Sand had him wishing he'd brought water. Selarom then turned right and began walking in an arc parallel to the curve of Zarad's cliff walls, pausing after a time and bending to the ground. The sand elf dug his hand into the sand and then pulled it up, holding a corner of cloth, revealing a hole under where the fabric sat.

"Have a look," he said proudly, and Harpis bent down, his eyes adjusting to the dark of the hole the elves had dug. He saw that it was almost as deep as he was tall, covered in buried spears, their tips facing upwards at slight angles.

"What is that stench?" Harpis said, trying not to gag as he handed the cloth corner to Aanaman, who recoiled equally as quickly.

"A mixture of scorpion venom, pufferfish bile, and camel dung we rub on the spear tips after they are buried. Kills them fast or slow," the elf said, lowering the cloth back in place and brushing sand over it.

"This is the last in a row of pits that stretches to the city walls. There are two more like it, one halfway between here and the sea on either side of the north gate," he explained, pointing with his hands at the location of the other mile-long trench lines.

"How long have you collected pufferfish bile and scorpion venom to coat so many spear tips?" Aanaman asked incredulously.

The elf shook his head, peering over his shoulder into the desert for a moment before speaking again.

"You haven't had time to explore the desert, our scorpions are nearly as long as my leg, and the pufferfish in the coastal corals weigh as much as you or me," Selarom laughed.

"Why did you dig them in this direction and not in rings around the city to slow the horde's advance?" Aanaman asked.

"Ah, because the horde is unthinking, they would just pile into the dugouts until they were full and no longer deadly, marching over the writhing corpses of their fellow subjugated man or woman towards our city. These are intended to split the army, not slow it.

228

This one here runs almost straight out from the north-facing main gate to break the army into two. It runs almost to the right side of the gate as we face it from here. The other two will similarly split the army in quarters," he said, making chopping motions with his hand.

"Three-quarters of the cliffs that wall Zarad are exposed to attack from the desert, the sea, and tallest walls are at the southern quarter," Harpis replied, shading his eyes and looking back at the city.

Selarom nodded, pointing at the sea to their right and then the western wall section closest to it.

"That is where Zarad is most vulnerable, aside from our main gate. The sand drifts that accumulate along the western facing walls rise almost half of the fifty feet to Daybreak's Rampart. If we let the horde advance on it, they would potentially be able to swarm over the top instead of being forced to attack the bottlenecks of our main gate and other much smaller side gates," the elf stated.

"That is why General Shieldborn's army and ours will assault from the sea on that side," Harpis said, beginning to understand.

"And according to the message sent from the flotilla, Erimo has been instructed to hit the other quadrant. Thus, the bulk of the army should be funneled towards the main gate and east, to the left. Erimo and your ships will pinch those here between them, driving them back into the trench line that will be in the middle of the horde forces there," he said, pointing to his right.

"Then what?" Aanaman asked, nodding in appreciation of the preparation that had been made.

"Then we fight until Konflict's hordes are spent, or our forces fail," the elf said grimly, motioning for them to follow him back towards the city after looking back towards the desert again.

"Come, the enemy will arrive in the coming days," he stated sternly.

*****

Ezera stood atop Daybreak's Rampart with Lorkin and the handful of storm priests and priestesses from Savja, their conversation growing quiet as the Exarch Vetlostis, and his clerics arrived.

"You have our most senior clerics and me at your disposal for the afternoon, Luminary Ezera," the elf said, motioning towards the other three elves and bowing to her.

"You do not need to use my formal title any more than you have allowed me to use yours, Exarch," she said.

"You had earned it, by your own admission, when you told me of your tribulations with Exarch Weksnor of Savja," he replied, and the other clerics nodded.

"Besides, we have never seen such a gift of devotion in any race besides our own. Your adherence to the old ways of priesthood in your pursuit is an appreciated divergence from the more bureaucratic clergy. Just because it is our method and the one Turin brought to Savja does not mean it is necessarily the most in line with our lady's faith," Vetlostis admitted.

Ezera brushed her blond locks from her face as she gave them a slight bow.

"We would like to see how your clerical gifts complement our own. For example, when we faced down the invasion by the Tormenta, I was able to shield our mages and necromancers from the lightning of their priestesses with my bulwark. I hoped we could practice the same to aid in defense of our forces, particularly the mages and archers," she said.

Looking over her shoulder, she noted the fidgeting Tormenta behind her. She smiled at Lorkin's stomp and severe glare that brought their attention to the present instead of their people's past indiscretions.

"We plan to assist in the coming battle, but not in the defensive way you mentioned," Vetlostis said, his jaw set in a slight grin.

"You have been blessed with spells beyond healing and our bulwark?" Ezera asked in shock at her own ignorance.

"No, we have access to the same Daybreak-given gifts as you, Ezera. We have simply perfected the use of the bulwark over the millennia, as Vicar Apwilla here will show you," the elf said smiling, nodding at the youngest of the three clerics with him.

The elf started walking away from them, stopping after close to a hundred paces.

"If you would oblige us by having one of your storm priests channel The Siren's blessing at Apwilla, she will demonstrate," Vetlostis said confidently.

Not wanting to insult the sand elves, she did not question the request and gave a look of assurance to the Tormenta, and one of the priestesses stepped forward, her hands outstretched in the air.

A second later, when the lightning arced from her fingertips towards Apwilla, Ezera gasped as it rolled off the dome of the cleric's bulwark. However, instead of dissipating, the dome of the bulwark bent upwards, causing the lighting to crash along its curvature until it appeared contained in a spherical ball. Apwilla then sent the ball of trapped lightning over the edge of the city cliffs into the desert, where it exploded in a thundering strike that formed a glass-like sculpture where it melted the desert sands.

"Stone Magus, would you now oblige us by summoning your elemental and have it charge at her?" Vetlostis said, pointing at the distant Apwilla.

Lorkin nodded in agreement, kneeling, and placing his hand on the stone.

"Mind you, be ready to release your hold from your elemental familiar. She will quickly have it neutralized and destroyed," the elf warned.

Lorkin nodded in acknowledgment as the stone beneath his hand began to grow into his wagon-sized stone bear. It thundered the ramparts as it sprinted at Apwilla until it came to an immediate halt as Apwilla stretched her arms before her, palms facing them. Then the bear's legs were forced out from under it as if an enormous unseen hand was pressing it down from above, squishing it against the ramparts.

Lorkin gasped and opened his eyes, watching as the stone that had been his elemental was crushed into powder by the collapse of the spherical bulwark the cleric had wrapped around it.

"Sleeper below me, that was impressive. I guess that means you are no longer the most gifted cleric I have ever met, lass," Lorkin chuckled, patting her back reassuringly.

Chapter 24
Intimidation

Harpis gingerly held Sudbina's hand as the woman did her best to greet and thank the well-wishers that had made their way to her bedside. Looking down at her, he had to choke back a tear at the gaunt visage of his dear friend. Itka and Jabruelle were the last to go, hugging her as she lay in bed. He watched as Sudbina kept a brave face until they walked out the door before clinching her frail fists around the pillow behind her head and pulling it over her face to muffle a sobbing scream of pain as another contraction quaked her frame.

Several panted breaths later, she cast Harpis a glare, and he returned her palm into his hand and squeezed it softly as she leaned back in the bed with her eyes closed.

"That's nice. I'll miss that. And you," Subina said, managing a tiny smile.

"Quit talking like that," he said, not sure he was even convincing himself anymore. It had been easy to believe Azahle had been wrong before. But, staring at the pain-wracked body of the woman lying next to him, he found that reassurance to be a growlingly blatant lie.

"Look what has become of the children of Kalt. You can sing to the gods. I will have rebirthed a gifted bloodline with strength unseen in over two ages, and Jabruelle is The Sleeper's Herald, even if by default," she said, choking on a laugh that turned into a cough.

Harpis couldn't help but snort at Jabruelle's expense, lowering her hand to the blanket and brushing a tear from her cheek.

"Help me sleep, God Singer. The pain is becoming too much again.

Harpis nodded and pulled his ebony violin and bow from their case, turning it over in the lantern light for a moment while watching the inlaid pearl stars come to life along its body and neck.

"Teach her to play," Sudbina whispered, tilting her head just slightly at the instrument.

"If you want her to remain unemployed and chased from taverns and inns across Quaj, I can teach her to play. Otherwise, it might be better that I ask Mahala," he said, straining for humor at the moment and cringing as she laughed again, the shakes of her body causing her to clutch her stomach in pain.

Closing his eyes, he began the lullaby he had long ago used to great effect on Aanaman's girls. For Sudbina, though, he wove his very being into the song. Notes and his gift alike caressed her mind until she was deep asleep, snoring before him. Then, after watching her chest rise and sink several times in peaceful slumber, he lay his violin and bow on the ground next to his chair and blew out a sigh of exhaustion, letting his head sink into his hands.

A gush of hot air flowed down into their suite overlooking the city from the rampart above and Harpis stared at the horizontal dance of the lantern flame clinging to life on the wick before eventually righting itself. Then, with the steady glow returned to the chamber, he noticed soft footsteps from the stairs and turned to look at the central section of their quarters, finding glinting swirling golden eyes approaching in the darkness.

Azahle came into the lantern light of the room, his silver silk robes shimmering in the amber glow. He stepped forward and lay his hands on her stomach. Harpis instinctively shot up from the chair to stop him from waking her, but the dragon's upheld hand, and something more subtle, held him firmly in place.

"Worry not, bard. I'll not wake her," he said quietly, releasing Harpis and softly sitting near her feet on the bed and motioning for Harpis to return to his chair.

"May I?" the dragon asked, extending his hand and nodding his head at the violin.

Harpis picked it up in both hands and half-rose from his seat to hand it to Azahle.

"As I approached, I could feel and see your song and gift swirling and floating out from Zarad like coils of steam from a hot spring on a cool winter morning," he said, turning the instrument over in his hands and raising an appreciative eyebrow.

"It is a beautiful tool," he said, handing it back.

"It was given to me by a good friend, gone too soon, much as she will soon be, thanks to you," Harpis said through clenched teeth. He knew better, knew that no one ever forced Sudbina to do anything she did not want to, but casting blame felt good all the same.

"She will pass into Maelara in the next day. She will do so knowing that her life has been well-lived and that she has left behind something greater than herself. Any being should be so lucky," Azahle replied calmly, unabated by Harpis' accusation.

"Easy thing for an immortal to say. You'll never have to be brought to judgment on either of those measures," Harpis returned.

"Immortal, no, just incredibly long-lived. From my vantage point, you humans benefit from an ever-present mortality to motivate you. Whereas I have nearly an eternity to misstep and falter at legacy or eulogy," Azahle said, his eyes twinkling.

"I can think of no greater legacy than helping save the mortal plane from Konflict's subjugation," Harpis stated, keeping his emotions and his gift unchecked as he did.

Azahle shook his head and smiled at the statement and the gifted attempt to convince him.

"Child of the harpies you may both be, but she is the one with a penchant for persuasion, not you, I am afraid," he chuckled softly.

Harpis crossed his arms and did his best to keep frustration from his face as he stared at the mighty creature that would not help them.

"Were I to help you fight against Konflict's forces, I would be sent back to the elemental plane from which I was born. Worse though, is the unknown outcome such action would bring forth from the gods," Azahle stated sternly.

"Worse than sending their little brother on a bloody yearlong conquest across Nysia?" Harpis asked incredulously.

"There are powers greater than Konflict's at play throughout the planes, God Singer," Azahle warned, and Harpis sat back in his chair with a defeated sigh.

"Play her that lullaby again. Let me hear and feel it up close," Azahle instructed, pointing to the violin.

Harpis picked it up, more to ensure they had not risked

234

agitating her slumber and returning her to the pain of wakefulness than to oblige the dragon. He pulled forth the Kaltese lullaby again, holding the notes around him and Sudbina with the same comfort his father's arms had given, holding him as a young child while singing the song off tune when he had a bad dream. When he finished, he saw a smile tug at the corner of Sudbina's mouth as she slept on peacefully.

Azahle stood from the bedside and extended his hand towards the violin again. Then, taking the instrument, he slowly ran his hand over its surface.

"I cannot get directly involved, and this is the last you will see of me while conquering god still walks, Harpis Akkeri, but I will offer what help I am permitted. As I flew over the Sea of Sand, I saw your enemy. Much of the horde will arrive tomorrow. The god general is not yet with it, though," Azahle said, closing his eyes and murmuring as he slid his hands over the violin.

Harpis felt the hot wash of the dragons surging gift flowing through and past him just as he had months ago when witnessing Parafano enchant Zarad's well. When he regained his senses enough, the view of the room stopped swimming in his mind and he saw Azahle handing the instrument back to him.

"It will echo with the very breath of my home plane, a zephyr to help carry the weight of your considerable voice, and a gift we can both leave behind to our daughter," Azahle said.

Harpis took the violin, feeling the hum of the dragon's enchantment as soon as he touched the ebony wood. Azahle began walking away but stopped at the door and turned, looking once at the sleeping Sudbina and then into Harpis' eyes.

"Konflict will hear your songs. Even he cannot resist the call of the winged women. Good luck, bard," he finished, disappearing up the stairs and departing with another gust of wind from his wings.

*****

It was rare for Enky to watch the same scenes for more than a few minutes, let alone days. Nonetheless, more than a week had been spent staring into the frame on his desk as he watched Sudbina experience the cost of her actions. Just above the scenes of his marionette were those frames containing views of Zarad, the

Savjan ships at sea, and the sand elven army of the desert. Just below those was the silver-framed scene of his brother.

"Is this what you have spent the past two and a half ages doing, brother?" The Siren asked sarcastically from behind him.

Enky turned in his chair to give her a severe look and to acknowledge his sisters before returning his gaze to what was taking place on Nysia.

"Is your plan unfolding as expected?" his red-haired sister continued.

"No, it has already failed," he replied without turning to glare at her.

"Then why do you still torture yourself to watch Enky?" The Wild asked in a caring tone.

"Because while my scheming failed to stop our brother as I intended, the mortals of Nysia themselves have yet to fail. Konflict has not brought order of his own design to every corner of the mortal plane, and still, armies stand to defy him. Where mortals are given free will, chaos will always have a chance," he said hopefully before deciding to turn and face his siblings.

"I don't see you doing anything to help their cause, Briny. At least I tried," he said, crossing his arms.

"I did not have to. The people of the sea have joined the other humans and sand elves in this cause just the same. What more could I possibly do?" she asked.

"Oh, I don't know, sister, you could flood The Sea of Sand until waves lapped against the very top of Zarad's walls and even the odds some," he replied, not bothering to watch the roll of her eyes.

"I wish more of my faithful were near to lend a hand. I would give as much of my gift as they could carry," The wild commented.

"Dear sister, you cannot be a mother to every living thing, especially in the desert sands," The Siren chided her twin.

"The greatest of my devotees stand atop the walls of the marble city. Perhaps they have a chance, as Enky suggests. Perhaps that means we do as well," Daybreak said quietly, and Enky and the two younger twins turned in surprise at the melancholy in the oldest sister's voice.

Don't worry, little sister. If the worst comes to pass and our brother conquers Zarad, our return to Nysia may be inevitable, but

236

at least we will be there again together," Enky said hopefully.

"Together with our order-obsessed little brother and his enslaved, red-eyed minions. I am sure he will not be mad at us for banishing him to that island prison for thousands of years," The Siren countered.

"It is worse than that. We would be trapped there with the mortals. If all mortal races have already fallen to our brother when we are cast back to the mortal plane, there will be no devotion to gain towards ascending again," Daybreak finished, hanging her head and turning her face away from them.

*****

Harpis startled awake as alarm bells tolled, their echoes rolling across the stone walls and surfaces of Zarad. He almost punched one of the two sand elf nurses standing by Sudbina's side when he first woke.

"How long have you been here?" he asked as they methodically examined and adjusted Sudbina.

"She screamed out in the night, and one of your fellow Savjans sent for nurses. When we got here, you were fast asleep. We thought it best to let you rest away your exhaustion rather than wake you," the one closest to him replied, while the other felt Sudbina's pelvis and stomach with her eyes closed.

"What is she doing," he asked nervously, quickly standing and holding Sudbina's hand.

"She is counting," the nurse replied calmly, and the other opened her eyes.

"She has a few hours yet. The contractions are still far apart," the other nurse stated.

"Your friends have headed to the front ramparts at the first sounding of alarms. The enemy must have been spotted from the walls. Will you be joining them?" the first sand elf asked.

He felt his hand squeezed slightly and looked down into Sudbina's eyes.

"Go, and then come tell me what it looks like," she whispered, her eyes closing again.

He didn't respond to her but looked questioningly at the sand elven nurses.

"Go human. Nothing will happen here for a good bit yet. You

have time to make the wall and return as she asked," the nurse stated, and he bolted out the door.

It took half an hour to reach the northern rampart over the city's main gate, where he found Aanaman, gratefully accepting a skin of water the man offered as he tried to find his breath.

"Is it here?" he asked in a labored and hoarse voice.

"Yes, and no," Aanaman replied.

Harpis peered out into the distance but wasn't sure he could make anything out in the shimmering heat haze at the horizon.

"It seems much of the horde is here, but no sighting yet of the god himself," Aanaman stated.

He then handed Harpis a looking glass. Pressing it to his eye, he closed the other and peered into the distance. Slowly sweeping from left to right, as far as he could see was an endless morass of shambling, red-eyed fighters. Many were heat welted pale folk, beat red by the sun. Some were olive-skinned, and others looked almost Quaji. The only common theme he could see besides their glowing red eyes was that they all looked like their clothes didn't quite fit or their armor was a little too large.

"They look like they are half-starved. How far away are they?" Harpis asked.

"They are not much further out than we were the other day. They quickly disappear into the heat haze even with the looking glass," Aanaman answered.

"Why do they not advance?" Harpis asked.

"I don't know. Neither does High Marshal Araho, who was up here a few minutes before you arrived. Perhaps they wait for their general. No one is sure. How is she?" Aanaman asked quietly.

"Not well. The nurses said she had a few hours until the baby will be born. I do not know if she will see the dawn tomorrow," he said, choking on the words, Azahle's observation about Sudbina's mortality foremost on his mind.

"I can't believe you slept through her agony in the middle of the night. I stayed with her and you until the nurses came. Her pained writhing in that bed may be one of the saddest sights I have ever had to witness. Go, be with her. The alarms will sound anew if they attack or Konflict decides to show himself. She should not be alone," Aanaman said somberly.

*****

Zolga stood on the *Torrent*'s steering deck with General Okliff Shieldborn, having just listened to the report given by the three Tormenta who had sailed a small sloop from Zarad. She had grown to appreciate dwarves and the gruff general especially so. They were a war-minded people like her own.

"I wish they would just move on the city. The anticipation is excruciating," she said, impatiently clutching the ship rail in front of her.

"Could be soon, could be days. Who knows how long the horde will wait there for their master to join them and order the assault on Zarad," Okliff said.

"If the message of how ragged the horde looks is close to accurate, they won't wait long. At least they'll not stay living for long in that furnace of a desert," Zolga stated.

She looked away from the city before them and at the twenty-four galleons moored together in an immense barge that held some six thousand Savjan warriors.

"Are you sure it's wise to stay within sight of Zarad? We could leave a scout boat and slip beyond the horizon so the enemy can't see us," Okliff offered.

"Konflict himself saw us at the Astinan River. I believe he would assume we will join the fray one way or another. He won't be planning on so many fighters disembarking from the ships. With us directly south of the city, his forces on the ground won't have time to react when we eventually make a turn for the city's east or west," she returned.

The dwarf respectfully nodded in agreement before heading back to the ship that acted as the headquarters for his flotilla-bound army.

Chapter 25
All Kinds

Sudbina's screams pulled Harpis from the formless nightmares that had greeted him in his stressful and exhausted sleep the past week. He was surprised and confused at the soft glow of dawn around them as he looked at the two elven nurses from the day before standing between her legs and then at Sudbina, grasping sheets in her fists as she clenched in pain trying to push the baby out.

"I guess you were wrong about her not making it through the night, dragon," Harpis whispered, hoping it wasn't the only thing Azahle had been mistaken about.

She screamed again, louder than he thought human lungs capable of screaming, and then he heard the shrill cries of a baby. The nurses wiped the babe clean, giving it an odd look before laying it on Sudbina's chest. Sudbina and Harpis looked into the child's green eyes, the same as her mother's save the glinting silver-flecks. Sudbina lay a hand on the baby, turning her head toward Harpis.

"Zalanica Akkeri," she said, squeezing his hand with her other before leaning back on the pillow, smiling as she looked up at the sky out their window.

"It's a beautiful name, Sudbina. I can't wait to tell her aunts she was named for them," Harpis said, smiling at the baby.

When he looked back at her, he noticed that her smile was unchanged, and her eyes were empty. He let out a sob as he extended his shaking hand towards her face, his trembling fingers brushing her eyelashes as he closed them. He looked to the two sand elves with tears falling from his face, and they both immediately rushed towards the baby and Sudbina. The one on the opposite side of her bed picked the baby up and reached into a leather satchel, producing a glass bottle with a thin round top that she placed in the baby's mouth as she coddled it. The other elf grabbed Sudbina's wrist, pausing for a moment and then jamming two of her fingers into Sudbina's neck before frowning and hanging her head.

"I don't understand. There is no reason she should have died," the elf said in confusion, gazing intently over Sudbina's body.

"I have never been part of human birth, but it can't be that different from the thousands of elves I have delivered. I am so sorry," the elf said, her shoulders sagging.

"The baby is oddly alert for a newborn, and something is unsettling about its eyes. Perhaps there was a complication due to some condition she was born with," The other nurse said, handing Harpis the baby and the glass bottle.

He was no wet nurse himself, but Zalanica looked much more developed than any day-old baby he could remember seeing.

"We will return with more for her to drink and linens for the baby. There are enough in there for at least the day. I will also have a cleric come perform Sudbina her rites, so long as those of Daybreak are appropriate," the nurse said.

"I will find our friend Jabruelle. I believe she would prefer those of The Sleeper. What is in the bottle?" Harpis asked.

"Camel milk, cactus milk, and spring water," the older nurse replied before the two elves exchanged odd glances, departing in hushed tones after giving him a slight bow.

Harpis watched them go, talking furtively amongst themselves before he looked back to the baby staring intently up at him.

"Maybe your mother was right to not trust the truth of your lineage to the elves or any others, Zala," he said, her name catching in his throat.

He was only able to keep from weeping for fear of sending the baby into inconsolable cries herself. He lay the swaddled infant next to her mother and drew his violin.

"Your uncle can perform the official ceremony, but I think I would like to send her soul to The Sleeper myself," Harpis said, smiling with lips that tasted of salty tears.

He lay the violin gently on his neck and reverently played *The Sleeper's Serenade*. He kept the goddess's true name from the lyrics and his gift from the song. The enchantment from Azahle made the violin sound as if it were crying for him while he pulled

241

the notes from its strings. Harpis played the woefully sorrowful lullaby as softly as he could. Holding the bow tight and dragging the last note forth, he watched the baby peacefully close her eyes and her blanket rise and fall as she breathed in innocent slumber. When the Alarm bells of Zarad rang out a moment later and the baby's eyes snapped open, he felt his skin flush in panic. The elves had not returned to help him, and Harpis knew he needed to get to the city gates if he was to play a part as Sudbina had demanded. He grabbed the satchel full of clinking bottles and linens, held the baby against his chest, and took the stairs up to the rampart three at a time.

*****

Harpis was amazed that the infant had fallen back asleep as he tried not to bump her against his chest while he walked as quickly as possible across the rampart to where Aanaman had been. He didn't know if he should be worried or relieved at the baby's return to slumber.

Reaching the rampart overlooking the front gate, he found Aanaman standing alone. Ezera, Lorkin, Jabruelle, and Itka huddled with the sand elven clerics off to one side. The High Marshals and several other senior officers stood with Vizier Mistis not far away. As he joined Aanaman at the wall, the greying red-haired former farmer shook his head, staring out at the distant horde.

"Never in my life would I have imagined I'd end up half a world away from my fields, staring down a god and his army from an elven fortress city," he said, turning to Harpis, throwing his hands in the air as his eyes widened in surprise as they looked upon the baby.

"Harpis, you can't have a newborn baby out here!" he shouted, drawing the attention of their companions who rushed over.

"Her name is Zalanica Akkeri," he whispered.

Each of them glanced down at the child in wonder and then slowly lifted their gazes to meet Harpis' eyes as he fought to hold back further tears. Their joint pain was an expected one. They had all been in and out of Sudbina's room over the past week. Still, it was difficult to accept the finality of Azahle's premonition. They

242

shared a moment of silence upon the ramparts for the passing of Sudbina.

That silence was rent by the distant rumbling thunder of the horde as they began their charge and the clanging of bells across the city and blaring of horns around the rampart. Staring out at the hundreds of thousands of humans and the black-armored general in their midst, Harpis knew his place was between them and Zala. He extended her towards Aanaman, who instinctively took the bundled and now awake but silent baby.

"What are you doing? Why am I holding her?" the older man asked in shocked surprise while Harpis slipped the satchel with linens and clinking bottles over his shoulder.

"I will figure out how we deal with that," Harpis said, pointing at the immense armored god wading through its army.

"I don't trust her with the elves. Keep her safe until this is over, Aanaman. Consider it as making us even for you having me kidnapped and brought to this cursed continent in the first place," he said so only his friend could hear as the rampart and city came to life.

Aanaman begrudgingly started walking back towards the southern part of the city.

"I'll be waiting for you in your quarters. They're closer to the docks should this not go as you intend, and we are forced to flee," the chancellor replied grumpily before changing his expression as he looked intently down at the child in his arms while departing.

Harpis and the others spun around to see the horde covering the desert ahead and on either side for as far as he could see. They came in a steady mindless advance, not even bothering to turn their heads towards those that found the spear pits as they moved forward. As they marched towards battle or died in the pits, not a one screamed out in excitement or agony. It was like a black funeral veil was being quietly drawn across the desert as they closed.

The sand elven High Marshal had been right. The horde cared not to avoid or swarm over the trenches. Instead, they just pushed forward towards the circular marble fortress. One comfort was to be found as they surveyed the encroaching enemy and found no dwarves, trolls, or wood elves amongst the red-eyed attackers. Konflict had swung south with his human horde to come for the sand elves first. Though they all would have preferred to fight alongside the other races of Nysia, not having to fight against them was no small thing. Thirteen months after he had played a part in waking the god, Harpis set his jaw to face it down.

The swarm-like hum of thousands of longbows loosed at once filled the air, and then they flew like a small silent cloud, casting a shadow that moved from the ramparts down into the writhing mass of Konflict's army nearing the walls. The elves need not even aim, so thick with bodies were the flats surrounding Zarad, but aim they did, resulting in devastating losses. Looking to either side, Harpis noticed that each elf had a huge wicker basket of arrows next to them with a shoulder sling in case they needed to move.

The plentiful supply had him questioning the slow cadence of volleys called forth by the officers commanding the ten battalions of archers.

"Are they trying to preserve ammo?" he yelled to High Marshal Araho, who had walked their way.

"No, we are trying to lull them into confidence before we launch the counterattacks," the elf said, surveying the death below with a grim look.

Arrows rained down and took lives by the thousands, and still, the horde pressed in, almost to the walls. Their rear ranks were finally within view, perhaps a hundred paces closer than the furthest spear pits. Harpis shook his head in horrified awe as the red-eyed fighters quietly stepped on or over the injured or dying.

The horde now encircled the three-quarters of Zarad not bordered by the sea. It was odd watching the momentum of close to three-hundred thousand warriors halt with a single-mindedness possible only through the solitary command of their godly general. Harpis was still amazed as the evenly distributed longbow units kept up a devastating but steady pace of fire as fighters from below were attempting, and largely failing, to scale the fifty feet to the top of their walls.

"There's no logic to it. If they simply stand below these walls, the only way they will take this city is if the elves run out of arrows," Itka said, standing on her tippy toes to look down.

After a second, she quickly ducked as an arrow haphazardly flew up from the crowd below, passing over their heads and landing harmlessly in the city beyond them on the lazily raised shield of a sand elf foot soldier. Twenty battalions of elves carrying spears and shields with sabers on their hips were stationed throughout the city and along the ramparts under the command of High Marshal Selarom. They stood ready to react to any perimeter breach or carry out a necessary counterattack.

As if in response to Itka's questioning of the attack's logic, several fireballs flew up from red-eyed, green-robed Necakan members of the god-dominated fighters. They were slow-moving and cast from deep within the enemy ranks. They rocketed up into the rampart and crashed down in the middle of where several archery lines had stood moments before.

The fireballs continued and grew in frequency as subjugated mages began casting them in earnest. Unfortunately, they were not the only gifted among Konflict's forces, as an unseen burst of wind from an air mage knocked several elves to their deaths, blowing them from the rampart back into the city's stone streets below. Heeding the magical threat, Harpis, Jabruelle, Itka, Ezera, and Lorkin huddled a bit closer to the front wall of the rampart.

Leaning against the stone, Harpis felt the shudder in the marble like giants began hammering the stone walls from outside. Jabruelle stuck his wiry-haired head far over the rampart, looking straight below them and pulling himself back to give them a look of concern.

"Stone mages, they are molding the stone at the base into wedge-like pillars and crashing them again and again into the base of the rampart," he said fearfully.

"You two want to do something about that, maybe?" Ezera asked the necromancer and mage.

Xissay appeared over Jabruelle's shoulder, and even the battle frenzied undead familiar was wide-eyed at the destruction. Several more fireballs came hurtling over the ramparts, and a small tornado touched down to the west, shredding several elves and sending many more flying off both edges of the marble rampart.

"I'd be careful, lad, if she flies down there and gets crushed by a stone mage or something, you're apt to go mind lost," Lorkin said, putting his hand on Jabruelle's shoulder.

The necromancer and mage did not have the chance to try their luck as dozens of sand elven clerics rose to the edges of the ramparts behind a handful of shields bearing warriors. Arrows and crossbow bolts from below skipped harmlessly off raised shields, and the clerics went to work neutralizing the green-robed enemy mages.

Some of the mages were simply crushed into bloody green cloth balls as clerics identified them and ensorcelled them in a spherical bulwark, collapsing it around them. The five of them collectively cringed at the sight of the effective, if not perverse, use of Daybreak's gifts. Their mouths then hung agape, awestruck as the more experienced clerics joined in the magical fray.

Several immense fireballs floated up from below. But, instead of crashing into the ramparts, they were turned and molded midair after colliding with clerical bulwarks. The raging maelstrom of the fire mage was sent back into the horde, killing the female mage that sent it and dozens around her. The thrum of giant stone hammers, too, had stopped. Curious, Harpis looked down over the wall to see elemental stone pillars being crushed under bulwarks, their heavy pieces falling onto masses of fighters squirming beneath them.

The handful of Tormenta priests came running up to them a moment later. The eldest and only woman among them spoke directly to Lorkin.

"Stone Magus, we came as soon as we felt the pull of magic raging. Shall we join in the fray?" she asked excitedly.

"Not yet. Let's not reveal all our tricks at once, eh? And the clerics seem to have dealt with the presence of mages below."

Harpis noticed that after the first few minutes of action, there were indeed no more sensations of others channeling their gift prickling at the edges of his senses, and no more was the rampart under siege from fire, air, or stone. The Savjans all turned at once and Harpis felt a huge summoning from Exarch Vetlostis and his three Vicars. They were standing over the north gate, palms outstretched and eyes closed in concentration.

"Who're they after?" Itka asked, following the gaze of the gifted folk around her but oblivious to the fact that Harpis could feel the very air tingle with the use of Daybreak's gift.

"Konflict," Ezera gasped, pointing at the glinting black-armored figure progressing towards the city.

The god's footsteps faltered for a moment, and then his feet sank several inches into the sand as if he was under immense weight. His head bent slightly, and his shoulders sagged under the pressure of the four bulwarks pressing against his very being. Then, slowly and deliberately, Konflict raised his right arm over his head to hold off the bulwark. Meanwhile, his right hand began a struggle to tilt his spear upright before slowly pushing it upwards above his head.

Ezera fell to her knees next to them, and Lorkin grabbed the cleric, hauling her back to her feet and smacking her face.

"Let go of it!" he shouted, and the blond woman's eyes snapped open to the shrieking wails of the four sand elven clerics. Harpis could feel the piercing tip of Konflict's spear sundering their joint bulwark.

Below, the god looked straight at the four mindlessly crying elves, pumping his arm in a mighty throw. His spear flew straight and level, not arcing in the slightest as it hit Exarch Vetlostis so hard that the sand elf was thrown from his feet into one of the Vicars, sending them back over the edge of the wall to their deaths. Before they even hit the ground, Harpis watched the black spear disappear.

He turned back to the rampart and the other two clerics as several of the shield bearers around them tried to stop their raving, and the spear once again flew in from the desert before them. It took one of the vicars through the chest, crashing into the stone walls and disappearing again. The odd blackish-red blood-like liquid dripping as it soared through the air landed on the last vicar and one of those holding up a shield. It burnt them like lava, scorching holes in their bodies and leaving black smoke curling from their lifeless bodies.

"We must find out a way to do something about Konflict. Zolga said he had turned their battle at the river in mere moments, but I have never seen the likes of that display," the mage said, and Harpis could not agree more, though how they might do that, he was unsure.

"The numbers alone make this fight a nearly impossible one. If he continues to have his way with the defenses, we will be done within the hour," Itka confirmed.

"I have an idea," Harpis said, looking around at his friends and the Tormenta storm priests that had joined them.

"Well, spit it out, God Singer," Lorkin said, pulling the cynosure that let him focus his spell casting from his robes.

"We will fight him," Harpis said, realizing as the words left his mouth how stupid they sounded.

"Oh, well, that's easy, you all wait here, and I'll just go deal with him then," Itka said, rolling her eyes as she pulled her maces from her belt loops.

"I don't know how we will get his attention, let alone keep it without becoming target practice for slung spears," Ezera added.

"Go and get as many of the sand elven clerics as will come with you and meet us down below," Harpis shouted, checking his boot for the dagger he found in Sikef and holding his violin case from bouncing around on his shoulder as he ran.

Chapter 26
By land and sea

Erimo sat in stunned silence, looking out at the breathtakingly terrifying visage of Zarad encircled on all sides by the endless mass of Konflict's horde. As Vizier Mistis' messengers had said, he could see two of the three trench lines meant to separate the enemy army into four sections. Half a mile to his right was the beginning of the line of pits closest to the sea, and half a mile to his left was the one that ran right into Zarad's north gate.

Even with the losses they had already suffered, the quadrant of the battlefield he would be responsible for still contained what looked like at least forty or fifty thousand enemy fighters. Being outnumbered three to one did not concern him. Especially if the allied forces from the sea were victorious and so long as the god stayed preoccupied on Zarad's north or east.

What worried Erimo was getting flanked or enveloped due to the sheer mass of their enemy. He and his brigadiers had planned out what he hoped would keep them tactically sound throughout the fight and maximize the amount of damage they could inflict. They had even discussed potentially boxing in their quadrant with lines of foot soldiers.

They would try to use their archers and slowly advance towards Zarad with the enemy trapped between spear-filled trenches on two sides, a marble cliff before them, and the elves at their rear. Erimo felt there was a danger that any number of forces could be sent around the back ends of the other pits and flank their rear as they tried. His elves would be strung out in thin lines, attacked on both sides if that happened.

Erimo knew there would be no help from within Zarad as High Marshal Araho and Selarom focused on defending everything from the north gate east into the sea. They needed to minimize the effect of the horde's numbers and hope to last long enough or kill enough to link up with the Savjan forces that were to land on the beach.

A red flag was hastily strung up on a pole atop the ramparts, signaling him to send in his forces, and he obliged by drawing his saber and waving it in several circles above his head before pointing it forward. He had lost several thousand elves in his skirmishes with the supply lines and the battle in the desert. Still, five thousand archers, eleven thousand foot soldiers, and almost a thousand camel-mounted lancers followed him down the dunes towards the flatlands around Zarad.

He stayed at the tip of what became a triangular formation, its point heading straight towards the distant wall of Zarad. One side slanted back from him towards the southern end to stay in contact with the edges of the spear pits. The natural advance of their formation would brush those between its angle and the pits into them. The tactic would allow them to maximize their use of the trenches.

They made slow progress but brutally pushed their way into the horde and advanced towards the city as the enemy fell before them. Sand elven spears probed and danced along more clumsily wielded weapons by gaunt, red-eyed fighters of the horde. He could tell he had successfully gotten the attention of those in his part of the battlefield as even those enemies closest to Zarad's wall gave up on assaulting it and turned to meet his army.

The flat rear of his triangular formation had passed through the initial lines now and he found his forces surrounded on three sides. Nodding to Nathken, he intently watched as the elf blew a signal horn. His soldiers started flank march, driving the tip of the triangle he was commanding towards the pit of spears until one side of his army was flush with the trench line. The enemies caught between were either forced into the poisoned spears of the holes or killed by his fighters.

He raised his sword above his head again, flicking it in a line back and forth towards Zarad, and several more horns blew. The elven foot soldiers from the side that now sat along the pits moved to bolster the two sides of the triangle that were fiercely fighting the crush of the horde. Once they were in place, the formation scraped along the trench line towards Zarad. If he could get to the city wall, he could make a single line of foot soldiers with archers behind them. They'd then have the trench on one side and Zarad's marble wall on the other to keep them from being surrounded.

He had his archers alternating where they focused their volleys to avoid his soldiers being simply pushed into the pits by the crush of tens of thousands of humans. They aimed deep into the enemy ranks to slow forward momentum in places where he saw his lines bulging inwards. He turned to see the few ranks of elves ahead of him were nearly spent, and the triangle point that ended with him at the trench line was getting squished backward as the elves tried to push closer to the city that was still several hundred feet away.

"Signal a charge on me!" he shouted to Nathken, who drew his saber and signal horn. The archers behind them parted as the camel mounted calvary with longer spears gathered around him. After a moment, Erimo drew the silver High Marshal horn from his tunic and blew as hard as he could before kicking his camel in the ribs.

He led the charge of thundering hooves on sand that turned to stomping on flesh and bones as he pushed the corner of his formation into the walls of Zarad. He grimaced and nearly fell from his saddle box as an ax blade clipped his calf while his camel trampled a red-eyed fighter between him and the marble wall. Then, he turned his riders left and cleared enough of the enemy for his formation to fall in between the wall and pit as they'd hoped.

He watched proudly as his elves surged behind the camel charge, forming a long singular front between the two defensive barriers, and began killing in earnest. The air stopped humming with angry arrows as his archers spent their last, drawing their swords and switching out with the tired and wounded at the front.

"That doesn't look so good, Erimo," Nathken said, riding to his side and pointing at the calf wound.

Erimo frowned at his tan trousers, stained dark red by his own blood. He pulled his sword belt from around his waist and placed it below his knee, twisting and knotting it several times while trying not to bite his tongue off in pain.

"I'll be fine, Nathken," he said through gritted teeth.

*****

Zolga and Galonica stood atop the bow of the *Torrent* as it sped towards the beach. Ahead, forty thousand enemy fighters were between the coast and the trenches dug a mile behind them. Zolga couldn't see them, but she knew they were there because there was a gap in the horde before her and those engaged by the elven army that had just charged in from the desert.

Behind her were two lines of ships. Six would beach themselves on either side of hers. The second line would tie to those as Okliff Shieldborn's army would flow from them once her raiders secured the initial beachhead.

"I did not expect to be greeted by mages. This could be a problem," Zolga said.

Galonica and fire mage Lyrnah beside her agreed as they watched a dozen green-robed humans wade into the shallows. Where they plunged their hands into the water, huge roiling elementals made of seawater took shape and began heading out to meet the *Torrent* as it neared the beach. Several others started huge sweeping motions, and Zolga felt the ship roll under her feet as rogue waves summoned by the mages slammed into the ship.

Lyrnah pulled her fire striker, flint, and oil from her robe, but Galonica grabbed her wrist.

"Save it to protect Zolga when they make the beach!" The Siren's high priestess shouted.

Zolga watched in shock as Galonica winked at her and her fingers bent out like claws from her outstretched hands, and a thick fog wall formed ahead of their vessel. Then, while maintaining the enchantment that obscured their boat, she let her hands fall until her arms were held out on either side, her head snapping back in a scream.

A dark cloud formed over the *Torrent* and moved out over the beach. Once there, it began raining down lightning bolt after lightning bolt, thundering the beach with the boom of their discharge. Zolga looked into the wide-open eyes of her lover and saw the flicker of lightning shimmer across them as strike after strike pounded the sands. She could not tell whether the flashes in Galonica's eyes were a reflection of the storm she had summoned or the source of it.

A moment later, Galonica collapsed in her arms and her eyes closed. The fog before them faded, and Zolga saw that they were nearly upon the sands. She handed Galonica to the helmsman.

"Get her safely to my cabin!" she shouted, grabbing one of her officers.

"Signal the assault!" she yelled, sprinting to the rail and jumping off the ship's side. She landed in one of the narrow raider sculls with her trident in one hand and a weighted net in the other.

Pointing ahead, she let out a savage scream and felt her leg muscle flex to keep her upright as oars snapped in and out of the surf, propelling them forward. She glanced behind her at the other galleons, still several minutes from the beach, and then at the beach full of tens of thousands of half-starved, red-eyed human fighters. She was thankful for the glassy melted sand spots where enemy mages had been, whispering thanks to Galonica before standing tall at the bow of her boat as it slid onto the sand.

"Tonight, we may find ourselves at The Sleeper's bosom!" she screamed, and her seven crew and those of the other ten sculls shouted in response.

Zolga waited for no one. She sprinted straight at the nearest enemy, burying her trident in the man's red eyes before sidestepping a lazy stab from a spear. She and the eighty raiders from the sculls found themselves immediately pressed back by the crowd of Konflict's forces despite the lack of combat skill among them.

She lost her net as well, using it to slow the chop of several swords to her right as she rolled to her left. Then, drawing her rapier, she began parrying and stabbing desperately to slow the advance as the enemy fell dead or writhing silently around them. Suddenly they were joined by the forty dwarves of the *Torrent's* phalanx, and the lighter armored boat crews fell in behind the shield wall as she signaled their retreat towards the sea.

Glancing at where the galleon was beached behind her, she saw her two assault boats carried onto the sand and flipped upside down. Her forty archers stood upon the hulls, firing as rapidly as possible to slow the fighters just beyond the dwarven shield wall. She let her forces fall back until they were before the archers and then halted them. The dwarves and raiders were killing the enemy as fast as they found the red-eyed fighters standing before them but the crush of their numbers was beginning to make even swinging a sword difficult.

She had lost several raiders, and a few wounded dwarves had been pulled from the front. Her archers had run out of arrows, drawing their weapons, and fighting off the flanking enemy on both sides of the shield wall. Zolga was about to order them back onto the galleon when a fire elemental in the form of a winged Pegasus began sweeping back and forth in front of them. Just feet off the ground, it scorched and maimed enemy fighters by the dozen with each pass, lighting many of them ablaze and carving a gap between them and the enemy. The dwarves quickly advanced into the space to give them more room to fight effectively.

Zolga nearly decapitated a red-eyed fighter with a crushing sweep of her rapier that bent its blade sideways. Then, already off-balance from the strike, she was almost knocked from her feet as twelve galleons crashed into the beachhead. The other thirteen ships broadsided their sterns from behind. A moment later, Water Mage Helki's house-sized seawater elemental in the shape of a giant crab began decimating the nearest enemies. As it went, it cleared a space between them and the red-eyed attackers before fading into a puddle on the sands. Within seconds, the chaotic mob on the beach was beaten back. In its place there was now a dwarven shield-wall a thousand shields wide with four ranks of experienced Savjan soldiers behind.

She saw General Shieldborn standing on one of the assault boats her archers had used for cover, and she climbed up beside him.

"You're the dumbest or the bravest fighter I've ever seen," the gruff dwarf said, shaking his bald head.

Looking out at the carnage on the beach and her raiders that made up the center of the Savjan formation, Zolga wasn't sure she could argue either accusation. The enemy continued to push toward them. So much so that there was a two-hundred-foot-wide gap between their rear lines and the spear pits. She could barely make out the immense elven line running at an angle from the city wall, a third of the way down the trench on the other side.

"Should we push towards the elven force?" she asked Okliff.

"Not yet. They may not be able to push us back any further, but we are outnumbered almost ten to one. I'd rather let them keep crashing against the shield wall until our archers on the ships run out of arrows," he said, and Zolga agreed as she watched volley after volley rain down from the beached galleons towering behind their army.

*****

254

Aanaman held the once again sleeping baby close to him as he took in the spectacle that was the battle for Zarad. He watched proudly from the rampart above the quarters as the Savjan galleons made the beach and established a hold on the coast.

"Your namesakes are the scariest women I have ever met," he whispered to the baby, shaking his head at what he knew to be Galonica's display of The Siren's wrath. The crazed charge of Zolga and her two hundred raiders to a beach crawling with tens of thousands of Konflict's fighters had him holding is breath in suspense.

He had a clear view across the city and could even make out some of the battlefields beyond its rampart. It looked to him as though the forces from the sea and those from the desert proved quite effective. Konflict's troops between the two trench lines to Aanaman's left were no longer engaged with forces along the ramparts. Instead, they faced the threat from the sea and the elven army outside the walls.

He heard several horns blown and a bell clanging. Ten battalions of archers had been spaced out around the city's walls. They moved into formations closer to his right, where the sand began, and the sea ended around the city's eastern rampart. There, he had watched slow and prudent volleys fly forth at the onset of battle. Aanaman now shook his head in wonder as ten thousand elves fired at will from condensed formations into the small section of the battlefield by the sea.

He couldn't imagine that anything on the ground where they were aiming could hope to live, but he wondered if it was wise to focus on the other seaside edge of the walls and not lay down clouds of arrows across Konflict's army. The elven army was still standing ready in the battalion formations across the city. However, as another bell rang out, Aanaman watched on, impressed as half of them rushed to where the archers compacted into a along the coastal portion of the eastern wall not far from him.

Suddenly, the archers started arcing their volleys further into the enemy as the foot soldiers reached them. Each battalion threw dozens of coiled ropes over the rampart's edge. Spear-carrying foot soldiers would reach the ramparts edge, throw their spear into the horde below and then slide down with a shield slung on their back and a sword on their hip.

His gaze went to the city's north as he heard what sounded like thunder strikes from outside the gate. Horns blew, and the remaining elven battalions massed into one formation as wide as the city gate, heading for the shaking Iron portal.

Chapter 27
The last finale

Harpis flinched as another of Konflict's spears slammed into the foot-thick iron doors of Zarad's north gate, shaking the ten-foot-tall gates. He turned from the door and looked back at the thousand ranks deep column of sand elves behind them until the heavy plodding of Lorkin's immense stone bear drew his attention to the dwarf standing atop it.

"If this gets me killed, I am finding you in the great dream and pummeling your soul for the rest of eternity," Itka said, her legs barely able to straddle the rocky neck of the stone elemental.

"Oh, don't worry, if this goes badly, I think you'll have to get in line," Harpis replied, pulling his violin from its case.

Craning his neck to peer up at the rampart above the gate, he found Ezera's eyes after shielding his own against the sun with his hand.

"Are they ready up there?" he asked.

"As ready as they will be," the blond cleric responded, disappearing back towards the front of the gate.

He could hear the scratching and grating of the enemy's weapons and hands as they tried to claw mindlessly through the thick iron. He raised an eyebrow at Jabruelle as the man busied himself, brushing dust from his robes and fidgeting while Xissay floated impatiently over his shoulder.

"It was good getting to see you again, dear Xissay," Harpis said, and the undead fire sprite floated over and slapped him gently on the cheek.

"Don't go dying out there, bard. The gnome won't forgive us if we show up to join him at The Sleeper's side anytime soon," she finished, and Jabruelle cackled and winked at him.

"A great many souls are sent to The Sleeper this day!" he said excitedly.

"Don't stay with us overlong, Lorkin," Harpis said to the bear, and the great stone head bobbed up and down once.

Harpis looked to the scores of elves that stood ready and held his hand up, waiting. As soon as another spear shook the gate, rattling the bolts and hinges that held them to the marble archway, he dropped his hands, and the gates flung inward under the press of the horde outside. Their momentum came to an almost instant halt as Lorkin's elemental blew through their forward ranks, charging straight ahead towards the obsidian armored behemoth that was Konflict.

Harpis stood in the middle of the archway with Jabruelle as the elven foot soldiers sprinted past them, five-wide on either side. Nimble and agile as any man could hope to be, they flooded like a possessed wind out from the gate. Harpis poured his gift into the strumming chords of *Panoryla's March*. The song enveloped the entire elven army, hastening their footstep, heartbeats, and the thrusts of their spears and slamming of their shields against red-eyed humans.

In only a few minutes, the last rank of elves rushed past, fanning out in a massive counterattack that ballooned the front of Konflict's forces back in a bulge that went from one trench to the other. The gates closed behind him, and Jabruelle walked off to the side and began picking and choosing corpses to reanimate, using them to help keep enemy fighters from them. Harpis stood alone in the archway of the north gate, gazing out at the mayhem before him. The iron behind him and the curvature of the archway overhead acted as a giant amplifier for the notes of song streaming forth from his dragon enchanted violin.

He kept on playing even though the instrument hummed and vibrated with so much gifted and enchanted power that he thought it would turn to splinters in his hands. Lorkin's familiar and Itka atop it had stopped a dozen paces ahead while they waited for the perfect moment. They hoped the ten thousand elves pushing the god's forces from the main gate would draw the deity's attention. They quickly found their assumption to be terrifyingly correct as he pumped his arm repeatedly, taking out several elves at a time.

Itka turned and gave him a grim nod before leaning towards the bear's head to shout to Lorkin. Harpis did not miss a beat, continuously looping his rendition of *Panoryla's March*. Without stopping his song, he began weaving and flowing the entirety of his gift towards only Itka instead of across the battlefield.

*****

Itka could feel the roar of adrenaline and blood coursing through every sinew in her muscles as she flexed her arms and legs, almost lightheaded from the effect of Harpis' focused song. With her elemental bear mount speeding towards the glinting black-armored giant that stood almost double her height, she was less sure of her decision to be the one to keep the god's attention off the rest of the soldiers around them.

She saw the void like vizor of Konflict's helm turn her way, and she sprang up to her feet, keeping perfectly balanced as the stone haunches of the bear rumbled beneath her. A moment later, she dove from the bear's shoulder as the god's spear soared through the air, barely missing her feet as she sprang from the mount. She came up after a roll, maces in hand, and began sprinting impossibly fast at the deity but not faster than the elemental.

Lorkin's stone bear crunched into the outstretched armored forearm of the god. The impact drove the god's feet into the sand so far, the toes of his boots were covered. It was then that Itka played her part, screaming at the armored god as Lorkin guided his bear beyond it to keep any of the possessed humans from attacking her while she taunted and battled Konflict.

Running as hard as she could at the god, she was glad for the lack of armor that let the decades of training under her uncle Braffen serve her well. Not like the steel plate breastplate would have stopped the god's weapon anyway. She barely dodged another spear as Konflict's arm pumped her way. The spear had just again appeared in his hands when she leaped in the air and struck him square in the chest with both of her maces as hard as her bard-empowered arms could swing.

The god took a half step backward from the strike, and she noticed a tiny scoff on his onyx breastplate.

"Now or never," she growled to herself, pointing one of her maces at him.

"May The Siren strike you down!" she screamed.

No sooner did the title of the goddess leave her lips did she feel the hair on her nape and arms stand on end as bolt after bolt of lightning rained down on the god from above.

Konflict gave a slight shiver as he shrugged off the initial volley of lighting. She took the opportunity to put even more distance between them. The god threw another spear as he walked her down, and she barely got out of the way, springing into a backward flip and then rolling to a kneeling stop.

"That's right, you big oaf, keep following me around while they blast you to pieces," she snarled, standing and pointing a mace again at Konflict and again lighting forked from the sky, turning the sand around him to glass as his black-plate boot stomped through it and kept after her.

"Now for the fun part," she whispered.

She watched as Konflict raised his arm again, spear pointed her way. The god was about to throw when Lorkin's circling familiar slammed into him from behind.

Konflict staggered forward and turned towards the fleeing elemental, raising his spear arm. Itka was on him in an instant. Sped along by bard-given haste and endurance, she slammed her mace heads hard into the tops of the god's armored feet, showering herself in sand.

She felt her blood go cold as she found herself in the shadow of the behemoth, looking up into the blackness of his helm's visor. He opened his hand to grab at her, and she activated the enchantment of The Stones of Fjall, and her mace heads crunched down, flattening the top of the god's boots to the bottom, holding them fast to the ground as she rolled away. She smirked in disbelief that the bard's idea had worked so far.

Her joy was short-lived as Konflict waded forward, a sickening pop and tearing of flesh coming from his ankles. He simply walked forward, pulling his legs from his trapped feet, trudging onward on black-armored stumps.

"Sleeper below us," she cursed as the god's arm hurled his spear at her.

She thought she had dodged in time, but her speed was difficult to judge with Harpis' melody flowing through her, and the spear nicked her shoulder. Itka had been wounded countless times. Cut, stabbed, bludgeoned, and slashed, but none of those pains matched the searing burn of the wound left by the spear. She

260

looked in horror at her shoulder as lavalike droplets turned her skin to ash and burned through her. She gasped then as she felt an odd warming sensation and her flesh regrew and then melted away again as the clerics on the rampart fought to heal the lingering wound.

It was pure agony as she watched her shoulder rot down to the bone and then almost return fully to normal, back and forth as over a dozen of Daybreak's clerics and Ezera tried to keep the dwarf from being consumed alive. She almost blacked out and found it impossible to run under the burning pain. She fell backward and began scooting with kicks of her legs and pulls of her other hand. She felt as though she were swimming in the sand to try and escape the approach of inevitable death as Konflict did not throw his spear. Instead, he was pointing it menacingly her way as he lurched forward on the remnants of his legs.

Her vision was a blur as she continued to fight for survival, and her shoulder continued to flood her with waves of pain. Still, she saw the indistinguishable form of Lorkin's familiar come between her and the god, rearing on its hind legs and charging in. She watched, tears flowing down her face as the stone claws of the bear hopelessly tried to rend the god's black armor while over and over Konflict stabbed into it with his spear.

She heard a guttural dwarven scream from the ramparts, and the wagon-sized stone bear melted away into nothing more than pebbles, and she realized that even if the clerics could keep the spear's wound from eating her flesh, from her bones, she would soon find herself with Konflict's sister.

*****

The scream from Lorkin as the dwarf's mind shattered into a thousand pieces pulled Harpis from weaving his gift, and he stared terrified as Konflict waded slowly through the sand at Itka, the lightning raining down on him growing more sporadic, having little effect on the god. Xissay shrieking as she melted the armor of several red-eyed humans that had closed on them was the only thing that tore his vision from the spectacle of Itka's impending death.

He saw Jabruelle, the wiry necromancer's black hair whipped by the wind, his necromancer scythe before him, and his eyes closed. Before Harpis could ask the man what he was doing, he felt a strangely familiar sensation and looked up to see the sky dimming and the color before him graying from the battlefield.

"Curse necromancers and their obsession with death," he shouted Jabruelle's way as he sprinted towards the necromancer to stop him from carrying out the same ritual Wren had at the battle of Kalt River.

Before he could reach the lanky, black-robed man, Xissay was in front of his face, holding up a hand to halt him.

"Don't you dare! This is the most important moment of his entire life. Jabruelle, The Sleeper's Herald will have done something that mattered for all of Nysia," she said.

Harpis stared dumbly from her to Jabruelle and then back to Konflict and Itka as he watched the grasping hands, claws, and tendrils of those within the great dream pull tug and grasp at the god. The sun above went dark, and Harpis knew that Jabruelle had successfully touched The Great Dream and the mortal plane together as Wren once had.

At a loss for what to do, he put the enchanted violin back to his neck and fought back the tears, watching Jabruelle age a decade with each passing moment. Then, Harpis saw that the god had stopped entirely. Konflict was sweeping his spear uselessly at the ghastly incorporeal appendages that held him fast in the sand. Itka had not been able to flee far, and Harpis knew that Jabruelle had only bought the dwarf a few minutes.

He closed his eyes and began to play the most terrifying song he had ever learned. One made for the violin. The slow sawing of his bow across the strings of his ebony violin wove the call of *Nyv's Threnody* across the sand to the god that was for a moment held by the necromancer's magic. Harpis couldn't believe that Azahle had been right about Konflict hearing his song. He found a heartbeat within the deity, forcing his gift around and into the god through the melancholy song's slowly rising and falling notes.

He could not read a sheet of music to save his life, but he could feel a sound. He could hear a thing and replay it with ease. It was the only talent that had allowed him to become a sanctioned bard of the Hall. So, he felt the gods' heartbeat, he heard it in the innermost canals of his own ears, and he matched it. The strings of his violin pulsed with the humming vibrations of the god's veins and arteries.

Then Harpis began to slow the song down. He felt the dying breeze, the setting sun. He let his mind wander to the collapse of Wren atop the bridge in Kalt. He felt all of it, and he poured those emotions into the waves of his song until he felt Konflict's heart slow in turn. Back and forth, his bow went across the strings. Slower and slower.

*****

Jabruelle collapsed to the sand, looking down at paper-like skin that clung, drooping, from cracking bones. He lay his hands on the sand and strained to hold his head up. He wept in joy at the sight of Itka further from the god. He struggled to hold himself up, to watch and see the dwarf live, but he had spent his life on the channeling of Maelara into Nysia. Finally, he felt both his arms give out under the weight of his slight frame. He collapsed to the sand, barely able to keep an eyelid open, watching the once again slowed advance of the god and uttering the final word of the ritual he had been desperate and fearful to perform.

"Rest, Jabruelle, Last Necromancer, Herald of The Sleeper. You have done well. Worry not. The bard has him now!" Xissay shouted, placing her hands on his cheek as his vision went black.

*****

The sleeper's eyes snapped open. Not for a moment and not in the darkness of her dream. Her eyes opened to the sun and the sand. Her nose smelled sea salt and felt the burn of desert air for the first time in ages. She smiled at the robed form of Jabruelle that lay across from her. Standing, she began delicately walking towards the black-armored figure. He was moving slower than he should be, stalking a female dwarf. She looked back at the bard, closed her eyes, and listened to his song for a moment, smiling at the thought of him eventually coming to join her under the stars of Maelara

*****

Itka's muscles felt heavy and weak, burning as she tried to continue crawling away from the specter of Konflict. The unnatural slowness of the god's movements was almost as unsettling as they were comforting. She would live a little longer, but her death felt imminent all the same. Suddenly, the pain in her shoulder stopped. The phenomenal torment of watching her flesh eaten away and then mended by the clerics subsided, and she almost passed out in sheer relief. Glancing down, she saw her arm, whole and no longer besieged by whatever foul magic the god had in his spear. Suddenly she found herself shaded from the sun, and yet strangely, the warmth of its rays seemed to grow. Through sand-scratched, sunburnt eyes blurred by tears of pain, she made out the white gown and blond hair of the woman standing over her.

"Ezera?" she asked in confusion before collapsing unconscious.

*****

Harpis felt the cool of shade as something walked between him and the sunlight while he played in the archway of Zarad's front gate. It momentarily blocked both his flesh and soul from the sun's light. He opened his eyes, and his song almost faltered as he watched the pale, nude form of the black-haired goddess walk away from him. Konflict did not notice her approach as he chased the crawling and screaming Itka away from the city. Harpis struggled to believe that the one whose eyes and voice had once shaken his very soul was there before him, walking after her brother.

Slowing the melody further, Harpis watched as Konflict's leg took what seemed like an eternity to step. Harpis looked on in horror as the god's arm began to rear back to throw again, even though it looked as if it would take the god an eternity to finish the motion. He felt his hold on Konflict's pulse strengthen. The crying violin keened out the dying notes of *Nyv's Threnody,* and he heard a languid, soothing hum wrap torpid comfort around the thread of notes he was sending towards the black-armored figure.

Then, tears started flowing from his eyes as he heard a sorrowful weeping lament intertwine with the warm comfort of another voice, ebbing and flowing together with his violin strings. He did not think he could play any slower, and he watched, amazed, as the god released the spear, which seemed to hang unmoving in the air. Harpis was halfway through pulling the last

264

dying note from the strings when a gold-haired woman in a white gown appeared between Itka and the spear, her hand extended before her.

Konflict's spear shattered as it reached her palm, and she turned to Harpis, her eyes warm and welcoming. Holding her finger to her lips, she pleaded for silence. Harpis could not help but oblige. He slowly let the fingers that held the fading note on the strings slide off into silence. The two voices behind him went still along with his violin strings, and he no longer felt the thrum of Konflict's heart struggling to beat. He gasped as the nude form of The Sleeper wrapped her arms around the black-armored god from behind. Her head hung sadly on his shoulder as she gently hugged him.

They both fell backward, toward and then through the desert, without disturbing a single grain of sand, disappearing from the battlefield altogether. It was then that the sun seemed to brighten, and the gold-haired woman vanished within moments of the red glow fading from the hundred thousand humans still alive in the salt flats around Zarad.

*****

With Itka finally safe, Ezera collapsed atop the ramparts, breathing heavy breaths of dusty air as she clutched her head and wept at the still form of Lorkin lying a few paces away. One of the few sand elven clerics left standing after their immense joint exertion helped her crawl to the dwarf.

"You old fool!" she said, slamming the barrel chest of the deceased Stone Magus with her fists. She then lay her head atop it, hoping against all odds to find a pulse.

"I don't forgive you for leaving us. However, I understand holding the channeling until your heart and mind gave out together. I'd not want to live as a husk either," Ezera whispered, closing his eyes with her fingers.

She heard the other cleric begin to utter Daybreak's funeral prayer and joined the sand elf, celebrating the dwarf's life. Ezera knew that Lorkin would want The Sleeper's rites too, so his soul would have to wait for Jabruelle. Like Sudbina's. Like so many others.

"You know, you look quite like her," the sand elf said when

265

they finished the prayer, looking at Ezera in awe.

*****

Harpis spun around and caught a glimpse of an olive-skinned woman that looked half Quaji and half Tuathian, garbed in moss and flowers as she smiled merrily at him and faded too.

The red-haired woman who stood with her, clad in a pale sheer gown that reminded him of the Tormenta priestesses, walked up to him, her hair billowing behind her as if in a gust of wind. She leaned in and put her lips to his ear, and he felt unable to move as she spoke.

"I was never angry with you, Harpis Akkeri, child of the winged women and descendant of the storm-blessed," she whispered, kissing him on the neck, leaving a burning sensation as the salt of her seas blistered his skin.

"Was that *The Sisters' Song*?" he dared ask.

"No sweet bard, but the sisters did sing it," she answered, fading before his eyes.

Chapter 28

Departure

Hardly believing what had transpired, Harpis shook his head and then ran out to meet the slowly limping Itka, who was already most of the way back to Zarad's front gate. Putting his arm around her waist, he tried to take some weight from her tired legs. He glanced back to see sand elves trying to calm an endless sea of starved and thirsty humans and aid injured on both sides. Several fights broke out as men and women of different countries realized they were standing next to old enemies. But, for the most part, the no longer red-eyed humans were too tired to do anything besides collapse and surrender.

"What'd that idiot do!" Itka said, pushing away from Harpis and hopping hastily to the frail, black-robed form of Jabruelle.

"*Yixia's Conjunction,*" Harpis explained, and Itka looked at him in confusion.

"He gave his life to perform a ritual that brought Maelara in contact with the mortal plane to save your life, slowing the pursuit of Konflict just as Wren had done when he halted the retreat of Tormenta forces at Kalt river," Harpis explained quietly.

"That wasn't the only ritual, though!" a cackling nervous voice said, muffled by the sand around its mouth.

Harpis and Itka both jumped back, brandishing maces and a ruby-pommeled dagger as they stared at the slowly standing form of the necromancer. When he turned to face them, they gasped together at the glowing purplish-blue light in his eyes.

"You'd think a man's stupidity would reach its highest potential in death, but no, not with you, Jabruelle," Itka said gruffly.

"Ah, but I did not die!" he answered sadly, his bluish

smoldering eyes looking down at shriveled hands.

"I gave the greatest gift of all, my death, and any hope of connecting again with The Great Dream. No more scythe. No more Xissay. No more voice of my goddess in my dreams," he said, what was left of his face furrowing into a frown.

"Why would you choose lichdom over a well-deserved afterlife with your goddess Jabruelle?" Harpis asked, confused but grateful to be conversing with what remained of their friend.

Itka walked up to him, poking his black-robed chest as if to make sure he was real, and inspected the necromancer's undying eyes and wrinkled face.

"She asked me to, as I lay there dying. I gave everything, my life and my death, in dedication to her devotion. I will lead a pilgrimage to Sikef and reestablish her cathedral in the deep city. At the moment before I became undying and she took Konflict into her dream, she told me there were witnesses to her presence on this battlefield. Witnesses who would take up our faith, several dwarves, humans, and even a sand elf!" the lich rasped excitedly.

Itka crossed her arms and glared at Jabruelle, and Harpis wasn't sure whether to feel joy or sadness. It was then that Ezera came out of the front gates to join them. She ran up to Itka, examining the dwarf's shoulder with her hands and eyes, smiling down at her before turning to Jabruelle and recoiling.

"Daybreak preserve us. What is wrong with him," she asked, staring wide-eyed at the smiling, ashen-faced Jabruelle.

"Ezera, where is my cousin," Itka asked, and the blond woman laid her hands on the dwarf's shoulders and embraced her. Itka pulled back from the crying woman after a moment.

"Thank you, all three, for saving my life, but I was not worth the cost," the dwarf said, looking from Jabruelle to Ezera and then heading through the gate towards where Lorkin lay.

"Oh Jabruelle, what have you become? The Sleeper has asked too much of her herald," Ezera said softly, gently holding the frail, bone-like hands.

"I can no longer herald her. I am the pilgrim that will lead her newly devoted on a sojourn back to Sikef," Jabruelle said, and Ezera shook her head in amazement and pity.

Turning to Harpis, Ezera wrapped her arms around him, kissing his cheek.

"Did you see them, bard? The sisters, they were both there

before our eyes!"

"I did. I saw all four of them," he said, winking.

She pulled back from him, looking around as if they still stood in the sands with them.

"Where?" Ezera asked incredulously.

"They stood here behind me, singing along with the notes of the song. The Wild and The Siren!" he exclaimed, tilting his head to reveal the mark of The Siren's kiss burned into his neck.

"How," was all she asked, touching the mark with a finger.

"I believe our friend the pilgrim had something to do with that," Harpis said, and Jabruelle nodded.

"When I gave my life, there was a moment where no mortal being on Nysia held devotion to my goddess, forcing her to wake," he explained.

*****

Standing on the balcony overlooking Zarad after sunset, Harpis finally let exhaustion envelop him as he collapsed into the stone chair and took in the winking stars above. To Harpis, the others, and the sand elves, the day's victory was greeted more with relief than cheer. Many dead needed burying, and even more living required tending. Aanaman had offered half the galleon fleet to begin transporting the survivors back up the rivers or to coasts closer to their homes. Harpis and Zala would join the those heading back to Quaj on the *Torrent* in the morning.

Itka would not be coming with them as she wanted to take Lorkin's body to the ancient dwarven capital in the country of Unkur. She said Ingar would understand and that she would return to Quaj after she had met with the older dwarven clans and lay Lorkin to rest. Jabruelle would stay, too. He intended to take new followers of his goddess to the abandoned city.

The lich had performed funeral rites for Lorkin and Sudbina with the sun's fading light, sending their souls to The Sleeper. They welcomed dusk on the rampart before their corpses were wrapped in oiled linens and draped in white cloth by the elves to await their respective processions in the morning.

Harpis did not know where to bury Sudbina, but he had a weeklong voyage back to Quaj to figure it out. They were all spending the evening in their own quarters, alone with their grief after sharing so much pain. Even Aanaman had left after the rites for Lorkin and Sudbina, saying he owed it to the dead of Savja to meet with Okliff and Zolga at the funeral pyres. Ezera had been the last to leave, saying she'd join him in the morning to greet Daybreak and walk with them to the *Torrent*.

"Not quite alone," he said to himself with a smile, glancing towards the archway into his room where Zala slept.

Aanaman had promised him the child would become more difficult as she learned to do more than eat and sleep. Harpis sat up sharply as he heard what he thought were whispers coming from the bedroom and rushed in to see a young boy holding a lantern over Zala's cradle.

"What are you doing!" Harpis whispered as loudly as he dared to avoid waking the baby.

The boy turned and flashed him a smile, setting the lantern down on the bedside table before sitting and staring at the baby. Harpis thought he looked oddly familiar, though he knew that no children had made the voyage with them from Quaj.

"Where will you bury her mother," the boy asked, an eyebrow raised Harpis' way.

"I don't know yet," Harpis answered honestly, still staring in confusion at the child.

"See, I told you!" the boy said loudly towards the balcony.

A strong breeze blew in from outside and then a light landing of feet was followed by softly rustling silk as Azahle stepped into the room.

"Shouldn't you be gone already? I didn't know your mother would suffer you to stray amongst Nysia overlong," Azahle asked the boy with a severe look.

"Oh, I won't be much longer. It is nice just to feel my body age, even if for only a day," the boy replied.

"Let me take her to rest in my home Harpis. I will carve her a tomb from the rocks with the wind," Azahle asked, and Harpis nodded numbly in agreement.

"Quite the performance today," the dragon said, resting a hand on his shoulder for a moment before turning to the sleeping baby in the cradle.

"When she is older, bring her to visit the memory of her mother, and I will teach her what the few Nysian mages left cannot," he said, touching Zala's cheek and then walking out to the

270

balcony, departing with another gust of wind.

"Dragons are always so dramatic. I guess it's understandable given how long they spend around you shorter-lived mortals. You should have been around when the whole lot of them were still watching over the flocks of Nysia," the boy said, rolling his eyes.

Harpis sat on the bed next to the adolescent and looked at the peacefully smiling baby.

"What are you?" he asked, realizing that he could feel the being's presence in the room like some unignorable puzzle demanding his attention.

"You know, for all their fussing about being sent back here, my sisters were sure making a whole lot out of nothing. All of them are happily back in their planes within breaths of arriving here on Nysia. I guess banishment would only be eternal and insufferable if our brother had truly extinguished all other devotions save his own amongst you mortals," the boy rambled, not quite answering Harpis' question.

Harpis' mouth hung open as he tried to reconcile what the boy had said.

"Now, you all can go back to killing each other on your own terms instead of Konflict's. Meanwhile, the upper planes will have to endure the rage of a father over the death of his son. Mother will see it through. She always does," the boy finished, hopping off the bed and walking to Zala.

"Unlike my sisters, I never felt love for a mortal before. But I will miss Sudbina. You aren't alone in that, God Singer," the boy said, pulling a large coin from his pocket and laying it next to Zala's swaddled and slumbering form before turning to Harpis.

"She will be the very best of you. Proof of the good that can come of chaos," he said with a wry smile, walking out of the room.

*****

The day after arriving back in Ravnice, Harpis had woken before the sun from the first good night of sleep in several years. He tiptoed down the stairs of Aanaman's home to find his friend sitting near a rekindled cooking fire, warming his hands. He opened his mouth to greet Aanaman, but the older man held his finger to silence him. The greying former governor then picked a kettle off the oven and poured its contents into a leather drinking skin, followed by a considerable pour of whiskey. Finally, capping the skin, he motioned for Harpis to follow and led him out the back of the house and to his stables.

"Come, bard. Join me," Aanaman said, pulling saddles and reins from hooks on the walls and preparing two horses.

Harpis paused for a moment, staring back towards the man's home.

"She will be fine, Harpis. If Zala wakes, Shanowen will tend to her until we get back," Aanaman assured him.

"Thank you again for letting us stay here," Harpis said, taking the reins to one of the horses from Aanaman and pulling himself into the saddle, nudging his horse to follow Aanaman's.

"It is the least I can do. I think Shanowen was more excited to cuddle a baby than at my safe return," Aanaman laughed.

"The girls did seem quite excited to have a baby in the house," Harpis admitted.

"Where do you think you'll raise her?" Aanaman asked.

"Ezera offered us a room at her little temple-fortress in Fjall, and I think I may take her up on it," he explained, leaving out his concern for having a first-generation dragon-gifted mage child around other people.

They rode in silence the short distance out of Ravnice city and went down the road north, the sea barely visible to their right, an endless field of clover stretched to the horizon on their left.

The steady plodding of the horse beneath him sent his mind wandering to the day before. He still felt the pain of guilt. Even though he hadn't slept with Sudbina, Kalna did not know that. He doubted she'd have believed him even if he had told her the truth. She had crumpled the letter he left for her and thrown it in his face as soon as she saw him with the baby when they visited her at The Siren's Scream.

He didn't blame her for her rage. If the child had been his, she would have been conceived with Sudbina during the very days he spent reconnecting with Kalna in Ravnice. He accepted the blame when she screamed at him that she should have known better after seeing Sudbina sneak in and out while he was staying there. Looking down into the eyes of Zala as he walked out of The Siren's Scream for the last time, he had to admit Sudbina had been right about one thing. In naming him Zala's father, she had given him a purpose, a reason not to flee within himself, and someone to love for the rest of his days.

The grey of the morning was starting to turn orangish golden around them, and Aanaman led them off the road, guiding the horses into the field of clover and eventually halting them next to each other after turning towards the sea. After a few more minutes, the sun peaked above the coastal waters and warmed their faces, turning the frost on the winter clover to dewy wetness and releasing the plant's telltale sweet scent.

"Life's greatest joys are in the small moments like this that peace affords us," Aanaman said, taking a pull from the skin and handing it to him.

Harpis drank the warm, rich mixture of dark Tuathian coffee and golden Reaper vintage. He smiled as the whiskey warmed his inside as the sun did his face. Closing his eyes, he inhaled the chill morning air, almost tasting the fragrance of the clover on it. When he opened them to the blissful sight of Ravnice bathed in the golden glow of a new dawn, he couldn't disagree with Aanaman's claim.

Epilogue

Harpis stretched himself awake in the small kitchen of Ezera's temple in Fjall. Pouring coffee from the kettle left warming on the low burning oven, he smiled at the sound of the blond cleric's enthusiastic chiding of Zala out on the grounds. He wasn't sure when exactly he realized he loved Ezera. They hadn't fallen in love so much as realized that it happened. Everyone that knew them had said it was only a surprise to the two of them that they were a match for each other after so much of their lives spent sharing in struggles and victories.

One night, not long after returning from Zarad nearly ten years ago, he had found himself in her bed after sharing several bottles of wine. Waking the next morning with her in his arms, he had spent each day since at her side, raising Sudbina's progeny. Sipping the brown Tuathian blend from his steaming cup he chuckled. With a resigned sigh at the increasingly impatient berating she was unleashing and pushed his way out the door to see what the fuss was about.

Only a few paces out onto the temple lawn, he froze, mouth agape staring up at the black-haired child floating twenty feet off the ground on a swirling wind. He looked to Ezera and the cleric threw her hands up in frustration before crossing them and looking at him expectantly. Harpis could not bring himself to interrupt the back-and-forth melody between Zala and a nest of baby birds in the boughs that she was whistling to.

When the last soothing note drifted from Zala's lips, Harpis steadied himself and did his best to keep a stern look on his face and tone in his voice.

"Zala, my dear, what have we told you about using magic so? You could be hurt or worse if your gift faltered while you were so

274

high in the air," he reprimanded.

"But Daddy, I did not do it on purpose. I simply wanted to hear their song better and found myself beside their nest. Are the voices of the sparrows not beautiful?" she asked in a voice purposefully much younger than her ten years.

He grunted and gave her a feigned glare as she slowly drifted to the ground, very much in control of the summoned zephyr before curtsying to Ezera.

"I am sorry for worrying you," she said bashfully as Harpis shooed her inside to breakfast and shared a look of concern with Ezera.

"Harpis, it is becoming almost a daily occurrence and we can't keep her hidden in Fjall forever. We soon must decide how and who best to teach her," Ezera said.

"I'd prefer to send her to Mahala before turning her over to her father," Harpis said quietly as they clasped hands and headed toward the kitchen.

Ezera did not reply but leaned her head on his shoulder and gave a slight nod.

*****

Harpis Leaned over The Hall's seaward balcony, allowing the upward gusting wind to howl past his ears. He was pulled from the meditative maelstrom by the opening of the balcony doors. Turning, he grinned at the stoic face and chestnut curls of the petite Troubadour Mahala. The female bard turned her usually unimpressed disposition into a smile as she stepped aside and Zala ran from behind her.

"Oh, Stinky! I missed you!" Harpis said, picking her up in a giant hug before setting her down.

"You know I hate that nickname!" she shouted, pursing her lips and crinkling her sharp nose in a look of indignance that was startlingly similar to one of Sudbina's.

"Go on then little one, collect your things, Ezera is waiting for us all to meet for dinner," he said as Zala rolled her eyes and skipped off.

He blew out a sigh and looked to Mahala, letting his shoulders sink.

"What happened to the little girl I brought here two years

ago?" he asked, refusing to believe during the monthly visits during her training at The Hall that she had changed so much.

"She's getting closer to being a young woman than a little girl Harpis. I'll tell you another thing, you may be the one called God Singer, but Zala may as well be the goddess of song," Mahala said in a rare compliment.

*****

Zala's heart was pounding with excitement as she gathered her belongings in her tiny room on the ship and shoved them into her mother's old satchel. It had taken the entire trip from Zarad for her to come to terms with what she had learned of Azahle, and what the dragon had taught her in the months spent in his castle of caves. At fifteen, she would be by far the youngest trainee taken in at the fortress of Southpoint. It was not being younger than her peers that made her nervous, more the potential of disappointing her instructors which terrified her.

Climbing up the ladder to the main deck she leapt from the railing and floated slowly down to the dock below, grinning from ear to ear at the two Tormenta women

"Aunties!" she said, crushing Zolga and Galonica in a fierce hug.

Zolga held her at arm's length, a firm grip on her shoulder and Galonica raised an eyebrow at her.

"What did you think of your real father and Zarad?" Galonica asked.

"Harpis Akkeri is my real father," Zala answered confidently and Zolga squeezed her shoulder in appreciation at the conviction.

"You could not have asked for a better one. Now come, it is time for you to be trained in talents that cannot be given by a goddess or inherited from a dragon," The short haired warrior woman said, leading them towards the circular stone walls.